As It Is In Heaven

Winslow Nicholas
Edited by Elizabeth L. Prince

For My Darling Wife, Debbie.

Introduction

I heard troubled voices call out, and then said, 'Why does the Great Spirit, God, allow all this pain, misery, and suffering, to continue in the world today?' And it went on to say, 'Why isn't he here with us, saving our desolate souls? Why is he not here with us punishing the wicked and stopping the suffering of the innocent children? Why is he not here to ease our pain and suffering? Why does he look on, while we pray and hope for delivery from the hands of the evil ones who seek to destroy us simply because of our way of life?'

Humanity blamed the Great Spirit for all the evil deeds committed in the world but forgot that he had already received free will, the power to make decisions of his own rather than depend on the Great Spirit or fate to determine his actions.

Man, and indeed woman were created at the same time, and were made equal, and perfect, except for the quality of divinity and immortality. One day men will understand and fully accept that the Great Spirit does not use his power to control everything, but for now, he chooses to tolerate those who misuse their free will to harm others.

Men used their free will once again, for the final time, to wage war on his enemy because of his insatiable lust for greed, wealth and power.

It was the year of our Lord, AD 2020 when the prophecy came true, and war raged upon the earth as before. But this time it was to be the final war, not one to end all wars, as they spoke of previously, but a war to end the eternal misery, hunger, and suffering. They hoped that it would eventually restore peace, prosperity, and eternal happiness on earth, as it was in the beginning. They called this one, not the third world war, but, the final 'Nuclear Holocaust'. Little did those poor souls realise that this impending event was to be the last war to ever rage upon the earth. It was to become man's last apocalypse.

At this moment in time, there are approximately twenty-five thousand nuclear warheads in existence in the world, more than enough to destroy the entire population of the world many times over. If that wasn't dire enough to evoke fear in the hearts of man, a few years earlier, a group of scientists, were busy working on the moon base, when they had discovered a new crystal, which they had not yet given a name. This crystal was indeed a valuable discovery, which those foolish warmongers did not fully appreciate. This useful crystal displayed some valuable properties, which would later become the main ingredient in the development of further highly sophisticated technology. Initially, they had discovered that this crystal could harness energy from light, as it was able to amplify it greatly. There was a hidden bonus; they found that it also had the power to suppress spirits of the dead.

The arrogant fools did not recognise these benefits, of course, as they were bent on war and destruction, and world domination, like children in the playground, arguing over who had the cleverest or the most energetic dad. They failed to see its higher purpose, so instead, they used it to destroy; to enhance the power of lasers, and for the augmentation of their nuclear weapons. Early experiments were indeed disastrous, to say the least, as whole laboratories, populated with scientists, would merely vaporise into thin air from the intense heat of the explosion caused by amplified light particles inside the laser. They tried reducing the number of crystals, to mitigate the effect, and then they increased them again, and eventually placed them into separate tubes. They tried crushing the crystals into smaller particles. It was then that they had inadvertently discovered Nova Nuclear Fusion; a nuclear explosion with all the effects of a nuclear blast, but void of all the devastating radiation aftermath. The crass fools put the crystals into their deadly weapons unaware of the overwhelming catastrophe that would befall them. Each warhead increased its power twofold, and each explosion produced a glow of such brilliant white light, hotter than the surface of the star by many times.

Suddenly, twenty-five thousand became fifty thousand, and one megaton became two megatons. The ignorant fools did not issue their entire arsenal, as each warhead could release enough energy that could almost bring about the extinction of all life on Earth.

Luckily for them, they had ceased fire early, as it only took a few deadly strikes to vaporise entire flesh and bones in a matter of seconds. Inevitably, individual missiles had missed their target entirely and went astray into the wilderness, where a limited number found their way into deep fissures beneath the earth's crust on both land and sea, where they had detonated and caused much devastation. These terrible events began the instigation of the 'Terrain Reformation', which was to alter the physical appearance of the earth's surface beyond all expectations.

The very few survivors, who witnessed this final Armageddon, preached it and passed it on through the generations by word of mouth, but did not write about it in history books. Although they maintained their reluctance to justify such atrocity of man against man, they were willing to confirm openly that the final Nuclear Holocaust served to pave the way for a new beginning and to bring into existence in the future a peaceful and happy world for all mankind.

After the war, some of them spoke of the Great Prophet. They questioned why has he not returned to earth to save their souls? They would repeatedly ask whether he would ever come to protect them from this living hell on Earth? 'Or will he just abandon them here in the flames of Hades?'

Well, that was almost half a millennium ago. I am Lord Bandersant. Today, it is the year AD 2914, and I find myself standing on the top of a hill. I am speaking to a man whom we have just rescued from deep within the earth's crust, in a chamber built by the ancients, we believe, but now troubled by seismic activity, so we saved him in good time.

He has told me that he was born. He claims that he was born, on a particular date and year given to me, but I am genuinely baffled because this time cannot possibly be correct, if so, and if his statement is true as he claims, then this man must be almost a thousand years old. He has shown me proof, which I thoroughly accept, but he cannot recall anything else to corroborate this bizarre statement other than what he has told me from his unstable memory. Either I am crazy, or he is attempting to fool me for some unknown reason, which I am yet to discover. He says his name is Newton Flotman, and I shall allow him to tell you his exciting story in person.

CHAPTER 1

The Discovery

"My name is Newton Flotman. It says so right there on my badge." I held it up for him to see, but he still had difficulty making it out. Perhaps it was the bright sun glaring in his eyes. I must admit it was extremely bright, rather unusual for the natural daytime sun. Then again, I have been living underground for longer than I could possibly remember. I shuffled around on my knees until I was facing the sun. He smiled and agreed that he could read it much better now, but it still read, only the words, "Newton Flotman" and below, was a faint image of what looked like a date, which I read out to him.

"I am Lord Bandersant. If the date you gave me is correct, you must have been in hibernation inside your life support capsule for... for a long period of time. I do suspect that there could be some urgent issues with your health, although you seem well and fairly active for a man of your condition. I must insist that we take you to a Recovery Room near the city, immediately, where we will be able to carry out a thorough medical examination as a precaution. You can rest there in comfort, and take all the time you need to recover."

I was reasonably comfortable here, and I certainly didn't feel as if I had any issues with my health. I kept on asking myself which city would that be? After I had asked him the first time, but he probably didn't hear me because he was engaged in a quiet conversation with one of the men in black. I just lay there on my weird stretcher, as I floated. I was actually hovering above the ground, on a flat stretcher bed of some sort, I must add, next to the Lord Bandersant, together with two of his accomplices, both tall men dressed in black suits. Neither of them was actually supporting this flat stretcher in any way whatsoever, which was extremely worrying, but it was incredibly comfortable nevertheless, so I had no real cause for complaint.

I could not make out where I was, in any case. The remote terrain surely did not look like any familiar country to me. I tried my best in the hope that by studying the ground, I might recognise something, but it was to no avail, and somewhat disappointing, as I always considered myself extremely good at identifying places. I felt strange because somehow I could perceive this fact, yet I had no memory to be able to recall anything specific beyond that.

The sky was dark blue, with a purple tint, which I found strange. It was warm and sunny, and all I could see around us was trees. Vast, dense forest of trees like no other I have ever seen. Somehow I could vaguely remember this fact, but not the details. How strange, because I remember buildings as well; their style, design, even shapes and colours flashed in my pitiful little memory bank. I saw no buildings in this place, no houses, towers or skyscrapers of any kind nearby or beyond the horizon. I caught a glimpse of an entire valley, filled with trees, sweeping down towards the horizon, which looked as though it blended seamlessly with the coast beyond. I did notice something extraordinary near to the horizon. Could it have been some doubtful atmospheric phenomenon, I wondered to myself? I was able to see the minute details of all the trees evident as if I had been looking at them through a pair of high-quality binoculars.

I was curious to know where these people were taking me, and how we were ever going to get to any city at this leisurely pace? I had no cause for complaint, as I lay comfortably on a giant hoverboard. My ride was as smooth as a floating feather. I had to look up occasionally to remind myself that we were still in motion. I eventually made an effort to sit up so that I could get a better look around, and perhaps see something of interest but it was hopeless. Just as soon as I tried to raise my torso, the man at the back end of the hovering stretcher had hastily, but gently, pushed me back down again.

Lord Bandersant was laughing, "Questions, questions, indeed, and more questions, Newton Flotman. I understand you are just as curious about us as we are about you. But it is vitally important that you rest your body and lay flat on the hoverboard to benefit from its healing energy, at least until we get back to the city, then we can run a full diagnosis."

Oh, that invisible city again. The one I cannot see, or determine how we are going to reach it at this slow pace. All I could see was a vast forest of trees. Mature trees. I pondered on the idea of making off into the dense forest to find my own way on foot. I felt that I could see civilisation much quicker by myself. Not knowing where I was or the dangers I faced out there, I decided that this would not be the best option. I wondered whether Bandersant was friend or foe; he could have hidden weapons, although I have not seen any yet, judging by the amount of technology required to run this hoverboard, If that were anything to go by I think their weapons would be equally formidable in power. With this thought in mind, I decided to stay put in my cosy, floating bed, which I believe was powered by something that I knew nothing about. Not a sound, not a hum or whisper of any hint of vibration or noise, which one would expect to be heard from such a powerful device. It was difficult to contemplate the enormous amount of energy required to lift and transport my entire body weight. Like a giant skateboard! A hoverboard! I had shouted to Bandersant, but he stared back perplexed as if he hadn't heard of such term. Perhaps I am on an alien planet? Or aliens have taken over my world, earth? If there ever was a time to make a run for it into the woods to find my own destiny, it was now.

The silence, which followed, was broken by the sudden appearance of a broad smile on Lord Bandersant's face as if he had found gold. "Here we are, at last."

I saw nothing but trees and more trees. Perhaps they are taking me to a tree house? A magnificent one, I trust, judging by the size of these boughs. I decided to attempt to sit up to get a better look at this beautiful city, which I couldn't see, and in doing so, I wasn't troubled or told by the men in black to lie back down like a sick and confused child.

"I'm afraid I see nothing but trees, and more trees, Lord Bandersant," I said to him.

"Look again, dear Newton," He said, as he waved his arm in the air like a magician.

I looked hard, and I scanned each and every tree. I realised just how difficult it was to suddenly acquire the ability of enhanced vision. I saw a flash of gold in the foliage, which I took to be some sort of firearm discharge. I panicked, and shouted to Bandersant to take cover, much to my embarrassment.

He laughed and then he urged me to calm down, and said there was no such danger in this world. As we got nearer to where I had seen the flash of light. I could see clearly what had caused it. I sighed with embarrassment, and smiled to myself and vowed not to be so hasty next time.

As we approached the object my eyes felt a little heavy, and I felt faint, but I managed to keep them open long enough to discern that my flash of light had indeed been a flash of light. But no weapons discharge, merely the reflection of the sun, through the moving trees from what I could only describe as being a large, round, shiny, golden hut with a dome-shaped roof.

"We'll be there quite soon now…" Lord Bandersant announced, in a voice, which seem to echo around the forest. At that point, my eyes became heavy like lead, and my faintness turned to acute dizziness, and then my eyes closed tightly as I succumbed to a deep sleep.

I woke up feeling worse than before. My whole body felt weighted down as if ten strong men were holding it down. Even my eyelids felt laboured. I needed to close them, however, to save my eyes from the profusion of golden light, which I presumed to be the reflection of the golden dome. So I hesitated a little before I opened them again. But when I did I didn't expect to see what I did.

I was seated, practically upright this time, not on my hoverboard but in a golden bed. Glancing up, I discovered the cause of the harsh glare. The walls and ceiling of the inside of this strange building were entirely covered in gold. Solid or plated I could not determine at this present moment, as I would need to touch and feel it first to corroborate this.

I must have decided immediately to do just that. I was sure that some subconscious action took over my whole body for a split second or two, only to be disappointed at the same time. The force was far too strong to overcome. The fact that there were no straps or any other bindings holding me to this golden throne proved that without any doubt. I conceded that there was no hope of trying any further as these gracious captives were far too intelligent and their technology was genuinely compelling. Resisting any longer was useless. I now resigned myself to the belief that I was a captured slave by a group of highly intelligent aliens, who had somehow erased my memory before they brought me to this planet for intense interrogation. I now need to find out for what purpose. Perhaps I am already dead and in one of the lower worlds, where these creatures are taking me to their god for me to be judged and punished accordingly.

I fear that I spoke out loud without realising it because just as soon as I had finished my supposition, I heard his voice again.

"Wrong on both counts, Newton Flotman," Lord Bandersant said with an air of passion, "wrong on all counts." He corrected himself. Then he went on, "But you do have a good imagination for an earth creature, I must say."

His sudden appearance made me jump with fright. I questioned myself did he materialise out of thin air? Or perhaps he had entered through an opening in the wall somewhere in this vast, golden prison, as I now called it because his tone and actions far suggested to me that all hope is lost. I didn't see him come through any door or opening, neither did I know one close behind him. There were no doors or seams anywhere to be seen, or indeed none where seams should have been, to indicate any hint of a door or opening anywhere.

I watched as he approached my bed. He appeared to glide smoothly across the smooth, golden floor. This time he was accompanied by two smaller figures, which, by now, I half expected to be little creatures with horns, perhaps a pair of evil devils incarnate, sent on a special mission to conduct my judgment and then inform me of my eternal punishment. I braced myself for what was to come, as I made a last futile attempt to free myself from the golden throne. Just as I conceded all hope and accepted that I was to spend the final few minutes of my life surrounded by more gold than I have ever seen in my whole life, although I could not remember any of it precisely, the two creatures stopped directly in front of me, then slowly removed their hoods.

I could only describe what was revealed beneath their hoods as being one of the most extraordinary sights I had seen since my capture by these so-called aliens. I felt my jaw drop and my eyes widen at the sight of what I witnessed. There before me stood two of the most beautiful looking young girls I had ever seen in my entire life. They had similar features, yet they were both perfect in every way. Clones? I thought to myself, but too loud a thought, once again.

What Lord Bandersant said next caused me great concern, as I knew for sure that my thoughts were indeed only thoughts and I honestly did not speak out loud this time.

"Clones, they are not!" He said in a deep and low voice, "And they are not horned creatures, and they certainly haven't come here to interrogate or punish you in any way; Far from it, Newton Flotman. Unless, of course, you wish them to?" He concluded in a higher-toned voice, and then he added a cheeky smirk. The first I've seen him wear since my capture or my rescue.

"Pranga? Karla?" He beckoned the two girls. They approached me with broad, friendly smiles.

"Are these your daughters, Lord Bandersant?" I said, in a kind voice, hoping to appease him.

"Oh, no!" He replied in a deeper voice, followed by a deep laugh. He gestured to one of them. She approached and sat beside me on my golden throne. In all the excitement I hadn't even noticed that I was no longer restricted, bound to the golden mattress by an unexplainable gravitational force. I took advantage of my freedom and sat up to make myself more comfortable. I could have easily made my escape at this stage if I so wished. But what a fool I would have been if I had done so, besides, how would I get out of this golden temple anyway? I couldn't even find a doorway!"

"Touch her." Lord Bandersant said suddenly as if she were a product for sale. She gave me her hand anyway. It felt quite warm and soft when I eventually touched it. I thought to myself, why should it not? Why was Bandersant testing me with his girls? Did he want a reaction from me? Why did he want a response? Just then my mind wandered, and I reverted to the judgement and punishment in Hades again, but Bandersant must have read my mind once more because he had quelled my fears immediately when his eyes closed and he shook his head slowly, as he gestured with his finger to his lips.

"They are all like this, no horns or tails," he said, with a smile, which was his second one so far. "We must get back now," he continued. "Karla will look after you; she's quite brave and adventurous. Like yourself, Newton."

"There are more like these?" I asked curiously, his frown made me change the subject. I went on, "Yes, tell me about myself, Lord Bandersant, as you seem more familiar with my mind than myself. I have forgotten... I know nothing. Start by telling me about this place. Where am I?"

He looked into my eyes, his countenance changed to almost that of an angel from a celestial world. I could practically read his soul through his eyes. They became a transparent blue, like the sky itself. He calmly closed his eyes and said in a soft tone, far different from his usual deep one, "Newton, my dear fellow man, you are in Heaven..."

I had many thoughts as I lay quietly on my hoverboard once more, looking up at gold, and the blue sky, then more gold. I have never travelled into space in a rocket before, although, I have piloted some fast aircraft during my brief time with the Air Force, some of which could reach high altitudes. I have never been in Heaven, not that I can recall, perhaps in a dream, which I cannot remember right now. It didn't take much calculating to figure out that after descending in yet another golden globe, this one is much smaller, of course, we were now hurtling through a tunnel deep underground at, what I believe to be an enormous velocity far higher than I have ever experienced on Earth. What is it with these people; they are obsessed with golden globes. I have never seen such extravagant use of the precious metal. What planet or realm could this possibly be where gold is so much in abundance, I would like to know, and perhaps take some samples back with me to earth? I kept asking Bandersant the same question, sometimes direct, and several times through insinuation, and I had lost count of the blank stares that he gave me in response to such queries and my incessant requests for gold. Perhaps he regarded me as an avaricious raider from planet earth who had come to pillage his precious resources.

"We are only a thousand miles from the city now." He announced. At that moment I relaxed knowing that I had plenty of time to question him without further distractions. My first question was going to be about this place called Heaven, as I wanted to know which star system it was in. Before I even had time to think of how to phrase the question without causing any offence, he had announced our arrival. I didn't notice we had actually moved anywhere. I believed that we were stuck due to some inevitable mechanical problem or delay, which I would have naturally accepted as a regular occurrence, while travelling, back on Earth. But these people were not so automatic as us earthlings. They could make machines move at high speed smoothly and silently. How is that possible? I hastened to ask Bandersant in case of yet another blank stare as if he thought this common knowledge and I should have known of such technology already. Well, he did express one anyway. This one had a smile attached to the end of it. He must have reread my thoughts. It seems he does that quite well, mainly when we are surrounded by gold. It must do something to amplify his unique mind-reading ability.

When I asked him about the construction of the city, whether it is made of gold, he laughed, and then he slapped his thigh as he told me joyously that indeed there is lots of gold in the city, as it is a natural element.

"There are also equal amounts of other natural materials that we use to construct many things, as you will see all in good time."

I was able to see much better sitting up on the hover-board rather than lying down, where I sometimes felt vulnerable, to what, I do not know. Perhaps it was due to the absence of motion that left me with this feeling. The ride was too smooth; no bumps and jumps, not even over steep hills. The warmth of Karla's soft hand in mine, which she would occasionally seise and then squeeze gently to reassure me, lessened my fears. However, all my worries were in vain, as I have never seen so many happy people in any city back on earth before. I had difficulty finding a face with a frown, or even a vacant stare.

"I don't recognise this particular city; remind me again which country this is, Lord Bandersant?" I put to him suddenly, in an attempt to catch him off guard, and hopefully goad him into answering a straight question. But this man was far too good for me. In any case, I should have known better for underestimating a man who had the power and ability to read minds. He casually smiled and said, "You won't, not now anyway." As we began to ascend up a set of broad marble steps, which lead to the most magnificent house that I had ever seen. I had to shield my eyes from the glare of the sun reflecting light from the pure white marble facade. In fact, the whole city looked as if it had been hewn from marble, and finished off with a little gold here and there. I have never seen marble in such abundance. Pure and white, and it looked so new. Its pureness complimented the gold in every way. The buildings were similar to the Georgian style; some of them boasted tall white columns, which were topped with the most detailed intricate carving, inlaid with gold, silver, and diamonds. Pure crystals flawless and cleanly cut, their smooth facets gleaming in the bright sunlight, irradiating a bright, dispersed rainbow of fire.

"This is the city!" Lord Bandersant announced as he danced on the smooth marble steps. His white suit almost rendered him invisible against the marble backdrop.

"What is it called?" I asked, excitedly.

"The City," he replied casually, as he danced up the steps.

I half expected such an answer from him, one void of details and reasons. Perhaps I was too pedantic. I should relax a little and go with the flow of things, instead of exerting my eagerness for answers to everything all at once. These people are an advanced race. They must have vast knowledge concerning almost everything in their own world, which is more than I could say about my own race back on Earth. I may be here for a while so I will need information, as my memory is unreliable. Somehow I suspect that Lord Bandersant is quite reticent with details about my rescue, or perhaps he is holding back for the right moment to tell me everything. Maybe he is concerned about my condition and is being careful not to reveal too much about this beautiful place in case I find it too distressing when I am ready to return home. I can say with the utmost assurance that these people are indeed friendly. I don't sense any hostility, and this place, most definitely, is no penal camp.

Just as I had imagined, the inside of the house was as equally splendid as it was on the outside. The doors were carefully hand carved from the most flawless oak, judging by its beautiful grain. I could see no joints, which indicated to me that each one was made entirely from a single piece of wood.

Pure Crystal Chandeliers dangled from immaculately plastered ceilings; their crystals emitted pure white light that reached every corner and every crevice of this spacious mansion. Hardly anything in the room had been marred by any shadows. The view was pure; the light was everywhere. At that very moment, I had recalled a dream, which surprised me much. Was my memory gradually returning to me? Karla sensed my sudden catharsis, I could see it in her emerald green eyes, and I honestly felt it through the gradual intensity if her warm grasp. The beauty of this planet, the architecture, and the friendliness of its people forced me to ask myself, should I really be concerned? Because from what I have seen so far I was beginning to come to terms with the fact that I was indeed in the very place they called Heaven.

CHAPTER 2

The Recovery

I remembered being taken, or hovered, to use a more appropriate term, up to the first floor of this immaculate marble palace, where I was lead through an oak door into, what I would describe as a grand hallway, similar to the one downstairs, but only smaller. Three large oak doors lead off from the marble facade, each one divided by an ornately carved marble column inlaid with gold, silver, and what looked like precious stones. Naturally, I assumed that I had arrived at a luxurious hotel where I would be made to rest and recover for a few days, and not at the hospital, where I was expecting to be taken. I was wrong again, and Lord Bandersant corrected me.

"You have already been to the hospital," he said, in a calm voice. "Don't you remember the golden bed?" He then pointed to the three doors and asked me to make a choice. I chose the middle one, as my instinct told me that it was probably the largest of the three, and somehow I felt that it was the grandest by the ornateness of the carving on the outside.

"Nice choice," Lord Bandersant barked, as he went on ahead and pushed the door gently. It opened gracefully as if it had been assisted mechanically, "This is where you rest, Newton," he said with a broad smile, "The other rooms are for you also, to use as you so desire, for your comfort and leisure while you recover."

I watched him for a while as he stood there his broad smile. His wild eyes filled with wonder, his dream-like gaze fixed on me for a moment as each of us waited for the other to speak, when, all of a sudden, Carla took my hand in hers. A gentle squeeze and a reassuring smile were all she needed to convince me of the kindness, loyalty, and trust. I was convinced by their warm hospitality. I reminded myself that I must remain positive at all times and try to banish any pessimistic thoughts, which I occasionally had, swarming around in my head like a lost fish in a fishbowl, because Lord Bandersant was an adept reader of my mind, in particular, the hopeless and distrustful thoughts.

I was led into the room on my hoverboard, and it glided slowly over to a large oak bed in front of an enormous window, where it suddenly stopped about a foot above the bed. I suppressed all my thoughts immediately after a quick scan of the spacious room. I saw that there was enough gold invested in the trim and inlay of the décor alone to sink a small ship. How foolish of me to go thinking naked thoughts like a ruthless pirate out to steal the treasure. I thought of how easy it would be to load it all onto a ship and then sail away somewhere. Lord Bandersant's sudden chortle made me snap out of my micro daydream. I looked down to see that he had touched the hoverboard with his index finger. He flinched as though he had just received an electric shock, which tickled him instead. Then he lightly tapped on the board with his fingers as if tapping out a da capo on an imaginary piano. Small lights flickered on the board, then it slid away fast from underneath me, and in a split second, I fell onto the soft, comfortable bed below. The bed was so sweet and warm that I could only imagine that I was suspended somewhere in space in a state of complete weightlessness.

The board slowly glided out of the room, and the two men in black followed it out. I caught a brief glimpse of them both as they trotted after it like two giggly school kids chasing a balloon in the wind. I heard laughter in the hallway, which surprised me, as I hardly heard a whisper from their solemn lips during the entire journey.

Lord Bandersant smiled at Carla then she turned to me and said, in a soft, warm voice, "I shall go and get us some refreshments." Before I could utter a word to her, she had left the room.

"You can lay there and rest until the morning, Newton Flotman. Carla shall see to your comfort and all your needs." Lord Bandersant said.

I must have been busy watching Karla, because I didn't see where he got the chair from or how he managed to be sitting down beside my bed, all of a sudden, wearing a broad smile. I hadn't seen that smile since we travelled from the hill. It was indeed a wide one, and he seemed much more calm and relaxed. Perhaps it was something to do with the sudden absence of the men in black, and Carla of course, and he felt that this was the right time to tell me the whole truth about this place. I returned the smile then I paused for a while half expecting him to address me further with additional information. Perhaps he is waiting for me to start with my many questions?

"OK, Lord Bandersant, will you tell me the truth now?" I blurted out suddenly, as if some invisible force had goaded me to do so, and forced me to step forward to ask the first question.

"What is it that you wish to know?" He asked in his usual calm voice.

"Why you captured me? How you captured me? Where you captured me, as I haven't a clue where this place is, this City, where you brought me, although you call it Heaven? How far are we from Earth? Are we currently at war with your planet and, if so, what do you intend to do with me?"

Lord Bandersant clapped his hands and laughed loudly, "War! You say? War with your planet, Earth?" He lay back in the large white comfortable chair. "There are no wars, Newton. Your planet had its last great war many years ago. All these people you see here know nothing of war." I sat up and turned to him. He went on, "Yes, we managed to keep the peace for many years after, give or take a few small wars in between."

He rose to his feet. His smile had gone. Instead, replaced with a look of concern, which also caused me concern. "Newton," he said, in a serious tone, "What I am about to tell you may come as a surprise to you. First of all, you were not captured in any war, as no wars are raging here on this planet. There hasn't been any conflict of any kind for at least..." He hesitated for a second, and then he looked towards the door with a blank stare. I sensed a degree of embarrassment, which surprised and troubled me at the same time. I tossed the comfortable duvet to one side and swung my legs over the side of the bed. They dangled down over the side, my feet almost touching the floor, like a child eagerly waiting to be told a bedtime story. But somehow I sensed that he was about to deliver me a nightmare.

He looked straight into my eyes and said, "Newton, the last nuclear holocaust on your... on the planet Earth, raged in the year of our Lord AD 2020.

I did expect that he would deliver some dire news judging by his actions and the tone of his voice, but I did not expect that it would be as grave as the complete destruction of the Earth and mankind. I tried my best to prevent myself from falling off the bed. I managed to cling on to the silky soft coverings as I fired a succession of questions back at him. I was confused and needed to know all the answers at once. Was he lying? What could he possibly gain by telling me such lies? I could only remember asking the last two questions though, which I considered being the most important, "What extent of destruction had the Earth suffered? Is there any chance you can get me back there to look for survivors?"

"Newton," he said in a deep and almost hypnotic voice, "the earth was completely destroyed... it was destroyed some time ago, yes, I am afraid to tell you that this happened not yesterday, as it may seem to you, but it occurred in the past; many moons ago, as your people would say. Newton, around eight hundred and ninety years ago, to be precise."

I sensed the feeling of both legs jar violently as my feet touched down hard onto the solid oak floor. I couldn't remember jumping down intentionally, I somehow lost my grip, as suddenly, I found myself standing beside the bed in a comatose state, just staring at Bandersant. I needed proof, so I felt my wrist, but discovered that I was not wearing my watch. I hadn't been conscious of the fact that I ever owned one until this moment.

"What year is it on Earth now?" I asked him, eager for an answer.

"Newton, there is another reason why you cannot return to Earth. The planet you are on now is the Earth, and the year is AD 2914."

I felt my head spin. The room became a blur, as if I was spinning violently inside a cockpit, in a fatal nosedive towards the ground, which was heading straight towards the ground far below. I suddenly found myself standing in front of the window; how I got there I could not remember at all. I could see people walking about in the perfect, pristine streets below. My vision became vivid and crystal clear. The people I could see all seem to wear broad, happy smiles. The scene? All happy, pleasant, and calm, like that of a movie set for a cheerful, bright and colourful musical without the music. I did not sense that Lord Bandersant had moved from the comfortable white chair, but I heard his voice directly behind me. It was low with a soothing tone.

"There's more, Newton," he said, "lots more."

"What happened to me?" I asked as I continued to stare through the crystal clear window, my eyes scanning every pixel of the colourful foliage, which had been carefully planted neatly in rows and borders in gardens and parks, and along neatly laid pathways that snaked through the city. I saw no cars or other dirty means of transport, only healthy people walking; happy children laughing. Even their pets seemed delighted.

Lord Bandersant took a deep breath, "During the excavation of our subterranean transport system, beneath the hill, where we discovered your capsule, our team found an irregularity in the terrain about a mile beneath the surface. Your scientists, they believe, had instigated this disturbance while drilling. They had constructed a vast network of tunnels and caverns, which we think was some sort of secret, highly advanced research centre. That is where our team discovered you inside the capsule, which we believe was a sophisticated life support system for its time. At first, they thought you were dead but later realised that your silver cord was still attached. Apparently, they could not retrieve the whole machine with you still inside as they had run out of time and had no other option but to perform a full rescue.

They had to carefully remove your body and bring you up to the surface as quickly as possible for further treatment. The team discovered that you had been the subject of a scientific experiment, details of which were somewhat vague, as there were no records to be found. However, somehow we assume that it involved the use of a life support system, which may have been energised around the time your nuclear war began. The team called me as soon as they brought you to the surface. I treated you to the best of my ability and brought you here to recover. As you know, I was unable to reinstate your memory. However there is still some hope yet, only time can heal this, so don't despair. You shall meet with Doctor Gabriel in the morning; he is more knowledgeable on such matters."

"Lord Bandersant, are you saying that I have been in a deep sleep, on a life support system for over 800 years? That's insane. I doubt if we even had such technology at that time. I wish I could remember. How could a machine sustain its power for so long anyway?"

"The team had to get you out of there quickly to preserve your life. There wasn't enough time to investigate the details of the technology, and they were unable to bring any evidence back up to the surface. Judging by the information, I was given, it seems that the on-going geological disturbance in the area had initially caused an anomaly to occur in the earth's core, which had instigated some sort of induced magnetic induction. It is possible that this action caused the production of electrical energy, which was sufficient to sustain a primitive kind of reserve power reservoir, which we believe had kept the necessary equipment running. However, they did report seeing an artificial light in the area where they found you."

Despite the nature and seriousness of it all, I had to laugh. "As a result of man's effort, in a quest to attain scientific excellence, all that we achieved was a lamp with a life expectancy of 800 years! Edison will be jumping for joy in his grave." I whispered to my self, or so I thought.

"Thomas Edison?" Lord Bandersant enquired rather casually with an air of surprise as if the great inventor had been his long-standing acquaintance, who lived just next door. "I communicated with him quite regularly during the construction of the sub-terrain transport system some seasons ago."

I turned around quickly, surprised at his remark, as I knew that Edison had been dead for over fifty years before I was born. I stared at Lord Bandersant for a moment as he lay back in the comfortable chair beside the bed. I sought to challenge his sanity, but he looked too relaxed to disturb. In any case, a sudden scream, which emanated from the street below, and sounded much like a child, added to the distraction, which prevented me from doing so. Instead, I returned to my window where I continued gazing out at the lively city people.

"That's a scream of joy," Bandersant said, with a tone of happiness in his voice, "there is no fear here, Newton. You won't find any fear in this place."

As I turned to him again, I caught sight of Karla. She entered the room, somewhat gracefully, carrying a large tray laden with an array of colourful fruit, some of which I have never cast eyes upon before, nor had I ever seen them in any recipe books, or encyclopedias, as far as I could remember. Her smile was warm and sexy. I felt an immediate sense of calm as soon as I cast my eyes upon her.

"What happened to the rest of the world after the holocaust?" I asked Lord Bandersant, as I deliberately distracted my gaze away from Karla by pointing out to the window, "This looks like paradise, is the rest of the world like this?"

Bandersant smiled at Karla and nodded his head. She placed the tray on a dining table on the other side of the room then she sat down in one of the high backed, comfortable dining chairs. I felt pleased that she had remained with us.

"Newton," He said, as he rose to his feet, "I don't know much about the history of the world that you left behind all those years ago. Doctor Gabriel, of course, has studied this era in depth, but that violent and chaotic age which you once lived in my dear Newton is no longer in existence. All its people of that period, indeed your loved ones, family, friends and colleagues, I am very sorry to say have all long passed on to another level of existence, believe me; they no longer dwell in the flesh. In spite of your temporary memory loss, we fully understand how you feel, as we too suffer loss, and indeed death, but we also enjoy certain conditions, which help us to mitigate the trauma of death and injury, as you will learn of later on.

I can only say that our world will surprise and astound you in every way, Newton. How we live and how we die is very different to how it was in your time due to many important discoveries and technological advancements that we have made in recent years. Although this is still your earth, the same planet you were born into, all those years ago, I hope you will discover that in time, you will grow to understand and accept the many changes that have taken place since then."

"Tell me about these changes, Lord Bandersant, I wish to know." I urged him vehemently.

"I can tell you most things," he replied in his soft, low voice, "but others you must see and learn for yourself. Man-made many mistakes in your time, as you are well aware. The violence, greed, suffering, selfishness, and the quest for world domination all came to a crux, which resulted in a world war, the very war you slept through almost a thousand years ago. The world population is not as it was in your time, Newton. It is now a fraction of what it was then, which was far too much in any case. There are no more wars. We have not had any conflicts or violence of any kind for over 500 years, thanks to a new common belief which resulted in the consolidation of the whole world."

I was confused, "What about religion and politics? Has that changed much?"

Lord Bandersant laughed aloud, "Changed? Yes, you could say there were many changes, all for the better indeed. The causes of violence, corruption and greed, were all instigated by the Neanderthal or Monkey Mind of mankind himself, in the primitive era and continued to flourish throughout the centuries. Even in your time, Newton, the so-called twenty-first century, when man considered himself to be a highly intelligent and civilised creature, yes, a creature indeed, as for highly intelligent? He thought he was intelligent, but he was merely a cave man with access to highly intelligent and sophisticated technology. Nothing else. Primitive creatures mixed with sophisticated technology was a bad alliance. It did nothing to change him into a loving and caring human being that he was meant to be, not until he banished false doctrines and embraced the true religion which was first given to him by the true prophet himself."

I struggled to keep my eyes open. The feeling of extreme comfort of my warm bed came over me all of a sudden, but I wanted to listen to Bandersant, as his facts were essential to me, to help me to understand what went on in the world while I was in a deep sleep. "Tell me about this true religion," I asked, "is it practised now? Here, in this city?"

"Yes, it is widely known, worldwide. It is a simple religion; it is the truth, the only truth. It is based on a belief, which in your time was feared by most men, in particular, those who were more engrossed and obsessed with matter and the material universe. Spiritualism is the true and only religion of today, Newton, as it relates to every living creature in the universe because each constitutes an obvious similarity of mind, body, and spirit."

I was lost for words for a brief moment in time, as I have never given much thought to religious matters and, in particular, the spiritual side of things. I was brought up in the Catholic religion, and I had no freedom to choose any other. I had been expected to attend church each and every Sunday lest I should be cast into hell to suffer and burn for all eternity, so I was told by the men of the cloth, and also the women, whom I feared the most. The only spirit that I was aware of in those days was the Holy Spirit, which was slightly confusing to a young boy anyway, as the details were never explained to me. The ghosts, of course, were even more puzzling; I feared them too and associated them with haunted buildings and the Hollywood and Pinewood film industry.

Lord Bandersant chuckled when I told him the extent of my spiritual experience, and he reiterated vehemently that ghosts did not exist in the world today because, naturally, there was no place for them anymore. He explained that they were no more other than disgruntled spirits of humans who had lost their body suddenly and tragically and had refused to accept that they were dead. Their reluctance to come to terms with this and move on to the next level of existence, as dictated by spiritual law, inhibited them from progressing spiritually thus they remained earthbound in spiritual form, which we knew and accepted as ghosts.

Karla grew impatient and made insinuations to demonstrate this from where she was seated in a cosy looking chair at the dining table. She had put in a great deal of creative effort in the preparation of the food, and I guess that she did not want her talents to go unnoticed. I learnt later that she had also developed an increasing attraction towards me in a short space of time, which she, or I for that matter, could not explain, so she did not wish to disappoint me at this stage.

Lord Bandersant took note immediately, "Ah, refreshments!" he cried, as he gestured towards the table then he began to make his way over to Karla, "Your Karla is waiting, Newton, let's go and eat. We shall talk some more, then you must rest before you see Doctor Gabriel in the morning."

I followed him to the dining table as I wondered how I would know when it was morning, as I did not have my watch and, strangely enough, I haven't seen anybody else wearing one. I didn't see a clock outside in the square either, nor have I come across one in this vast mansion as yet. Not even on the mantlepiece, where one would expect a clock to be.

When I mentioned this fact to Bandersant, once we were comfortably seated and enjoying the excellent fresh food, he laughed and said, quietly, "There is no time here." He must have felt sorry for my ignorance and lack of knowledge and understanding of his world when he saw my expression in response. Somehow I guessed that he did not want to explain it in detail right now, so I left it at that. "Karla will be your keeper of time," he uttered suddenly and succinctly, in between a mouthful of papaya fruit. My Karla will be my keeper of time? I was slightly confused by the statement he had made earlier. It led me to believe that she had been explicitly assigned to watch over me and to accompany me during my stay, for security reasons perhaps? Or was she his spy?

Although I have no long-term memory or short term for that matter, I was still able to distinguish the sensation of taste from an experience from the past, which I was sure had derived from a memory bank somewhere deep inside my mind. A mind, which I had no direct access to; perhaps it was affected by some unexplained force here in this place? I decided not to question Bandersant further, as I was enjoying the taste of the food. Fresh fruit, a selection of cooked meat and vegetables, which all had a distinctive feeling of organic freshness, and a natural earthy flavour. This enjoyable experience took me back to my childhood, the one that I had no recollection of, and reminded me so much of my early life, in the days of natural and unprocessed food.

Karla made an attempt at reading my mind this time. Just as I had finished my thought she leant over and kissed me on the cheek and told me, in a warm, soft voice, that none of the food here is processed, it comes straight from its own source. I could still sense her soft, moist lips and the warmth of her gentle breath against my skin. That sensation and a full stomach did much to contribute towards the best nights' sleep I have ever had, as far as I can remember, that is.

Before that, Lord Bandersant answered my question concerning crime in this world. I was eager to know how they managed to eradicate it thoroughly, and what measures of punishment and deterrence was enforced to maintain such prolonged bliss? He did not enter into any detail, as he wished to tell me more in the morning when I was regenerated, as he put it. However, he did leave me a clue to ponder over, but nothing else. He wasn't about to give away too much; He merely said, in his low, serious tone, "We invented Ghost Crystal."

After the most refreshing shower I have ever had, in a comfortable, hi-tech shower system, which looked so beautifully constructed, and most generously finished in natural luxury marble, with copious amounts of gold trim, I climbed into my warm, comfortable bed and fell into a deep sleep. Shortly after, I had experienced what I had thought was a lucid dream. I dreamt that I was awake, and in a daze, lying in bed with the covers on. I heard a noise as if somebody had entered the room. I wasn't too concerned because of the dream-like state I was in, which didn't seem real in any case, and the fact that I was in a crime-free world, contributed to my unperturbed condition. Suddenly I felt the thick quilt peel back. Somebody had climbed into my bed. I felt soft, warm hands on my bare skin. As I attempted to turn over to catch a glimpse of the intruder, I felt a long slender, smooth leg entwine with mine, and then a warm, soft, familiar voice whispered in my ear, "Newton, what is your desire?" I was startled. I became more aware but still in a dream-like state. "Karla? Is that you?" I whispered, then I realised that I must have been dreaming about Karla because of last night at the dining table. I shouldn't have looked at her so much, and I believed this thought was imprinted somewhere in my mind. I immediately relaxed and decided to play along with the dream, as it was like no other that I could ever remember. It was so vivid and so real. I stroked her long silky hot legs. Suddenly, she threw me onto my back, and then she mounted me like a steed. I began to caress her soft body as she heaved into me, too and fro. Then like a killer whale toying with its prey, she rolled over and tossed me into the air like a seal. I clung to her arms desperately, but the moisture under my fingers caused my hands to slide, as I slowly lost my grip.

She clasped my torso with her long slender legs and wrapped them around my back in a vice-like grip, like a snake entwined with its prey. I can remember thinking to myself 'what a dream! And I wondered whether all women in this place they call Heaven were as strong as this one in real life or was it just my wishful thinking?' My body was tossed in all directions like a rag doll as she screamed out in a state of frenzy.

After what seemed like half an hour of extreme ecstasy and passion, we both collapsed on the bed, our drenched bodies bounced up and down until they finally came to rest in a heap, embedded into the soft, comfortable mattress. I questioned myself as to why I hadn't woken up just before the best part of the dream had begun? As I had always done so many times in similar lucid dreams, which culminated in pleasure or fear. For instance, if I were to jump off a tall building in most of them, I would always wake up just before I hit the ground.

This particular dream felt too real in every sense, and the desirable experience wasn't over yet. As I lay on the bed panting for breath I felt a soft hand glide across my chest, then the other hand began to work on my legs; slender fingers gently stroking my skin, arousing a desirable sensation over my entire body. This state of bliss continued until the soft hands had visited every inch of my body. I reciprocated, my fingers sensing every contour of the petite, curvy torso. I toyed with her light golden blonde hair and was charmed by its silky texture, which flowed gracefully and effortlessly between my fingers. This dream was so real I just didn't want it to end. I didn't want to wake up from this one. But all things must come to an end, I thought, even in a place that they call Heaven.

I opened my eyes. It was daylight, the morning I guess, judging by the voices I heard in the street, "Good morning!" "Good morning to you too!" I felt refreshed just as Lord Bandersant had said I would, in the morning. It must have been the fantastic food that I had eaten yesterday. I checked the bed. No signs of Karla, or anybody else. Of course, why would there be? After all, it was only a dream, a realistic one no doubt. Lord Bandersant did warn me about the effects of the natural, organic food on my delicate digestive system, much used to additives and preservatives. He stated that only time would help my body to become accustomed to this natural and highly nutritious sustenance. If this is the result after my first meal, I hasten to wonder what my dreams would be like after a year or more in this heavenly place.

CHAPTER 3

Heaven On Earth

"Newton! Good morning!" I heard his voice, but it was distant. Somewhere out in the hall, it echoed around the intricate, ornate carved cornices.

"Good morning! Come in, Lord Bandersant!" I called back to him, as I sat up in my bed.

He entered the room carrying a tray of multi-coloured fresh fruit, and he had a broad smile on his face. He approached the bed and made a gesture towards the floor at something, which was out of my field of view, "I see you and Karla acquainted yourselves last night? Good, excellent, Newton. Now eat up and get dressed. Doctor Gabriel will be here to see you later." He placed the tray on the small table by the bed and then left the room before I could question him. I wondered how he could have known about my dream, as I had deliberately blocked all thoughts of it from my mind just before he had entered the room, as a precaution, or so I thought; yet he still managed to pick up on it. Admittedly he couldn't have read my sub-conscious memory?

I decided that a nice hot shower before breakfast would calm me down a little. Perhaps I will adjust the temperature and have a cool one, if I manage to find the controls, or understand this new technology, as everything seemed to be touch control in this place.

I leapt from the bed and headed towards the cubical, but something strange and obscure caused me to freeze in my tracks. A little fear ran through my entire body for a single moment. I had caught sight of something in the corner of my eye. Whatever it was, it was laying there quite still on the floor at the foot of my bed. Thoughts flashed through my mind at the speed of light, just like when one is about to face impending danger. My head erupted with thoughts, could it be animal? Creature? Robot? My old twenty-first-century mind, or Monkey Mind, as Bandersant succinctly put it, raced on ahead conjuring up a string of bad images, then I remembered what Lord Bandersant had said about Karla when he brought in my breakfast. I distinctly recall seeing his eyes wander in that direction when he made the gesture. I couldn't see it at the time, as the bed had obscured my view. It was quite clear now. Oh, no! I slumped to the floor in a state of shock, knowing entirely what I had done. I strolled over to where the thing on the floor was. I could see that it was a heap, of something, tucked in well against the bed, and partly under it. I bent down to discover to my horror the identity of the contents. I picked up one of the items from the top of the heap. I didn't need to examine the rest to confirm my fears, as I was quite sure that these garments had belonged to Karla. Who else?

I did not enjoy my morning shower, not as good as the first one I had last night, despite my discovery and eventual understanding of the sophisticated controls. The whole experience was incredibly invigorating and artificially generated quite skilfully by thirtieth-century technology. My constant tweaking with the controls made it even more comparable to standing under a waterfall in a real rainforest, experiencing all the natural sounds and the distinctive aromas one would expect to find in a tropical jungle. But I was unable to concentrate properly. I guess I was more worried about meeting Karla again after what had happened last night, more than anything else. So I abandoned the controls and dried off before making my way to the dressing room to examine the wardrobe, which Lord Bandersant had promised to stock up with a plethora of clothing to replace what I didn't have. He must have sent his men in black while I was sleeping last night. They had stocked it up entirely with a wide variety of quality garments and shoes, and other useful paraphernalia, for which I was genuinely grateful.

After my delicious fresh fruit breakfast, I rested a while on the comfortable sofa. I must have dozed off and dreamt of a beautiful tiger with the most amazing colourful stripes. It had calmly strolled into my room, placed its paw on my knee as if to greet me, and then it calmly sat down on the floor by my feet. I was sure I was dreaming this time because this animal didn't make any attempt to maul or devour me. I'm sure that would have been the case had it been real. I fell asleep stroking its fur, which was ultra soft and warm like that of artificial hair of a stuffed toy. Hours past, or so I thought, it was actually less than one to be more precise when I was woken by a child calling.

"Alice! Oh, there you are! I told you not to run off like that, you naughty pussycat." The girl's voice shouted to the tiger, as it lay motionless at my feet. My countenance must have given her an indication that I was about to get up and run for my life, as soon as I opened my eyes. At that very moment, I had realised that I was wrong again and that this experience was yet still the real deal, and not a dream.

36

"Hello," she said, quite calmly as she knelt before me, hugging the creature as if it was a stuffed teddy bear, "my name is Sophista, and this is my pet cat, Alice."

"My name is Newton Flotman," I replied calmly. I soon realised that I wasn't about to be eaten or mauled by this giant man-eater, so I decided that it was best to just keep calm. I stroked the cat's fur, as she lay motionless, her heavy bulk resting firmly down on my feet, the weight of her huge body held them fast to the floor. "You're young to have such a big cat as a pet," I said, somewhat regretfully, fearing that I was out of touch with life on earth for almost a millennia. As far as I was concerned, big cats could have been the new common house pet in this century which every little child desired to possess, and I had no business to dictate to a child what was right or wrong in her own world, a world which I knew nothing about? I quickly disguised my embarrassment with a broad smile.

She returned the smile,

"I'm Ten," she said, "How old are you?"

"I am…" I struggled with my words and decided that a real answer would not go down too well. However, Lord Bandersant saved me, when he strolled into the room wringing his hands, "There you are, Sophista, with that big pussycat!" He exclaimed, jovially, "Your father is searching for you, he is in the dining room next door with Prangalistra," He gave her a gentle pat on the head, "go and join them; we shall be along in a moment."

The striped beast got up and followed her out. My aching legs were free at last, although I wasn't able to stand up properly just yet due to the numbness permeating in my toes.

"You will be all right to walk in a few moments, once the blood has circulated again." Lord Bandersant said, rather casually, as if it was quite normal to have a fully-grown tiger sitting on your feet, then he sat down on the sofa. "Doctor Gabriel is here. He's next door with Karla."

"Is she all right?" I asked, perhaps a little too hastily, before he had barely finished saying her name.

"Of course she is," Bandersant, replied, with many surprises, "she is much happier now. Come, let us go, eat and talk. We all have much to learn."

The dining room was opulent and grand like a kings' palace from what I could remember from photos of kings' palaces in books. This one was adorned with more gold, silver and precious gems than any palace I have ever seen in my time. The centre of the room was decorated with a large round dining table, which was laden with food. The perimeter of the room was lined with comfortable looking well-upholstered chairs, which seemed much more inviting than the sofa in my room next door. I could have kicked myself for being so absent-minded. Didn't Lord Bandersant show me three rooms, including this one, and told me to use them at my own leisure? I could have slept for another thousand years in any one of these comfortable chairs.

"What are you thinking of, Newton, with that smile on your face?" A soft, familiar voice rang out beside me. It was Karla. I asked her where she had been all morning, she responded by kissing me gently on the lips. I was startled, not by her kiss, but only by the embarrassment, it may have generated, as there were other people present in the room also. She reassured me, "Don't worry, Newton, we are as one now." She said gently, and she kissed me softly on the lips again, this time it was a lingering one. I wanted it to last forever, but she slowly backed away, her lips still pursed, "I will see you later," she said. Somehow I thought she was teasing me.

"Introduce me to your primaeval specimen, Lord Bandersant!" Said the tall, blond curly haired man, who had entered the room while I had been busy admiring the furniture. He was accompanied by a tall olive-skinned woman, who had attractive looking almond eyes. She came straight over to me and offered me a long-fingered hand. "Excuse Doctor Gabriel, he loses himself when he gets excited about something of great interest. My name is Prangalistra, I'm the Doctor's soul mate."

"I haven't divulged that information to Newton yet," Lord Bandersant said as he glanced over at Prangalistra, "in fact, he knows little of this new world, so we all need to enlighten his soul first."

"How do you feel?" Doctor Gabriel asked.

"Tired, sometimes," I replied.

"Impurities, Doctor?" Lord Bandersant inquired.

"That also, and an acute accumulation of free radicals, charged with who knows what lethal dose of chemicals those primitive souls used back in those days. I will try a cleanser, and leave the rest to self-extract." Doctor Gabriel looked into my eyes as if he were looking for something of great interest in them, "Do you like the food here?" He asked.

"It is the best food I have ever tasted, as far as I can remember," I replied most sincerely, "I think it is doing something to my mind though because my dreams have become more vivid. Do you enhance the food with chemicals, or treat the soil in any way?"

"No!" Doctor Gabriel roared, in a jovial manner, "No such primitive acts here, not in this day and age, as you will soon find out, Newton. You'll be surprised yet." He concluded with a smirk.

"Come, let us eat!" Lord Bandersant announced, and then he led us all to the round table in the room where we sat down on high backed, comfortable dining chairs, in our designated places. Doctor Gabriel sat to my left side. Beautiful Karla was on my right, close enough to me that she was able to grab my hand underneath the table and squeeze it gently as she blew me a kiss. Little Sophista, seated to the right of Karla. Sophista giggled when she saw what Karla had done. I looked around for her tiger then I gestured to her that it was nowhere to be seen. She smiled a cheeky smile, then pointed at the table and promptly held her finger to her lips. I chose not to disturb the silk table covering to take a peek underneath just to confirm the animals' presence, in case she saw me and decided that my lap might be more comfortable than the floor.

"Here's your cleanser, Newton," Doctor Gabriel said as he thrust a small clear crystal into my hand. When I suggested to him that it was too large to swallow, he laughed and said that the pill was inside the crystal case and I had to take it out and swallow it with some water.

It was only after I had swallowed it that he had warned me to be cautious first, let it rest in the mouth with a little water, he said, so that it may become accustomed to your system or else you may experience an overload. I thought he meant that the overload would come later, so I envisaged that if I were to swallow the pill first, the food would follow and then digest inside my stomach together with the pill. Lord Bandersant reminded me that I was no longer in the twenty-first century, but the thirtieth and that the 'monkey mind' was incompatible with their advanced ultra-technology, so I should take great care to adhere to specific instructions when dealing with delicate matters of this nature.

"These pills have been around for almost a century," he said, as he began cutting into a large steak, which was almost the size of his plate "Although, they have a limited effect on our people. However, we still find a use for them in exceptional circumstances."

"Just in case you come across a cave man from a primitive world?" I quipped, in jest, which caused the whole table to erupt with laughter.

"Tell me, Newton," said Doctor Gabriel, "Can you not remember anything from your past? Do you know what type of experiments your scientists were carrying out at the time?"

"No, Doctor, I can remember nothing of these events," I replied. "I only know that I am on earth eight centuries later, but at first I did believe that I was on a different planet far more advanced than the earth, judging by the level of technology that I had witnessed. When Lord Bandersant and his guards rescued me, I was under the impression that I had been captured by aliens, and I will admit now that I seriously considered a means of escape."

"Why didn't you succeed?" Prangalistra asked, in her deep, commanding voice.

"I changed my mind once I had been taken to your gold dome building."

"The Golden Dome," Doctor Gabriel said, as he enjoyed a mouthful of steak. He chewed a little more then he continued, "Our recovery room. Your ancient tribe called them hospitals."

He must have noticed the puzzled look on my face, "The room was bare. I saw no instruments to indicate that this building was a working hospital, apart from the interrogation table."

"You must not assume, dear Newton," he replied, "you are eight centuries late indeed, what do you imagine man has achieved technologically during all that time? Mankind has finally reached his true potential only because he progressed in the right direction, unlike ancient man, who chose to regress instead and in the wrong direction, despite correct instruction from the great Prophet. Since around the time of the birth of Christ, man relied on war and oppression to maintain control of his fellow man. His greed for even more power led him to invade other lands to destroy the inhabitants, and seise their wealth, while the potential for peace and prosperity has always been present and well within his reach. Two thousand years later, your kinfolk still suffer the very same symptoms of greed for power and ownership. You were once given the opportunity to create and to utilise sophisticated technology, which had the potential to enhance your way of life beyond your wildest dreams, yet all that you ever achieved, in the end, was war… and more conflict until, ultimately, you reached the point of no return where the only outcome was total self-destruction.

"We were able to reconstruct a totally peaceful new world from the ashes of your old one within eight centuries. Thanks to a great man called, Samuel Page. In the year AD 2520 after mankind had consumed his belly full of destruction and greed, it was decided that these same mistakes of the past should never be repeated ever again. But to achieve this, we needed to head in a totally new direction, a direction, which eventually was to lead us to where we are now, Newton. We are living in a total utopia."

I started to feel the effects of the pill. My head began to spin wildly, then it stopped. It spun faster in the opposite direction, and I tried to ignore it by drinking glass after glass of deliciously sweet fruit juice in between mouthfuls of steak.

"It is true that we have had some difficulties and disagreements, which caused the odd war or two along the way, but we are not perfect, Doctor Gabriel." I said to him, "What did this Samuel Page achieve? Was he the new prophet who had come to save you all from evil and sin?"

Doctor Gabriel took a deep breath, "He wasn't a prophet as such," he said, as he started on another thick, juicy steak, then he glanced at Lord Bandersant, who nodded his approval. Doctor Gabriel continued with added enthusiasm, "Samuel Page made a discovery which was to shake the foundations of every religion on the face of this, formally sick and pitiful, little planet. It was a discovery, which would expose the true faith, one, which all mankind could understand, and follow. It was a pure religion, a religion that was explored as early as 6750 BC by the Borean race of the Herman tribe. Mankind needed a common belief that was familiar to all men throughout the world, a system to bind their souls as one and not to cause any division, which could eventually lead them to disagreement and conflict. There are three primary paths of progress, the first being, the development of the intellect; and the second one is the purification of human love; and finally, the transformation in Divine love, where one would eventually develop a relationship with God and receive God's divine love. The worship of false prophets and futile heavenly beings was banished from the world by AD 2530. And we continue today earnestly requesting divine love directly from the pure divine spirit, our true creator, known to all mankind as God.

I paused a while, as I anticipated that he would elaborate on this, because he told me nothing new, except for a brief history of the Herman tribe. I needed more.

"He, Samuel Page, discovered God?" I asked, with conviction. There was laughter in the room, something I half expected, but didn't mind, as I wanted to goad him into revealing all the facts to me.

"He knew God, truly," Doctor Gabriel replied, "But most importantly, as far as man is concerned, he had developed a new method of communication with discarnate spirits on the other side."

"To communicate with the dead?" I asked, curiously.

"No," he replied firmly, "One cannot communicate with the dead, simply because there is no death. Samuel Page developed a method of communication by way of Ghost Crystal, a crystal made from several thin layers of various natural crystals, which had been embedded with gold and silver particles along with an equal quantity of various other chemical elements in a complicated process, which I shan't explain at this moment. This highly balanced combination, when induced with an enormous boost of electromagnetic radiation, he found that a phenomenon had occurred inside the crystal formation, this somehow made it possible for him to observe and communicate directly with the spirit world. At last, mankind had made a great breakthrough in the discovery of a true gateway for the direct communication with the spirit world, which was one hundred percent accurate and true. This invention revolutionised spiritualism beyond all expectations."

"This happened in AD 2520, almost three hundred years ago?" As I was curious to learn how far they have developed this thing in all that time. Somehow he had sensed this, perhaps from the tone of my voice, or could he read a mind better than Lord Bandersant could?

"Newton, to us, progress does not develop in the way that it did in your time," Doctor Gabriel replied, as he started feasting on the fresh fruit now. "We progress according to our requirements, and not for greed, profit, or world domination. Those vices no longer exist here in our perfect, happy world."

Prangalistra's intense stare alerted me to thinking that she too was adept in mind reading. Her low tone projected directly towards my ears. "Perhaps Newton thinks that we are a world in which its people still trade with each other for gain, just as they did in his time?" She looked around the table at the others, searching for assurance, "I have read some history on his time. They traded with finance, which was the cause of much of their conflicts."

I was utterly baffled now. However, I did have my suspicions when I first realised the vast abundance of wealth here; the gold, silver, and precious stones. Practically all their buildings were adorned with opulence.

"What about all the wealth here, it is surely the result of acquired spoils of war, perhaps in the past?" I dared to ask.

"No, Newton!" Doctor Gabriel corrected me rather vociferously, and then I realised he did so not because he had read my mind but because I had unknowingly spoken aloud something that I should have kept in my thoughts. A habit I had acquired since my rescue, as with my dreams, I found myself suddenly unable to discern reality from the dream world, or was it the spirit world? Each melded seamlessly into one complete experience, and the feeling was growing stronger each day.

He continued, "Not from war, Newton. Perhaps Lord Bandersant has not informed you yet, but we do not trade here, or anywhere else in the world, for that matter. This may come as a surprise to you, Newton, but for you to fulfil a happy and successful life here, you must..."

"Dispense with the 'Monkey mind!' Lord Bandersant interjected. "I did inform him, but not, I'm afraid, with the specifics. Newton, we do not trade here because we do not use currency... of any type. It was abolished since around the time of Samuel Page because it brought nothing but misery and suffering to man, in the past. Our forebears became tired of a world controlled by tyrants, thieves, murderers, and liars, who almost always seemed to own and control most of the world's wealth. Without money, they were rendered totally useless, as most of them lacked knowledge and wisdom, and indeed compassion and love for their fellow man. As the paucity of money increased rapidly, they noticed a great change throughout the world. Wealthy cretins were no longer in control of anything important, only their slow demise. Instead, the intelligent and practical rose to power, and so did the teachers and the carers of this world. They were the ones who were suddenly important now. They were the ones now in demand, they instigated the new beginning."

I gestured to the table, which was filled with, what looked like, a generous variety of food from every corner of the globe, "Who is paying for all this?" I asked. Karla grabbed me around the waist and gently pulled me towards her. "Newton," she whispered in my ear, but it was enough for the entire table to hear, "the food comes from the ground. It grows from the earth. We just pick it and eat it. Nobody pays for it."

If ever there was a moment when I was to display my real ignorance and confirm my original status of the 'Monkey mind' it was right now, at this moment, during this pause. Embarrassing abeyance of time, with all eyes on me, like in theatre, spectators staring in silence awaiting the performer's next move, his following deliverance of speech, which I did not have. I could not find. I needed a saviour right now, so I imagined that Alice would leap from underneath the table and grab me with her giant paws and drag me under, out of sight; A clean stage left exit.

Alice did not save me; I didn't think she would anyway because I was quite sure that during the embarrassing silence I had heard her snoring heavily under the table.

It was the sheer intimacy of Karla's wet kiss on my cheek that caused the silence to suddenly break, and then diverted the subject of the discussion to love. Prangalistra boasted about the abundance of human love, which existed in their world today compared with that in my time. I had no option but to agree with her, after all, wasn't the lack of love one of the main reasons our society had descended into darkness and depression? They all nodded in agreement.

I sat and stared at the happy faces around the table, wondering when I would wake up, and perhaps this joy will suddenly end, and I would find myself back in my old world listening to the same old news of violence, greed, and suffering. 'You're not going to, Newton,' Lord Bandersant would say, 'this is your world now.' He told me, that to have a basic understanding of this world, I would need to explore it a little and find out about all the new things for myself. And there was plenty to see. A wealth of modern science and technology, which you only knew of in your childhood science fiction stories, is waiting to be discovered. "You can sit here in the comfort of the city," he said, "and hide away from the reality of it all if that is what you desire, but in our opinion, we would advise you to devote some time to catch up with what you have missed out on in the past. But you will need an open mind to be able to ingest it all, and to accept it all."

I liked the look of those massive islands in the middle of the ocean. I read about them in a brochure I found in my apartment, or should I say my little palace, as I felt like a king here. I was indeed treated like one. Bandersant corrected me about the islands and informed me that they were not islands at all but ocean liners that sailed continuously around the world on a perpetual cruise. Somewhat surprised, I asked him if they carried any cargo on the way? And where do they berth to enable the passengers to board? He laughed on both questions and corrected me once again stating that they were solely for the purpose of recreation and that they would be far too slow to carry cargo, and in any case, they never berth, as we have no dock large enough to accommodate them. It was decided and agreed at the time of construction, that it would be much easier to board them by air.

"So they have airports on deck as well?" I asked, sounding much like an overexcited kid.

"Yes, they do have provisions for airships." He replied.

As a former pilot, as somewhere in my memory I perceived a desire for flying, and I felt that I knew the basics. I was confident that I still knew how to fly; I had an interest in aircraft, and airships of all kinds. I did mention to Lord Bandersant that since my time here I have never seen nor heard any aircraft in the cloudless blue sky. He, of course, laughed, and then told me, in a quiet voice, 'Perhaps you are thinking of 800-year-old aircraft? Things are a lot different today, Newton. We don't bounce around on air like you did in your time. We destroyed the laws of gravity a few hundred years ago. Our ships are much faster and quieter than any you have ever seen in your lifetime.'

With that, he said, quietly once more, that there is some craft, which is docked on the landing platform on the roof of the building, just above my bedroom. "Perhaps you and Karla could take one out and go exploring a little. You needn't worry about getting lost, as she has detailed knowledge of the entire geographical area, and the ships have advanced built-in navigational systems anyway."

The feast went long into, what I assumed to be, late afternoon, judging by the position of the sun. The annoying absence of timepieces made it quite challenging to manage time efficiently each day. 'Live for the moment,' Doctor Gabriel would say, 'the pace of life is how you wish it to be each day. Sometimes relaxed, and then sometimes a little slower; we are not governed here by time."

I found this difficult to comprehend, as, in my time on this very earth, time was of paramount importance. Every detail of our lives was controlled by the clock; it told us when to go to bed, when to wake up, when to eat, when to work, and when to stop work. Doctor Gabriel shook his head violently from side to side when I told him, 'No, no, no,' he would say when I explained my experience with time. Time even told us when to retire, and it often dictated when we should die! Which galvanised Doctor Gabriel into a lively discussion about death.

"Monkey man feared death," he began, in a lively tone of voice, "ancient man used death as a punishment. In your time, Newton, you still feared death, and you also believed it to be a punishment and so, used it as a weapon of fear against your fellow man. I realise that you even fear it now, even though you should by now, be long dead and buried. What if you had died in that chamber, Newton, where do you think you would be now? 'Living on borrowed time' I believe is the phrase that you used in your period on earth?"

I couldn't find an answer to such a complicated question, but I replied anyway, "I'd be dead, of course."

He shook his head, "Just as I thought," he mumbled, and then added a few sad words, which were too quiet to decipher. "We need to enlighten you first." He suddenly said with a raised voice. Then he went over to Lord Bandersant and spoke a few quiet words with him.

I had an inkling of their next move, perhaps to educate me in some way with details and facts about the way that they live in this fabulous new world. I was brought into it like a newborn baby, with a limited knowledge of instinctive ideas, half of which were gleaned from the residue of my former life. However, I must admit that with each day, the ones I bother to count, that is, my memory seems to increase in strength. Not in a way that would allow me to remember how I had ended up deep in the belly of the earth inside a complex life support system, and why I was there in the first place, as my memory lacked specific details, which were crucial to the complete understanding of my existence here. I had no idea where I lived, or what country I had originated from, whom I loved, or indeed of the many influential people in my life, or the few. But memories of little experiences, which were usually associated with instinctive habits or desires were sometimes triggered by, I believe, the consumption of excellent and natural highly nutritious food that this desirable world provided in abundance.

Doctor Gabriel said that this was due to my 'Monkey mind' becoming more aware of the spiritual universe, but sadly this progress had been delayed by the abundance of residual impurities present in the physical body. He went on to state that the problem was reinforced by my Neanderthal attitude and thinking, which would only serve to postpone this development. Doctor Gabriel concluded that I should continue to consume, in abundance, a variety of the natural and excellent food that I adored so much, and drink from the natural rivers to improve my soul inspiration. Lord Bandersant agreed when I told him, he claimed that the food contained nutrients like I had never seen in my time when the earth was a dirty cesspit and sickness, and disease was rife, and the health benefits of these clean foods constituted the capability to nourish and cleanse the physical body beyond belief. My tainted self was perhaps the most contaminated organism on the planet at this moment in time, and presently it was undergoing an enhanced spring clean.

"Newton, do not be deluded by the true value of pure water!" He exclaimed, "As your forebears did when they polluted it with their futile chemicals for the sake of profit and gain, which resulted in disease and death. The water here is clean and pure, and it has the potential to speed up the cleansing process tenfold. You should feel the effects, and benefits almost immediately."

I did enjoy the food very much, and I was willing to try almost anything new or different. So far, the incredible experiences, which I was lucky enough to benefit from in this peaceful modern world, were as evident and real as the most lucid dreams that I have ever experienced in my entire life. On the physical side, I could not fully understand my relationship with Karla and why it had been developing at such a rapid pace. I held her soft hands in mine and looked into her beautiful bright eyes. All I could see was a warm loving and kind heart. There was no pain or sorrow, not from her or any other living creature that I had the pleasure of meeting since my inception into this beatific realm. Even Alice, bless her furry soul, who was much considered a wild and dangerous animal back in my time, with whom I would never dream of coming so close to, as I had done so already, without the thought of being eaten alive. I know she has not been drugged in any way as, on close inspection of her eyes, they reveal a great deal of love and compassion. As far as my instinct serves me, I would never ever recommend looking into the eyes of a fully-grown tiger, in particular, while it had its paws resting on one's feet, except, perhaps, in a dream. Provided that I was capable of discerning this from reality.

That's it! There is no fear here in this blissful place. I see no fear in the eyes of my Karla. I see no fear in the eyes of any of the other living creature, simply because, unlike in my time on earth, it seems that fear may have been completely eradicated.

"You see no fear because there is no fear." Said the voice to my left.

"There must be fear, what about jealousy, hatred, and envy, do they exist?" I asked Doctor Gabriel, as he stood up wringing his hands, "They do not indeed, simply because of the abundance of two things in this material world, love and truth!" He announced and confirmed with an inflexion. "The monkey mind is truly ready for the complete revelation of love and truth. You shall learn of the Ghost Crystal, Newton Flotman! And only then will you know of love and truth."

If it weren't for the look on Karla's face, I would have had my reservations about Doctor Gabriel's offer. Her warm and robust hug convinced me entirely, as I trusted Karla immensely. We shared something more profound than love itself, something, which I would later learn, would change my whole concept of life and death forever.

CHAPTER 4

The Ghost Crystal

"In the past, man relied on clairvoyance to communicate with the dead. The dead? No, not the dead because, in simple terms, there are no dead, only living souls that have passed on to the next level of existence."

They lead me to this place where I am now standing bewildered having been taken there directly from the back of my apartment first through to a lush green garden. I witnessed enough fruit and vegetables growing to feed a small army. I remembered descending in a lift shaft and down into a concealed underground chamber, I would not for one moment believe that this place ever existed, Just feet away from where I had been sleeping each night.

"This is it, Newton Flotman. The Ghost Crystal. The largest piece of handmade crystal ever made, and the most powerful of all on this earth." Doctor Gabriel announced to his small audience, which consisted everybody on our entire table, and even those underneath it. Yes, the overgrown pussycat came too. Alice sat quietly in the corner of the room licking her paws as if she had just swallowed a man, whole. Karla was by my side, clinging helplessly to my arm, rising up and down onto her toes with excitement. Little Sophista displayed her eagerness as well by tugging relentlessly on my other arm. Her childlike animation almost caused it to dislocate from its socket. And it would have done so quite quickly, if Prangalistra had not intervened to save me with a simple gesture, one that I shall remember to use on Sophista the next time the little girl becomes too overexcited. A gentle ruffle of her soft brown hair was all that was required to appease her.

The room was quite spacious with an array of comfortable soft furniture. Somehow it reminded me of a luxury cinema dimly lit by crystal lamps of a strange design and technology that I had very little knowledge.

The light seemed to emanate from the crystal itself yet not project as straight as light should typically, but it transmitted somehow towards solid objects, and then it reflected around them as if it had passed straight through, in a strange but unusual way. I struggled to find sufficient words to explain this phenomenon, as it makes it quite impossible sometimes to identify the actual source of the light. It appeared to me that these smart earth dwelling inhabitants had conquered the laws of light as well as that of gravity.

"We managed to bend everything else," Lord Bandersant said, proudly, when I enquired about this impossible phenomenon, "So light was no exception." Then Doctor Gabriel told me that I could have done the same back in my time if only my people weren't so engrossed in conflict and greed. "You were far too busy making...that useless stuff, you call - Money!" He said, sardonically. "Instead of making progress with technology and spiritual development."

The room was peaceful and tranquil, perhaps ultra soundproofed, as it had an atmosphere similar to that of a recording studio, for what I could remember of one. A large recording studio, because the crystal screen was huge, it measured at least eight feet from the ground to the ceiling, and it was like a giant concave lens, and it emitted soothing light, which had a golden hue.

"Come, Newton, see for yourself," Doctor Gabriel beckoned me to approach the screen, "touch it," he said. I did, and I flinched when my fingers made contact. I expected the screen to be hard and cold like that of glass. It was soft and warm, yet silky. Close-up the light it emitted was a bright, diffused light, which made it look warm and frosty. Doctor Gabriel continued, "In simple terms, the spirit world is merely a world beyond the comprehension of the five senses of man."

"And you have conquered that too," I said, without thinking. Prangalistra stepped forward and ran her slender fingers over the screen, "Newton, you have an obsession with conquering. We don't control the spirit world, we have merely mastered an extremely effective way of communicating with the spirit world and conversing in real time to spirits who wish to communicate directly with us."

Doctor Gabriel expressed his agreement, and then he threw himself into one of the comfortable seats in front of the screen. He beckoned me to the place next to him. The others took their positions in the front row too. Lord Bandersant was standing up directly in front of us.

"Well, Newton, I bet you are dying to know?" He asked.

"Yes," I said, rather excited, much like little Sophista, who had now left the clutches of my arm and had gone over to tend to Alice. "A demonstration would be a great start," I said.

"OK," Doctor Gabriel replied, he then signalled to Karla, who promptly let go of my other arm and walked over to the screen and placed her right palm flat against it. The area of the screen around her hand developed an aura of glowing light, which began to glow as it increased in intensity.

"Why Karla?" I asked, somewhat concerned about her, why? I did not know because of sheer ignorance of this new, unfamiliar technology. I knew for sure that no harm could come to her, not from these people, as I have not yet come across any hostility of any kind, neither from man nor animal, except when Alice tried to lick my face with her papillae ridden tongue. I guess, the most disturbing thought for me was the presence of this vast, bright, ominous screen, bolstered by my morbid fear of ghosts. The fact that I was the only one in the room who could not possibly predict what would happen next made the whole experience much more frightening.

Sophista had joined us again, as she took time out from tending to her cat. Her countenance puts my mind to rest. My monkey mind, forever suspicious and alert with the potential of fear of aggression from predators, or an unprovoked attack from opponents with hostile intentions, was now at ease, as I knew, for sure, that fear cannot dwell or manifest itself here in this room. Sophista, with her beautiful little face, so cute and joyful; its broad smile in excited anticipation for something good; eager for a something to happen; a message from the other side from a long-lost relative, or a friend, in a conventional procedure with which she seemed entirely comfortable.

"Because Karla has the key." He replied, much later than I had first asked the question, and without elaborating any further. "Look!" He shouted. I observed as the entire screen began to glow in a multitude of colours. Karla removed her hand from the screen, and then she took her place on the chair next to me and took hold of my hand once again, squeezing it very gently.

"It's happening," she whispered loudly in my ear, "they are coming through."

"Who?" I asked, in a nervous whisper, my eyes fixed on the bright, changing screen. I could see emerging figures moving about, but I could not tell what they were as they had no definite shape or form, and then, gradually they became much clearer until I was able to discern them. They appeared to be of the human type. I felt the bones in my hand click, as Karla grew more excited, as she increased the pressure of her grip on my hand with gradual intensity. She did so in perfect sync with the steady focusing of the figure in the centre of the screen, which we could see distinctly now as a young man dressed in clothing that I could not make out. He walked towards the screen, and came so close and was so sharply focused on a comparison with the others in the background who were blurred, and appeared to be waiting in line behind him. I was astounded by the absolute clarity of the picture for a brief moment until something strange occurred.

In spite of my temporary absence of memory, which has been improving each day steadily, I can vaguely recall my fascination for three-dimensional movies back in my time which I viewed with the aid of specialised equipment. Three-dimensional eyewear, some of which were somewhat bulky and uncomfortable, and today would widely be considered as ancient technology, indeed by the folk in this world. However, to me, at the time, the results were as close to the real thing as one could expect. What I was seeing with my naked eye on the giant screen directly in front of me right now was, without a doubt, technology far beyond the limits of mankind in my time, and was, in reality, entirely outstanding.

"It is Androgen!" Doctor Gabriel shouted, somewhat excited, yet not too surprised as I expected him to be. I was practically falling off the front edge of my well-upholstered, comfortable chair, with awe at the perfectly formed, three-dimensional figure that had appeared before us. An ethereal glow of light radiated from every portion of his body. His garments were well designed and well fitted. They looked as if they were made partly from leather and thick woven wool fabric. I could not place the design in any era that I knew of in my past, except that they resembled some distinctive, futuristic character from a typical science fiction movie, in my time, that is.

"Who is Androgen?" I asked, nervously, my eyes fixed firmly on the bright, angelic character on the screen.

"Ask Him yourself, Newton," Lord Bandersant replied, with childish excitement, and much delight at the fact that I was awestricken by the whole experience.

"He can see us?" I asked, surprised, I felt my whole body quiver.

"Yes, he can hear us as well, Newton, just as we can see and hear him, even better, no doubt. So don't say anything to him that you wouldn't say if he were alive." Doctor Gabriel said.

I could have reached out and touched this character, as his form was as solid and bright as any of us in the room, even more, apparent in detail, and so shiny and perfect, clean and unblemished. He gazed at each of us in turn, and then he reverted his attention to me.

"Newton?" He said, with a perplexed expression on his face.

Something made me flinch. It was Karla; she had hold of my upper arm, which she gripped with excitement. Too much drama, I hasten to add, enough that I felt her nails slowly pierce my tender skin as she intensified her grip, "Talk to him, Newton! Talk to him!" She urged, gripping me even tighter.

I could not think what to ask, although I had a head full of unanswered questions on how and why I had ended up here in this time, but somehow it didn't seem fair to hijack the séance with my selfish desire for information, even though I had been invited here as a guest. Besides, it was my first attempt in my life, all 800 years or so of it, to communicate with spirits of the dead, an activity I would never have dreamt of participating in back in my time. I've often heard stories of such meetings where the lack of evidence usually provided much disappointment for some of the participants. Without a doubt, even the most hardened sceptic would be forced to agree that the evidence in this room was indeed highly credulous. Unless, of course, they had been showing me a movie, in very, very high definition, three-dimensional, 30th Century technology?

I was yet to discover, as I know for sure that you cannot communicate with the actors on a movie screen. It was either live or recorded. I was about to ask a question, any question, just to relieve my poor arm from little Karla's grasp, but the spirit had beat me to it.

"You are Newton?" He asked, curiously. I nodded, with my mouth gaping. "You do not belong here. You belong in a different sphere." He continued, and then he looked at Karla with a smile and said, "You are unseen, lest the cord be released."

"What does he mean by that?" I asked her. She immediately loosened her grip on my arm.

"I do not know, Newton. Perhaps he has no message for me, because nobody has seen me, or come through yet, that's all." She said succinctly. "Ask him a question?" She blurted out suddenly, in the hope that I would not question her further.

"Never mind me, where do you come from?" I asked him.

"My name is Androgen," the spirit replied, "I live in the first sphere, the one near to your earth. It is not very bright there. I have been here for about one century. I am trying my best to move away from the darkness and hopefully enter the light, which I think is in the second or third sphere, but I find it so difficult to achieve this sometimes."

"Why can't you just move away from the darkness into another. You ghosts can fly there, can't you?" I asked, somewhat naively, I later had learned, because everybody in the room had looked at me as if I was a naughty child. I'm sure Alice did as well.

Even Androgen laughed at my ignorance of the spirit world. Well perhaps a slight exaggeration there, he smiled broadly.

"There are certain rules here, Newton, I cannot move up to a higher sphere until my soul condition allows. I have performed some good deeds while I was living in the flesh, and I have equally done bad things in my time on earth, for these, I must pay the price. That is the way of the spiritual law here. This sphere contains the least light, and it is a place where spirits are paying the penalty for their wrongful thoughts and deeds while they dwelled in the flesh on earth."

"Will you be sent to hell for these sins?" I asked, foolishly I guess, judging by Karla's chuckle, which she followed with a gentle squeeze of my arm.

Androgen walked towards the screen. It looked as if he was about to walk right through it and end up in the room with us, but luckily he had stopped in time at the very edge. "I was a scientist and inventor in my time on earth," he said in a much more quieter tone, "I created robots for my fellow man. These particular robots were crude in design in the first place, and as the years advanced and the technology changed I developed more sophisticated ones, but I soon grew tired with the mundane actions and mannerisms of these mechanical creatures, so one day I decided to add an extra flair to make them more intense."

I was becoming more curious at this stage hoping that he would mention my era, even though I didn't know of him. "Was this in my time?" I asked him.

"It was in your future, Newton, around the year AD 2814." He replied, and then he said something, which made my entire body shiver with shock and fear. "This was a long time after you had died." Then he paused a while and looked around the room before he continued speaking. "You too were unseen, as the cord is circumscribed."

I looked at Karla, she wasn't shocked or surprised, and when I asked her why, she just said that he might be confused, and she went on to explain that there still exists confusion and ignorance in the spirit world, in particular in the lower spheres. I wondered why the others were so silent. Lord Bandersant sat back in his chair, deeply relaxed with a big smile on his face, while Doctor Gabriel looked as though he had a permanent grin, with his eyes fixed firmly on the screen, watching intensely. I was about to disturb them with a question when Androgen just faded and vanished into thin air. I immediately turned to Karla. She could tell by my expression that I required some explanation.

"Don't worry, Newton," she said rather flippantly, "it happens quite frequently, they lose contact, and then they go off somewhere else."

When I looked at the screen again, I saw the other blurred figures just standing there; I presume they were just looking at us, but I couldn't tell for sure because their faces were blurred. The ones in the front row began to come into focus as they stepped forward towards the front of the screen.

When he had come into full focus, I saw the man dressed in a white robe made from a thick, dense fabric. His arms folded and he looked slightly nervous.

"I desire to come to you with a message to bring hope to all men." Then he went on, "My name is Darsaus Cornelius, and I belonged to the Holy Order of the Brotherhood in the 30th Century in the time of Androgen. I have committed many undesirable acts while I dwelled in the flesh., Since I came here to the spirit world, I brought with me nothing but regret, which has not left me in peace since. I have met a bright spirit who calls himself Swedenborg; he claimed that he was selected some time ago as an instrument through which the spiritual truths could be revealed to and understood by mankind. He came to earth in your era, Newton, around AD 1753."

I was indeed, astounded by his reference to me, but the date was inaccurate. I decided to converse with him anyway, "Darsaus, what do you know of me?" I asked, in the hope that this man could provide me with some useful information, anything to help restore my lost memory.

"I know that you lived in the place in your name and that you conspired with others to interfere with the master's time and space by using primitive machines in your fruitless experiments."

"Did we succeed?" I asked, not knowing what he meant by this, but I was hoping that he would reveal more anyway.

"No." He answered, dryly, "Your insatiable desire to wage war against one another took precedence over progression and human development. Your primitive race could not live in peace and harmony, although you had the entire world at your disposal. It was given to you all by the great spirit, yet greed consumed you all until eventually, you depleted your race, and within a small space of time your population was diminished to such a level where it had almost become extinct."

"Tell me more about this Swedenborg?" I urged as Darsaus began to fade away. Suddenly one of the other figures stepped forward and came into sharp focus. She was tall, middle-aged, with long dark hair. She smiled as she glanced around the room, and then she focused her attention on me. "Newton," she said in a soft, sweet voice, "don't be afraid of what you see here. It is of no consequence who I am or what I achieved while in the flesh, other than my sole desire to become one with God through faith, truth, and divine love, which I continuously request through my prayers. You are unique, Newton, you had walked the earth at a time when man developed ignorance, selfishness, and greed. Your kin attained to such level of perfection in profanity and sin that they had convinced themselves that the very nature of its ugliness had become essential for his survival, which he believed was his sole destiny to immerse himself in this banal ritual of death, destruction, and evil.

"He preached and practised this dark art to perfection until the world became rife with sin. In the end, the fools destroyed themselves, and then they dared to blame God for their offensive behaviour. You have seen these unjustified things, Newton you must show these good people here that sin is not the path to bliss and everlasting life, lest they stray from their perfect ways. You must tell them not to stray unto the path of death and destruction lest they end their blissful world, just as your people did in your time."

I was perplexed, and I looked to the others for support, but I got nothing but blank smiles. I asked myself what could I possibly tell these people that they already knew. What influence would my life experience have on them? And how will they benefit from what I had to say to them of the sordid past?

These advanced people had already created their peaceful world, and judging by what I have witnessed so far, had made an excellent job of it. Why would they need my intervention? It seems that this world of spiritual communication is quite mysterious and personal, and specific messages, no matter how cryptic they may seem, can only be interpreted on a personal level.

I started by asking her name, but she would not tell me, she just kept on saying that it was of no consequence and that it was more important that I prepare myself first before I went out to spread the word to the people because it was my destiny.

I was much surprised by what Doctor Gabriel said to her; he suddenly spoke out without any hint of a warning, not even a gesture, "He is not yet ready to see the revelation yet!" He said. But I hadn't a clue what he meant by that.

The spirit immediately looked at him and replied, almost in a harsh whisper, "It is not a matter of being ready, dear Doctor, as the whole procedure is, in itself, an inevitable consequence, that can be easily regulated by a careful administration of a controlled proportion of revelation. As you know, Doctor Gabriel, this purpose must be served upon all, and endured by all who walk the earth in the flesh to maintain stability and to fulfil the journey towards eternal progress."

Doctor Gabriel stood up, this time he made many gestures, with his hands as he spoke, "His mind is of inferior development, and far different from ours; he is from the primitive era. He may not..." he searched for the words, but could not find them, or perhaps he did find them but had restrained himself as not to scare me with the truth. He made his best attempt to rephrase it and continue. "...I just meant that his level of tolerance might not be sufficient to sustain the force of the Revelation, and his mind may suffer as a result. I fear that there could be a possible risk of potential misfortune."

"Oh, come now, Doctor Gabriel," the spirit replied, " You have chosen your words very carefully, no doubt, but surely you do realise that there is a risk in all that we do, especially for you mortals on earth. Have you no faith in your fellow man? Even though you may consider them inferior of mind? How can you be so certain that the monkey mind, as you so succinctly put it, is any less capable than that of your own?"

At this point, I was slightly worried about the content of their discussion, and I accepted that I was the subject to some impending ritual or experiment, but to what extent, I needed to find out. I began to stand up when suddenly a soft, warm hand gently took hold of my forearm, and somehow, at that very moment, I felt a sense of belonging. I felt the love and caring nature through the warmth of her smooth fingers against my skin. Karla pulled me back down, so gently, without uttering a single word, and I was in no mood to offer any resistance. I decided that I should speak from the comfort of my seat, where I would be calm and at ease. "What is it that is so formidable that my monkey mind would not be able to tolerate, Doctor Gabriel? What is this revelation that I am not ready to see?" I asked as I attempted to focus on the Doctor and the spirit on the screen.

"It is nothing that you need to see yet, Newton, don't listen to that spirit, she is ahead of her time." Doctor Gabriel continued.

"I would like to know what I am up against, Doctor Gabriel," I replied, and then I turned to Lord Bandersant, who had been quite reticent up until now, "Lord Bandersant, tell me what is it that I need to see that is so crucial, and inevitable?" I asked him; at this point, I stood up, without any objection or restraint from Karla.

Lord Bandersant rose to his feet and turned to Doctor Gabriel, "Surely, Doctor Gabriel, Newton is wise enough to decide for himself? None of us here know for sure what effect or outcome the revelation would have on Newton's mind. I trust that any decision which he needs to make should be decided only by Newton, and not us. Surely the whole principle of becoming oneness with God is based on love, faith, wisdom, and trust? Is this not true?" He paused for a moment. Doctor Gabriel sat back in his seat, and he made himself as comfortable as he could, "very well, Lord Bandersant," he said with a smile, "show him the revelation if you wish. Show him the revelation and let him decide for himself his level of endurance."

The decisions that they made were indeed conclusive, although I had not a clue or indeed any idea of their intentions concerning the so-called revelation. Doctor Gabriel indicated that I should decide my level of endurance. I took this to anticipate an impending mind-painful experience, or some futuristic ritual, which, I think, somebody would have to explain to me in detail before I agreed to involve myself.

Later on, when I questioned Karla about it, back at the apartment, she just shrugged her shoulders and said that she didn't know much about the revelation. Although, she did mention the fact that she had already experienced it anyway but, strangely, in spite of this, was unable to explain any of it to me. Karla honestly could not remember any of it, as it happened a long time ago when she was young.

I believed every word she said, as I trusted Karla, she seemed uniquely genuine to me, and she would never withhold any information from me. She had the temperament of a saint, yet she could be sensuous, caring, respectful, and vivacious, the perfect woman. In fact, probably the ideal woman I have ever met, as far as I could remember, that is. At times, I thought that her level of perfection was impeccable. Often I would allow myself hints of a shadow of a doubt to invade my clustered mind during these occasions, and then suddenly she would say or do something so pleasing that would immediately dispel all my reservations. It was as if she was tuned into my mind telepathically, or electronically, and she could please me remotely at will. I had even had the cheek to check myself, several times, for signs of bugs while having one of those fabulous rainforest experience showers, but pinching and prodding alone is hardly sufficient investigation to expose concealed bugs or foreign objects in one's body, or clothing.

In consideration of the level of technology in this era, any such bug in existence is likely to manifest itself as a tiny crystal so small, perhaps even the size of a grain of sand. Such minor device could easily have been implanted into the glorious food that I had been enjoying so much and had eaten in abundance since I've been here in this utopian paradise.

I have never once been close to danger, or indeed come to any harm during my time here, so I do often urge myself to remember that I must endeavour, from now on, to quell my suspicions, and to control my suspicious, pessimistic, monkey mind.

CHAPTER 5

Revelation

That night I went for a long walk with Karla, strangely, after she had said that she wanted to take me on a short tour around the city. Short indeed not because she was tired and wanted to go to bed, but because Lord Bandersant had requested that we stay close by as we had a challenging day ahead of us in the morning.

He continued with his secrecy; his reticence proved his reluctance to divulge any details concerning the Revelation; he would not even provide me with a hint of what it entailed, and all my questions put to him seemed futile. He wasn't going to give anything away at all, so I gave up and decided to forget the details and instead concentrate solely on my gallivant around the city with little Karla.

I wasn't particularly sure which country we were in as I could see no distinctive landmarks, either manmade or by nature itself, that could provide me with an indication. These people were not very efficient with names or labels, in any case, they were so relaxed in their happiness that they hadn't bothered to name anything, not even the streets. Luckily I had Karla with me. Lord Bandersant told me that she knew every street, every town, and every city on the entire planet. Of course, I do believe that he was joking with me at the time, although he does not fool very often, in fact not at all, at that particular time we were engaged in heavy eating and drinking. 'Just sampling the wine' as he put it, and I must say, the wine is undoubtedly plentiful here.

Many people in my time on earth thought that they could achieve happiness by attempting to impress everyone around them, these people did not appear to do that at all, there was no need, as it was as if they had nothing to prove. One young couple told me that the happiest people are those who can be themselves, and the people here are probably all as happy as they want to be. That wasn't too difficult to believe, I guess, judging by the abundance of wealth I had witnessed, considering that the use of currency had been extinct for years.

Karla was somewhat confused by the term I used to describe opulence and, indeed, wealth itself. These people did not consider their wealth, the word I used that is, as a fortunate consequence due to some economic success. They described it as a gift from God, the Divine Spirit, from whom they inherited the Earth and all its wonderous things.

Our table at the lively restaurant where we sat that night was full of happy faces, a selection of people of all ages, eating and drinking, and in deep, meaningful conversation. I, of the monkey mind, seem to be the main centre of attention, as they regarded me as a primitive creature from a different world to theirs, in their eyes, but most pleasantly and curiously, I must add. Almost all of them were intrigued and very eager to know what life was like back in my days in this world, nearly a thousand years ago. I had received a somewhat incredulous reaction when I told them that is was not much different to what I see right now. If I happened to open my eyes this very moment and had suddenly found myself here in this place, I would swear that I had been transported not a thousand years into the future but just to another country; perhaps, to a high class, luxury seafront restaurant somewhere in the South of France, maybe. Without the high technology, that is.

I received not gasps of awe and excitement, but a crowd of doubtful stares from a table full of puzzled, but happy, faces, and as if that wasn't enough, I added the fact that the supposed restaurant, where I had opened my eyes after my arrival had been filled with wealthy people! The puzzled faces grew even more puzzled because the term 'wealth' in this world was not the same as it was in mine. In a world devoid of money and ownership of material possessions, wealth has no meaning because it applies to everybody with spiritual wealth and not material wealth.

A middle-aged woman, with fingers, adorned with gold rings, garnished with perhaps the most enormous and splendent precious stones I had ever seen, sipped from a tall glass.

"Newton," she said, just after she swallowed a mouthful of the sweet, pink bubbly liquid, "I have studied some history of life dating back to your era, and it did not sound too promising."

"I know," I replied, "I share the same view. Our history doesn't amount to enjoyable reading either, we've suffered wars and more wars until eventually, world war three."

"Yes, we do not have any wars here, not anymore. They are a thing of the past."

Just then, a well-dressed waiter came over with a tray of silver and gold pots, "More coffee, Sir?" He asked me casually.

"Yes please," I replied as he took my cup. I don't know why, but I looked at him with a smile and said, "Can we have the bill please?" He just looked at me then he glanced around at the others for a reaction, and received several smiles, and then he smiled back in return, bowed his head, and quickly walked away.

"See, Newton?" The woman said. " That was a prime example of your insatiable obsession with commerce, wealth, and greed and, as always, in the end, the entire fate of mankind is decided with a thermonuclear weapon. Look around you, Newton, what do you see?"

"I see lots of happy people," I said, "delighted and contented people."

She slapped her thigh, almost spilling her drink, which she held firmly in the other hand, "Exactly, Newton, and you didn't see any of them giving money to the waiters, simply because they have none to give. Do you know why?" She studied my puzzled expression for a moment, her wild eyes darting around in every direction, impatient for an answer.

"I haven't seen any since I have been here, but in my day, rich people did not use cash anyway, they obtained most things on credit."

Her darting eyes suddenly stopped darting. They stared intensely into mine instead. "Because Newton we don't use money here anymore. Not in this city, not anywhere in this world. We eradicated The evil tender long ago, and it will never return, we will not allow it to return." Then she took another swig from her pink bubbly before she stared deeper into my eyes and continued, "Because we don't want the filthy stuff to return. We are all delighted here without it."

I had a string of questions to throw at this woman, but Karla had whispered her gentle persuasion and used her soft fingers to slowly massage my hand, which was more than enough to persuade me from entering into an even more profound detailed discussion with an inebriated woman, as Karla had put it. She advised me not to pursue with a street discussion about delicate matters of this nature, not with this woman anyway, as I needed to be shown and not just told details about life in my new world. She suggested that we enjoy the night, and in the morning I should ask Lord Bandersant anything I needed to know during the Revelation, which was of paramount importance, as it was crucial to the instigation of my spiritual development.

"Oh," I said, "Does this Revelation involve a journey, Karla? Travel to other countries perhaps, to see how they live, to gain further experience?" But she did not answer me. She knew immediately of my intentions, and she wasn't going to fall into that trap so easily. "You will just have to wait and see, Newton," she said, "I shan't tell you anything," and she squeezed my hand, and gave me a sexy grin, which I could not resist.

After much drinking, talking, and occasional dancing, with our table of newfound friends, we left them and took a peaceful stroll along the waterfront, admiring the luxurious restaurants along the way. The whole scene resembled a place in one of my happy, peaceful dreams. I had to stop to admire the architecture and design of these fabulous, man-made, structures, which I believe were probably built by angels from Heaven, and I would have agreed with Karla quite willingly, had she told me so.

"They were built by Androgen." She said, tersely, as she pulled me along to hasten my pace.

"He must be the best architect in the world," I replied, not paying much attention to anything but the magnificent hand-carved marble cornices that adorned the walls.

"They are, Newton," Karla replied as we picked up the pace.

These people knew how to construct buildings with immaculate perfection. The brilliant white Roman-style arches, every detail carved with precision. One particular structure displayed an abundance of pure oak, which had a perfect, silky smooth grain, just like the doors in my apartment. I slowed down so that I could run my fingers along the grain, and caress the soft, warm marble façade. I scrutinised every detail but found no flaws, no grime, no dust, dirt, or indeed evidence of age or wear whatsoever. I asked the waiter, who was standing at the entrance, 'how old are these buildings?' He just smiled at me and said, they have been here longer than I can remember, then he tried his best to tempt us into his restaurant with the promise of a selection of the most delicious looking seafood, which he showed us using a small square crystal in the palm of his hand. The gem glowed brightly and then projected a stable looking, three-dimensional image into the night air just above his hand.

This hologram technology was so advanced and so realistic that it convinced me entirely that he had, hovering above his hand, a substantial live lobster in full glorious colour. Like a fool, I tried to feel it with my fingers, to the amusement of Karla, who gave me a playful slap as my hand passed right through the hologram, almost knocking the crystal out of the waiter's hand. He gave her a 'you better take this inebriated jester home' look, and then he smiled and strode back into his restaurant.

Further along the wonderfully illuminated waterfront, more waiters had emerged from their restaurants. Each of them had the same idea in mind, to entice us in for wine, food, and entertainment. It seemed quite strange to me that their primary motive was not for trade or profit, but to please and care for us, and at the same time demonstrate their culinary skills. This practice was a far cry from my time on earth when the primary motive of business was solely for the sake of money and profit, which ultimately led to greed. I do have a lot to learn from this world, in this era, but sometimes I wonder if I am capable of ingesting it all. Lord Bandersant told me that it would be much easier to absorb information once I had suffered the Revelation. I find this difficult to believe; however, only time will tell, so we shall see tomorrow.

We strolled further along the front taking in the warm night air. I was told by Karla to keep my hands firmly behind my back whenever an enthusiastic waiter approached us, to avoid embarrassment again, no matter how attractive his three-dimensional visual display.

A combination of fresh night air, followed by a long leisurely stroll, not to mention copious helpings of food and wine, left me feeling tired and ready for sleep in my soft, comfortable bed. Karla had other ideas. Sometimes I wonder where she had got all her energy from, as she never seems to tire, unlike me. I probably need a couple more years on the pure organic food, and the crystal clear natural water before I was ready to compete at her stamina level.

My body felt wrecked when she had finished with me that night. Somehow I felt as if she had just used me and then cast me aside like a rag doll. I vaguely remember her saying that she was thirsty and that she needed a drink. Soon afterwards she flew out of bed and went off to get one from the kitchen. I just lay there, trying to regain my breath, looking up at the ornate ceiling. I made a futile attempt at counting the gold beads around the cornice. Perhaps I was nervous and anxious about tomorrow. I decided to put all the random thoughts at the back of my mind to help me to relax, and I hoped that I might get enough sleep tonight to replenish my depleted carcass.

"You must be positive, Newton," Karla said as she approached the bed, fully quenched from her trip to the kitchen, "Don't think deeply of it too much, and you must trust your... human instinct, and your, human soul." She spoke soft and slow as if she was unsure about something else that she needed to tell me but just couldn't bring herself to say the words. She climbed into bed and proceeded to smother me with wet, playful kisses, which I reciprocated, with satisfaction, until I eventually passed out.

I slept like a newborn baby that night, and when I woke the next morning, Karla had gone. I assumed that she was taking a morning shower and at any minute now she would stroll in from the shower room, her petite frame wrapped in a thick, cosy white towel, and she'd be drying her soft flowing hair with a smaller towel. At the same time, she would attempt to urge me to get up because the morning was so beautiful, just as every morning had been ever since I arrived here in this peaceful world of uninterrupted blue skies. Bright sunshine, and the sound of a multitude of tropical birds singing in the trees. All that beauty, she said, I would miss the moment by wasting time laying in bed... my warm, comfortable, cosy bed, which I suspect possessed the capability to respond organically and ergonomically to my every body movement. I would then say to her, 'I know that the sky is blue and the birds are singing because this is Heaven.'

My instant morning daydream was suddenly interrupted by an audio announcement from somewhere in the room informing me that somebody had called at the main door out in the hallway. A soft female voice had confirmed this, as it reverberated around the room. I could not discern where the sound had originated, and I could not find any speakers on these immaculate marble walls or ceilings to provide me with any clues. I gave up on Heavens' highly advanced technology, which seemed quite confusing and frustrating for a nine hundred and twenty-nine-year-old man. I decided instead on a more traditional method to answer the door, one that was more familiar to my epoch. I considered the thought that it might have been quicker than searching for a hidden button or console in any case, after all, I sometimes had a ball trying to find a simple light switch.

When I opened the door, I was surprised to see the same two men in black suits, who had brought me here on my first day by hoverboard. They both greeted me with a short smile, and one of them spoke and said that they had come to collect me for my Revelation, as it was Revelation Day, and Lord Bandersant was waiting for me on the roof. I cannot remember him ever telling me their names, Bandersant never introduced them to me directly; he had only referred to them as his accomplices. It probably wouldn't have made any difference anyway, as I could hardly tell them apart.

I let the men in black in and told them to wait while I got ready. They told me not to rush, 'just take your time', they said, so I did. I had a hearty breakfast before showering in the rainforest shower, and then I got dressed. The clothes provided fitted me quite well, as the material was naturally high tech yet again. It felt so comfortable and light.

I kept asking myself, on the way to the roof, why was Bandersant taking me to a ship, after all, he did tell me that he kept them docked on the roof and that I could go exploring in one whenever I was ready. Perhaps the Revelation is a journey around the planet where I will learn of the real beauty? This possibility seemed plausible to me, or we could be travelling to a different part of the earth? These thoughts went around in my head several times, along with some more bad ideas, which I cannot think how they even got into my mind in the first place. It was as if some form of baleful spirit had been trailing me, and its sole aim was to frighten me into submission. Perhaps it did not want me to complete the Revelation for some unknown reason?

My reverie was cut short by the booming voice of Lord Bandersant, which came from an open cargo deck of, what seemed like the largest ship of the fleet if this collection represented the entire fleet. At least eight spacecraft were basking in the bright hot sun on this smooth, whitewashed rooftop area. The ships themselves were pure white but a few shades lighter in contrast to the background, but I could not discern clearly, and each of them looked quite magnificent in the bright sunshine. I was somewhat disappointed in Lord Bandersant, as I half expected gold. I also expected him to laugh at my jest when I told him so, but apparently, the whole mission was quite critical. He smirked when he said, "Gold is far too soft to stand up to the rigours of space. The fuselage consists of a white crystal, which can tolerate extremely harsh conditions."

I had followed the men in black up the ramp into the belly of the cargo hold. I felt like a condemned man being taken to his doom, as I walked between them. I was greeted with a handshake from Bandersant, but not before admiring the other ships; with their gleaming white bodies reflecting an array of white light onto the smooth, white unblemished surface of the marble roof. There was something strange about the light here, the way it refracted. In such a situation, with the late morning sun high on the horizon and bright as it was, I should have suffered snow blindness; at least I should have been wearing shades to mitigate such a fierce intensity of light. It seemed somehow subdued, soft, diffused, and calming to the eye.

Lord Bandersant called it the God Principle, the fact that all sin had been removed from the Earth by man through his efforts to become one with God, the rewards for this was a brighter, cleaner world. He seemed to relish on the success of the pure water. He told me that one could drink directly from any river, lake, or stream in the entire world, as they are all pollution free. He said that this way of life started after the war and continued to grow and develop for hundreds of years after, through man's effort and determination.

It began first with the abolition of money, trade, and commerce, much to the reluctance of the criminals and the wealthy money grabbers, as he called them; those few who ran the entire world on lies, corruption, and greed. They resisted, fiercely kicking and screaming, because of their morbid fear and concern for their loss of wealth, rather than rejoicing charitably for the rest of mankind. The wealthy few had failed to recognise the real potential of continuous long-term wealth and happiness for all throughout the whole world.

By this time the world population had diminished mainly due to conflict and other misfortunes, and the lucky few survivors were reluctant to continue procreation on a similar scale like they did in the past, which had brought about starvation for many, and almost total oblivion. They had no desire to witness a repeat of history, so they agreed reluctantly to take another route.

I noticed that the ship was equally as white and clean on the inside, as it was on the exterior. The front console and almost every wall and ceiling space were covered in illuminated buttons that looked like they were made from crystals of various colours, some glowing lustrously in a bright array of colours, and others dark and unlit. Two black leather looking seats with high backs faced the large windscreen to the front. They looked extremely comfortable. I had an immediate urge to fall into one of them to check it for comfort and size. Lord Bandersant must have read my mind because he gestured and told me where to sit. I was seated in sheer comfort in the left seat before he had uttered the last word.

"Not that one, Newton," he said rather sharply, "you are going to pilot the ship today."

Judging by the complexity of the controls in this craft, I fear that I will require much more than a simple crash course in the piloting futuristic spacecraft in the year 2914.

"Perhaps you can brainwash me?" I suggested to Bandersant, rather jokily, "Because my terse knowledge of piloting twenty-first-century fighter jets does not extend to thirtieth-century technology as advanced as this unless you don't mind losing one...does this one have ejector seats?"

Bandersant did what I expected him to do. He clapped his hands and roared with laughter before he fell into the co-pilot's seat next to me. Even the two men in black couldn't resist a giggle while they made themselves comfortable in the two other places behind ours, which had a smaller console immediately in front of them.

"Newton, you must have faith," Lord Bandersant said, as he touched several buttons on the console, "let me show you." He continued, as lights flashed, and then the cargo door closed silently. In fact, everything on this ship operated quietly. I felt a smooth lifting motion as we ascended high into the blue sky.

"We are about one thousand feet above the city," Bandersant announced a few seconds after we had taken off, "Newton, you take it from here. See if you can crash this ship."

My countenance must have revealed something unfavourable that caused Lord Bandersant to substitute his smile for a more thought-provoking frown, "Relax, Newton," he said in a rather calm voice, "this ship, like all the others in the fleet, is far more advanced than you can ever imagine. Take the controls." He indicated to a cluster of buttons built into the armrests. There was a significant round button in the centre, which was surrounded by several square ones. I ran my finger over the square one on the right-hand armrest. Almost immediately I felt the ship bank right. I tried the left side; the ship went left.

"Forward, reverse, up, and down," Lord Bandersant said as he pointed to each button in turn, "they are all highly responsive. The whole ship is powered using a highly sophisticated technology, which you will not have seen in your time. This technology is in the form of a solid-state crystal drive system, which generates energy by splitting light particles, or photons, similar to that of your old nuclear reactors but a thousand times more powerful, and indeed much safer. And, no, you cannot build a bomb with this technology, if at all you are thinking such thoughts, Newton, as the various principles prohibit this negative action. There are no moving parts, which makes them all maintenance-free, like most automated devices in this world today. It is impossible to crash a ship because while it is in the confines of the Earth's magnetic field, the drive system creates a powerful gravitational field, which opposes that of the earth. So, in effect, the ship can hover in mid-air, at any altitude, even an insignificant distance such as a few feet above the surface of land or sea, for an indefinite period, if you so desire." And then he laid back in his seat, "Go on, Newton, fly it!" He said.

The thought of an aircraft that couldn't crash, either by accident or neglect, seemed like a dream to me. The response from the controls was efficient and smooth. I felt an almost organic connection as if I could will this gentle giant to glide effortlessly through the air in any direction and speed that I desired. Lord Bandersant claimed that the process of Revelation would alter my spiritual perception, which will enable me to connect to this advanced technology. He said it would only make me a better pilot if I maintained true faith and understanding. I asked him would it be possible to predict and evade a collision from an external source, which I had no control for example?

"If you are inferring that another ship, or any other machine on this planet as the hostile invader, then a collision could not possibly happen due to the safety technology indigenous to all our machines."

This information helped me to relax more, but I also needed to see for myself. Well, Bandersant did tell me to fly it. So I did; high and low, across the entire city, above mountains, down into valleys, to the coastline, and up high into the stratosphere, and then back down. There was no method to my crazy piloting. I was like a child with a new toy. Well, I was on the way down, intending to try to land, when Bandersant told me to stop. We hung there in mid-air several miles above the earth. When I looked down, I could not make out any of the continents, as I knew them. They appeared distorted as if the whole of Europe had condensed and shifted towards the equator. And both North and South America looked like one mass of land centred on and around the equator. I couldn't see Australia; perhaps we were out of range and needed to go south to get a glimpse of it.

Bandersant pressed a few buttons on the front console. As he did so, the ship repositioned itself and pointed at an upward angle perpendicular to the earth's curve.

"Where are we going for the Revelation?" I asked casually, displaying my newfound confidence. "Do you have a base on the moon?"

Lord Bandersant chuckled, "Newton," he said, "Why does primitive man always think inside the box? The Luna Region is for manufacturing. The Earth is your paradise. What reason does man have to occupy a dead planet? Your people used it for storage." Then he put on his serious face, the one that I have seen before, but this time it had appeared somewhat different. I could see the concern in his eyes. "We are destined for a place of far greater distance, you may have heard of it," then he paused a while, "a place called Andromeda."

It was my turn to burst out laughing now; of course, I did not, due to his seriousness I managed to restrain myself. I took a deep breath, "Are you serious, Lord Bandersant? Andromeda is two and a half million light years away from the Earth?"

"Yes, indeed it is," he replied, "but we will not be going all the way there. Let me explain. We, humans, are sent to Earth by the Great Spirit for a purpose. The earth is an image of the realities of the spirit world. The material world exists for the individualising of the soul. When God created man, he was made perfect, then he sinned, and he fell from the condition of his higher state. Before the time of the Ghost Crystal man continued to sin thus increasing his distance from the Great Spirit. And as you know, Newton Flotman, in the time before your sleep, when you walked the earth, this same world, it had been contaminated with the sin of the so-called modern man, which culminated in full-scale nuclear war. After the discovery of Ghost Crystal, and up until now, man was able to banish sin and become purified and retain harmony with the laws and will of the Great Spirit.

"Newton, you now find yourself among us almost a millennium after your death, you are astounded by what you see, a peaceful nation with their hearts filled with abundant happiness, kindness, and love. How is this possible, you ask yourself? Well, Newton, today you will find out why we are so peaceful and why there is no sin in this world today. On this very day, Newton you will shed the monkey mind and leave behind your earthly, material thoughts, the very ideas that cause mankind to err in his ways and stray unto sin.

"The most potent force in the whole universe is not a supernova, Newton, nor is it a black hole. It is merely 'love', and there are two types of love, the first is 'the natural' love, which is human love, and the second is the most crucial, 'divine love', which derived from the essence of the Great Spirit, God. And the natural love, endowed in the soul upon its creation. This natural love is the love that we have restored to its original purity through effort and goodness. The divine love, however, is a remarkably different quality, as it is not endowed or self-generated, the Great Spirit bestows this love directly upon the soul. Every human being is entitled to receive this love, but to secure it one must long for it and pray for divine love whenever the opportunity arises.

"Newton, the Revelation is a process, which we use to expose your soul to awaken its awareness of morality and virtuous behaviour. As your mind, body, and spirit are of another time, a time, which we consider today a primitive epoch, we must conduct the Revelation initially for this purpose. All our children have done so in the past, and indeed, will continue to now and in the future to maintain the purity of the soul and to preserve our happy existence on Earth."

"Wait a minute," I had to interrupt Lord Bandersant, "you bring your children up here for the Revelation?"

Lord Bandersant laughed, "No, no, of course, we don't, that would be highly impractical and wholly unnecessary. Besides, we don't need to, as there is another way. They can perform the Revelation indirectly through the Ghost Crystal."

"What are we doing out here then?" I asked somewhat puzzled at the fact that Bandersant held this information from me all along.

"No, Newton, do not believe for one moment that this is a wasted journey," he said, with a smile, "Ghost Crystal Revelation would not work for you initially, Newton; in fact, it is more likely to harm you. We need a more direct approach, in your particular case, which is the method that we use now. I shall explain it all to you later. You will understand it far better then".

I just had a sudden vision, which triggered a swift rush of negative thoughts through my mind like a burst of light. So I decided to play safe. I asked lord Bandersant, what I considered as one of the most critical questions. "Lord Bandersant, how many times have you performed a successful Revelation in this way?"

"Well, Newton, to be quite honest with you, success depends much on the individual rather than the process itself. However, I can safely say that this is the first," He replied, and then he paused for a moment, "well, we don't often have the pleasure of visitors from the past, so there is simply no demand for this particular method. Don't worry, Newton, you are quite safe here," he looked at the ship lovingly, "the ship will protect you."

I wanted to know the risks that I faced during this so-called Revelation. Bandersant was adamant that there were very limited. He said that it was a spiritual experience in which man had no control or influence over. The spirit world guides the entire process, and they have strict laws in place, which they consistently adhere to, unlike the inconsistent laws of man. One of their most valuable laws involved the cause of interference and harm to those spirits still in the flesh; us humans, so I've been told. The Great Spirit strictly forbade the destruction or harming of any human being by a spirit, so any detrimental effects that you experience during the process are deemed to be the fault of your own, determined by the condition of your mind, body, and soul.

He asked me if I was ready and I said that I was, as I was eager to get this thing done. I was about to ask him to explain the process, but he did anyway.

"There are certain things that you may not understand, Newton, but do not fear; you will come to learn of them in good time. In layman's terms, the process of revelation is to allow the soul to be exposed to the afterlife momentarily so that it can experience all the wonders that await it after death. History informs us that no man has ever returned from the dead. I don't mean by merely recovering after the heart had stopped for several minutes or so after an illness or injury. When we are born into the physical world, the body is connected to the soul by a silver cord. This cord is said to join a person's physical body to its astral body. And during out-of-body experiences, and vivid dreams, the spirit leaves the body and travels to the spirit world, where it can experience all the wonders of the afterlife. But the spirit will always return to the body so long as the silver cord is still attached. When the body dies, however, the silver cord is severed, just like the separating of the umbilical cord, when an infant enters the physical world for the first time, and it cannot be re-connected. The spirit leaves the body forever and can never return to it. So, if a man says to you that he had suffered trauma or died on the operating table and then went into Heaven and met the Great Prophet, or even the Great Spirit, God, he is undoubtedly telling lies. The silver cord would need to be cut first so that the soul may reach far into the spiritual realms. Which would ensure that his spirit would not be able to return to the body again, thus it would be rendered dead, and he would be unable to tell others of his experience.

"The spirit world is so wonderful, Newton, that once there, no man would voluntarily want to return to his body and continue to live on the earth plane, as it does not compare to the wonders of the spiritual realms. Even in this present day in our paradise on earth, much less in your time when greed and violence were rife on this earth."

"How do we get there in a spaceship?" I asked him, with some degree of curiosity.

"You will go there, Newton, not I. We will head to Andromeda at high speed, faster than light itself, but we will never reach Andromeda because it is physically too far a distance. Don't ask me for details, but it is just a known fact that if you travel towards the galaxy at the right speed, you can create a vortex, which provides a path of direct entry to the spiritual spheres. This vortex will manifest itself as a band of golden light around the top of the ship. You will see the light above you, by the top console. To enter this realm, you just place one hand in the light, and you must exercise true faith and earnestly ask the Great Spirit for divine love. There must be no doubt in your mind whatsoever, just pure faith and divine love.

"Newton, it is imperative that you observe control; you must regulate the time you spend in each sphere by simply pulling your hand away from the light whenever you wish to leave that sphere, and you place it back into the light when you wish to enter once more and so on. I warn you now, do not spend longer than one minute in the second sphere, as such is the euphoria there that on your return to this lowly physical realm, in contrast, your suffering may be greatly enhanced. The effect is similar to that suffered by men in your ancient times when they took narcotics to simulate an artificial mental high, and when they ceased taking them the sudden withdrawal hurt their mental and physical well-being. If you linger unnecessarily in this sphere, you will suffer similar reactions, but it shall be a thousand times greater in strength."

"Anything else I should remember before I commit myself to mortal doom, Lord Bandersant?" I asked, sardonically.

"Yes," he said with a broad smile, which was made more prominent by the light from the silvery moon, as it cast a vein of lustrous, greyish, white light against his natural, pristine teeth. "That was the easy part, as you will be entering the second sphere first, and after that, you shall enter the first sphere, which is considered moderate, a place where average souls dwell until they had, by repentance and suffering, progressed to a higher one. On this level, they are sometimes in a state of semi-darkness where they have to suffer the recollections of their life on earth. Others may be in a better condition. Your time in this sphere must be brief, as it is considered a lowly place with much suffering and depression. Five seconds would be considered far too long for any mortal, so I suggest that you exercise a degree of caution here, or else you will experience great suffering on your return, so be aware of this, Newton."

"Do any records exist of cases where one had spent too much time in the spiritual realms?" I asked.

"In the past," he replied, "some cases recorded results where subjects used the Ghost Crystal to communicate and to perform the Revelation for frivolity. They had entered the lower sphere and spent considerable time there in the belief that they were able to help those fallen spirits, but evil spirits who only wished to harm them had subsequently lured them further into the lower realms of sin and depression. Others are known to have gone further and ascended to the higher spheres in the hope that they might meet the True Prophet, Jesus. Others hoped for an encounter with God's Messenger, the prophet Muhammad, and other prophets. They all failed to understand that one cannot simply visit the higher celestial realms, where these higher spirits dwell, unprompted, especially directly from the lowly earth plane, until one's soul is ready and worthy of spiritual progression."

I was eager to learn what became of these people so. Naturally, I asked him directly and, just as I had expected, he gave me a circumlocutory answer, perhaps to save me from the real dangers which I was about to face, and to mitigate my concern. He said that I could have backed out at any moment. However, I knew for a fact that Lord Bandersant wished me to continue with this Revelation to the end, as it seemed to be a mandatory procedure which was expected to be carried out by all earth-dwelling humans. I was curious by this stage in any case, and I wanted to see it through to the end because my curiosity provided me with an aspiration to discover whether the process would clear the Monkey Mind or not, as I sometimes had experienced unwanted thoughts, which could have related to my Neanderthal instinct. And secondly, but just as important, I did hope mainly for the reinstatement of my precious memory. Perhaps I was asking too much? One more valuable asset, which I considered a bonus, is the fact that I could be the first man, in my ancient world, to travel at light speed.

Lord Bandersant astounded me by revealing that we are not only going to travel at light speed, but astonishingly, and somewhat impossible so I thought, we are going to exceed it!

"Thanks to a Mexican physicist, the Alcubierre Drive system, in your time, Newton, the Twenty-first Century, pioneered a new development of light speed system, which our ancestors developed and improved over some years and we now use the improved process in our advanced ships today. Without becoming too complicated with scientific detail, as you know, Newton, our craft is powered by photon fusion, where atoms of light are enhanced and accelerated using a combination of special crystals. This complex process, together with the ability to alter the fabric of space both immediately in front and behind the ship, enables the craft to move in space at speed faster than light itself. As we accelerate to plus-light speed and travel towards Andromeda, we create a vortex in which the spiritual phenomenon occurs."

My short physics lesson provided very little additional reassurance to alleviate any fear that I had about this whole mission. There was no time for fear, or to express it. Bandersant didn't comment any further, nor did he answer me directly when I had asked him 'why Andromeda?' he just got on with the business of pressing buttons and proceeded with the Revelation. I saw a flash of white light at the front of the ship.

The two men in black, who had been passive up until now, were pressing buttons frantically too. Both their consoles lit up with an array of lights. I felt my whole body tighten, and then there was a white flash of light at the rear of the ship, which seemed as though it had lit up the entire fabric of space. The stars suddenly appeared blue and began to elongate and move towards the ship creating an extreme Doppler effect. It was as if we were travelling through a tube of light, with shifting colours, as the ship accelerated towards light speed.

Suddenly my attention was drawn to the ceiling of the spaceship. Just as Bandersant had described it, the halo of golden light appeared. Something told me to wait until it had reached maximum intensity. But how was I going to know? I just paused and trusted my instinct. I was right. It glowed brightly. I could swear that I heard angels singing in the background. Perhaps that was my cue. I immediately placed my hand on the ray of light directly above, taking great care not to point my fingers too much and accidentally press the buttons on the console.

I am unable to explain in words what happened next. The nearest equivalent would be to imagine the best dream one has ever had in their entire life and then multiply it tenfold. The experience I had was so real, it was so peaceful and tranquil, as I found myself in a location filled with scenic views and beautiful bright, vivid colours. Grass that was so green, sky so blue, and water so clean and crystal clear. It somehow resembled where I lived now, but yet it felt somewhat different; more real and dreamlike at the same time. My body felt much lighter if ever I had one because I bore no mental or physical burden. I could merely think and the thought would happen. I was in one place, but yet in another.

Time and space just did not exist in this realm, as I felt neither hurried nor delayed, I only existed for the moment. I found myself shifting seamlessly to other places where I encountered various people that I had never met on Earth before, yet I knew them here in this paradise, I knew them in every detail; I knew of their present, their past, and their future. It was indeed a remarkable experience. So fascinating that I was reluctant to leave. I wanted to stay here in this new found paradise. Something triggered an alert, just like the instinctive message you receive that tells you to wake up just before the alarm clock goes off in the morning. I thought of Bandersant and his warning, which prompted me immediately to withdraw my hand from the golden light. I did so, and as quick as a bolt of lightning I found myself back in my seat surrounded by controls and indicators, soaking wet, drenched in sweat, seated in the pilot's seat of the spaceship. I had to pause for a brief moment to recollect my thoughts, as I had a temporary lapse of all sense of perception. So firm was the belief that my physical body had been present in another realm, like waking up from an exciting dream, I had momentarily forgotten everything about the ship and the purpose of the mission. I forgot about the existence of Lord Bandersant himself and his two men in black! I did not, for a split second in time, remember any part of it, and then suddenly, like a rushing stream, it all came flooding back to me, just as a computer suddenly receives a full download of information.

I looked at the panel on the ceiling and saw that the bright golden light had suddenly turned colour. It was now a darker gold. The first sphere, the first sphere, I thought to myself as I slowly raised my hand and plunged it into the light above. Somewhat reluctantly, I hasten to add, as I had just emerged from what Bandersant called the second sphere, which to me, seemed like complete heaven. I just wanted to return there and remain in that blissful place forever, and I almost did so.

A sudden plunge into the lowest sphere, the first, is likely to do great harm both mentally and physically. I kept repeating to myself that five seconds it too long, five seconds is too long. Just as soon as my hand had entered the light, I counted to three then I hastily pulled it out again. I found myself slumped in the pilot seat, trembling uncontrollably. I closed my eyes, and then I heard Bandersant's voice. Another voice, which I did not recognise, said, "Is he dead, Lord Bandersant?" I thought for a moment, if I was dead when I open my eyes I should be back in the second sphere paradise again. That prospect suited me fine.

Of course, I was somewhat disappointed when I had opened my eyes; I saw no paradise, only Lord Bandersant's face staring down at me. The men in black stood over him, with their eyes wide open in shock. "He is dead." One of them said, "I said it was dangerous," the other said. I looked around and saw only the inside of the ship, the cockpit, the controls, the view from the large front windscreen, which was just black space with a few visible stars scattered about, no distortions or streaks of bright, colourful light. I observed a small blue planet below. It looked like the other paradise, the one that they call the first material sphere where humans come for the individualising of the soul. It was our planet Earth, my home, the Earth Plane.

When we had landed safely on the roof of our building back in the city, Lord Bandersant told me with much enthusiasm that the mission had been successful. I was doubtful about my last entry into the first sphere, and I said to him that I thought it was too brief because the length of time I had kept my hand in the golden light was minuscule. This misunderstanding led me to believe that the whole thing had failed, and was ineffective, as I could not remember much of it.

"Believe me, Newton," he answered, vehemently, "the whole thing was truly a success. You exposed your soul to the first and second spheres, and not your mind, which is yet to catch up and become synchronised after you have had adequate rest." He went on to tell me that I had, in fact, I had spent all of four seconds in the first sphere, more than any man in my condition should have done. I guessed he meant a man of the Monkey Mind mentality, with an undesirable mind filled with the effects of troubled events, from my time on earth, such as war, destruction, hatred, and greed.

I didn't feel any of those things at the moment. I felt indifferent to them, in fact, to all things negative. Bandersant told me that this feeling should significantly enhance after much rest. I took his advice and made straight for my big comfortable bed. But not before visiting my rainforest, where I had the most invigorating shower ever. I had no idea of the time, nor did I care about time, as I had no desire to find out about it either because I no longer had a yearning to study the position of the sun as I had done in the past, which I thought strange and surprising. Was this the new beginning of my long and fruitful journey towards my spiritual perfection? Which I find so pleasing, I did wonder?

CHAPTER 6

How To Create Heaven

I woke up the next day feeling refreshed and wholly vitalised. I had no idea how long I had spent in bed, in a deep sleep, and I cared even less about time now as I did when I got into bed after my last beautiful shower. My mind felt crystal clear like it had been rested, reset and cleaned. I was relaxed and ready for anything that this beautiful day, or the world, had to offer me.

I went out onto the marble balcony expecting to see Karla sitting there taking in the warm morning sun. Although she didn't spend the night with me last night because she wanted me to rest, she said that is important to do so immediately after the Revelation to instigate the regeneration process, and I assumed that she would be along later on. That was before I heard her voice call my name from the bedroom, which brought me nothing but a sudden flood of happiness and joy. She came out onto the sun-drenched balcony looking tanned and gorgeous in her tight little mini dress. She beamed a radiant smile, as she spread her arms and leapt at me. She greeted me in her typical way, clasping me with both arms, and at the same time grasped her long legs tightly around my back, this time she almost crushed me to death.

"I missed you so much," she said, in between repeated kisses on my face and lips.

"I know," I choked, "I missed you too, Karla, very much too," I said, as I held her tightly with both arms.

"I am so relieved that you are safe."

"Did Lord Bandersant tell you anything about it?" I asked in a matter of fact way.

"No, he just said that it all went very well and that you are now better prepared for this world."

I loosened my grip and looked into her eyes, "I want to see everything. I want you to show me everything; tell me everything about this world, Karla."

Her eyes widened, "yes, Newton, I will show you, I will show you everything, but we must travel. Lord Bandersant said that we could use one of the small ships up on the roof port, the ones that you were admiring so much on your way to the Revelation."

I kissed her beautiful thin lips, several times. I have never felt so strongly in love with anybody in this way. I felt genuine faith and love like I have never done so before, although I could not explain or put these feelings into words, the intensity of these feelings seem to be increasing at a rapid pace.

Karla grabbed my hand and led me towards the dining room, "Let us eat first," she said, "I had some food brought up from the kitchen."

"Oh, you had some food brought up?" I jested to her, "My little Karla doesn't prepare her food anymore? Has she kitchen servants to do it for her now? Is that a privilege of the Revelation?"

She looked at me somewhat bewildered, "What are kitchen servants, Newton? You are crazy. The Androgen from the restaurant prepared the food, they always do. Are you sure you are OK or do you need more rest, Newton, my love?" She said, and then her serious look faded into a smirk, which indicated to me that she had been teasing me, or so I thought. I was far too hungry to contest her right now. I laughed, as I chased her around the dining table with the promise of a severe tickling if I managed to catch her.

We settled in comfortably at the dining table where we had enjoyed a delicious, hearty meal of fresh fruit and vegetables. Afterwards, we made our way up to the roof port to look at the ships. I couldn't wait to get up there, but I managed to contain my inner excitement all the way there. I felt a feeling in my mind, which had suddenly opened up a memory channel that prompted me to recall a past event a long time ago when I was a kid on my way to the toy store to buy my first big toy, a radio-controlled aeroplane, I believe, ironically.

These ships were huge toys indeed. We walked right past the very craft that took us beyond light speed, towards Andromeda for the Revelation. A much smaller spacecraft, which looked tiny in comparison, was positioned right by its side. I suddenly drew my attention to this one; I felt a connection as I began to experience a déjà vu. Its sleek body was pure white, streamlined, and futuristic looking. These machines were a vast improvement in aviation in comparison to the flying machines from the Twenty-first Century. A helicopter could easily appear cumbersome and out of place amongst this line up of beauties.

I approached my chosen ship, and I placed the palm of my hand over a flat square crystal plate adjacent to the doorframe. Karla looked at me with an expression of expectancy.

"Have faith, Karla, please," I assured her, with an exaggerated smile, "I believe I am logged into the pilot database... according to Lord Bandersant, anyway." After an agonising three seconds of uncertainty, the large curved door swished open and slid up into the cavity of the roof of the craft, revealing a large doorway to the plush white, shiny interior of the neat little spacecraft. The layout inside was similar to that of the more significant craft, but this one was snug, and the incredible handcrafted seats looked rather cosy. I wasted no time by jumping straight into the pilot's seat. I sunk down into the leather-like fabric, which fitted my body like a hand in a glove. I pointed out to Karla that I could have sworn that the seat had adjusted itself automatically to accommodate my body contours, as if there was somebody inside the upholstery pushing and to pull it about in sync with my body movements.

She just shrugged her shoulders, and laid back into the co pilot's chair, "It is a possibility," she said, "As these ships are new. Our creators are always working on improvements with new technology, that is how we progress, Newton."

"Let's see what this baby can do," I said, with much confidence as I began to press buttons on the console.

"I noticed Karla's look of concern. "Do you know how to fly this craft, Newton?" She asked, looking a little apprehensive.

"Yes, of course, I do, Karla; you look nervous though; don't worry, I was a pilot on earth back in my time, I think so anyway... in any case, I was given a crash course by Lord Bandersant, and he assures me that all these ships have a built-in safety mechanism, and they are impossible to crash. Is that true, Karla, or was he just trying to reassure me?"

She didn't answer me directly. Instead, I got a cheeky smile, and she leant over and kissed me on the cheek. "Let's go then, Captain Newton, and try not to hit anything," she whispered in my ear.

I ran through the necessary instructions, as shown by Lord Bandersant, just by remembering the pattern of the sequence of button pressing and tweaking, plus a little bit of sporadic pressing action with the large round button and the square ones on the console. I tweaked with the other buttons until the craft moved forward, and then it lifted off slowly and effortlessly from the roof of the building almost silently. To my surprise, this spacecraft seemed much more comfortable to control than the larger one, as I found that the controls were highly responsive.

I climbed high, at least two thousand feet, with no trouble at all, and then I circled, I descended, I turned, I ascended slowly, then I accelerated fast, and then slowed down again until I was familiar with the controls and was able to perform smooth and steady manoeuvres effortlessly. My inner feelings played a significant part in the control of the ship. I could influence such manoeuvres, by a degree initially, just thinking about them, something I wasn't aware of before the Revelation. Karla said that this was usual, as I would later discover more surprises and delights, which would equally astound me. She suggested that we head to the foot of the mountains; there was a valley there where a great warrior lived as a hermit, which I found rather astounding and incongruous for a heavenly world until she told me the correct facts regarding this character.

"What is a great warrior doing in a heavenly kingdom such as this? I thought there was nothing but peace and tranquillity here?" I asked her.

"He thinks he's a warrior," Karla replied.

"But how could he think of war? Surely he has seen the Revelation, how can his heart be filled with any violence at all?"

"He is not violent, Newton. Nobody on this earth is violent; not anymore. He just thinks that he is a great warrior, and believes that he is a descendant of a long line of great warriors from the past."

I was curious now. "Does this great warrior know about war, and of my time, the Twenty-first Century?"

"I doubt if he has ever experienced war as such, but he does seem to know a lot about your Century," Karla replied.

Somehow I sensed her hesitation; why would Karla hold back on me? She didn't even mention his name, which I find very strange indeed. Perhaps Karla was trying to protect me from something? But, then again, surely she would not have suggested that we go and see this character if he wasn't entirely upright and honest? Perhaps she believes that his knowledge about my Century may prove valuable in some way, and she feels obligated to help me to glean as much information as possible to bolster my soul development.

I decided to keep quiet about it and not push her for any more information about the hermit until we reached the valley. I bought the ship down to a lower altitude until I found a clearing suitable for landing. We found an ideal spot directly in front of a natural high waterfall, which cascaded straight down into a deep blue lagoon beneath it. One could determine its vast depth mainly because the water was so crystal clear, and I could see the walls of the lake as they dropped steeply down into a chasm far below the surface of the water to almost a pinpoint.

The whole scene was reminiscent of a dream I had just before the Revelation. It was a peaceful and tranquil dream, in a place much like the Garden of Eden.

"It's beautiful, isn't it, Newton?" Karla said.

"Yes, it's amazing. How deep is it?" I asked.

"Oh, it's endless," she replied, shrugging her shoulders.

I set the ship down on a flat piece of ground just in front of the waterfall, and we both went outside to admire the scenery. The large clearing was surrounded entirely by a dense, lush rainforest. A variety of tropical birds sang their sweet chorus in perfect harmony, which filled the sultry air with an ambience of peace and harmony. We approached the edge of the lagoon. I stooped down to feel the water. It was cool and so unbelievably clean. I scooped some in my hand to smell the aroma. Karla urged me to try some; she assured me that the water was safe here. Having drunk a mouthful, as I was thirsty anyway, I noticed that it tasted just like the water we had back in the city. Karla assured me that the water was utterly natural, and it was the very same substance as that of the city, acquired from the same deep springs. There were no chemicals added, or any goodness extracted from it.

Suddenly we heard a noise, which came from above us. It came directly from the cliff top, about two hundred feet up, on the flat summit of the waterfall; we heard screams and then laughter. They sounded like kids, teenagers. Suddenly I saw a silhouette of two figures on the top of the rock, and later another two emerged.

"What are they doing up there, Karla? Surely they are not going to jump?" I asked, somewhat concerned, as it was extremely high. But she didn't seem too worried.

"Watch, Newton. Do not fear," she said, "whatever you see don't worry, they are safe."

I watched, astonished, as all four figures leapt off the edge of the cliff, practically one after the other in quick succession. "It's a suicide mission!" I exclaimed as I witnessed their rapid descent. Arms and legs flew in all different directions as they fell towards the deep blue lagoon, screaming and shouting as they fell. Cries for joy or fear, I could not discern. Just then a remarkable thing happened, so strange was this unexplainable event before my eyes that I had to slap myself twice only in case this was all a dream.

Karla grabbed my hand and squeezed it tightly, "You're not dreaming, Newton. Just watch them." She said, somewhat coincidently I thought.

I watched and observed as they reached a distance of about one hundred feet from the surface of the water, a remarkable, unexplainable phenomenon occurred right before my eyes.

Their bodies, which until now, had been in perfect free-fall for the first one hundred feet or so, suddenly slowed down rapidly, it was like watching a slowed down a movie, until all of a sudden they appeared to be entirely weightless, just hanging in mid-air.

"How could this be, Karla," I asked, as I run up and down the bank to get a better look at these floating bodies. "Is this the result of some zero gravity?" I asked, but I doubt if she heard me. "Karla? Did you hear me?" I shouted, but I didn't dare turn around to look at her lest I miss this remarkable phenomenon. My eyes fixed permanently on the four bikini-clad teenage girls who floated down gracefully in mid-air above a lagoon, and I didn't want to miss what was about to happen next.

All four girls, giggling, screaming, and laughing uncontrollably, glided down like feathers in the wind towards the water, but not before each of them gave their aerobatic performance. One of them performed perfect summersaults in mid-air, while another moved her arms and mimicked mid-air swimming. The other two just tumbled over and round with arms and legs flying uncontrollably until, one by one, they plonked gently into the deep lagoon.

"Strange phenomenon, isn't it?" A voice uttered behind me to my right, just where Karla had been standing, but it most definitely wasn't Karla's voice that I heard. I turned quickly to see a man on horseback, dressed in a modern looking bearskin coat. He had a beard, and his hair was dishevelled. My immediate thought was the hermit of the valley. Who else? I called out for Karla, but she did not answer me.

"Oh, she went back inside the spacecraft," the man on horseback said, "I think I must have scared her off." He dismounted and offered me his hand. "My name is Louden. You must be Newton, the man from the twenty-first century?"

"Yes, I am," I said, as I shook his hand. "I am pleased to meet you, Louden. How did you learn about me?" I asked, somewhat curiously, as nobody has yet discussed anything with me concerning my popularity, which surprised me.

He signalled to the four girls who emerged drenched from the lagoon. They nodded and smiled, and then they made their way off into the forest.

"How is this possible?" I added, staring into the lagoon.

"Everybody knows about you, Newton. The thousand-year-old man, who displays an aspect of a man of thirty years of age," he replied, as he looked me up and down.

"No," I said, "I meant the lagoon, how is it possible that an anti-gravitational field exists here?

He looked puzzled. "My name is Louden," he suddenly blurted out with an air of pride, as he placed his clenched fist across his chest. "I dwell here in the valley of Kings, and I descend from a long line of warriors as far back as the first century. Newton Sir, I have no time for trivial, gravitational phenomenon,"

He waved his hand in a dismissive gesture toward the direction of the lagoon, "this thing occurred during the great quakes, after your foolish scientists, if you can call them that, almost destroyed the whole planet with their primitive, thermonuclear weapons. They damaged the earth's core and caused it to somehow alter in such a way as to cause this phenomenon. It is no good for anything but a playground for the kids. Another one, which I believe is much larger and more powerful, exists somewhere in the ocean, but nobody knows where as yet."

"Has any nation ever fought a war on earth in recent years, Louden?" I asked, in a futile attempt to test his sanity.

Louden laughed out loud; his voice reverberated around the valley, "That is preposterous," he said, "we are all peaceful here, Newton." Then he walked off into the forest in the same direction where the girls had gone earlier. "Come! I have wild boar soup prepared for us all! Let us eat while I enlighten you of the foolishness of your people of your time!"

"I'll get Karla!" I shouted back to him as he disappeared through the dense foliage without waiting.

I don't know if he heard me, but just as I had reached the door of the craft I listened to his faint voice in the distance, "Leave your ship there, Newton, it is quite safe! Just follow the path to my humble abode!"

When I entered the ship, I noticed that Karla looked somewhat dejected and worried.

"There you are, Karla. Where did you disappear? Are you all right?" I said in my most gentle voice.

She looked me in the eyes, void of her usual smile, "What did you say to him, Newton?" She asked.

"He has prepared some food for us. I told him we would follow him. His daughters are nice. Does he have any sons?" I asked innocently. Karla attempted to ask me something else, but she stopped midway. She looked rather doubtful. I embraced her tightly to appease her, but for what I've yet to find out. At a rough guess, I could sense that she was uncomfortable around Louden, something I would never have been able to feel before the Revelation. I decided not to push her. I told her that if there were anything that she needed to say to me about Louden, she'd let me in her own time, but for now, Karla should just concentrate on being happy, and that she should live for the moment.

Through the dense tropical jungle, we followed the path, which leads us to a valley in which stood the most substantial and grandest log cabin I have ever seen. It boasted at least four levels, and each level boldly displayed its balcony, which extended all the way around the house, I guess to afford a full panoramic view of this near perfect paradise.

An unseen voice called to us from the side of the house. We followed it until we arrived in a beautifully landscaped garden. A pure white marble terrace extended from the house to the edge of a grassed area, which contained a large rock pool in its centre. There were tropical plants everywhere, naturally, and intricate tree-lined pathways leading to other areas, which had beautiful wooden huts with comfortable looking loungers outside of them. A beautiful, naturally created man-made river extended off the main rock pool, and meandered its way past the cabins and beyond, perhaps to the sea, or a large lake somewhere. I saw mountains in the background, and a steep valley in the foreground, which we could observe in detail from our elevated position.

The atmosphere was indeed crystal clear and unpolluted, as I was able to observe and witness an event never seen in my time on Earth before. I stood staring in fascination at this spectacle. Karla, by my side, could not understand why a grown man had such a keen interest in an everyday triviality such as this, which she claimed had occurred on a regular basis, in particular out here in the jungle. Loudens' bikini girls were swimming in the rock pool and shouting desperately in an attempt to attract our attention. I was only interested in the spectacle of animals down in the valley.

Although I could see them enough from that distance, I waited a while until they were much closer to us so that I could confirm with certainty what I was observing. The animal in front was a lion, a female no doubt, running at full pelt, from what looked like a small gazelle. I moved closer to observe the lion, which had now reached the lawn at the edge of the garden, and then it suddenly stopped and rolled over onto its back. The little gazelle leapt on the lion's stomach and, to my astonishment, both animals began to tumble around and play on the grass.

"What's wrong, Newton?" Karla asked, pulling my arm in another direction, towards the rock pool where the girls were swimming. She took no notice of the animals.

"Did you see that?" I asked, with much excitement, like a kid on his first visit to the zoo.

"Yes," Karla said, casually, as she pulled on my arm even more, "It's just the animals playing, Newton. They do it all the time.'

"You made it then!" The voice of Louden echoed across the valley. He stood by a table stirring a large pot. He had comfortable loungers set up by the pool. Karla kissed me on the cheek then she apologised briefly and then said that she was going to join the girls in the rock pool.

"This is pure paradise, Louden. They described you as a hermit. I wouldn't go that far." My eyes panned the valley, as I spoke. The tiger and the little gazelle were still cavorting on the green, now accompanied by a variety of other animals, which, in the real world, or in my time, I should say, would by now be tearing chunks of flesh from one another. "How did you tame them, Louden? Was it a difficult task?"

He just burst out into laughter, "They are not tame, Newton, they are just wild animals from the jungle!" He said, "They have always been like this." Then he sighed, "Look, Newton," he said quietly, "there is an old tale, I don't know for sure if it is entirely true, but many years ago two young, mischievous boys thought it rather amusing to bring a chimpanzee to the city and show it the Revelation. Fact or fable, the story goes that the damned thing went crazy, scratched and bit them half to death, and then ran off into the jungle, never seen again." He paused and waited for a reaction, and then he changed the subject and spoke instead about all the effort and toil he endured during the creation of this beautiful paradise.

I raised my eyebrows, as I only half believed Louden's story of the chimps, I at least expected him to finish it, or provide me with answers to my questions. Did this particular chimp have any influence over the other animals? If so, was it the catalyst for the taming of the entire animal kingdom? I soon learnt that Louden had a penchant for telling a bad story; he was somewhat disappointing at completing them as well. Perhaps this attributed to his natural short attention span. However, I must say that he is highly creative with his hands if all this beautiful handcrafted work is to be considered an illustration of his ability and success.

His delicious tasting soup contributed many points towards his culinary genius, which distracted me from his disappointing storytelling. When I managed to steal a little time alone with the girls, they told me that they had to put up with Louden's poor storytelling most of the time. 'Every night before we go to bed he would sit with us around the fire and tell us a bad tale or two,' one of them told me. Another said that he always centred his favourite stories on a crazy inventor who made mechanical dolls and other primitive things of the past.' 'Perhaps he reads too many books from your world, Newton?' One of the girls said to me in jest, but I couldn't tell which one precisely because they all had such similar features. It was difficult to distinguish one from the other, and when I approached one to finish a conversation, she would say that it wasn't her that I spoke to about this particular subject, and then she would point to one of the others, and she too would deny our conversation.

Despite Louden's storytelling, he had a fair degree of knowledge about twenty-first-century life on Earth. In particular, he was adept at the details of the inadequacies of such men from my time, their foibles, and their follies. He had the perfect remedy to rectify their bad behaviour and to establish perfection within their society, albeit almost a thousand years too late, it's a pity he wasn't around in the twenty-first century, perhaps we would have enjoyed Heaven much earlier than now.

"I'm glad you're here, Newton," he said, with great enthusiasm, "I can't converse of such matters with the girls, all they want to do is play with the animals, and swim and lay in the sun."

"I don't blame them, the girls are so young, and that's what kids did back in my days on earth," I said, much to his displeasure, which I read clearly from his face. "Don't they read any books about the past or your history?" I asked, attempting to appease him.

"No. Never!" He spat. I couldn't tell whether it was the potency of the strong fruit drink that he consumed in vast quantities, or just coincidence, that he happened to choke on a piece of pork from the soup as he spoke the words.

Karla had warned me about his behaviour, that it would decline after two glasses of the red juice. I told her for sure that he has consumed at least eight glasses of the stuff, I watched him drink them all...one after the other, as I only had two glasses during the same period. I just decided to continue drinking the stuff for one reason alone, because it had tasted so good. Louden seemed quite sane to me anyway, after such a massive consumption, apart from his sudden vocal reiteration of opinion on man's downfall, and his increasing vehemence in expressing them. Although, I believe this supposed potent beverage had no adverse effect on my faculties whatsoever. Not like alcohol did in the dangerous world that I left behind, long ago.

We settled down onto large comfortable loungers facing the pool. Louden held a full glass of the red juice in his hand, and he had reserved, a whole large bottle on standby on top of the wooden table right beside him. The girls were still in the water, laughing and joking, swimming up and down the tree-lined river, which lead from the main pool and snaked around the vast grounds. There were no boundaries here. The animals could roam freely. And they did, but within reason, because they seemed much better disciplined than the animals had been in my time. I saw the lion sunbathing on the grass. I became slightly concerned because there was no sight of the little gazelle. Then I heard a noise further away in the distance, where I spotted the small creature running about with two others. I sighed a sigh of relief. Louden must have sensed my concern.

"Newton, I share your concern for the animals, but you must leave them to get on with their lives. Mankind has a history of interfering, especially with things that he should not try to control, to the detriment of his body and soul. And of course, the poor innocent animals suffer as well."

"So you made them intelligent so that they had become aware of their fate?" I asked.

"Not at all, Newton," he replied, "something was revealed to them, which made them alter their way of thinking. Like us, they became more passive and less aggressive, to begin with, and later on, they integrated with us more to a level where, eventually, they were able to understand emotional perceptions."

"And this had nothing to do with Ghost Crystal?" I asked him, knowing that I wouldn't receive a straight answer anyway.

Louden took a mouthful of juice and shook his head, "The story of the chimpanzee? Some say that it was a myth; others say that the experiment developed further to include several other species, which began a chain reaction within the animal kingdom. The Ghost Crystal hadn't existed until around AD 2520 and developed by Samuel Page; the animals were cleaver by then." He took another mouthful of juice, and almost choked while trying to swallow it down in one gulp. "The trouble with people of your time, Newton, they were masters of interfering. They would interfere with the science; they would interfere with nature; they would interfere with geology! If a war started in another country..." he banged his fist down on the wooden table, "...they would get involved. If famine resulted from bad leadership, corruption, and rebellion, they would involve themselves to the point where they would lose all control of the situation, and the whole thing would descend into chaos."

"Are you suggesting we should let people starve then, Louden?"

"Exactly!" He retorted, "Newton, You have answered my question exactly. Your history informs us that you had interfered, in this particular case, and this meddling resulted in large-scale war, which brought about more misery to the world, and eventually, as you are quite aware, nuclear war." He lowered his voice, "Newton, sometimes one has to allow nature, and the Great Spirit to do its work. I cannot think of any benefit to humanity, which we still enjoy today, that was created or instigated by the people of your time, Newton. We had to reset the whole system. It all went crazy after the war, which served to quell the growing population; I suppose the only good idea your people ever had. Even if you took 'war' out of the equation, then famine, pestilence, or perhaps another asteroid strike would have been the inevitable consequence that would eventually serve to reduce the population."

I could only look around at the peace, the happiness, and tranquillity, the abundance of fresh, unpolluted, organic food, clean water, which one could drink directly from the source, not to mention the absence of war for over 500 years. I heard Karla, and the girls call my name, come on in and cool down, Newton, they said in unison. Joyful and happy they all were, enjoying the peace and tranquillity in the perfect climate, warm and sunny with an endless blue sky.

"Louden, how did mankind create all of this out of chaos?"

He sighed as he lay back on the lounger. He told me to lie down and observe the blue sky; he must have read my mind. I did, and as I stared at it for a good few moments. I concluded that I, Newton Flotman, was the only living creature on this entire planet who had ever had the pleasure to compare sky in the twenty-first century to that of the thirtieth century. And in my conclusion, I declare that the atmosphere in the thirtieth century was of a much more profound blue, just like the same blue sky that I had seen in holiday brochures, where they had cheated and used filters to enhance the colour.

The world is a living filter; Louden had told me after I shared my observation with him. He said that I was looking up at pure, fresh, clean air. There is no pollution up there. He sat up briefly and took another sip of juice before he proceeded to answer my question. "Newton, a recipe for disaster is greed! First, we got rid of the desire. Mankind was told one day that he can no longer own material goods as property and that his time for running and controlling others has now ceased.

"The Spiritualist Movement decided that religion was too varied, so they agreed on a simple religion based upon the true teachings of the Great Prophet, directly through The Great Spirit. And all men on earth would abide by these rules alone and banish all other religions, which were considered malicious lies and deception. Our new world would thrive on perception, awareness, and love. Fortunately, we were able to utilise Ghost Crystal to provide tangible evidence of life after death, and quite soon the fear of death diminished to such a degree that it almost became revered and even welcomed. Sad funerals, mourning, and weeping for the dead became a thing of the past. Instead, the mourners would be invited to communicate with the deceased directly through Ghost Crystal where they would learn that the person did not suffer death at all but the soul left the body and merely passed on into the spiritual realms and is now at peace and much happier than ever. The discarnate soul was almost always asked the same question by the relatives. His answer would always be the same, Newton, even to this day it remains constant; they would say, 'No I would not want to return to earth in the flesh if I had the choice to do so right now.'"

"So how did you achieve to free the world of violence, and at the same time deal with the non-believers?" I asked.

"Newton, that was the easy part. Ghost crystal was the Spiritualist Movement's weapon of mass destruction. It took very little convincing once the recidivist saw his future and his past. The revelation of such facts forced the murderer to become a saint overnight. So too did the atheist, as he converted to an avid believer, and then he suddenly developed an insatiable appetite for spiritual knowledge."

"What about sex, Louden?"

"What about it, Newton? Aren't you getting enough from your soul mate?" He joked, rather curtly, as he gestured with his head in the direction of the pool. I swiftly laughed off his remark, as I did not want to distract him from the main topic of the conversation while he was doing so well.

"I meant, how did you manage to control promiscuousness and immoral behaviour, Louden?"

"Ghost Crystal!" He affirmed as he took a mouthful of his deadly concoction. "It worked immediately for the normal deviant. But for the ardent debauched fool who chose to defy nature and stray into licentiousness, a brief spell in isolation on the Luna Region was their only hope for reform, until years later their kind became extinct."

"How could that be?" I asked, quite surprised, "You mean they died out?"

"Newton, in your time on this mortal coil, all manner of wantonness occurred due to pressures and demands, which was forced upon the individual because of the iniquity of mankind, in particular, his irritating desire for self-gratification. The Great Spirit explained the three basic phases of the soul. Incarnation, being the first, is when the soul splits into its two respective parts of male and female, known as soulmates. Phase two refers to the physical life of the two souls on the earth plane, and their quest to find each other, either on earth or in the spiritual realms later on, as they are soulmates. And I believe phase three to be the return to the spirit world where the two can reunite and live together in harmony and happiness for all eternity."

"So, Louden, you mean, male with male, and female with female, is a sin against the Great Spirit?" I enquired after a short while.

"Such deviant conduct is considered a futile act, which has no place in the celestial realms, and serves no purpose on earth but to enhance sexual gratification, Newton, as it goes against the grain of nature and is considered only to gratify lust. Instead, such intense affection is better expressed through human love, and ultimately Divine Love. You cannot create offspring as a result of such visceral, physical acts, whereas for platonic love, which exists in abundance in the spiritual realms, and indeed here on earth too, if mankind is ever bothered to look for it, there are no boundaries or restrictions. It is the degree of desire that is the main cause of the problem, as such physical acts do not manifest itself in the spiritual realms."

"Did you banish them to the Luna Region?" I asked.

"Samuel Page did, indeed, in the twenty-sixth century, around the time when all manufacturing on earth ceased, and they transferred it to the Luna Region. He made all prisoners into workers and miners, until much later, after his time, when robots took over the task."

"What of the reluctant ones who still refused to conform? The selfish men with violence instilled in their hearts, what degree of persuasion did it take to convince them that the peaceful spiritual way was best?"

"As I said before, Newton, it was somewhat tricky at first to convince them with just knowledge and wisdom alone, but the discovery of Ghost Crystal made it possible to communicate adequately with the spirits in the spiritual realms. Such séances weren't crude like in the early days, where you had clairvoyants, clairaudience, clairsentients, a little tap here, a wrap there, a series of knocks and a shadow would appear, and then the moving of specific objects. No, this was real, Newton. The spirits came to us in full glory on a crystal screen so that everybody could see them all at once. There were no misgivings or any question of doubt, or trickery. Of course, the scientists and sceptics had the opportunity to poke and prod, and they did, for a long time. Eventually, the doubters walked away in silence, and the scientists walked away scratching their heads.

"In the next three hundred years, Newton, the world went from being a polluted, crime-ridden cesspit to what it is now, a peaceful paradise."

"I'm baffled," I said, "who runs it all?"

Louden sat up and looked me in the eye, "Newton, you're crazy. Did you not experience the Revelation? Man cannot run this paradise; only the Great Spirit himself can oversee total control of such a world as it is today. In the past, your past, Newton, as you know, man trusted in man, which was wholly wrong. Today we no longer believe in man, we trust in God, and we are right to do so, as our utopia is the proof of our success.

"We have advanced greatly since the discovery of Ghost Crystal. The world is devoid of crime because we eradicated all the causes of crime. Men only committed felonious acts for one main reason, and that was the greed of want. They simply wanted material things from the earth. Material things that the Great Spirit has already given us all, but the men of greed chose to deny others their given right to these things. Instead, they forced them to labour for their share of earth' material benefits, which they knew had already bequeathed to them all. That is wrong, Newton. A man should not toil for a man just for the sake of making the few wealthy."

I sat up and looked around. I gestured with my hands, "I have seen people working here, just as they did in my time."

He laughed loud and hard, "I need a drink!" He said, as he leant over the table and grabbed his empty glass and then he topped it up with more of the green stuff from the bottle. "Newton, trust me, you have not seen people work here." He stated, with a degree of conviction. "And you will never see people working anywhere on this planet. Not the kind of toil you did in your time." He took a sizeable long mouthful of the potent fruit juice.

I sat there bewildered, wondering what he meant by this. I was just about to ask him when suddenly a shadow cast over me like an eclipse. I jumped with fright thinking that it was one of the big cats; perhaps it had come over to play. But no, it was the soft voice of my own lovely little kitten Karla that caused me much relief.

"What are you two discussing so vocally? We can hear you from the river." She said in her sweet voice. I sensed some awkwardness between Louden and Karla. However, this wasn't the time, or place, to enquire after such matters, and I thought it best not to question Louden further anyway. So in an attempt to divert her attention, and perhaps interrupt the awkward silence that followed. I grabbed Karla by the waist in jest and pulled her towards me, but she fell into my lap giggling and wriggling around. Her slender tanned legs were kicking about in the air. I needed to find out more from Karla later on, and not arouse Louden's suspicions right now, perhaps when we are alone.

Later on, after much discussion and some laughter, we had consumed enough wild boar soup to fill the bellies of a small army, if ever such a group existed in this peaceful world today. Louden had drunk more than a fair share of the potent fruit juice for an average sized man. It didn't seem to have any detrimental effect on his mind because he wasn't ranting or raving, and his words were steady as his lies were true.

He invited us to stay the night much to Karla's disliking, but I managed to persuade her otherwise with the promise that we would leave as soon as the cock crowed at first light. I do believe that Louden had compounded her decision by a condition, which he had insisted. He said that we could stay but only if we occupy one of the luxury beach cabins by the riverside. I haven't seen any beach here, but the huts were exquisite, made from a mixture of high-quality wood, marble, and crystal, and they were as comfortable and cosy inside as the house back in the city. I hadn't noticed them when we first arrived, as they appeared to be hidden in a secluded area a little way down the valley, on lower ground, away from the main house. There were four in total; each one was a reasonable distance from the other. Like with the rest of the garden, the grounds were well kept, and landscaped to a very high specification, just as the gardens were back in the city.

We retired after much eating and drinking. I didn't drink any more of the potent juice, although it did not have any noticeable effect on my system. Louden claimed that it was because I still possessed a trace of the monkey mind and that I needed more Revelation to clear my soul of these ignoble instincts completely. I told him that he was mad, and I needed to know more about how this world operates just in case I woke up one morning and found myself back in my old world, at least I would have the necessary tools to save it.

Louden said that I was mad too, to think such a tortuous thought, "Even the Great Spirit would never subject you, Newton, to such a devilish process. Have you not suffered enough at the hands of your crazy scientists, who were bent on avarice and greed for power and control of the whole world?"

He then told me that I needed to go to the island to speak with those of vast knowledge and wisdom, as I could learn a lot about this world from them.

"Where is this island?" I asked, "Out in which sea?"

He laughed profusely, "Nobody ever knows where the Island is, Newton. You are expected to find it for yourself. Your girl Karla can take you there, she knows, I'm sure."

We must have slept soundly that night because we woke late morning and missed the cocks crowing. Only the delightful sound of tropical bird chorus could be heard calling from the lush tropical gardens around us, and the wet feeling of Karla licking my face. I struggled to try to understand what delight Karla would attain by licking my face, first thing in the morning, something, I admit, that she would not usually do. Immediately when I made any attempt to open my eyes, they would be swiped shut by her wet tongue, as if she was engaged in some kinky game. It became too much in the end, as I needed to open my eyes and get out of bed. I had to speak to her firmly.

When, at last, I was able to open them without further hindrance from her wet tongue, the sight I saw before me shocked me greatly, and almost caused me to leap out of bed. There, sitting on the bed staring straight at me with its big, bright, shiny eyes, was a little tiger cub, no doubt, a cute one. Its fur was colourful and bright, and very soft to the touch. I held it in my arms.

Karla woke and turned to me, "Newton, where did you get that from?" She asked,

"I was about to ask you the same question, Karla. I woke up to find it licking my face. I thought it was you. Did you leave any doors or windows open?"

She laughed, as she gently stroked the cub. "No I didn't, Newton, It must have wandered off from its mother and somehow got locked in here last night," she said, and then she grabbed the cub with both hands, leapt out of bed, opened the door and put it outside. She watched as is scampered off into the tropical wilderness.

We didn't see Louden that morning, but his girls came by to tell us that he was still asleep in bed, and was unlikely to wake up until later on in the day. I wasn't surprised judging by the amount of potent juice he had consumed last night. At least my head seemed clear, and I felt a whole lot better after a refreshing shower.

We hugged the girls and said our goodbyes, and then we made our way back to the craft. As we boarded, I jokingly asked Karla to check the ship for stowaways, in particular, 'cute little furry ones'. She had almost got out of her seat to carry out my command but suddenly realised my cunning deception, for which I paid the full price with a playful slap on the back.

"Karla," I said, once we had taken off and were hovering high above the forest, in the upper atmosphere, "show me where to find this, so-called, fantastic Island."

CHAPTER 7

The Island

I could not recognise any familiar shape landmass at all from this altitude. It looked to me like a belt of land, which spanned around the equator, and displayed a variation in thickness in certain places, with the vast North Sea above, and a substantial south sea below. It was as if all the land had been compressed into a continuous slim belt and then strung around the equator like a colossal bandana.

"What happened to the rest of the world, Karla? How could geological changes of an extreme nature occur in such a short space of time?"

"Some say that it was the result of the nuclear explosions that triggered a disturbance in the core and somehow caused it to collapse and alter its shape." She explained, "and it had a devastating effect, which altered the oceans and the continents in a short space of time. I know it won't seem feasible to you, Newton, with your old science mind, but during your absence, many strange things have happened. There is one particular story, which some doubt to this day, about a stray missile, which somehow had entered the core of the earth through a fissure in the earth's crust. The explosion caused devastation to the earth' core and altered it in such a way that resulted in a change in its proprieties. This crazy phenomenon enabled our scientists to discover a means to conquer gravity. When we reach the Island you can get more information from the captain, he has more knowledge of these things."

"All this happened while I was asleep, Karla?" I enquired with a degree of doubt, "Roughly how many years are we talking about here?"

"I don't know for sure, Newton, but we do know that this period began, and perhaps ended, between the time of your war, which I believe to be around AD 2020, and the terrain reformation ended about AD 2414."

"Almost four hundred years? How could all this happen in such a short period?" I asked, somewhat curiously, but I naturally didn't expect Karla to give me an answer to such an equivocal question, which I was asking myself, in all honesty. She did, however, shrug her shoulders instead; a gesture that she had hardly ever used.

Geology has never been my strong subject, but I felt confident enough to recognise the difference between obsidian and white marble. These land formations baffled me. I had to bring the ship down lower to get a better look. We were about ten thousand feet. I could distinctly make out the broad band of land that encompassed the equator.

"It all looks tropical," I said,

"It is all tropical, Newton, the entire world. Even the Polar Caps have melted. There is no more ice left on the entire planet."

"This must have had a devastating effect on sea levels," I said, slightly concerned.

"Not, Newton," she replied as she stroked my hand, "It all happened slowly and carefully, as if was all planned." Her eyes wandered, for a split second, upwards towards the ceiling of the craft, and then, without much warning, she gave me a gentle, lingering kiss on my lips.

"Newton, you will need the coordinates for the Island," She blurted out, halfway through the kiss, which I was enjoying immensely. I felt my lips vibrate from the pressure of her sweet breath as she spoke. She quickly pressed a series of buttons on the centre console, as crystal lights flashed, and the craft banked to the right and then accelerated at high speed, and made a gradual ascent as it did so.

"Louden said that we would have to find the Island, Karla. How is it that you know the exact coordinates?"

"I am only taking us to the area where the Island originates and not to its exact location, which we will have to discover for ourselves when we get there."

She sensed my confusion. "I suppose that we can't miss an island, as I presume it is quite large. Does it have mountains and white sandy beaches, Karla?"

"No," she replied, "just hills."

"Tell me about the Captain, Karla, does he live on the island?" I enquired further.

"He sails around, but he has a home on the mainland as well."

"Oh, I see, he's a sailor too, with his boat?" I asked, totally confused at this stage. Perhaps we were talking about two different characters. I decided at this stage to ask her, what would be highly considered, in my time, as a stupid question, as sometimes this was the only sensible way to deport any misunderstanding and expose the facts. So I took a deep breath and asked, "Karla, tell me, why do they call him the Captain?"

She reacted to my question just as I expected, a mystified stare in complete silence. "Newton," she said quietly, with an expressionless mien, "Didn't Louden tell you anything about the captain?"

"No." I replied, while at the same time, trying hard to recall our conversation, "He just told me to go to the Island to meet people of great knowledge and wisdom."

"Well, they call him the Captain because he is the Captain of..." Her voice trailed away. She now stared beyond me and out through the front viewport. He is the captain of that ship, which they call, The Island!" She announced as she pointed to the front.

I followed her finger and was astounded at what I saw out there in the deep blue sea. From here it looked much like any regular Island that I had seen from a plane at a similar altitude, but this island was different. Its shape was odd to begin with, somehow elongated and tapered to a point at both ends. But the most peculiar phenomenon I observed was the appearance of a wake in the sea, which seemed to be trailing from one end of the island. I could see the foamy line precisely as it had extended far out into the sea as if it had been created by a moving ship in the water. This monster was an island, and it appeared to be moving along in the sea, as any sea-going vessel would. I decided to descend to take a closer look. Karla agreed and said that was good because we need to land on it soon anyway.

Karla smiled and joked about my flying. After warning me to take it slowly, she also reminded me of the fact that this little craft was utterly watertight, just in case I decide to misjudge the landing of this supposed un-crashable ship.

I couldn't believe what I was looking at from this altitude, about five hundred feet above the surface of the floating colossus below us. I could see almost everything in detail. I saw trees, landscaped gardens, marble walkways, and buildings. The whole thing resembled an island, yet it moved along on the water like a ship.

"See, Newton?" Karla said, rather joyously, "He is the captain of that ship, down there."

"It's an island, Karla, how can anything as big as that float on the sea?" I cried like an overexcited kid who was just about to unwrap his much desired birthday present. I compared its size with the enormous ocean-going vessel of my time and conceded defeat just as immediately as I begun, without even bothering to gather any comparable data. It was apparently a floating island. I further concluded that even the largest ship of my time would comfortably berth in the middle of the vast lake, which graced the centre of this man-made giant, and one would hardly notice it there.

"Karla, please tell me this is the largest man-made structure in the world today?" I asked tentatively.

"No!" She retorted, but with a cheeky grin with it. "It was built by Androgen, so it is the largest Androgen-made structure in the world today."

"This Androgen must be a knowledgeable guy," I replied rather naively, and then I made the situation even worse by asking another silly question. I asked her if this Androgen will be on the Island and, if so, would it be possible to meet him? She just smiled and said, "Yes, Androgen will be down there, and you will be able to talk to them about the Island, if you so desire, Newton".

It's a pity I didn't pay much attention to her answer; it would have saved me further embarrassment, which was soon to come. I was distracted by the view outside, the sheer size of the hull of this beast, as I caught a glimpse of its enormity when we began our descent. It was the same colour as most of the buildings I had seen so far, pure white, with a texture like quality marble, gleaming happily in the bright sunlight.

I briefly counted the multiple rows of enormous windows, and although I expected to see portholes at least on an ocean-going beast, the large square ones looked quite fresh and fitting. I lost count at ninety-six. The whole structure stood high in the water, at least a couple hundred feet above sea level. This titan was indeed a floating Island, the one that Lord Bandersant had told me about, which I briefly read about in the brochure back at the city, but I had never imagined that it would be so huge. I couldn't wait to get down there to explore it all.

"Newton, The people you will meet on the Island, have a great degree of intelligence and wisdom concerning spiritual matters. They have all, of course, experienced the Revelation, some of them more than once, and others are in constant contact with the spiritual realms."

"Karla, I feel like a warrior on a final brief before an important military mission. Did Lord Bandersant put you up to this? Or was it Doctor Gabriel?" I asked her in jest in my heart. But she shared a stern expression with me, but she did manage to finish it with a smile after I had pulled a face at her.

"Newton, seriously, you know there are no wars in this world or military people, they have all gone on to the next world." She said, and she placed her hand on my knee and smiled, "This is a peaceful place." she continued, "You'll find nothing here but love and kindness."

I descended and brought the craft down and landed on a patch of green grass, next to the other ships, berthed on the deck of the beast. Well, it certainly looked like a deck from high above, until we touched down, then the view of the surrounding sea was no longer visible. Its sheer size gave the impression that we had landed in the middle of a busy town, except for the fact that there were no roads or cars, only marble walkways filled with holidaymakers. Some of them were walking around at a leisurely pace, and others were lying down on comfortable sun loungers on the green areas. Most were in conversation or just taking in the moment.

A few well-dressed men and women walked among them carrying offerings of snacks and drinks. I noticed that they could move around at a smooth and rapid pace, much faster and efficiently than their relaxed customers, which they served fondly and efficiently. This fluidity was because they sported roller skates; well that is what I thought at first glance. I made the mistake of assumption; I assumed that the skates must have had wheels, until I had reminded myself, once more, that I was no longer in the Twenty-first Century, but the Thirtieth Century. These people were the Kings of gravitational manipulation. Wheels were no longer an option in this new world of peace and tranquillity. Friction and attrition was the mechanical burden of free and rapid movement, which these people would no longer tolerate in this modern world of anti-gravity and photon-crystal energy.

I ignored, at first, the lingering stare of the attractive, tall, olive-skinned woman who had approached us on the green just as we had finished closing the door to the spacecraft and was about to go off to explore. I stared back at her but I said nothing, even though she seemed familiar to me, I wanted to avoid any further assumption.

"Prangalistra!" Karla cried, as she took her tanned hand and greeted her with a hug.

"It's good to see you, Karla," Prangalistra replied, "You are looking well as ever."

"So this is where you spend most of your time," I said, as I took both her hands to greet her. She pulled me forward and gave me a robust and lasting hug.

"Newton, I am glad you are here, you shall learn much here on the Island from the knowledgeable and the wise, now that you have experienced the Revelation. Be concise and profuse with your questioning, and your answers will be rich and fruitful."

"I shall do just that, Prangalistra, there are many things that I wish to inquire. Is Doctor Gabriel here?" I asked as she released her grip on my waist.

"Of course!" She roared in her deep voice, "He is on the bridge drinking with Brodar. He will be most pleased to see you both. You must go up to see him." She gestured to one of the well-dressed skater waiters who promptly approached carrying a gold drinks tray laden with golden champagne glasses. Prangalistra whispered something in the young man's ear, and he nodded his head in agreement and smiled. "I shall leave you both now, but I will see you later," Prangalistra said to us, "but Darus here will look after you. He will escort you to the bridge; I must go now." She shook our hands and then promptly walked off and disappeared into a crowd of happy people, who were browsing casually, and laughing and joking merrily, as they strolled along one of the many paths.

"My name is Darus," The young waiter said, as he handed us both a golden goblet, "here you are; compliments from the Captain." He then, boldly, took one for himself, which he knocked it back in one single gulp.

"What is it, Darius?" I asked, fearing that it might be the same potent red fruit juice, which did not affect me when I drank copious amounts with Louden.

"It is golden Champagne," Darius replied.

I hesitated at first, but after further scrutiny, I decided that it would be much safer to sip it first, as I am not yet familiar with most of these new potent drinks. Karla had already taken a mouthful, and she was enjoying it thoroughly, so it must be safe, I thought.

"It isn't as strong as the red fruit drink; you will only get one today anyway," Darus said.

"And how many have you had today, Darus?" I asked, as I took my final mouthful, which I rather enjoyed too.

"Only one." He replied with a mischievous grin. He took the metal vessels from us and placed them on his tray. "I only ever drink one," he concluded, with a glint in his eye.

"How do we get to the bridge? Is it far, Darus?" I was worried about his condition, and I whispered my concerns to Karla, she just laughed and said something about the safety system in my craft, however, I did manage to catch some of what she said, but with all the noise around, it was somewhat tricky. The whole deck resembled a scene from a party in full swing.

We tried our best to keep up with Darus, although he wasn't skating at full speed. His motion was fluid and dexterous as he weaved effortlessly in and out of the crowds without even the slightest contact with anybody or any object. He glided flawlessly as if his skates had contained its memory bank filled with every detail of this leviathan, and he performed his movements with sheer confidence, such that he appeared to read every mind and then synchronise with and anticipate every intention to avert a collision.

He led us into a crystal dome building, its framework made of gold, which stood out from all the other domes that were of pure bright, dazzling white. Crystal, no doubt, I thought to myself. He stopped next to a large round door, a sight that immediately brought back memories of my first meeting on the hill with Lord Bandersant and his men in black. The look on my face must have given Darus cause for concern.

"Have you travelled in a Golden Globe before, Newton?" He asked.

"Yes, I have," I replied, as the doors slid open silently, "I travelled underground..."

"Ah!" Darus interrupted, "The Terrain Globe, one of the fastest earthbound modes of transport."

"Yes, I'd say it is fast but steady as a rock. One could hardly tell if it was moving," I replied, as I glared into the globe through the open door.

"Don't worry, Newton, this one is not as fast as the Terrain, there is no need for speed here, you are always in relax mode when on the Island," Darus said as he beckoned us towards the entrance of the globe. "This Globe will take you anywhere on the ship, or should I say Island to be more precise. All that is required is a simple voice command, and your wish will be granted. If at any time the system is unsure of your request, it will soon let you know," He continued, and then he turned to Karla," I am sure you are familiar with such technology being..."

"Yes, Darus," Karla interrupted rather suddenly, "I think we are quite capable of managing this level of technology. I do use the Terrain quite frequently anyway."

Darus just smiled as he leant towards the crystal panel, which was set flush in the gold control panel by the side of the door. 'Your command, Sir?' A soft, friendly, female voice echoed around the smooth, golden walls of the dome.

"Take us to the captain's bridge, please," Darus replied, with a cheeky tone in his voice, and then he sat down next to us on the ultra comfortable, built-in sofa by the rear of the globe. I continuously struggle to understand how the inhabitants of this world manage to design such comfortable furniture. It is somewhat surprising what man can achieve when such motive as greed is removed from the equation and then substituted with compassionate values like comfort, care, and wellbeing. These people apply such amounts to almost everything, is it any wonder that this is a pure and perfect functioning utopian society? The world in my time could never replicate this bliss, not before the holocaust anyway. Perhaps war was our inevitable providence to cleanse the world of sin and evil, to separate the wheat from the chaff, remove the wolves from the lambs, to clear the way for the Shangri-La? But this one is genuine.

Perhaps the holocaust was not part of God's plan, and it was inadvertently forced by man's hand, his stupid, ignorant, hairy Neanderthal finger, on the nuclear button? I do hope to find Ghost Crystal here on the Island, as I need to make contact and find out more reliable information about the spiritual realms, and perhaps contact some of my long-dead relatives and friends in the hope that they can help me to revive my memory. I spoke briefly with Karla on this subject when we spent time at Louden's little paradise down in the valley. She told me that I could learn what I am allowed to know. However, there are certain things even the spirits cannot divulge just because such information is not yet available to them. Also, there are specific risks involved if you desperately seek information from the other side, as you could expose yourself and be made vulnerable to unsavoury spirits.

Lord Bandersant taught me about some of the causal laws of the spirit world, oh, yes, surprisingly rules do exist there as well, and they are much more straightforward than those of our material world. He said such laws are set like gravity. For example, if you drop an apple from a tree, it is sure to hit the ground, every time, unless you have an anti-gravitational field in place! Unlike the laws of man, which can be mitigated, reformed, and manipulated by the will of man himself.

Punishments make good examples, Doctor Gabriel told me, he said in your time, Newton, men were quite lenient with punishment for some criminals, and, on the other hand, totally harsh on others for perhaps the same crimes, how could that be so? Not so in the spiritual realms though, he said with much satisfaction and delight in his heart. Punishment is constant and justified; there is no bargaining or reprieve. You cannot turn back the clock. The apple dropped; therefore it must hit the ground, that is spiritual law, laid down by the Great Spirit himself.

In this utopia I find it strange that crime does not exist at all, not because they have just removed all the causes and temptations of sin, but because of a marvellous discovery. This marvellous one enables them to see the consequences of crime in full glorious colour with their own eyes, collectively, the result of which is so disturbing that even just a brief glance at this vision is quite enough to deter any potential criminal, hardened or petty. Children are encouraged from a young age to experience this concept, a process that they call The Revelation.

I have had the pleasure of a mollified version of the Revelation, and I must admit that although I am unable to remember much of the detail of my experience, I do believe that my subconscious mind has been dramatically affected. As for my so-called 'Monkey Mind,' this has been waning since the inception, and it has, somewhat, almost diminished into infinity.

I find it difficult to put these feelings into words, but the closest I can get to any comprehendible elucidation is to imagine the most pleasant dream where you find yourself surrounded by everything beautiful. The love you feel for others is so deep and intense and higher than the human love. It is such powerful love; perhaps an essence of divine love bestowed by the Great Spirit, through the Holy Spirit?

When we reached the bridge, which was much quicker than I expected, I must say. Darus did not step out of the Golden Globe with us; he said that he was going back down to the deck to look after more guests. And he added the fact that he didn't have time to babble about worldly matters, or spiritual ones, for that matter, which made me relaxed and at ease. He probably wanted to get some more of that golden champagne which I assumed was his favourite drink.

We arrived at the entrance to the bridge where another waiter at the door greeted us once more. This one had no gravity-defying, hover skates, just a pair of well-polished shoes.

"We are expecting you, sir, Madam," He said as he opened up the large wooden double doors. I glanced towards Karla and shrugged my shoulders.

"Did you know about this?" I asked her, as I did not expect such a formal welcome.

"No," She replied with a smile, "Perhaps Louden had something to do with it."

We entered the bridge, I half expected a medium-sized control room, but this one was vast. A large curved front windscreen from which one could see the entire view below, as well as the front and sides, dominated the room. Full glass surround, all made from one cut piece of glass, pure crystal, no doubt.

We must have been at least three hundred feet up from the surface of the deck. The deck itself did not look like any deck I had seen in my days at sea. It looked much like an inhabited island than a typical deck of a luxury liner. It boasted trees, small buildings, a large lake, and marble white winding roads, which served as pathways for leisurely strolls for these happy folk. I took Karla by the hand and lead her towards the front screen to get a better look. She looked at me, strangely, but I explained to her that I didn't wish to lose her in this enormous space. I guess I deserved that playful slap on my back, which followed, and it felt much harder than the previous one.

A large man stood by the console in the centre of the screen. He suddenly turned and looked at us, his eyes widened as he flung his arms out, "Newton!" He cried with joy, in a much deeper voice than Louden, "Newton Flotman, the man awaken from the dead; the great prophet has returned to save us all!"

"Oh, I wouldn't go that far," I replied rather sheepishly, "Judging by what I have seen of this paradise so far, you are in no need of a prophet or a saviour for that matter, especially not one from the Twenty-first Century."

"Now, there's a troubled era," he said, as he grabbed me with both arms and greeted me with a manly hug, "You poor thing, Newton, you were present in the world at the time of war?"

"I'm sorry to say, yes I was, but only just before the nuclear holocaust; and after that, it was all deep sleep and memory loss... I take it you are the captain of this ship?"

He let go of me, and then he greeted Karla briefly, then he slapped his forehead, in an exaggerated manner, as if to indicate that he had forgotten something of great importance. "Silly me! You have to excuse my manners, not enough Green Rum. Yes, I am the captain of this vessel!" He said in his deep voice, and then he reduced it to a whisper, "But, Newton, we don't say the 'S' word, we like to call it the 'Island'. The 'S' word is for the smaller vessels." And then his voice changed again, "I am Brodar, the Great Captain of this fantastic vessel, The Island!"

"Pleased to meet you, Captain Brodar, Louden told me about you. How did you know about me?" I asked.

"My boy, you are known throughout the land by every soul. The man who slept a thousand years? What great news, it travels well here, Newton, like the speed of light it travels well. How is the old hermit, Louden?" He suddenly asked in a lower tone.

"Oh, he is fine," I replied, "Enjoying his little paradise."

"Still drinking the red fruit drink, no doubt, when he could be enjoying Green Rum, the fool!"

"Tell me about the Island," I enquired, "Is it true that it can never visit a port due to its size?"

"It is true, Newton!" He boomed, "The Androgen constructed it in the only port in the whole antipodean region. We take it there on certain rare occasions if we have to that is, but it is far too big to berth anywhere else."

"Do you mean Australia?" I asked, rather curious why he had referred to the antipodean region, as we used to describe the region of Australia and New Zealand back in my time. He looked at me with a blank expression in any case, and he openly admitted that he knew nothing of such place of that name.

"Come!" He suddenly exclaimed, as he walked away from the bridge towards a large wooden double door, which leads into an enormous ballroom, "let us go and have a meaningful conversation with our eminent people."

We followed him into the spacious room, filled with well-dressed people talking in small groups. I spotted Darus skating in between them on his invisible skates. I turned to Karla, "Did you know anything about this?" I asked her, but I don't know why because she had been with me the whole time and it would have been quite difficult for her to organise something of this magnitude without me knowing. She shook her head and shrugged her shoulders. She looked as surprised as I was.

Darus skated over towards us with a tray full of an assortment of drinks. "Darus," I called, but he was stopping anyway, "what is the special occasion?" I asked.

He looked at me bemused, "What do you mean, Newton?"

"The party?" I replied, trying my best to gesture with my hands.

Darus laughed, "A party, Newton? This is no party, this is The Island," he gestured with his free hand, "they celebrate like this all the time. Life is one big party on the Island. Life is one big party here in this world, Newton. Here you are, choose a drink, take the big ones, this heavy tray is upsetting my balance."

Karla chose the larger glass, which contained a bright rainbow coloured drink. I had no choice but to opt for the next size down, which happened to be a green liquid.

"Newton, I see you are accustomed to our traditions, I take it you have met Captain Brodar then?" A tall blond man said. It was Doctor Gabriel. He was drinking with a group of people not too far from where we were standing. Brodar was beside him; he turned to me and called me over. I took Karla's hand, and we went over to join them.

"Have you found your watch yet, Newton?" Doctor Gabriel asked, in jest. "The last time we spoke, you were quite concerned with time. How are you now, after the Revelation?"

"Oh, to be quite honest with you, Doctor Gabriel, I haven't even had time to think about it, since I lost my monkey mind."

"Good, good," he replied, and could just about be heard having been drowned out by the uproarious laughter. He raised his voice to compensate. "You have shed the Neanderthal thinking. Tell me, Newton, do you ever think of war and violence?"

"No, I don't. I certainly don't miss anything from my time, not as intensely as I did before the Revelation. In fact, I am quite eager to learn more about the spiritual realms. Is there Ghost Crystal on the Island?"

Doctor Gabriel laughed, "Of course, Newton, although not as large and powerful as the one back in the city, but adequately sized for reasonable communication with the lower levels."

"Why is it that we are unable to communicate with the higher levels?" I asked as I was curious to contact knowledgeable spirits who possessed bounds of wisdom.

"That is because there is nothing to seek from these higher spirits but divine love and bliss, which you hope to attain on your journey to the higher levels, eventually. You only found souls from the lower levels because you are expected just to help them to shed their evil habits so that they can progress freely to the higher levels. In effect, you are assisting them. That is your prime objective, Newton.

"There are only two professions in this world today, Newton, and they are the most important occupations known to man. Your people, in your world, made a serious mistake by undervaluing these important professions, which they senselessly considered inconsequential and worthless."

"And what are these important professions, Doctor Gabriel?"

He drew in a large breath, "Teaching and caring." He replied, with an air of dignity.

I half knew that, because back in my time, in this world, our governments failed to offer teachers or carers the respect that they deserved, and they treated them as low reward professions. I took a mouthful of the green liquid, which I was told was green rum. It was a mistake that I could not reverse. I cannot explain, in mere words, what had happened to me just as soon as the sweet, thick liquid found itself in the depths of my stomach. The sensation was akin to a sudden catharsis. I needed to engage in meaningless conversation to take my mind off the effects of the rum before it blew my head off, so I asked a stupid question. "Who makes the rum then, if there are only two professions, Doctor Gabriel?"

He scanned the room, as his eye caught Darus, who carried a full tray in each hand skating dextrously between the groups of people, who were drinking and chatting amongst themselves, and he followed him until he approached us. "Newton, there's plenty of food at the bar, go help yourself!" Darus shouted, smiling as he whizzed past without stopping.

Doctor Gabriel looked me in the eye and paused for a moment, and he smiled, then he said, "The Androgen, of course, they perform all the tasks here in this heavenly world."

I felt the bones in my hand click as Karla's hand tightened. I hadn't notice Doctor Gabriel's sudden disappearance; he must have excused himself or was dragged away by Captain Brodar because I saw that the two of them were in deep conversation immediately behind us. I guess Karla's prolonged handgrip had lasted longer than I thought; I must have momentarily become lost in the concept of time. I was about to question her on the subject of Androgen, as he or she seemed quite popular here... Ship designer, and builder? Master rum distiller? What next? The innocent look on Karla's face informed me that she was hiding something important.

She was saved the embarrassment of providing me with an explanation, for now anyway, by a sudden tap on my left shoulder. When I turned to look for the perpetrator, a young girl, who had similar looks to Karla, greeted me enthusiastically. My mind went into temporary overdrive for a split second while I tried my best to identify her or remember who this pretty, young, familiar looking girl was. I blamed it entirely on the profusion of Green Rum, of course.

"Hello, Newton, it is me, Pranga!" The little girl said, "Have you forgotten me already?"

"Pranga! Yes, I mean no I haven't forgotten you. I remember you...with Karla and Lord Bandersant. How silly of me to forget. Where have you been lately, Pranga, we haven't seen you?"

She nudged Karla, and they hugged and greeted each other. "He's drinking Green Rum, that won't do his memory any favours," Pranga said. "I have been on the Island since I saw you both last," she went on, "We have a lot of catching up to do, Karla. Why don't we leave Newton here and we can go for lunch at one of the new seafood restaurants?"

Karla stared at me with a half smile, as if she wished me to grant her permission. "You both carry on," I said with an air of indifference, although I'd rather her by my side, I wasn't about to deny her freedom. "I'm sure we can meet up later. Be careful." I called after her, as they walked away. Karla turned and said something about the dangers of my world and then reminded me of the peace and tranquillity that existed in this world today, and with that, she blew me a sensual kiss, and they both disappeared amongst the crowds.

I stood there staring, for a moment, although they had both left the room, I was just thinking to myself about the journey I had taken through time, almost a millennium of history had passed me by, most of which I had been denied the experience of earthly life due to my slumber.

Since the Revelation, my spiritual nature had become more prominent, as before I was incredulous about such matters and would only be prepared to view such phenomena with an air of ignorant scepticism, especially in the absence of evidence. Whereas now I can comfortably agree that I have developed a healthy appetite for matters about spiritualism and the afterlife, and I sought to discover more.

A soft, warm hand touched my shoulder, and then it was followed by a gentle kiss on my neck. Karla is back! She missed me already, or she had forgotten to give me a proper goodbye? So I thought until I turned around and caught sight of the tall woman with exotic almond eyes.

"What troubles you, Newton, and what do you wish to know about spiritualism and the afterlife?" She whispered in her grave, distinctive voice. It was Prangalistra. I had recognised her immediately.

"Hello, Prangalistra," I replied, rather staggered by her question, "have you been rereading my mind?"

She shook her head slowly. "No, Newton, you have improved post-Revelation, but you are still predictable. What is it they used to say in your time? 'A penny for your thoughts?' Or something like that?"

"You are familiar with my history, Prangalistra?"

"Of course, it is difficult to ignore it, living with a historian."

"Oh yes, Doctor Gabriel. You are his soulmate, I believe?" I enquired, as I wished to know more. "Please tell me how that relationship works because I haven't been informed about this process yet. Does one choose one's soulmate?"

She laughed, as she caressed her glass with her long, slender fingers. "No, one does not choose, it is a simple understanding, Newton, one which ignorant men in your time failed to understand. You are not just given a soulmate, but the process itself begins just before incarnation. The soul splits into its two respective parts, that is male and female, as the Great Spirit intended, and it is these two halves of the one soul that are called soulmates. Come with me, Newton." She said, and she took my hand and led me to a seating area at the rear of the bridge. We sat in an enormous, comfortable circular couch, which had a large table in the centre.

"When physical beings procreate," she continued once we were both comfortably seated, "they produce an egg, as you well know, Newton, which is given a soul by the Great Spirit himself, God. The two halves of the soul do not necessarily incarnate at the same time, as one goes before the other."

Prangalistra suddenly raised her arm in the air. There wasn't time for me to see whose attention she was trying to attract. All of a sudden a tall young waitress arrived on hover skates carrying a large tray, which was laden with fresh food. She set it down on the table in front of us, smiled broadly, and then skated off at speed.

"So tell me, Prangalistra, when did you find Doctor Gabriel?"

She laughed out loud as she carefully selected some food from the tray. "This world today is idyllic and peaceful; I grant you that, Newton, we made it so, but close to Heaven we may be, we simply cannot interrupt spiritual law whenever it suits us. God wishes soulmates to find each other while on earth, true, but it does not always work out that way, even in our wonderful world, which has a close resemblance to Heaven. So we continue to search, unaided by the spirits due to spiritual law, but most will never find their soulmate while in the flesh because soulmate recognition is a spiritual skill."

I helped myself to the food, in particular, the large selection of cheeses on offer. Variations of colour seem to enhance the appearance of the display, and I considered it somewhat shameful to disrupt such beauty. "So how did you find yours, Prangalistra, you must have the spiritual skill?"

"No, I haven't found mine yet."

"What about Doctor Gabriel? I thought you, and he was..."

"We are both humans. We only live as soulmates temporary while we dwell in the flesh, as it is almost impossible to find your true soulmate while here on earth. That is why you were given Karla as your soulmate. "

I closed my mouth rather quickly, as I realised that the sight of a gaping mouth half filled with masticated cheese would not be an excellent example of table manners.

"Karla is...human," I said tentatively, unsure if I should have asked a question or make a statement.

"Karla is Celestial." Prangalistra argued.

"Karla is an angel?" I asked, confused.

"Newton, Karla is a highly advanced synthetic – organic being."

I suddenly lost my appetite; I had to put the last piece of cheese back on the tray or else it would have slipped from my paralysed fingers and dropped onto the floor. My mind raced at the speed of light, thinking of all the intimate moments we had since we met. The warmth of her body, the beating of her heart, all the things she said to me. "She can't be a robot! She's real, and she is human, I felt her, I tasted her, I smelt her, she is real, Prangalistra!"

"Newton, you are from a different epoch, robots in your time were extremely primitive, they could not think, or reason and they could not feel emotions. That was almost nine hundred years ago. Many advancements have been made since then."

"How did I not know?"

"Newton, you did not know because it is virtually impossible to know. There is only a subtle difference - which is - " She suddenly moved closer to me and put her arm around my shoulders. She began to caress my hair, and then she ran her long fingers up and down the nape of my neck. "This, Newton," she said, a little louder as she rubbed harder, "The difference, Newton, is in the nape of the neck."

Her actions confused me, as I believed that her sole intention was to console me, and now she began to talk about my neck. "Explain this to me, Prangalistra, I don't understand you."

"The vertebrae of Celestials is made entirely of organic crystal," she said, as she removed her hand from my neck and then continued to pick food from the tray. There was now a selection of drinks on the table, which I had no idea of how they got there; neither did I see who had put them there. "You can discern them from us humans only by the seven cervical vertebrae in the nape of the neck. When you rub this area, it will feel much more solid in a Celestial than it does in the neck of a human."

I began to laugh, as I could not find any other reaction for which I considered a complete joke. Prangalistra wasn't laughing, and I believed her to be a rather serious person who seldom laughed, only if she had to. "Who created these Celestials?" I asked.

"Newton, I am afraid it gets more complicated...," she began, devoid of a smile, and then she continued, "the Celestials were invented and created in the year twenty-eight fourteen, about one hundred years ago. They were created and built by the Androgen; these are the synthetic androids that are less advanced than the organic Celestials. The Androgen is used mainly to carry out manual labour in this world. The Androgen is responsible for the design and creation of this enormous and complex vessel that we are on at the moment, called The Island. They grow our food, and they make almost every material thing you see on this planet."

I tried desperately to retain my sanity, and I had to ask myself once again if this had all been a dream. Or worse still, had I died and crossed over to the lower world where robots ruled over man, and I am paying penance for the evil sins I had committed on science and technology while I dwelled in the flesh?

Prangalistra looked at me with her big, bright almond eyes. I could see the sorrow in them, the pity; the shame she felt for me, having to tell me these things now, after a long absence from reality. "It is important that you know everything, Newton," she said in almost a whisper, as she took both my hands in hers and squeezed them tightly. "All of these material things that you see before you have no significance in the spiritual realms. This realm is still just a material one, where we are allowed, through our God-given free will, to create technological advancements to make our mortal lives, in the flesh, as comfortable as possible."

"Prangalistra, be honest with me," I said to her, "Tell me sincerely, does Karla have a soul?"

She quickly let go of my hands, and I thought for a moment that she turned away from me briefly as if ashamed, and then she suddenly turned back to me, or it could have been my imagination, as nothing seemed real anymore. I was just hoping to wake up at any moment now.

"Newton, you cannot ask me such a question, I do not have the answer to this." Her hands were busy gesticulating. "To be honest with you, Newton, we do not know if this is true, it is rather confusing," she concluded, in a low tone.

"You are an advanced race, you have a super-advanced technology, which I have never seen or heard of before in my time on this planet, not even in science fiction films. You have Ghost Crystal to enable you to make contact with spirits of the spiritual realms, you have conquered the laws of gravity, but you cannot tell me if Karla has ever made contact with spirits from the other side?"

"Karla is a catalyst for instigating the process that drives the Ghost Crystal; she has no desire to communicate with spirits. As far as I know, she has never done so."

"Do you know how old Karla is?" I asked.

"Newton, you know that time has no concept or significance in our world, and we chose not to be governed by it. That is the very reason your people failed and ended their existence with war. Their obsession for counting and recording every minute of each day, each month, each year, contributed to their impatience, selfishness, and greed; such methodical time-wasting, in the end, it does nothing but exacerbate psychological trauma, and eventually, it consumes you. Time has no place in the spiritual realms, likewise here on earth, as it is in Heaven, we are no longer slaves to time, we simply live for the moment."

She paused for a while, then she stood up and held her arms out, "Newton, look what we have created. Are you pleased here, or do you wish to go back to your world? Your way of life, Newton?"

"I hope you are not about to tell me that you have also conquered time, Prangalistra and that you can send me back to the past?"

"Newton, there are two things that we found out from the spiritual realms which are considered as spiritual law and also confined to the law of material things. The Great Spirit forbids these two things, one is the transportation of solid matter, and the other is time travel into the past. Just think of the confusion and chaos this would cause if we were able to control these phenomena."

"I wouldn't want to return, in any case. I am delighted here. This old planet is now Heaven on Earth." I stood up too; I wanted to know more about the Celestials and the Androgen. I hesitated, knowing that I might be asking for the impossible, but I needed to know more details. "Prangalistra, can you show me the 'creation' process of the Celestials and the Androgen?"

She looked surprised, at first, I thought that I had asked the impossible, or crossed the boundary of secrecy. She sat down again and began to wring her hands. I sat down too.

"Newton, why would you so desire to see a baby being born? What purpose would this event serve in your spiritual development?"

"It's just curiosity I guess, a desire which was common in people of the primitive era. Was it not?"

"I can take you to see some of the Androgen processes, but it is highly restrictive, only because it is considered a highly delicate procedure, and not because of fear of malice, as you know does not exist here, but I cannot guarantee that you will accomplish anything from this. As for the Celestial process, this is more complicated though…" She paused to think for a moment. "You do have a spacecraft here, Newton?" She asked.

"Yes, I do, it is docked in the park, down on the deck."

"Which one?" She asked, which now confused me.

"There is more than one?" I asked.

Her facial expression alone told me that I was a fool not to expect that there was more than one deck on a vessel of this magnitude.

"The one by the big lake. The main lower deck, I presume." I declared suddenly.

Luckily, Darus had just passed by with a tray of drinks, and then he stopped to greet us and asked if we required more to drink. He had also overheard our conversation about the whereabouts of my craft. Of course, he knew for sure where I had docked it. He leant over to Prangalistra and told her. She smiled and nodded her head, and then she took my hand and led me to the Golden Globe, which transported us directly to the park by the lake, where we boarded my spacecraft.

CHAPTER 8

Artificial Intelligence

We took off from the Island and headed straight up into the stratosphere, as instructed by Prangalistra, from where she sat, somewhat comfortably, in the co-pilot's seat. She explained to me that whenever you wished to land or take off from the Island, the safest way to accomplish this was to use the vertical altitude method to avoid the busy airspace.

"I was told that these ships were safe to fly and that they were furnished with a safety mechanism to avoid all types of collision?"

"Yes, Newton, this is correct, but you are still required to manually avoid the object and make a detour each time, which can become rather tedious and disruptive especially if you have to negotiate your way through space debris."

I had to agree with her, although I had not yet had the pleasure of experiencing a potential collision as yet, one that would force me to take all necessary steps to avoid, and then re-route.

As we reached a high altitude, I could see very clearly through the ultra clean atmosphere below. To my surprise, I could see the bright outline of Northern Australia.

"Is that our destination, mainland Australia?" I asked.

Prangalistra looked at me with a puzzled expression. "Do you mean the Antipodean?" She said, and then she laughed, "Sorry, Newton I almost forgot, you referred to it as Australia in your time. We have always known it as the Antipodean or the Antipodean Region; it is the only landmass in the Southern hemisphere, except for the Zealand in the south, and a few scattered islands to the north, where the vessel 'The Island' sails on its continuous voyage."

I gazed out the front screen in a daydream state as I began my descent, thinking to myself that I had to accept the many changes made to my world almost nine hundred years ago, and the fact that there was no going back. I still needed to ask more, rather than make my assumptions about what I thought was right in my time on earth, primarily where names were concerned. Names didn't seem to matter much here.

Prangalistra punched in some coordinates on her console and told me not to land anywhere yet until she gave me specific instructions. Soon we were a few hundred feet above an enormous, white structure, which resembled a roof of a vast building. It was at least a couple of miles square. However, I couldn't determine the height of the structure, but considering our present altitude, I would say it was rather high.

"Go around the perimeter." Prangalistra urged, "That's good, Newton, slow right down."

We made a complete pass of the perimeter of the building at an altitude of about two hundred feet. I could see now from another angle that the height of this smooth, pure white structure must have been at least one hundred feet from the ground to the flat roof. I saw no doors, windows or openings of any kind.

"How are we going to get inside?" I enquired.

"We don't," Prangalistra replied, "The building is airtight."

"It's a vacuum?" I asked, somewhat surprised.

"Yes, Newton, completely, but don't worry there are no humans or Celestials inside, only Androgen."

"What do these Androgen look like?" I asked her, realising from her immediate expression, that I may have asked a ridiculous question, once again.

She rubbed her hands and laughed. "Newton, you fool," she said in a low, deep voice, "have you not been talking to one today?"

She paused; her almond eyes stared deep into mine. I reached for the nape of her neck and quickly fondled her cervical vertebrae. Her eyes widened, and she did something I have never seen her do before – She erupted into a fit of laughter.

"Newton," she said, in between bouts of laughter, "that green rum has certainly gone to your head. What are you thinking? I am like you, Newton, I am human." Then her laughter ceased, and she adopted a more serious manner. "Darus, the waiter, is an Androgen, the men in black who accompanied Lord Bandersant on your rescue mission, they are Androgen. All the workers, the carers and most of the teachers on this planet are all Androgen. They have similar uses like the machines your scientists created back in the twenty-first century, but ours are much more highly advanced. They have organic intelligence, which can evolve, just as it does in humans, and it continues to do so over a period as it develops by absorbing information externally, rather than by direct input, which your primitive folk used to refer to as programming."

"Computers that can think and reason. Now that's a first."

"Newton, they are not computers like the type you used in your time. They are much more sophisticated than that. Androgen are artificial life forms – Look! Down there, Newton!" She exclaimed suddenly.

When I looked out through the front screen, I could see a large white land vehicle moving away from the building. Well, I believed it to be a land vehicle, at first, until I witnessed that it appeared to be running straight over rocks, shrubs, dips and holes in the ground, and even boundary walls. The terrain was undoubtedly rough here, indistinguishable from the indigenous outback terrain. And it was hot, dry and arid, like that of a desert, one that I wouldn't like to be exploring on foot.

"Take it down, Newton!" Prangalistra said as she pointed to a clear piece of land free of rocks and obstacles. "Land there." She insisted. I was reluctant at first, but I maintained my faith in the belief that nothing was hostile or evil on this planet, not even what we had discovered inside the land transporter down there.

My suspicions were confirmed once we had landed. The large white vehicle was heading directly towards us at a smooth, keen pace. And yes it had been defeating gravity all along just as I suspected, although its name suggested that it was a vehicle that travelled on land. However, it did, in fact, hover comfortably about ten feet above the ground without any visible means of support, although it sported a perfect set of wheels. The vehicle reduced speed and stopped beside our ship.

The climate wasn't as bad as I anticipated. It was hot and dry indeed, but just bearable. After securing the door to our ship, we stood on the burning dry sand waiting for the land vehicle to lower itself to the ground and open it's doors so that we may meet its occupants. I wasn't so sure that this was a good idea, and I made it clear to Prangalistra, several times, which she ignored. I had no idea who or what we were about to encounter inside this strange looking vehicle, but she seemed confident enough that we were in no danger, but somehow I suspect she concealed a hint of doubt.

The bright hot sun sent a dazzling light, which reflected directly from the white marble-like surface of the land vehicle, this was so intense, that it played havoc with my ability to see clearly.

It landed gracefully in complete silence directly in front of us where it became shadowed by one of the large rocks near our ship. We watched intensely as the door slid open slowly. We saw no movement inside only pitch-black darkness, and silence. Suddenly I thought I heard a shuffling sound coming from the inside.

I looked hard through the blackness, but I could see nothing. I heard the sound again, this time it was much louder. I felt Prangalistra jump; it was at that moment that I realised that I was holding on to her arm. I was about to let go when total fear came over me, the fright that was so intense and uncontrollable only for a brief moment. Prangalistra let out a sharp cry of despair, a sound that I have never heard her make since we met.

What we both saw standing in the doorway of the land vehicle contravened all the rules and laws of this blissful planet. Its form was the head of a creature so hideously deformed, with large canine teeth and huge bulging eyes. I quickly scanned the ground for a rock or a stick, or any other handy weapon available on offer from nature's garden, but I found none. My mind raced, this was all wrong, I kept telling myself that there is no fear or danger here on this blissful earth?

The creature made no noise, it just stared at us, and then suddenly it revealed itself, the rest of its body slithered from the darkness and out onto the ramp. It was all black - and then I suddenly saw legs and arms, they were black too! I felt Prangalistra go limp, and then she let out a deep sigh. I stood there bewildered as she left me standing and began walking casually towards the creature.

"Fortinell!" She said in an angry tone, "You little bastard! You could have given us a heart attack!"

The now frightened creature quickly removed its head, which I immediately recognised as a lifelike, latex mask – a hideously well-made one at that! Prangalistra grabbed the mask and threw it to me.

"Newton! Put this in one of the photon jets; we'll destroy it on take-off!"

I stuffed the mask into the largest of the three jets at the rear of my spacecraft, and then followed Prangalistra into the land vehicle.

"So you're the famous Newton I heard about?" The unshaven little man, dressed in black garments said, as he greeted me at the door of the land vehicle. He removed his leather cap and offered me his hand. " Fortinell is my name. Sorry about the creature show, it gets lonely out here sometimes, and with the heat and the dryness, it's no good for a man of my condition. I sometimes need a little diversion to take my mind off the job."

"Fortinell, there are thousands of Androgen inside that building, if you were to converse with each one you would be in the spirit world before you got halfway through them all!" Prangalistra said, as she sat in the driver's seat and began pressing buttons on the console. She suddenly reached down the side of the seat and pulled out a large glass bottle, which contained a green liquid. "Fortinell, here's your diversion." She held the bottle up high, "Green Rum! Quite enough to take your mind off anything."

I took my place in one of the large seats opposite Fortinell, which faced an oblong table. "It is fairly hot out there, Prangalistra," I said, perhaps in sympathy for this sorry looking man, "enough to drive any man to madness."

Prangalistra laughed, as she pressed a button on the console. The door closed and locked with a clunk, which was followed by a hissing sound.

"Don't fall for that one, Newton; he is not affected by heat. He is Androgen – Hang on, we are going for a tour of the plant."

The land vehicle slowly elevated to about ten feet above the ground, and then it travelled towards the building at a moderate speed.

"So, you are Androgen?" I said to Fortinell.

"He's not sure what he is, Newton!" Prangalistra shouted from the front of the vehicle. "He thinks he is human sometimes. He was a prototype, created to run the plant by a man called Celebrias; he was one of the pioneers of all this technology."

"I'd like to meet him. Can we meet him?" I asked as I scrutinised every detail of Fortinell's lined face from across the table.

"You will need Ghost Crystal," she replied, "he progressed to the spiritual realms around AD 2844. Too much Green Rum."

I was slightly puzzled at the fact that a robot could consume and digest organic matter. I do recall Darus drinking golden Champagne back on the Island. I put this question to Prangalistra.

"Most Androgen are of the advanced type," she informed me, "they can digest organic matter by a process similar to that used in your ship's photon jets, the solid state crystal drive, but on a much smaller scale. Fortinell is one of the first of the advanced types. Unfortunately, his ability to digest matter is more efficient than that of the others, but his liking for the green rum does him no favours at all."

"Just like his creator, Celebrias?" I said.

"Yes, Newton, some claim that it is the result of psychological behaviour, as he seems to be mimicking his creator."

I watched as Fortinell reached down under the table and, from a wooden cupboard, brought out a green bottle and a small glass and placed them on the table. "Drink, Newton?" He asked as he waved the glass at me.

"No thanks," I said politely. "Tell me, Fortinell, what exactly is your function here?" I asked as the vehicle pulled up in front of the massive white building. Shutters opened on both sides of the vehicle, which revealed extensive glass windows allowing us an unobstructed panorama of the outside.

"I am the controller and operator of the Androgen processing plant." He said, with a degree of pride.

, "We are going in now!" Prangalistra announced.

A hidden door opened up within the walls of the building allowing us to enter. Prangalistra drove the vehicle forward, slowly until we were inside, then the vast doors closed behind us. It was dark inside, all except for a few flashing lights here and there. Then came an announcement, 'Caution! Do not attempt to leave the vehicle, airlock system in operation!' It repeated twice in a soft female voice.

We were still for a moment, and we remained to hover above the floor, although I could not tell at what height because I couldn't see any floor below due to the lack of light. Then suddenly there was a hissing sound, and a pair of doors on the opposite side slid open. The female voice announced that we were now in a vacuum and it would be wise to remain in our pressurised vessel at all times. I wasn't planning on going anywhere. I decided to go and sit with Prangalistra at the front of the vehicle while Fortinell drank himself into a stupor – if robots can do that? Perhaps this advanced type could, due to the capability of organic matter digestion.

"Where are you taking us, Prangalistra?" I asked her, as I placed myself in the comfortable seat beside her.

"I am not doing the taking, Newton. This place is a highly restricted facility with highly efficient security, which even I am having trouble with clearance. This system will only allow access to certain areas, and I am unable to override anything."

"What about him?" I indicated to Fortinell.

"Yes, he can take you anywhere you wish to go, Newton, – on foot." She replied, tersely, and then she pointed to the sealed door. She lay back in the chair and folded her arms. "It's a tour from here on, and I'm afraid I no longer have control."

We were about fifteen feet above a walkway, in a hermetically sealed land vehicle, moving slightly faster than walking speed. Below, we could see rows and rows of containers stacked side by side.

"What is this place?" I asked.

"It is the storage facility," Fortinell replied, as he downed another glass of green rum.

"Why do you drink that stuff?" I asked, "It does not affect your system."

"Green rum is good, it helps me to concentrate," he replied, as he poured out another glass.

"Do you have any Celestials working at this facility?" I asked.

"No, only Androgen." He replied.

"How many Androgen?"

"Fifty-five," he replied before he took a long swig of the green rum.

I turned to Prangalistra, "Didn't you say there were thousands in here, Prangalistra?"

She smiled and pointed to the containers below.

"The sleeping ones," I said, and then I turned to Fortinell, who had suddenly appeared to be in the seat directly behind me. "Do you mean fifty-five workers, and the rest are in containers, Fortinell, is that correct?"

"Why would you want to know all this information, anyway?" He asked, his words becoming slurred.

"How many humans?"

Fortinell suddenly perked up; then he put his glass down on the console by his side. "There is one human here in this facility." He said in a clear voice.

I turned to Prangalistra.

"So much for the effects of green rum. Surely Fortinell is faking intoxication?" I said to her in a low voice. She nodded profusely, in agreement. I then turned to Fortinell, "I need to talk with that human, Fortinell. It is important that I speak to him about information regarding this facility. Do you think you can take us to him?"

He paused for a while, and then he suddenly burst out laughing. "You are crazy, Newton, I am the only human here in this whole facility – Tell him, Prangalistra – I know everything about this facility. You can ask me anything!"

"Show me the complete process of how the Androgen are created."

He paused for a moment as if he was in deep thought. He suddenly stood up, as if he had received new instructions from elsewhere, and then he pointed to Prangalistra. "I will need to operate the land vehicle. You two go and sit at the table, out of sight."

I went over and sat down at the table, and was later joined by Prangalistra, who sat directly opposite me. Fortinell made himself comfortable in the driver's seat, and as soon as he had settled in, he began pressing buttons on the front console. The shutters on the side windows closed, obscuring our only clear view of outside. We just had the front windscreen view to rely on, which was too far to see any real detail. I was about to protest when Prangalistra touched my arm gently. She was staring awkwardly at the table, which made me look at it as well. 'What are we looking for?' I thought to myself because all I saw was a cloudy white surface. Then suddenly, just as I had decided it was time to of resume my protest with Fortinell, the surface of the table glowed, and it revealed a pure, crisp picture of the outside of the vehicle.

I was forced to praise Fortinell instead, for pressing a button and turning a simple crystal glass table into an ultra-high definition TV monitor screen. I witnessed an advanced technology that employed precise microscopic pixilation, with a degree of clarity never seen anywhere on earth before. I had no words available, nor could I think of any, to describe the quality and the beauty of these images.

Prangalistra explained briefly, devoid of technical detail, in her own words that such simple devices and their underlying workings, atomic photon particle imaging, was commonly used throughout the world to receive TV images, and most vehicles had them.

This marvel was the first working system I have seen since my arrival, apart from the Ghost Crystal, which I was told later, utilised a more complicated method of operation, far beyond the comprehension of most ordinary mortals. It was at that point that I gave up examining the underside of the glass table for any clues of how this technology ticked.

"Newton, what are you doing?" Prangalistra asked as she posed in a head cant and an expression of perplexity with it. "You are not in the twenty-first century now. There is no need to touch the screen, or pinch it." She demonstrated by waving her hand over the table, and then she made a simple beckoning gesture. The images in front of her enlarged and then they appeared to zoom in at the same time, in sync with the movement of her fingers. "This is how you control it, Newton, like this. There are no buttons."

I followed her example, although it took me a few attempts to master. I was highly pleased with the results. The detail was astounding. I zoomed into one of the containers below us; I could see the texture of the material itself of the container as if I had been right up close to it.

"We are going into the processing area now," Fortinell announced, somewhat discreetly.

I observed another area of the facility; it was large, white, and clean. The walls were bright white, so too were the floors, and space was vast. We travelled above the floor, at least fifteen feet above it looking down at the busy activity below.

"There are people down there," I said to Prangalistra.

"Those are Androgen down there, Newton." She replied.

I zoomed in on one of the figures, which I noticed was carrying a component in his hand. His movements were like that of a human. His gait, the way he interacted with the others, even his facial expressions.

Prangalistra looked up at me from the table, "Don't let it fool you, Newton, there is no air inside this building; they are working in a vacuum. Humans cannot survive in such conditions. Remember Darus? You couldn't tell if he was humanoid. You assumed that he was human."

I scanned the others; they all had similar facial features. Prangalistra informed me that, unlike the workers outside, these never leave this facility so it would be pointless to give them distinguishing features, hence their facial similarities.

We moved along further to a more delicate section of the facility where the rooms were smaller. We observed Androgen heads, floating in mid-air with, what I could discern as fibre optic cables trailing from the spinal column of each one, which led to a massive machine, which looked much like a large computer, with an array of multi-coloured flashing lights.

"This is the Neurological and Cerebrovascular section," Fortinell announced, rather proudly, this is where all the information is processed and added to the brain."

I zoomed into an Androgen working on one of the skeletal heads. I wanted to know if this contained any organic material. I was able to observe the most revealing detail of its internal workings. The equipment and the components seemed entirely alien to me, as I could not even recognise anything that I could associate or compare with my dated technology from the twenty-first century. It seemed that all the components had been designed explicitly for photon and perhaps other electromagnetic technology. The faculty of such advanced technology was far beyond my comprehension. I would require about eight hundred years of teaching just to catch up with it all.

I sat back in the seat and wiped the sweat from my brow. I asked myself what am I trying to prove here? Am I attempting to satisfy my understanding of Karla's existence? Her origin?

I leant forward and looked Prangalistra in the eyes. They widened, enough to ask me, 'what now? Are you not satisfied with what you see?' I grabbed her hand and locked my fingers in between hers. Now I had her full attention. "Prangalistra, tell me please," I said, in my most commanding voice, "If those intelligent humanoids down there built Karla, why is it that she is much more advanced than they are?"

"Newton, they did not build Karla!" Fortinell interrupted before Prangalistra could even utter a single word in reply.

I stood up and approached the front and sat down in the seat behind Fortinell, in full view of the windscreen, unconcerned about being discovered at any moment by the Androgen below. They would raise the alarm without hesitation. But I was only interested in what Fortinell had to say about Karla.

"Karla?" He said, "Is an advanced Celestial from the Luna Region."

"Newton! Get down, they will see you, and we will be discovered!" Prangalistra called. But it was too late; I was already in full view of the Androgen, who now had a clear view of the windscreen from the ground. It was only a matter of time until they realised that we were human imposters, and then they would raise the alarm. Fortinell kept calm and continued at a steady speed as not to raise any further suspicion.

"Fortinell, tell me all you know about Karla!" I urged him.

"All?" He asked in surprise, "You need to visit the Luna Region. You may find all your answers there – the dark side, mind."

I turned to Prangalistra. "What will we find there, Prangalistra?"

"I told you it would get complicated, Newton!" She said in a loud whisper, "It is difficult enough to get into this place, you won't have any chance on the Luna Region. The security there is high, and the fact that the whole planet is a vacuum makes it all the more difficult." She then turned to Fortinell and whispered a loud command, "Fortinell! Abandon the tour! Please get us out of here immediately!"

"I'm doing it now! Don't stress me, please!" He shouted back before he reached down and picked up a bottle of Green Rum, from which he took a long, nervous swig.

We eventually reached the airlock at the opposite end of the building, as we were unable just to turn around and go back to the inside. Such careless action would have most definitely aroused suspicion and get us caught.

We had just left the airlock and were heading out into the open air and bright sunshine when we heard the alarm warning sound inside the building. Fortinell was still in control of the vehicle, which he resumed at average altitude, at a constant speed, heading away from the closing doors in a somewhat leisurely fashion, I thought, which I made clear to him with the suggestion that it would be more prudent to perhaps go into escape mode. It was just when he had heard a second warning, which came in the form of a human voice this time, and carried a much more dire advice; he had made an immediate decision to suddenly accelerate and bank to the left in an attempt to turn the vehicle around. And then he quickly headed in the opposite direction.

"Why doesn't he ascend into the atmosphere, perhaps we can lose them in the thin clouds up there!" I shouted to Prangalistra.

"Not a good idea, Newton!" She shouted back, "These are advanced land vehicles, not spacecraft. We are practically at maximum altitude right now!"

I observed with great concern as we neared the side of the building, almost clipping it, and then we travelled away from it at full speed, judging by the sound of the engines. After a while, we found ourselves back to the location where we had left our spacecraft, right beside the rocks. It was a fast and rough ride, bouncing up and down on air, but Fortinell managed to get us there all in one piece, considering the amount of Green Rum he had already consumed.

He hovered behind a rock a little way away from the ship and told us that it would be a good idea to jump down to the ground, as it was too risky to land because if he did so, the Androgen would discover that he had dropped off imposters. I protested because I didn't want to break my legs, my ankles, or my neck, when all he had to do was to land quickly or, at least, hover a bit closer to the ground instead.

"You got us here in one piece, Fortinell, and I would rather stay that way please, so if you could, I would be most grateful if you can get this thing closer to the ground so that we can jump to safety?"

Prangalistra peculiarly looked at me as she pursed her lips and shook her head slowly, and then she opened the hatch door and shouted to Fortinell to pass her the gravity belts. He threw her two, which she caught dextrously, and then she gave me one and then told me to put it on and to press the button – just before you jump! She stressed.

I quickly put on my belt carefully copying her every move, and then I watched her as she approached the opened hatch door. We both stood at the edge of the threshold. I was nervous, but I trusted her. She unexpectedly grabbed me by the arm, and we both leapt out through the hatch. I later discovered that we hadn't fallen fifteen feet at all. Although at one stage, we had been hovering at that height, while I was airing my worries over the dangers of such a long drop, Fortinell had ascended the vehicle to a height of fifty feet from the ground.

I did express my grave concern about my safety immediately before we hit the ground, but that was due to my sheer ignorance about the workings of thirtieth-century gravity belts. I believed that the device had malfunctioned because it did absolutely nothing.

I had underestimated their advanced technology once again, as I waited, in vain, for the belt to inflate. Assuming that a thick envelope would fill up with air; the only logical explanation my primitive brain could comprehend, that would be capable and sufficient to save my fragile body from crashing feet first onto the hard ground below. But instead, a beam of light, and a strange magnetic force, ultimately took over space around my entire body, and in a split second had temporarily cancelled all the laws of gravity in that vicinity. I slowed down and floated safely to the ground, like a feather in ultra slow motion.

We both rose to our feet unscathed and unharmed, save for a little dust in my throat, which I got rid of rather quickly. And we brushed off the rest of it from our clothes.

"These should come in handy for our next mission," I said to Prangalistra, as I removed my belt and was about to take it with me to the craft. She grabbed it from me and then threw it into the air along with hers. Fortinell, who was standing at the open hatch, caught them both expertly with one hand. He then waved goodbye before disappearing out of sight. We watched as the door closed, and the vehicle sped off through the air.

On the way to the ship, which was just beyond the rocks, Prangalistra explained the reason why she had returned the gravity belts to Fortinell. She said that all vehicles have them as a safety measure, including yours!

We took off and headed back to The Island, which was now out in the middle of the ocean somewhere in the Southern Hemisphere. I was hungry and tired, but most of all I couldn't wait to see my little Karla.

CHAPTER 9

Communication

I found out later that Prangalistra had secretly arranged, with Captain Brodar of the Island, for Karla and me to occupy one of the grand and extremely opulent honeymoon suites to make our stay on the Island more comfortable. I believed she did it to take my mind off going to the Luna Region, which she thought was a bad idea.

I had a strange feeling when I got back on the Island, one that I could not explain. It is what you humans call ESP Extra Sensual Perception, Darus had told me when I met him on board. He was taking me to my cabin, the honeymoon suite; he said that it was an exclusive suite designed for soul mates to share special memories just after the bonding. Darius tried his best to explain, but he did it somewhat awkwardly, so I was inclined to help him. I mentioned about couples in my time and the marriage ceremony. He said that was in their history, as they did practise this in the past, but now they just call them soul mates, and there is no actual official ceremony as such, they naturally found each other and bonded.

We decided to take the long route to the suite because I wanted to see more of the vessel on the way instead of travelling inside a golden globe with no windows to look out of, although it was much faster when you consider the size of this vessel. I was in no hurry anyway because nobody had seen Karla, so I assumed that she was still out with Pranga, eating, drinking, and enjoying herself, which is precisely what I could do with right now.

After getting the door for me, Darus left a bottle of golden Champagne on the table, and he told me that he could send up some food as well if I liked but I said to him I would be going out to eat soon, and I thanked him, and he left the room.

The view from the door of the entrance to the suite was of sheer luxury. I saw an open veranda that led straight down onto a sun deck, which had six comfortable sunbeds arranged neatly in a row. They were facing a large swimming pool with a Jacuzzi and hot tub at the side. The dining room was quite spacious and cosy too, as it reminded me of my own back in the city. There was an arch that led to a spacious hallway, and then on to the bedroom; the master bedroom, I believe, because this room was vast. The bed itself was huge, with enough space all around to walk, or even to run, if your heart desired. The bed appeared to be even more significant, in comparison to the figure lying face down in the centre, and half covered by the silk sheets. I had to look twice, and it was only then that I had concluded that it had belonged to a small-framed girl who appeared to be sleeping face down in the middle until I heard her sobbing quietly.

I had to stop and listen carefully to confirm what I saw. I wasn't at all startled at what I had discovered, as my mind was racing along with questions. Perhaps Darus had shown me into the wrong room? But he's Androgen; they seldom make mistakes especially with such trivial details as this, according to Prangalistra.

I approached her carefully and touched her arm gently. Something flashed in my mind, her hair looked familiar, but the colours were somewhat different.

"Karla? Is that you?" I asked, a little unsure and with a degree of embarrassment. She turned to look at me. I could see her tear filled eyes. The look of sorrow on her face saddened me greatly. But I sighed with relief as soon as I had recognised her.

"Newton, you won't love me anymore," she sobbed, as tears streamed down her cheeks.

I held her close to me; I was confused, and at the same time worried. "What are you talking about, Karla? What do you mean I won't love you?"

"You know about me; Louden told you everything!"

"Karla, what are you saying, Karla? I haven't seen Louden."

"He said that you know everything about me, and I am afraid, Newton, I am afraid that you won't love me anymore because of what I am!"

I held her tightly.

"Don't be silly, Karla, I will always love you no matter what." I looked into her eyes. "Now, listen to me, Karla. I did find out something today, but nothing about you. I have been to the Androgen facility on the mainland with Prangalistra. I insisted that she take me there so that I could learn more about the Androgen."

She stared at me, her gorgeous green eyes wide open and still, not even a blink. "And the Celestials?" She asked in a soft whisper.

I kissed her gently on her lips, "Karla, you are so beautiful, how could I ever stop loving you? I could never give you up, no matter what happened. It's not about who you are, or what you are, Karla, it is about me finding out about my past. I have lost almost nine hundred years of my life." I kissed her again, this time a lingering one. "Yes, it is true I do know you are Celestial, Karla, but I don't care. I couldn't distinguish you from any human on this planet. I couldn't even distinguish between Androgen and human. To me you are my beautiful Karla, that's all I know, and I want to be with you forever. Look," I waved my hands in the air, "why do you think I got us the honeymoon suite?"

She laughed, as she wiped her eyes.

"And what have you done to your hair?" I said, teasingly, "I almost took you for somebody else when I walked in and saw you laying on the bed."

"I went to the salon with Pranga. She's crazy. Do you like it, Newton?"

"Of course I do, my darling, Karla. It becomes you."

I held her tightly in my arms; the warmth of her perfectly proportioned sylph-like body drove me crazy with passion. I caressed her and ran my fingers through her hair, as I whispered 'I love you' in her ear. She responded with a soft purr, like a cat. I whispered into her other ear, "I love you more than anything in this world, my dear little Karla." Her purring turned to groans. I picked her up from the bed and carried her into the shower, where we spent at least an hour or so, but I wasn't counting, as I was no longer concerned about time, only lasting happiness. After our impromptu shower tryst, we got dressed and went out in search of an excellent restaurant to eat.

I had no idea how high we were from sea level on this big ship, or floating 'Island', as they called it, or referred to, I should say. Because nobody was too concerned about names here, as it was considered Heaven on earth, and here we are required to live for the moment, and not worry at all about material possessions.

I looked out to sea towards the bright blue horizon, with the warm tropical breeze gently kissing my face, in deep thought, thinking of the vile world I had left behind. Here I was on the most significant luxury vessel ever constructed on this entire planet, an enormous ship that sails continuously around the globe in the tropical zone, and at any time anybody in the whole world can come aboard solely for the benefit of relaxation, pleasure, entertainment, and recreation. And guests can eat and drink as much as they like in any of the three hundred and sixty-five of its luxury restaurants.

In my time on this same planet, such luxury was reserved only for the super-rich, and they had to pay for the privilege, with their hard-earned cash, which they claimed they had acquired quite honestly. This so-called elite, as they believed themselves to be, had elected to segregate themselves from the rest of society, in particular, the less affluent, which they had made impoverished initially through new slave labour, and then this very pseudo-elite dared to consider themselves above the less well off. They all seem to forget one thing that God made all men equal. They then would justify their actions by claiming that they are the virtuous and respectable citizens who provide the jobs for the uneducated, unskilled, proletariat.

In many cases research had proved, in my time, that some of these so-called successful innovators of commerce and finance had turned out to be nothing but flawed instigators of baleful conspiracies who sought to deceive to benefit financially.

This world has conquered greed, poverty, crime, war, sickness and disease, just by the freeing up of all material possessions. Is it communism? No, it is not. Communism is worse than capitalism, as harsh dictators, who have an unhealthy obsession with arms and domination, usually control the people. There are no military bases in this world. I have not seen any weapons or defence systems anywhere.

There is only one thing I could consider as a weapon, in a way that it has high power to suppress man's evil desires, and at the same time encourage him to live in complete peace and harmony with his fellow man. To love and care for one another, and to seek and follow the path of the Great Prophet towards spiritual enlightenment. That powerful weapon is the Ghost Crystal itself. According to Louden, within the space of about three hundred years, this very substance had wholly changed the world without taking a single human life. Not through fear or control of any kind, but only because of what it had revealed to mankind, the truth.

We found a somewhat comfortable and luxurious seafood restaurant, and according to Darus, it was considered the best one on the entire vessel. He said that he would recommend it always. Just like our honeymoon suite, it too was located high up on the roof of the Island with an uninterrupted view of the horizon. Across the way, on a level below, from where we sat, we had a perfect view of a large platform. It was green and lush, with a large lawn in the centre, and a generous collection of tropical trees and plants scattered here and there around its perfectly kept walkways.

People gathered on the green outside of one of its restaurants. They were drinking and socialising on the green. It was evident that they had been waiting for something to happen. I mentioned it to our waitress, an attractive young girl called, Alana, while she was on her way to the kitchen with some empty plates.

"A fireworks display?" I asked her, curiously. She just laughed, as she perhaps had never heard of my twenty-first-century term.

"They are waiting for something to arrive from the air." She said.

I immediately sensed a negative feeling from Karla. She was upset about something.

"They are waiting for Louden to arrive in his balloon." I heard one man say at the next table.

"That old hermit is coming here, by balloon?" I said to Karla, although she did not respond in a way that I expected. "Will he bring his young daughters? I can never tell them apart. Do you know their names, Karla?"

"What does it matter," She replied, "if you cannot tell them apart anyway?"

"Karla." I said, "You are upset about something, and I suspect it has something which relates to Louden. Karla, you were acting the same way when we stayed at his place." I held her hands across the table. "Now, Karla, remember what I said to you earlier? If we are to be together forever, there should be no secrets between us. So before we can settle down and enjoy this meal together, I would like you to tell me everything concerning you and Louden, if there is anything. Trust me, Karla; it will take a lot to shock me. Remember, I am from a time where one man would not think twice about killing another just for looking at him in the wrong way."

I felt her flinch, and then she tightened her grip. She sighed, as she looked me in the eye. I could see an expression of regret in her eyes. I kept silent and waited for her to begin.

"I shan't go into too much detail, Newton," she said, with sadness, "No, you are right, he hasn't done anything as bad as in your world, but I am concerned for Muriel and Cassie."

"The twins?" I asked quickly, as not to break her flow. "What about the other two?"

"Newton, He only has two, the others are Androgen. I am not aware of their names. Louden was working at the Androgen facility with Celebrias, who built one of the first Androgen, it was a prototype called Fortinell."

"Karla, I found this out on my recent visit there with Prangalistra."

Her eyes widened, "So you know all about them?"

"Yes I do, but you must tell me where you fit in here. Prangalistra didn't mention you at all."

"Well, Louden requested two Celestials for companions and arranged for Fortinell to transport them from the Luna. I am not sure if Fortinell carried out his request, or if he brought them back by himself. But he got them back to earth somehow, and they lived in the city for a while, that is where I got to know them because they stayed with us. I was surprised that they were so young, but I just assumed, like everyone else, that he wanted daughters, that he and his wife could not have."

"She left him?" I asked.

"She left this world."

"Oh, sorry – Karla, do continue, please."

"When the girls moved in with him, in his hermits paradise, they were not very happy at first, and I thought it was because they missed the good times we had together while they were living in the city."

"Did you visit them at his paradise?"

"Only once. The second time was a brief visit; I had gone there to take some of the clothes back for them, which they left at our house – That is when I caught him."

I squeezed her hands tightly, she yelped. It was the first time I had accidentally hurt her. "Sorry, Karla." I apologised profusely and caressed her hands, then we both let go of each other's hands and folded our arms on the table instead. "You caught him?" I asked, somewhat afraid of what she was about to reveal to me.

"I caught him in bed."

"In bed?"

"Yes, Newton, in bed with the twins!" She reiterated.

"And he saw you, Karla? Is that why you both have issues?"

"No, Newton, he didn't see me, but he guessed that I found out because I had left the twin's clothes outside his door, and then I just left without seeing them. He knows that I would never do that."

"And you told him that you knew?"

"No, not exactly," she replied, "I just limit my communication with him."

"What about when you went swimming with them, did they say anything to you? Were they all right, because they seemed all right to me?"

"Yes, they were fine. Both seem to be happy when they are around the Androgen kids."

"They do most of the work for him around the estate, I imagine?"

"Yes, and they also find time to conspire with the twins to subdue him by plying his drinks with red juice, and sometimes Green Rum. It makes him tired, so he spends most of the time sleeping."

"Have you told anyone else about this, Karla?"

"No, Newton, I have not. But it will do no good anyway because when Celebrias and his team developed the Androgen and Celestials, they specifically stated that they were created solely to assist and to satisfy man's earthly desires."

"If the twins are unhappy couldn't they just leave him?" I asked

"No, Newton, it doesn't work like that. They are brought into creation specifically for him, and he is not allowed to disrespect them or mistreat them. He cannot do so anyway, as it is in his nature. Like it is with all humans on the planet, who have experienced the Revelation."

"Perhaps he needs more revelation. Is it possible to increase the efficiency by implementing multiple exposures?"

"You will have to ask Lord Bandersant or Doctor Gabriel about that," Karla replied.

Alana came over again; this time she was carrying shiny, golden tray with a black and a white wine bottle and two glasses. She was smiling, and she wasn't wearing any hover skates, yet she displayed a graceful gait, her long slim legs scissoring under a tight black skirt, which seemed to synchronise in perfect harmony with the restaurant's mood music, as she approached our table and set the tray down.

"Compliments of the house, Newton," she said, " as our special guest this evening, you are invited to indulge yourself with one of our best wines. You have a choice of the black or the white; do try them both if you so desire." She popped the cork of the black and filled two glasses with a good degree of graciousness and dexterity. "I shall bring you your starter menu," Alana said, as she beamed a friendly smile and then she told us, in a kind and pleasant manner, to enjoy the wine, and then she quickly walked away with the same graciousness that she had displayed when she had first approached us.

I smiled at Karla as I raised my glass. "Now, she is most definitely Celestial," I said, as I was about to take a sip of wine.

Karla gave me a playful slap on my arm, "No," she said, "Newton, you are crazy, she is Androgen, all the servers here are Androgen. No Celestials are serving on the Island."

"How could you tell?" I asked, slightly mockingly. She just slapped me again, and then I proposed a toast to everlasting love and happiness.

We ate seafood for starters and then we had more seafood for our main dish. I have never seen such huge Langoustines before. Usually, they were nine or ten inches long, in my time that is, these were at least double that in size, served on large square plates of equal proportion, and the taste? I could not explain in mere words alone; I should require sound effects and music, and perhaps employ all five senses to erupt in gastronomic ecstasy, all in one instance, to describe such a delightful experience. The wine too – well, the two bottles were empty by the time we had finished eating. The additional bottles, which Alana had brought over to our table just as we had finished eating the dessert, were both almost empty as well. It was indeed the best wine, and wholly addictive too.

I toyed with the smooth, white, marble-like bottle, as we sat drinking coffee, admiring the sunset over the horizon. It was almost down; with not much idea of time and not a clock in sight it was difficult to tell exactly, not that I wanted or needed to know, but I estimated another thirty minutes or so before it submerged into the sea, ninety-three million miles beyond the horizon.

Colourful lights, gleaming and shimmering, turned on everywhere around us, one by one casting clean, sharp, fresh light on pathways, in foliage, from rooftop and park restaurants, and on balconies and other areas in every corner of this enormous ocean-going Leviathan. The colourful matrix of lighting seems to transform the whole vessel into a floating heavenly kingdom. I was eager to see how it would look in complete darkness, and I even suggested to Karla that we go on a night flight to observe its entire beauty from above.

She just laughed, and said that it would look equally beautiful from up there, just as it did from here where we were sitting, but smaller. Only then, her gaze was interrupted by something outside.

"He's here." She said, in almost an angry whisper.

Her sweet voice drowned out by the melee out on the lower balcony, where a good number of people had gathered earlier and was now drinking, chatting, and cheering. They were all looking up towards the sky.

I stood up to take a look. "Louden?" I said. "That's no balloon; it's a floating house."

We both walked outside to the balcony through the large open glass doors, which led out from our restaurant. There were more diners seated out there on the terrace, eating and drinking, and enjoying the warm tropical evening. They were all looking up, admiring the vast object that had suddenly appeared in the sky, and had taken up much of it too.

"Where is he going to land that thing?" I said quietly to myself.

"In the sea, perhaps," Karla said quietly to herself.

"It looks as if he has brought his whole house with him."

"This is what they were all waiting for." A little voice said in my ear. I turned to see Alana suddenly standing by my side; a kaleidoscope of colourful lights cast reflection upon her shiny, bright, blue eyes, as she expressed total surprise and delight at the huge spectacle above in the star-studded night sky.

"Alana, where will he land that thing?" I asked her.

"Over there, on that platform, on the green," she said, without taking her eyes off the balloon, pointing to the lower platform where the crowd had gathered. "They just love the balloon." She continued.

"How is it powered, does it contain gas?" I asked.

"Yes, it is pressurised," Alana replied.

"It has a solid-state crystal drive system, like the one in your craft, Newton," Karla said, "But with much lower power than yours. It is designed just for low-speed cruising and just enjoying the view."

We watched as the balloon headed for the lower platform, and then eventually it landed on the green without much bother, as the green itself was vast enough to accommodate it, and more. A loud cheer suddenly erupted from the crowd, and some of them surged forward to get a better look.

I took Karla's hand, and we made our way back to the table, where we sat down again and enjoyed another cup of coffee. All of the wine had gone, which surprised me because I have never, in my whole life, ever drunk even one single glass of wine without feeling a little bit tipsy afterwards. And here I was with four empty wine bottles, and a belly full of one of the world's finest wines, a fresh sea breeze on my face, and yet I felt no adverse effects whatsoever.

I am told that the potency of such beverage is almost akin to that of Green Rum. Perhaps the combination of the cleansing drugs given to me by Doctor Gabriel, and the Revelation, is affecting my entire system. This process must be strengthening my spiritual side, which in turn is causing changes, relating to matters of the flesh, making them more unimportant and insignificant.

A stronger spiritual side, now that appeals to me very much. It was at that point that I had one of the most bizarre experiences I have ever had since I arrived at this heavenly paradise. I had a dream one night that I was taken to a place by Darus. It was a place on the Island, a secret place, where I discovered the largest single piece of Ghost crystal ever found on earth, although I am fully aware that Ghost Crystal cannot be found and that it has to be made entirely, the dream continued and developed further anyway.

With this valuable find, I was able to not only just see and communicate with spirits from the other side, but I could also visit them in the spirit world with my physical body, and interact with them in their world. I am told by Lord Bandersant, that sometimes spirits can and will communicate with you during your dream state, as this is the best time when the chakras are active, and this could be during a lucid dream when you have an out of body experience. He claimed that it was entirely possible to enter the Ghost Crystal using the physical body, but he never did fully explain what he meant by this, and I never bothered to pursue him with further questioning because I thought it quite bizarre and doubtful.

There was just too much information to take in. I've yet to find out many more things about daily life in this world. Some of my questions remain unanswered, or exasperatingly incomplete, which leaves me with a half finished jigsaw puzzle, and many pieces still missing.

Just then, I remembered something about my first encounter with the Ghost Crystal. There was a character called Androgen, who also featured in my dream, and he had said something about Karla being unseen.

"Why did he say that to you, Karla?" I asked her in my most gentle, pleasing voice.

She displayed a worried expression, as she toyed with her coffee cup, then she took a deep sigh. "He meant that he was unable to feel my soul, Newton."

"He is saying you don't have one?" I asked, rather confused. She did not answer me. I stood up and approached her. As she got up from her chair, I embraced her tightly, "Karla, Do you feel that you have one?" I asked her.

She smiled at me and said, "Yes I do, Newton. I feel it mostly at night when I am dreaming, and sometimes during the day when my heart is troubled."

"Well, that is good enough for me," I said, as I squeezed her even tighter.

Darus suddenly barged into the restaurant like a crazy kid on a skateboard. He stopped and greeted us both.

"Did you see the balloon?" He asked, trying desperately to catch his breath.

"Yes, we did, and it is still down there, Darus."

"Louden," he said casually, "they are having a meeting."

"Darus," I said, as I suddenly remembered something in my dream, then I lowered my voice, "Do you know of any Ghost Crystal on the Island? I need to make contact to develop my spiritual side."

"I know just the place," Darus replied, "follow me."

I was surprised by his reaction to my question as I never thought there would be any trace of Ghost crystal on this vessel due to it being for recreational purposes only. But then again, nobody works on this planet, apart from the Androgen of course, so it would be quite impossible to mix business with pleasure. They only sought to achieve higher learning and spiritual enlightenment, and happiness, of course.

Darus had warned us that there would be a long ride in the Golden Globe because this particular location was situated on the other side of the river at the far end of the vessel. He gave us no details at all about the place, nor did he take my hints when I attempted to question him. However, I did manage to ask him about the character named Androgen, who appeared in the last Ghost Crystal Séance. He was vague with his history, but he established that Androgen was the name of one of the scientists who had invented the first Androgen robots back in the last century.

I wasn't too concerned about the history of cyborg or humanoid technology, and I didn't have much of an appetite for any new information regarding this. I was only concerned with spiritual matters and not material ones. I wanted to know about Karla, but at the same time, I didn't want to say or do anything that would hurt or upset her. Perhaps I should try to be the key to the instigation of the Ghost crystal this time, instead of Karla?

I expected to meet others here if this was the only Ghost Crystal on the vessel, but Darus corrected me, as I must have misapprehended the information he gave me earlier. We arrived at a place on the far end of the vessel, after crossing a small river, and then we made our way through a jungle, would you believe, on a ship? But this was no ordinary vessel.

There was a significant, white, circular shaped building, which was several storeys high, and recognisable only as you approached the front entrance, due to the dense foliage that surrounded it. It was undoubtedly designed to be inconspicuous.

It wasn't until we had entered its grand front entrance, and was shown by Darus to one of the rooms inside, that we discovered that the building was not round at all, but in fact, it appeared more 'D' shaped, which suggested to me, an auditorium of some sort. Darus led us through a large wooden door, which revealed another room. It was a medium-sized theatre similar to the one we used back in the city. There were four rows of comfortable seats against the flat wall, which faced a large screen, about eight feet tall and the same in width. It was curved, concave, against the 'D' shaped wall, where it fitted into it nice and snug.

"This reminds me of the one back at the city," I said, as I checked the ultra soft, cosy carpet beneath my feet.

"There are all like this," Darus said.

"How many are there?" I asked, curiously.

"There are six in this building, and I think the captain has one on the bridge, and there is a smaller one right down below," Darus replied, as he pointed his finger towards the floor. "I shall leave you now," he continued, "because I have to get back. We thanked him, and then he skated gracefully out through the doorway, closing it behind him.

"Do you want me to initiate the process?" Karla asked as she sat down in the front row directly in front of the screen.

"No, Karla," I replied, "Let me do it this time. I am curious to know what would happen if I initiate the process instead of you."

"Are you sure it is safe to do so, Newton? Did Lord Bandersant advise you on this?"

"No. He did not, but we will soon find out."

I approached the screen and stood there staring at it for a few seconds before turning to Karla. I smiled at her a hopeful smile, with much faith in my heart, and I thought to myself what possible harm could occur to us if I do this incorrectly? If Karla has the key, absolutely nothing can go wrong. If I do not possess the key, nothing can go wrong. And if I do own the key?

I wasted no more time speculating on the outcome, good or bad. I quickly placed my right palm on the screen at shoulder height and waited with trepidation. Nothing happened at first, and then all of a sudden I could feel the screen as it began to get warmer, or perhaps it was my nervous hand transferring heat to the surface of the screen. I could not tell which. The temperature gradually increased until it reached a point where I decided that this idea was a bad one. And it would be best for me to remove my hand before something more sinister unfolded, which I may live to regret.

Just as I was about to lift my hand away from the glass, it began to glow, and then it pulsated a warm golden colour. That was a positive sign, as this was supposed to happen. After a few more seconds or so, my hand returned to its average temperature. I removed my hand from the glass and took a step back.

"It is working, Newton! You have the key!" Karla shouted, rather excitedly.

I sat down beside her and smiled approvingly. "Don't be too hasty with praises, Karla; we've yet to see who comes through."

The screen flashed from gold to a multitude of colours, and then a figure appeared. It was difficult to discern at first, but it soon became much clearer. It had the appearance of a human, but its head was a different shape, enlarged, and the top part had what looked like spikes, or horns, sticking out. I took Karla's hand. I felt her whole body tremble through her soft, warm fingers. Oh, Karla, what have I done? What vile, evil creature have I summoned from the lower world? I began to regret; to regret that I had been hasty in insisting that I should initiate the session instead of Karla, the genuine key. I should have heeded to what Doctor Gabriel had said, 'only Karla has the key' Not me.

I closed my eyes, and I thought to myself, how do we turn this thing off before this creature appears? And will it possess the ability to leave the screen and wander around the vessel, refusing to return through the Ghost Crystal? Or even worse, it may decide to follow us around, or somehow latch onto my soul forever?

Next, we heard a sound, which almost stopped my heart. I felt Karla's shock too as she nearly crushed my hand this time. I opened my eyes, and then I nudged Karla. What we both saw on the screen in front of us confirmed my worst fears, and indeed Karla's, much to the sudden relief of the crushing bones in my hand.

A Red Indian in full costume, including feathered headdress, the same one that we had mistaken for the head of a horned creature from the underworld, appeared, not as a silhouette as it did at first, but now, as a bright, sharp and clear image on the screen.

"Who is this man who defies death and transgresses time but yet still walks the earth still clothed in the shameful garment of flesh?"

"I think he means you, Newton," Karla said, as she gave me a playful shove.

"I am Newton Flotman," I replied, "born on earth around AD 1985, I seek enlightenment from the spirits from the higher spheres. Who are you, my friend, and how did I summon you?"

"Newton Flotman, you say, from earth? The material realm, filled with men of evil desire and greed? I was once poor and naked on earth, but while there I was the chief of the nation. We did not want riches, but we wanted to train our children right. The offer of riches did us no good, as we could not take them with us to the other world. We did not want riches. All we wanted was peace and love. I am Red Cloud, I dwell in the higher spheres, and I seek peace and Divine Love to ascend to yet higher realms. You have reached me, Newton, because you have a good heart. You have shown no sin for almost a millennium, a feat considered impossible for most mortals, yet you still dwell on the material earth plane?"

I looked at Karla, she too expressed the same level of surprise, and I could see it in her eyes.

"I have never thought of it like that, Red Cloud. But what about Karla?" I asked, quickly and precisely, as I knew Karla would disapprove. She protested with a look of disdain; I could see her glare in the corner of my eye.

Red Cloud studied Karla with a gaze filled with perplexity, which made me nervous. I sighed with relief when I observed his expression as it morphed into a smile, he then he turned to me to speak.

"She is seen, but unseen, and her faithfulness is from the heart. Newton, what do you see in Karla?" He asked.

"I see the love and a kind heart," I replied, without really thinking about the question first.

"Then you are true as one." He said succinctly, as he folded his arms, and then he quickly faded away.

I was somewhat disappointed at his sudden departure, as I knew for a fact that the North American Indians were adept in their knowledge of the spiritual realms, which they acquired proficiently during their existence on the earth plane. They were close to nature and had an understanding of environmental wisdom and spirituality, and were known to be equally respectful towards all animals, as well as their fellow man.

My disappointment soon turned to hope and joy when another spirit appeared and gradually came into focus on the screen. I had seen this one before, no doubt. Karla confirmed this with a short gasp.

"Do you know her?" I asked Karla.

"No, Newton I don't know her, but she has come through before, during your first session before the Revelation." She said, in a low whisper.

The spirit looked directly at me, and then she smiled, "Newton, I see you have completed your first revelation."

"Yes," I replied, "It is good to see you again too. Your name has slipped my mind though, and I would be most grateful if you would remind me of it again if you would, please?"

She smiled and folded her arms. "Newton, your presumptuousness astounds me yet it is amusing all the same. I have come to you again indeed, as you have earnestly requested, now that you have the gnosis, the knowledge and insight into the Divine Love I believe that you are ready to learn more?"

"True, I would like to know more about this planet. I would like to know who you are."

"Newton, your persistence delights me. For this reason, I shall reveal the information that you so vehemently request, however, you must not allow such knowledge to interfere with your pursuit for self-improvement, nor let it quell your desire to attain the Devine Love from the Great Spirit."

I am glad that, this time, I had decided not to take hold of Karla's hand during the Ghost Crystal Session (or GCS, as I would later learn from Lord Bandersant). The level of excitement that she expresses is incomprehensibly high, and most of that expounded energy is concentrated through her hands. Instead, I rubbed her arm, gently. She reciprocated, and we both waited in awe to learn the true identity of our anonymous, disembodied spirit.

Her long, dark hair flowed as if disturbed by a cool summer breeze. She stood with her arms folded, as the light behind her caused a silhouette like an outline of her tall, svelte frame. You are not supposed to have a body in the spirit world, are you? I put the question to her.

"You fool, Newton," she replied, "let me explain this concept of death to you. Upon death, the soul is released from the earthly body encased in its spirit body. The soul's home is in the spirit body, as the soul is never without its spirit body. The appearance and composition of the spirit body are determined by the condition and state of the soul. Remember this, Newton, and you shall not fail.

"Now I shall reveal to you both who I am. My name is Marla Page, I was born in the year AD 2502, and I returned to the spiritual realms in the year AD 2560 where I am now, in the third sphere and still progressing."

I turned to Karla, and we both stared into each other's eyes without uttering a word. Then Karla broke the silence.

"Are you going to ask her, Newton?" She said.

I turned to the screen to see Marla Page smiling in anticipation of my impending question. I paused, thinking that she knew, exactly, what I was about to ask, but she kept silent.

"Are you related to Samuel Page?" I asked.

Her smile increased, "Newton, you fool," she said playfully, "Of course I am. I was his wife on earth. He is in the higher realms, above the fourth sphere, I believe. He does visit me sometimes, but you will not be able to make contact with him yet, in case you are thinking of doing so, however, not before you enter the second Revelation can you accomplish this."

"I am not too good on my history of this period, as you may well know, but did you have much involvement with the Spiritual Movement when Samuel Page started it around that time?" I asked her.

"Indeed, I did," She answered, as she walked forward towards the screen, I feared that she wouldn't be able to stop in time and perhaps continue to walk straight through and end up falling into one of the comfortable chairs in the front row. However, she stopped, and then she went on, "After a great deal of initial work in the early years, Samuel set up the movement in AD 2520. Our first problem was to expose those vile and corrupt members of the pseudo ecclesiastical fraternity, who sought only to satiate their desire for power and wealth. The Great Prophet warned that there would be many false prophets to lead many astray with malicious and destructive heresies.

"In your time, Newton, the world was rife with ignorant fools who denied the Master who brought them into existence and provided them with all the comforts that those spiteful idiots could ever hope for, but eventually their foolishness led them to self-destruction and almost total annihilation. Save for a few brave and fortunate souls who were left with the involuntary task to repair the world and put it back in order. Your people stated that religion was the cause of war. But this is not true, as it is the teaching of false doctrines that cause men to turn against one another and then to violence. Fake preaching from the place of worship, where insincere preachers do their utmost to obstruct the road to the truth, as their only interest was to fight for their existence.

"We began the New Spiritual Movement at a time when this chaotic world needed a new religion, which could be accepted by everyone. With the creation of Ghost Crystal, we were able to eventually replace all other religions with what we called the true religion. As a religion, Spiritualism is concerned with evidence based on facts rather than faith. The development of Ghost Crystal enabled us to prove to everyone on earth, including the hardened sceptics, that life indeed continues after the death of the body. Nobody was able to deny this as the truth anymore, as they did in early times, even well before your time on earth, Newton.

"The Great Spirit manifests his truth only to those who are of good will. In the past, the false preachers waged war on The Great Prophet and his doctrines just to save their fruitless and inept livelihoods. Their desire to promote falsehood and venality commanded the mutilation of the Holy Scriptures, and they also mutilated their once perfect world with hatred and war."

"Tell me, Marla Page," I interjected, "Is it true that the result of the nuclear holocaust caused a change in the earth's crust, and made the plates move into formation, as they are today?"

Marla laughed, "Newton, dear Newton, what serious enquiry you ask of me with such emphasis on geological material detail? You must seek out a learned professor from your world to furnish you with answers to questions of this nature. I qualify only to assist you in matters relating to spirituality, and not of earthly, material matters."

"I had the understanding that the spirits were enlightened with boundless knowledge and wisdom once they had crossed over to the other side?" I said.

Marla laughed yet again, but this time it was prolonged and loud. "Newton, you astound me. From which false preacher did you acquire such misleading evidence?"

"I assume – "

"You assume?" She interrupted. "Newton, let me enlighten you with the correct facts on these spiritual matters. When I passed over to the spiritual realms around AD 2560, although I no longer had a physical body, my spiritual body contained all the faculties of my mind and all my memories and desires of the flesh from when I walked the earth. Nothing changed, and nothing was added or taken away.

"So let me conclude by stating that truly you will take nothing more with you to the other side than the knowledge and wisdom that you received while in the flesh, although you are free to increase this once in spiritual realms. It would be better to endeavour to acquire first, the Divine Love, as well as knowledge and wisdom, while you dwell in the flesh here on earth."

"Marla Page, can I please ask one more question concerning Karla?"

"Newton," she replied in an angry tone, "you should not persist with matters of a frivolous nature when you have all the answers already within your reach. When a teacher sets an exam for you, do you also expect the teacher to provide you with the answers as well? If so, then how do you expect to pass the test of life?"

I guess she knew that I wanted to ask a question about Karla and her supposed soul. I should have known better than to ask a spiritualist who has inhabited the spiritual realms for over three hundred and fifty years, such a predictive question. If Lord Bandersant can read my mind, occasionally and with such ease, I don't think Marla Page would have much difficulty doing so, but just to assure myself that I would not suffer further embarrassment, I decided to keep away from the subject of Karla's soul, for now.

"Marla Page," I asked, "can you please describe to me what it is like to be dead?"

"I don't know, Newton." She said, abruptly, which amazed me, Karla, too, as I felt her fingernails in my forearm.

Marla walked away from the screen; she appeared to be in deep thought. I was worried that I had upset her with my common questions, and she had, had enough, and was leaving us for good. We both exhaled with relief when she turned around to address us once again.

"Newton, do you know why I don't know what it is like to be dead?"

I shook my head in silence. I was eager to hear her explanation, so too was Karla. I dare not to speak a word to throw her off the subject.

"Because I have never been dead, Newton." She replied, "I have never been dead. There is no death as such; the word is merely a definition to describe the state of the material body. Just like any other inanimate material object, such as a rock or a piece of wood. It is not you, but your body that dies. The body is a vehicle for the soul, and the soul contains the spirit body. The spirit body is a duplicate of the physical body, but it is not the actual body. There is also a silver cord, which connects the soul to the central nervous system of the physical body.

"Everything that you experience on earth, while in the material body, is recorded by the mind, and simultaneously, in the soul, both which cannot die. Therefore, Newton, I tell you this, that when the body dies, and the silver cord detached, all your thoughts, experiences, knowledge, wisdom, and love, have already been stored safely within the soul. Newton, do not listen to those fools who tell you that they have died and come back, and when asked what was it like, they say nothing but blackness and nothingness. I tell you now, Newton, such ignorant fools have never died.

"One of the important laws of the spiritual realms states that once the silver cord has broken, it can never be attached again. The dead cannot return to life in the physical body. Those who claim that they have returned, have never died but slept in deep or shallow sleep where the soul has become separated from the body but is still attached by the silver cord, and it can wander at will to the spiritual realms but close to the earth. The effectiveness of Ghost Crystal is a proven fact of this present moment, Newton. If I was dead, Newton, tell me how would I be able to converse with you with such garrulousness?"

Marla began to fade, as she did so she stepped back a couple of paces. I was fully aware that this phenomenon could occur, on certain occasions, when the spirit was required elsewhere, or when it needed to regenerate its energy levels.

Karla pointed out another figure on the screen behind Marla. I couldn't see it at first, but then it gradually emerged shortly afterwards. It was that of an older man with a white beard. He advanced towards the screen at the same time as Marla Page blended into the background.

"Greetings," the old man said, with a smile, "I am Samael, I dwell in the higher heavens. Newton, I walked your stinking, vile earth in the year AD 2414, and with much pleasure and delight I gladly shed the garment of rotting flesh around AD 2494 and entered into the spiritual realms."

Karla grabbed my arm with both hands, as she gasped, "So that is what he looks like! I had read stories about him in the history archives; he is Samael The Soul Gatherer. He will speak overtly, truthfully, and painfully, so I must warn you, Newton, it is your decision, if you wish to carry on with him?" She urged me, in a loud whisper.

What possible harm could an old man in a robe inflict upon me? I asked myself. But my opinion was to alter, as I was yet to discover.

"Greetings, Samael," I said, "My name is Newton Flotman, and I –
"

"I know who you are, Newton Flotman," He interposed, as he adjusted his hands underneath the large black sleeves of his thick robe, "I know where you hail from, Newton Flotman. You are known here as the man who slept a thousand years!"

"I am known in the spiritual realms?" I asked, slightly surprised at such acquired fame.

"Don't let your head swell, Newton, indeed, there is no such thing as fame here, not the type of futile notoriety that those vile, sodomitic cretins from your century worshipped and yearned. Like lost sheep, wasters, wallowing in their epidemic of depression and lack of self-esteem."

"What was your function on earth, when you dwelled in the flesh, Samael?"

"I was a preacher, and a philosopher to all those hollow and meaningless sinners, after the Reformation period."

Karla reminded me that this was the period almost four hundred years after the nuclear holocaust when the complete physical structure of the earth's crust altered from within and changed the appearance and the positioning of the continents to what they are today. A full band of the land formation around the equator, which divides the two oceans, the north and the south.

"Were there many survivors during and after this period, Samael?" I asked him.

"There was much pain and suffering due to the rapid change of the physical terrain. This misery continued unabated for the next century until the discovery of the Ghost Crystal."

"Is it true, Samael, that you once led an army of rebels?" Karla asked suddenly, which surprised me, as up until now, she had been entirely passive during the Ghost Crystal sessions.

Samael expressed shock and delight, at the same time, but not for the same reasons as I. He raised his eyebrows.

"History books! Oh, History books, where would we be without history? Where would we be without books?" He pointed a bony finger at Karla. "But I ask you, Karla Flotman, is this truly the truth?"

I glanced at Karla, waiting for her to look at me, but her eyes, firmly fixed on this historical hero, his life-sized, irradiated image glowing, ghost-like, with eyes wide opened, staring wildly into the room. I wanted to know why he had referred to Karla as Karla Flotman? She didn't hear him, or perhaps she hadn't noticed, or she would have surely reacted or made a comment by now, or at least glance towards me only to confirm this confusion. I decided to let it go, happy to conclude that it had just been an innocent slip of the tongue. Samuel continued.

"I am afraid that we only contend with the truth here, on the other side. Lies and deceit can only work to hinder one's progression. So I will be truthful to you both. After the Reformation period, when the physical world was stable, but man himself scarce in numbers, confused, and doubtful of his future, the temptation to revert to old habits was powerful indeed. Certain groups, of ecclesiastic origin, sought to grow and increase their sect, some eager to spread the same poison, lies and false doctrines, just as their fathers did in the days of old. We did not want this to flourish, as we sought for change for a better world for our children. We began by imposing a complete reformation of all religion to strengthen spiritual development. We recognised that religion should be simple and accessible to all like it once was, as it is nothing more than the relationship and harmony of the souls of men with the soul of God. One God, one religion, common to all, and made simple for all."

"So, what of the adversaries, did they comply or did you resort to force?" I asked, not meaning to challenge him in any way.

"Of course, Newton!" He replied as he wrung his hands. "Indeed, there was vehemence, as certain conditions warranted this as appropriate at the time. Yes, Newton I fully admit that I have wronged in the past, and for my sins, I have been punished in darkness and misery in the lower worlds. Eventually, after many years of suffering in such dark and lonely realms, my persistent longings of the soul for the inflowing of divine love was my only salvation. So you see, my reputation as a warrior, leader of rebels, bringer of death and destruction to all who opposes the spiritual doctrine, was exacerbated by rumours made by my opponents."

"What of all those women's hearts you broke?" Karla asked.

Samael laughed aloud, and clapped his hands, "My girl, what have you been reading? I take it that you refer to the romantic stories written around AD 2465 by a lady called Anniotte Moby? She was an extrovert. If it were true what she claimed I had done to all those poor, innocent women, in her book, I would have lived until I was two centuries old!" Then he lowered his voice, "Rumours, nothing but rumours for entertainment, like in your terrible world, Newton where this sort of thinking was rife."

"Yes, I believe so," I agreed. "Samael, please tell me more about Heaven, as I am in a beautiful place now, here on earth, which is far more beautiful than the world I left behind, as you know. When I eventually reach heaven will I be astounded by its beauty, as I was when I first discovered this world?"

"Newton, are you an insane creature from the swamp?" Samael replied, in a voice so high that it almost broke when it reached its peak. "Your ears have heard these words many times before; I'm quite sure. I tell you now, Newton I cannot express the joy and the exquisiteness of this place in mere words alone. You say that you are in a place of sheer beauty, most pleasing to the eye, and also to your other four earthly senses? When you are asleep, and engrossed in one of your most vivid dreams, you see bright colours, you hear wonderful sounds, you feel love, and all other emotions like you have never done so before, and yet, your eyes are closed, and the other senses are subdued. Think how great it would be if you can perceive all this beauty tenfold, not with just five senses of the material body, but through all the senses of the spirit body? There is no comparison between the wonderful, bright spiritual realms and your dull, miserable material world of matter, Newton. None whatsoever."

"But I am happy here, Samael, this is a wonderful place. I have everything I need here, everything I have ever dreamt of exists in this perfect utopia." I said in defence.

"Utopia? Newton, you are indeed a wild creature from the swamp, or perhaps you are just inherently half mad? To you, it may seem that you have arrived in a perfect paradise, in contrast with the hell world that you left behind, and good riddance I say to that over-populated den of shame and misery, but just wait. Newton, just wait until you shed that shameful, earthly garment. I tell you from my heart, that just as soon as you arrive in the wonderful, spiritual realms, I can assure you, Newton, that you will look back on the place that you are in now, and you will notice, immediately, that there is no comparison to the beauty of the spiritual realms. And for sure you will forget all about the material world in no time at all, as you will be so enthralled by your new home, just as I was when I first arrived here."

"Do you have any idea exactly when that will be?" I dared to ask him, but he just glared at me for a while, before he replied.

"That's some impertinent question, Newton, from a man who should have shed the earthly garment a long time ago, and should be long dead by now? Perhaps you can tell me some things that I don't already know?"

"I cannot remember anything in all that time. Please tell me, Samael, if I was dead for almost a thousand years, where was my soul during this time?"

"New-ton, New-ton," Samael replied, as he clapped his hands in sync with each syllable of my name. "Have I not told you that there is no death? There is no end, to anything not in the material or the spiritual worlds. Can you show me where I might find the end of the universe, Newton? No, you cannot because I cannot show you the end of the spiritual realms, as an end just cannot be conceived. Will it be in the form of a wall perhaps? Then what lies beyond that wall? Another wall, maybe, and so on, and so forth? Do you see now, Newton, why there cannot be an end because there is no end?

"You were brought into the world, Newton, on the very day you were born. You have not seen death yet. Therefore, your soul lies within your mortal flesh. Your silver cord has not yet broken therefore your soul will travel out of your body and is restricted only by the limitations of the silver cord."

"Did I travel out of my body for that length of time? Surely I would remember some of it?"

"Perhaps, Newton, but your body was in a deep sleep, and it is entirely possible that the soul was at rest too; in abeyance, similar to that of a healing process, during trauma, which allows the body to regenerate.

"But all this is rather insignificant and does nothing to contribute to your spiritual development," he pointed his finger directly towards us, "Newton, you need to explore your new found Utopia and discover things for yourself. There is still a lot to learn, as many changes have taken place on earth during your absence. Stop wasting time with miserable spirits, Newton. Go out and explore your material world first before your second Revelation!"

Samael must have used up all his reserve energy because his image began to fade but, strangely enough, it did not disappear entirely. Karla reiterated my thoughts by giving me a more detailed explanation, which involved time and space, something that was not recognised by spirits but they still tire during lengthy communications, just as we do in our physical bodies when we are run down and exhausted. Since the invention of Ghost Crystal, the demand of exertion a spirit required to expound to materialise and appear to us in complex physical form had increased tremendously, compared to that of the past, when spirit communication was simple with no additional energy requirement for visual and vocal communication to consider as well.

The advent of Ghost Crystal changed the whole concept of spiritual communication, transforming it way beyond all boundaries of comprehension. This new spiritualism destroyed and demoralised the sceptics and the non-believers of the afterlife, as well as those of limited religious wisdom and understanding. Samael had told us that it wasn't until after the time around AD 2520, Samuel Page's era that the fragmentation of the old religions began. Their doctrines and creeds were being disproved and then abandoned with regularity, much to the infuriation of the clergy and indeed other religious groups, especially those of spurious nature, who feared much for their precipitous decline in power and control over their weak minded followers. This inevitably led to a significant financial loss for them in the end. It seems that the motivation of money, greed, and power was their primary concern rather than their apprehension for their true beliefs.

Samael had also delved into the past, at least one hundred years or so before my birth. He said that it had taken a long time for the early spiritualist movement to become accepted as a true religion, mainly because of law and attitudes influenced by the Bible. My concern was how he happens to come by this information. He casually waved his hand and accused me of having a limited understanding about the spiritual realms, amongst other things, and he reminded me that every living soul that had ever walked the earth in the flesh and have now left their bodies are currently resident in the spiritual realms, across the seven spheres. They can visit, or he may visit them in some cases, and communicate, share information, wisdom, and love with one another.

He also told me that many years after the third world war in AD 2020, a new spiritualist movement began, and had suffered the same ignorance and scepticism as the first campaign did in the 1800's. That was when the Fox Sisters established meaningful regular contact with the spirit world, which was then considered as the birth of modern spiritualism.

Samuel Page and his wife, Marla page experienced a great deal of opposition from the ignorant cynics of the twenty-sixth century. An era considered populated with wise and erudite inhabitants; it was only the discovery of the Ghost Crystal that helped to facilitate the new and final spiritual movement, which contributed much to the necessary fabrication of our Utopian world today.

I had depleted all my energy. Karla was tired and hungry, having fallen asleep in my arms several times during my banter with Samael, only to be woken at intervals whenever our voices were raised momentarily during the heat of our discussion.

A remarkable and highly unusual situation occurred just as we were about to end the session. We saw another spirit behind Samael, and like the others, it gradually came into focus as it approached the front. We recognised it immediately, both Karla and I, and believed it to be that of Red Cloud, the North American Indian. We were both confused as to why he had returned. Then he was recognised by Samael; he seemed to know him well, as he greeted him with much enthusiasm.

"Red, how pleased I am to see you." He said, and then he turned to us and smiled, "I must go now, this time, Newton, and you dear Karla. I leave you with my capable friend, Red Cloud. Goodbye now..." He faded and eventually vanished into thin air. Red smiled at us. "Greetings, my friends, I have some wise words for you. Brother, you say there is but one way to worship and serve the Great Spirit. If there is but one religion, why do you people differ so much about it?"

Before we could even think of providing him with an answer, or finding out whether one was required or not, he was gone.

We had no concept of time here. It wasn't encouraged, and I didn't want to know anyway, as nobody rushed around or performed any tasks to the beat of time. There were no windows in this theatre so that none could tell day from night. I didn't care much about that. I had other goals to fulfil. I wanted to explore the planet on my own, and perhaps take a trip to the dark side of the moon to find out more about the Celestials. But I thought to myself that it wouldn't be very wise to take Karla along with me just in case I was to discover something unpleasant.

We made our way back to the honeymoon suite, drank some golden champagne, and retired to bed for the night, although there was not much night left to enjoy any sleep. Yes, it was still dark, but I wasn't concerned about the time remaining before sunrise, and I made no attempt to find out. We both slept until the next day, when the sun was up again, whenever that was, I did not care much.

CHAPTER 10

Soliloquy (The Second Revelation)

I must have been relaxing in the Jacuzzi when Darus brought us breakfast in the honeymoon suite. Perhaps Karla had let him in. I left her in bed sleeping when I got up to take some morning coffee. The sun was bright, as usual, and the sky was a deeper blue, than usual. I had put it down to the reflection of the deep blue Pacific Ocean. I had no idea of our position in the South Sea, and I could see no land anywhere in sight to confirm this, only endless blue sea, all around us. That hideous golden balloon was still in the same position where it had landed, on the green, in full view of all the apartments, on various levels, on this side of the vessel.

It was the piquant scent of the delicious, freshly cooked breakfast that prompted me to get out of the Jacuzzi. I did so immediately and headed straight to the dining table, where I found Karla, seated comfortably with her legs tucked in underneath her. She had been eating two lovely, fat brown sausages, with a portion of scrambled eggs, and a slice or two of fried bacon, all on a large square crystal plate, which I thought was almost the same size as the one that I had in the seafood restaurant.

I have never seen a breakfast so colourful and bright. The taste and texture of the cooked sausages were enough to cause a mini-catharsis and at the same time an eruption of my taste buds. I was in Heaven by the time I started on the scrambled eggs, not to mention the bacon. Karla didn't speak much. She was pre-occupied with, what looked like a sliver of ghost crystal, which she held in her hand. I soon learnt that this was some sort of communication device, similar to a mobile telephone from my primitive world.

Karla explained to me that she had spoken to the twins, Muriel and Cassie, this morning. They told her that they had given Louden a barrel of green rum disguised in various containers. He had been drinking non-stop all last night, and now he is fast asleep, almost comatose, in bed on board the balloon. The twins wanted to get away and spend the day exploring the Island with Karla. I, of course, took advantage of this opportunity and urged her to go out and enjoy herself with the twins, as I shall just go and do some exploring on my own.

She felt sad about leaving me, but I told her not to worry because in this perfect world we no longer follow schedules and time slots, we merely live for the moment – and we should enjoy it immensely.

The purpose of this action today was to explore and see the world, and also pay a visit to the dark side of the moon. I am relatively confident that I shall achieve these goals without encountering any difficulties today, as I have access to state of the art, light-speed ship. I am sure that it is quite capable of handling a mere two hundred and forty thousand miles, which it could comfortably achieve in about one point three seconds, travelling at light speed.

I was suddenly daunted by a frivolous thought, the fact that I could also reach the sun in about seven minutes, travelling at the same speed, but for what purpose, other than to burn up in space like an over-cooked pig in a clay pot. Truthfully, I wasn't about to charge to the moon at light speed. Such an act would have been highly irresponsible, and dangerous for the fact that I have no knowledge or details of the current pollution levels out in space in the way of spent satellites or any other space debris floating around out there between here and the moon. I wasn't planning on finding out the hard way either. The thought of being struck by a one-tonne missile travelling at a velocity of one hundred and eighty-six thousand miles per second was quite daunting, to say the least.

I managed to find my ship without the help and guidance of Darus, although it had taken me a little longer than it should have done, due to the extra number of detours I was forced to make along the way. I took off and headed straight up into the blue sky. The Island looked magnificent from a few thousand feet up. I was able to make out the wake in the water, which trailed the Island, suggesting that the vessel was moving at top speed. By the look of its position and heading, I reckon it was about a few hundred miles off the coast of the central band of land, which circled the Equator, and was heading West towards the Americas. That, I had learnt from my last trip in space with Lord Bandersant, had no longer existed in the same formation as it did in my time on earth.

Once I was clear of the airspace around and above the Island, I descended to a lower altitude and continued heading west towards the Equator. I planned to circumnavigate the globe by flying around the Equator while observing the land below just to familiarise myself with the new terrain, and to see the extent of the physical changes of the continents.

My first encounter was the sighting of a simple belt of land to the North. The instruments, which I sometimes struggled with due to the vast difference in technology, confirmed that I was indeed over the City. I needed to see which continent my beautiful home had been located in, because of Lord Bandersant's taciturn for details and place names. When asked, he would tell me not to worry about such trivialities, just enjoy the moment, as you are now closer to Heaven than any man has ever been who walked the earth in your time. He would then conclude by reminding me, once again, that the progress you see before you is the result of the work of men who had no real regard for inconsequential matters, as such encumbrances which can only lead to disagreement, war and destruction. And he was right; he is always right when he makes such statements. I do believe that our obsession with money, wealth, power, time, and names, had inadvertently contributed towards our final destruction.

I climbed high into the atmosphere, just enough to be able to discern the shape and position of the continent. I could see that the outline resembled Australia but, surprisingly, it was much bigger. I checked my altitude. I climbed higher. Bang! Then it hit me. Not physically, but mentally. The land mass was not Australia at all, but the continent of Africa. It looked as if it had been rotated anti-clockwise by a few degrees, and now, what was once the North, was now pointing northwest, towards North America! My next task was to find the Americas.

It wasn't too long before I had spotted Bahia Thetis, on the Mitre Peninsula, and judging by its present position it looked as if the whole of South America had rotated, and the southern Peninsula had crashed into The Gambia. Further observation confirmed that the whole of the Americas had remained intact and had turned considerably. The whole continent was now lying almost horizontally along the Equator.

I had seen enough. I made a heading towards the West and accelerated to about five hundred miles per second. As I approached the area which was once North America, in no time at all, I must add. I couldn't see Alaska, which should have been pointing southwest down into the north Pacific. I decelerated and made a decent. My worst fears were confirmed.

Alaska, along with its mountains and forests, and abundant wildlife, no longer existed. As I descended further, I could see, over a large area, some mountain peaks protruding from the Pacific Ocean, just below the tropic of Capricorn. I noticed an abundance of sea life in the choppy seas below, and the air filled with a healthy variety of birds. It was a fantastic sight from my observation point, directly above them, looking straight down into the deep azure sea below. The ability to defy gravity, and to allow the craft to hover in mid-air, just to observe these beautiful creatures in flight, made the entire experience even more delightful. Back in my day, I would have had a limited choice of suitable flying machines. The line-up would have been, a capricious glider, a noisy aeroplane, or a cumbersome helicopter. Perhaps an airship would have also qualified, however, one would have to consider its immense bulk, which would have been more than enough of a physical threat to scare the birds to death. One would also have to consider the dangers of getting back to the mainland, especially if a strong wind had picked up, which is what I was experiencing right now, and I hasten to add, without even suffering a fraction of turbulence.

I headed north and then banked right and continued along the coast towards the East just to observe what was once the East Coast of North America. I couldn't see Baffin Island or the smaller islands around Foxe Basin. I consider these all to be submerged due to the increased sea levels. The coastline along the north side, and also the south, was made up of beautiful white sand, from what I could see from my present altitude. I decided not to descend to the coastal areas just yet, as I wanted to observe the entire globe first.

I was further astounded when I reached the United Kingdom, or so I thought. The shape of the land mass was somewhat confusing. I was forced to gain altitude to observe it from above to establish a better view of the whole region. I could see that Spain and France, although still linked, had broken away from the rest of Europe and had moved south and subsequently collided with what was formerly known as the east side of the African continent, Egypt and Ethiopia.

I could see now that the United Kingdom, in its entirety, had shifted south and locked itself against the north coast of Spain, and it sat comfortably in the Bay of Biscay. One could efficiently travel by land, starting from the United Kingdom, across Spain, and then on to Africa without having to cross any seas.

I couldn't see the rest of Europe beyond France, which prompted me to continue east, across Northern Europe towards Asia. There was nothing but vast, blue sea where Russia had once been. I travelled south in search of China, but found nothing but sea, until I reached the Equator.

A narrow band of land ran from west to east, from South Africa towards an area in the Pacific Ocean just above the northwest corner of Australia. Further investigation confirmed that this band of land consisted a total of three countries, Pakistan, India, and Thailand, which had broken away from Southern China in one complete section, moved south, and then finally settled along the Equator.

I did not study geology or any other related subject, but what I had witnessed today, so far, was quite confusing beyond all comprehension. Some new and devastating phenomenon must have occurred to influence the continents in such a way to make them shift to that extent. And to remain intact, rather than just the existence of a natural plate shift, which usually resulted in the accumulation of tectonic tension where the plates collide or scrape together and release energy. What makes this so bizarre is the fact that the whole process occurred over a concise period in geological terms, less than a millennium.

I descended to several hundred feet above sea level and proceeded to circle the globe once again, but this time solely to observe its beauty and natural wonders, and also to admire the many manmade structures, or I would be correct as to refer to them as Androgen-made structures. I did not accelerate to such high speeds, not over the most populated areas, for safety reasons. I was, however, tempted to land several times, in various places which I considered to be a resemblance to a miniature paradise.

The most beautiful thing about this world now is the sheer freedom. I could land anywhere I desired or considered suitable, walk into any restaurant, and sit down and enjoy a meal of my choice from the menu. I could sample from a list of the best wines in the house, and it wouldn't cost me anything, but my time, because here there is no price on anything, there are no costs or charges on goods or services. The need to create or produce products in exchange for financial advantage and profit no longer existed in this world. Where the motivation was once for profit and wealth, it was substituted for happiness and health, and it worked quite well. The inhabitants of this beautiful and peaceful world firmly believe that the Great Spirit has given them the earth not to divide up and sell on to the highest bidder, but for all material beings to live in peace and harmony, and to enjoy and live life to the full.

I wanted to find out more information about the military if ever they existed at all in this world. In the time I had been airborne, I have not yet experienced, or encountered, any military vessels or aircraft of any shape or form, or had any announcements or warnings from the ships' computer system, which related to an airspace breach or any other violation or impending threat.

The onboard computer informed me that there was a significant knowledge facility nearby, which I had guessed was a reference to a school of learning for the children, or a university of some sort. I decided to land the ship in front of the main building, which was, of course, made entirely of the highest quality, pure white marble, and it was set in the most beautiful landscaped garden I had ever seen. The building itself, although not very tall, like most of the other buildings I had seen here, except the Androgen Facility, (located in the Antipodean region), covered a large area of land bordered by a perimeter of a mature forest of oak, ash, and elm.

A young woman, who called herself Professor Anne, and Her colleague, an older man, by the name of Professor Stagston, were delighted to see me, both greeted me enthusiastically at the entrance of the facility. Professor Stagston seemed to know a lot about me and of the dirty world that I had come from, as he put it, and he made it quite clear that he intended to deliver a diatribe on the failings of my world. He said if I'd rather not hear it, I had better get back into my spacecraft right now and fly off home.

I was quite happy to bear his denunciation on behalf of mankind, after all, I was the last man standing, it was only fair that I accepted the title of scapegoat for the defects of my ancestors. In any case, I like to hear the truth, which was quite common in this world. Such openness no longer bothered me, after my first Revelation. Perhaps the Monkey Mind had diminished somewhat since then, and the Revelation helped in the removal of the ego.

Professor Stagston made it quite clear that I would require a second Revelation to destroy the Monkey Mind once and for all before I could enjoy my life to the full here in this perfect world. But he warned me that it would be dangerous if I were not prepared for it. My lowly, material mind should be cast away and instead concentrate on knowledge, wisdom, and love. I was curious to know what particular subjects were taught here in this beautiful, spacious, knowledge facility.

We walked, as we conversed, throughout the entire complex, and I was left astounded at what I saw, and indeed what I had discovered. Every conceivable subject had been covered. Nobody was forced to adopt a particular topic, as these teachers were incredibly intelligent, they understood that no two pupils were the same. Each was given their own choice of subjects, which they were able to focus on in their own time, and for as long as they wished, to familiarise themselves enough to decide if the subject was a suitable one for them. If however they were dissatisfied in any way, they would just choose another topic until they found their desired aptitude.

Professor Anne reminded me that each person has their skill and talent for a particular subject of their liking, and it would be a waste of time forcing them to do something which they were not suited for – 'Just as teachers did in your old world,' Professor Stagston would interject. He went on to say that in my time the ignorant religious nuts were to blame for the cause of the third world war. Professor Stagston made a point about spiritualism, which I concurred was impartial, but until now, I hadn't given it much thought. He wondered that, since AD 1848 when the Fox Sisters established contact with the spirit world and started the first modern spiritual movement, why my people back then did not take advantage of this moment and force a religious revolution and establish spiritualism as the prime religion. It almost incensed him why those earthly cretins, as he put it, had ignored this golden opportunity and instead continued preaching their lies and deceitful doctrines.

I argued the point that their motivation was purely wealth and power to establish world domination. The religious superpowers, as they became known as, in time, were not going to let anything, or anybody for that matter stands in their way. Professor Stagston said that this prolonged corruption and deceit, although it served well to keep the ecclesiastical fraternity in power throughout history, did not do anything positive to help its followers. The real truth about spiritualism within the Biblical text had been hidden away for years, and evidence suggests that some ancient texts may have been forged to deceive its readers and to keep them ignorant about the truth.

Professor Anne reinforced this concerning a discovery made 'in my period' as she succinctly put it, of the missing text, 'Gnostic Gospels' discovered in an Egyptian town of Nag Hammadi in AD 1945. It relates to a belief that the material world was created by an ignorant emanation of the highest God, trapping the divine spark within the human body, and that it is possible to liberate it by gnosis of this divine spark. I wasn't at all interested too much in past religious history, but only with the Ghost Crystal through which I was able to contact spirits of the past and discuss with them real authentic history. This method was reliable proof beyond all expectations, although it could not safeguard against the evil mendacious souls who purport to be genuine and helpful but surreptitiously cause harm and ill will. Nevertheless, this method is considered to be extremely reliable, more than any crystal ball in my time.

I was shown all the indoor activities, which the pupils could select and undertake at their leisure, and there was an enormous choice of subjects to choose from, more than I have seen or ever known in any school or university in my time. And they all consisted of exciting topics, although I wasn't familiar with the thirtieth-century technology, they all looked quite interesting to me. I was taken to a room, which had a forty-foot-high ceiling. I refer to it as a room, but in fact, it was more like an enormously oversized aircraft hangar. I could have flown my spacecraft around the inside of this place with ease, and at a reasonable velocity, without worrying about colliding with any of the walls, or the ceiling. But there were no spacecraft in sight, only flying kids.

I could see several platforms suspended in mid-air at one end of the building. One by one, pupils leapt off the highest one and descended slowly towards the highly polished wooden floor below, and as they fell they managed to perform intricate acrobatics in mid-air on the way down. Some of them leapt from the next highest platform, completed a few somersaults, and then landed on their feet onto the lower platforms. This performance reminded me of military training back in my day, even though I couldn't remember whether I took part or not, but the practice was without the aid of gravity belts; that much I can remember. We had to rely on a simple harness or bungee, and then hope and pray that it held fast.

The reminiscence prompted me to ask the professors about the military presence in this world today. They both laughed, of course, and informed me that no such service existed today, as it was no longer required. There were no enemies as such, as the world was now one big, peaceful domain. In another area, we passed through a large glass tube, which elevated and continued outside of the building and across a vast field below. I was able to observe, through the glass, about fifty feet down, an immaculate playing field which, to my surprise, was not like any playing field I had seen before, but round and concave, just like the inside of an enormous bowl, and coated with lush, green grass. I saw players running and jumping around. They were pursuing a large, luminescent, orange ball, which they punched and kicked in all directions. The ball came straight towards the glass tunnel, from below, and then it shot past and continued skyward until it fell back down again, bouncing off the roof of the glass tunnel. I saw a group of players flying through the air in pursuit of the ball. They were moving in slow motion, but I could not see any gravity belts around their waists.

Professor Anne reassured me that they were safe, and she continued to explain to me that an artificial anti-gravitational field, created within the bowl, enabled the players to defy gravity during their game of Skyball. I saw no goals or nets, only field. I learnt later on that the object of the game was not to pass the ball through any hole or net, but it much depended upon touch. An opponent would hit the ball, with any part of the body he or she desired, and if it were received and struck immediately by a teammate, they would acquire points for their team. If, however, an opponent interrupted the ball in mid-flight, the team would not receive the point, and subsequently, the opponent could claim a point by hitting it to his teammate, and so on. The game was dynamic and energetic, as it could be regulated by altering the gravitational field, which would both speed up the ball and increase the ability of the players to fly faster or slow it right down during a practise session for instance. I had wondered about how they managed to keep score, but my curiosity quelled when they told me the ball recorded all detailed information required, including the totals, automatically and then relayed the relevant report back to the scoreboard.

After we had watched an exciting game or two of Skyball from the glass tunnel high above the bowl, we continued to another spacious building further on in the complex. This one had a glass roof, and inside consisted an indoor jungle complete with real rivers, plants, trees, and all other natural elements of nature that one would find in a jungle. I could see pupils below; they were training and working with a variety of wild animals. Both professors assured me that they were not artificial, or wild for that matter, that included the tigers, panthers, and bears. I did not express my wonder, as I had already witnessed such phenomenon at Louden's ranch.

Later on, I enjoyed a fantastic seafood lunch with both professors, washed down with superb best quality wine from France. (yes, they were still producing good wine even though their location had changed: situated on the Tropic of Cancer now, I believe), and later on, we were joined by some of their colleagues. I also had the opportunity to converse with some of the pupils, who were all eager to ask me a lot of questions about my world. One of them even asked me how old I was, I replied that I was in my early thirties, but I had overslept for almost nine hundred years.

Education had changed dramatically since my time. The pupils were undoubtedly happy here, and none of them was forced to attend or were they compelled to study specific subjects, as not all topics were relevant in the workplace of the year AD 2914, not when they had an army of Androgen at hand to undertake most of the laborious tasks for them. So it seems, gone was the days when students took up boring, manual jobs, such professions no longer existed, and were not required because demand for such work did not exist as it did in my time. These fortunate students of the modern age reserved themselves for exciting careers in science, technology, research, teaching, caring, and of course spiritual science.

I indeed gleaned a lot of information and knowledge from my visit to this particular education establishment. It was immense and well equipped, as there were no money problems here, the stuff just did not exist in this perfect world anymore.

The people in this world owned the world, and it was theirs to do with as they please. They espoused the idea that if a man wished to create and live successfully in a Heaven on earth, he would be required observe and replicate the true spiritual way of life in the spiritual realms. For instance, since crime and money does not exist there, so too must they be made extinct here on earth also, and so on, as it is in Heaven.

Professor Anne said to me, 'the pupils can have anything they wanted, we simply take it from the very world that belongs to us all, and nobody may get rich as a result'. She is entirely right in her statement, as before my first revelation my Monkey Mind would not have readily accepted this to be true, but now I have become more tolerant towards spiritual matters, I fully understand the concept of true spiritualism and except the laws of the spiritual world.

In my time, governments made feeble excuses with much protest in respect to concerns regarding expenditure for the provision of the essential services, which they were obliged to supply on behalf of the people. Their failure of duty to provide even basic needs such as food and education for the population was due to the lack of funds, and their ability to eradicate crime and pollution was marred for the same reasons. Money and the shortage of it was the encumbrance that encouraged them to harvest false ideas, which led to wastage when over-funding occurred, and total inactivity during periods of under-funding.

These people had the right idea when they abolished the evil tender, around the same period when they discovered Ghost Crystal, in the twenty-sixth century, and they survived very well without cash for the past three hundred years or so. I haven't met anyone yet who wished to reintroduce the evil green tender, which they all agree served no useful purpose other than an incentive for the wealthy, powerful, and corrupt, to use against the poor to keep them subdued and to coerce them into slavery for a pittance.

I spoke to many of the pupils here, and they all seemed extremely happy in this education establishment. The good thing about it was the freedom. There were no set rules about time, or complicated schedules to follow, as one could come and go as they pleased. I did not encounter any unhappy pupils, nor did I witness any leaving or wishing to leave. In fact, it was the total opposite, as the activities and studies here were so exciting and diverse that pupils were eager and willing to attend. In my day, it was a chore, which some pupils loathed. Here today, they all enjoy it immensely, and a considerable majority informed me that they looked forward to learning and couldn't wait to get to school each day.

I ventured to inquire about Ghost Crystal because I was curious to know if and when the pupils had their first experience with the Revelation. Professor Stagston informed me that back in time, in the same world I had come from, the Christian sacrament of admission and adoption was carried out by the use of water on infants and adults alike. And that the Revelation today serves as admission and acceptance into the spiritual realms for everybody who has a soul, and is not determined by any particular religion. He stated that Baptism, as it was known, (the sprinkling of water on one's head) is solely of man's creation. The physical activity has no virtue to save any man from his sins nor does it assist in making him at one with God, as it cannot affect the condition or development of the soul. He concluded in stating that young children have a pre-Revelation, and when they attend an education establishment, they undertake the complete Revelation, which is quite adequate for most.

When I explained that I was whisked into space at light velocity towards Andromeda during my first Revelation, he laughed and told me the reason why Lord Bandersant and Doctor Gabriel had decided that this rather prudent method was apt for me. He went on to inform me that this process was a form of pre-Revelation, similar to the experience of what the young children would encounter via Ghost Crystal, without the inclusion of light speed travel into space, of course, as this would be highly impractical.

I was almost ready to depart because I needed to continue my journey when Professor Anne asked me about my second Revelation. After telling her that I felt prepared for it but there was no mention of it as yet, and I was instructed to learn more about this new world first, she went on to suggest that I should conduct my Revelation right here in the education establishment. They have here one of the best-equipped theatres in the land, which has a large screen with a dissolvable surface. She had to explain to me in detail about this unique crystal dissolvable surface screen. This apparatus was able to, somehow, cause an increase in the vibrations of the molecular structure, and then synchronise this with that of my body, which would eventually enable me to physically enter the screen so that my material body can dissolve through the crystal and present itself on the other side of the glass. Once there, my spirit body would be free to leave my physical body and wander freely at will into the spiritual realms.

Of course, my first question was that of woe and dread, as this sounded much like the stuff of science fiction. Dissolving solid matter into matter? What if I get stuck and I am unable to get back; what if there is a power outage halfway through the session. She replied that the first question would be quite impossible because you cannot take your physical body away from the screen because it acts as an anchor for the silver cord, which is attached securely to it. She clarified by stating that, usually, in an out-of-body experience, the spirit body leaves the physical body and travels away from it while the silver cord remains anchored to the body. With the dissolvable surface, your physical body is dissolved with the unique properties of the Ghost Crystal glass, so your body and the crystal glass becomes one. The glass acts as a retainer for the physical body, which remains just behind the surface of the glass. The spirit body would then be able to leave the physical body at will and roam into the spiritual realms while still attached to the physical body by the silver cord.

Professor Anne assured me that this method was quite safe, and there have never been any mishaps since the discovery of Ghost Crystal. She explained that Ghost Crystal was the gateway to the spirit world. And that Dissolvable Ghost Crystal was an advanced gateway that enables the physical body to pass through the gate and wait on the other side while the spirit body performs an Out of Body Experience, (OBE), it can leave the body while still attached to it by the silver cord.

THE SECOND REVELATION:

The convincing and reassuring words from Professor Anne, concerning this new technology of Dissolvable Ghost Crystal, verified by Professor Stagston's passionate assertion that my ability to attain Divine Love, to develop my intellect through thought and reason, and to purify the human or natural love, shall be significantly enhanced.

All this was more than enough to convince me to proceed with the second and final Revelation right here in the educational establishment, without first acquiring sufficient wisdom, knowledge, and experience about this world, which I intended to seek out today. In spite of this, both professors believed that I was ready to take the next step, as the knowledge and wisdom could be assimilated another time, which would enable me to advance closer to spiritual enlightenment. I agreed and was eager to learn of this fascinating and exciting new technology.

The theatre was just as the professors had described it, plush and well furnished, similar to the one on the Island vessel, but much smaller, with a close, cosy atmosphere. It would have cost a small fortune if money had existed in this peaceful world. A few older pupils occupied the comfortable seats, which encircled the theatre. The screen was the same size as the one on the Island, but it was not concave, but dead flat, with a constant golden glow from its enticing, sheen-like surface. I was tempted to run my fingers over it, but something in my head told me not to. I sat down in the front row of seats directly in front of the screen, next to the two professors.

The whole process seemed somewhat informal but well organised, as each person knew their role, which they conducted with confidence and skill. There were no speeches or announcements, just the dimming of the lights followed by a warm, friendly silence. I sensed that there was much more communication going on but on a much higher level than my inexpert natural senses could comprehend. ESP or telepathy could not be ruled out, after all, I had noticed the existence of a particular department, which was dedicated to this subject when I passed by the room earlier but I was not informed about the place, or shown inside. Perhaps they assume that I was not ready to absorb such an advanced speciality yet, which would need more time to develop naturally. They may reconsider after the Second Revelation, perhaps, when I rid myself of the Monkey Mind completely.

When all was dead quiet, and the room dimmed of its crystal light, Professor Stagston turned to me and spoke briefly of my expectations from this Second Revelation. He advised me to always seek the Divine Love from the Great Spirit during the process, and then he instructed me o the process itself. I asked him about the time restrictions, which I had to adhere to for safety reasons, in the first Revelation with Lord Bandersant, but he shook his head in disagreement and said that Lord Bandersant was just over cautious with you because of your origin and physical condition. He clarified that the Dissolvable method is safer because you physically take the earthly body through the ghost crystal and onto the ledge, which overlooks the spiritual realms, and from the safety of the ridge you can release the soul from the body safely while it is still attached to the silver cord.

The time had come, finally, unexpectedly; I only went to this educational establishment to learn more about how they teach in this new found world, its people, and their way of life. Where best to start but with the young, the innocent. I am young to this place; I am naive and inexperienced in contrast with the young that is why I find myself here in a school, filled with experienced pupils. This establishment is indeed the best choice for me to conduct the second Revelation.

Professor Anne advised me, just as I walked towards the screen, she said that this Revelation is more potent than the first and if you conduct it right, and you are serious about attaining enlightenment, you will reap the benefits ten-fold. I thanked her, and then I approached the screen, raised my arms, as instructed by Professor Stagston, and placed my hands, palms down, flat against the glass.

It didn't feel like glass at all, but the texture of warm water, but dry water without any wetness. My head began to vibrate; it was a slow pulsation at first, and then it increased as it transferred into my whole body. The vibrations reached its peak, a higher frequency, which I could barely discern in the end. Suddenly my hands pushed forward into the liquid glass, then my arms. My whole body felt the sensation of weightlessness. I attempted to turn around and look at the audience, and the two Professors; I wanted to see their facial expressions. Had it all gone wrong? It was too late. A strange force prevented me from doing so. My face suddenly sucked into the liquid, and in a split second, my whole body followed. I went right through to the other side of the glass, into complete nothingness, or so I had thought.

I endured the sensation of falling but soon realised that I was outside of my body. I was floating in mid-air. I turned to look behind me, and to my surprise, I saw my physical body standing on a ledge in a fixed in a pose, as if it were caught and frozen in ultra slow motion by a three dimensional, high definition camera. The ridge was smooth and black like granite. There was a golden glow in the background immediately behind me, which I assumed to be the inside of the screen from which my physical body had just passed. I saw intermittent flashes of light coming from my body. They looked like laser flashes, but I soon realized what this was. I observed my silver cord as it swayed to and fro, catching the light intermittently, and reflecting it in pulsating bursts of high-energy photons towards my spiritual eyes.

I remembered the advice from the Professors. Divine love; earnestly seek Divine Love from the Great Spirit. I repeated this over and over again, and then suddenly I felt a sense of total euphoria, happiness, and ecstasy like I have never felt before. It was indeed an experience comparable to the best dream I have ever had in my whole life, but only ten times better.

I was quite sure that I had experienced the true explanation of death itself. I wasn't using my physical eyes to see, I didn't need my ears to hear, nor my hands to feel, or my legs to stand or walk, because my body was dead, suspended, in abeyance. I could see it with my spiritual eyes from where I was floating, and I felt it with my other spiritual senses, as It stood alone, lifeless, on the base of the granite ledge, on the edge of the spiritual realms, awaiting the welcoming return of my soul.

My spirit has left my material body still encased in my soul and is floating somewhere in the first sphere. I continue to yearn for Divine Love direct from God earnestly. The divine spirit or Holy Spirit is the higher spirit, the very essence of the spirit of God that emanates from God's being and blankets the whole universe, as it carries God's divine love to the human soul. It takes Divine Love to every human soul, as well as divine qualities of wisdom, goodness, power, justice and mercy. I desire for this love so that it is bestowed upon my soul; then it shall become divine itself.

The more I yearn for divine love, the more I can perceive the beautiful ambiences. It is nothing like I have ever seen on earth. I see bright, natural surroundings; beautiful white marble buildings besieged by beautiful green fields filled with colourful flowers. I observe plants and trees with pure green leaves, some overflowing with a variety of ripened fruit. I see people gathering before me all with happy, smiling faces, and children playing, running about the fields. Faces look familiar in a strange way, and the surroundings resemble the City where I live, and some of the other beautiful places I have visited lately. I can discern the stunning scenery more than I ever did during the first Revelation. Also, my mind, or should I say, my spirit, is more active, and fully aware of everything. I can think and reason instantly without the slightest hesitation, and I begin to fully understand now how humans had managed to achieve the creation of such a perfect utopia on earth. They merely used the blueprint from Heaven.

Just like in my dreams, I experience various scenes, in different locations; perhaps different times in the past, or the future yet to come. Everything is clear and bright, sharp, and detailed like I have never seen before. I see people in front of me as if I am understanding them when wide-awake. I can see every detail in their faces, yet I do not know of them either from my new life or the previous one before the holocaust. Perhaps they are relatives and friends, who have long since died and passed over into the spiritual realms. There must be at least thirty generations of ancestors who walked the earth in the flesh during my time of absence. My brothers, my sisters, if I can ever remember any?

A young woman approached me; an older man who had a white beard immediately accompanied her, from where I did not see. They are both telling me that it is time to descend into the lower realms – so prepare yourself, they kept saying to me, and do not absorb any spirit there. Somehow they managed to relay this information to me without actually speaking, as I cannot recall hearing actual words nor did I witness any movement of lips, but somehow I became aware of the imparted information in an instance, as I could sometimes achieve in my dreams. This experience is an enhanced dream. As I glance back at my material body poised on the granite ledge, I began to accept the fact that it is not my five bodily senses that are actually doing the perceiving, but the work of my spiritual body contained in my soul.

Somebody asked me if I was ready, a voice from nowhere, and before I could answer them, an extreme veil of weirdness took over. First of all, I experienced intense fear, followed by fright, and then pain, but not like bodily pain but spiritual pain, much more intense, as it seem to pervade all the spiritual senses all at once. Then came the worse part.

I saw visions of figures in a miserable place void of all light, colour, and contrast. It was pure darkness, yet I could see my way clearly in the darkness, which they claimed was due to the condition of my soul. There were no beautiful landscapes here, with colourful plants, or joyful animals cavorting merrily in fields, just black darkness, filled with fields of grey thorns.

Many troubled and dejected souls shifted about aimlessly in darkness and suffering. Lost souls, engrossed in anxiety, troubled with fear, wandering perpetually. There were no endless pits of burning fire down here; such punishment was fitting only for earth dwelling material bodies, and not the troubled spiritual ones here. I saw no ogres, devils, or multi-eyed monsters, nor did I witness any punishers with burning whips flaying the damned.

A deeply troubled spirit approached and enquired about my presence in this dreadful place. It knew that I did not belong here because it sensed the love and kindness emanating from my soul. It explained to me the reason why the other spirits, which had gathered around me, were all kept in darkness. It told me that the darkness in which they live is determined by their recollections of deeds done or not done while they dwelled on earth in the flesh and that no one punishment exists for all. Evil spirits do not reside in pleasant places, and each of them suffers only from the penalties that their recollections bring to them.

Some have been suffering here for a very long time. Perhaps hundreds or even thousands of years in rare cases, and they shall continue to do so until, by the operation of the law of compensation, they are relieved from some of their evil tendencies and desires, so they may be allowed to progress further.

I attempted to descend much deeper into the lower realms to enquire even further of regrettable punishments from greater sins. I saw the bedraggled souls of those who had committed the most heinous offences against their fellow man. I attempted to perceive them but was almost struck down with utter evil and fear so great and powerful was this force that it was only permitted, by spiritual law, to last for a split second or more. The bearded man appeared again, this time he admonished me for being foolish and inquisitive to transgress so deep into such a dark and dangerous realm. He reiterated that I shall, by the power and law of compensation, feel the full force of my foolishness when I return to my waiting body, and in good time, lest the silver cord shall fail and leave me stranded here in devil's province. At that point, I thought of nothing but divine love, wisdom, and kindness direct from the Holy Spirit. And at that very moment, I found myself in a beautiful place.

I appeared to be in a lush green meadow, looking down into the brightest and most colourful valley I had ever seen. Mere words could not describe the beauty of this place. It was quiet and peaceful, only broken by the sound of sweet, gentle, birdsong chorus that was relaxing and pleasant. A song so charming, fresh, and melodious, and never been heard on earth before. The sky was blue like that of the present earth but darker and purer. Everything around me was so colourful and bright. There were no shadows or darkness, only light. Even the bearded man was light.

He sat on the grass with his legs crossed, directly in front of me. He thanked me, for what reason, I do not know. Maybe because while I had languished for a moment in the lower realms in a potential state of complete lack of hope, and was about to descend even lower, I duly saved myself, deciding to pray earnestly for the divine love from the Great Spirit, and found my way back to paradise. He said that I had proved with just that if one desires the divine love earnestly, significant results could be achieved, as you now find yourself in the third sphere, a most beautiful place where good spirits reside and prepare to ascend to the higher spheres, such as the fifth, or the seventh.

As with most of my dreams that I had experienced while asleep, there was no chronological order of events, but a juxtaposition of random scenes without continuation or storyline. The bearded man told me that was because time did not exist in the spiritual realms, and it certainly does not follow on linearly as it does so on the earth plane.

I was once again surrounded by spirits, but these were very different. They were glowing bright, and I could sense an aura of love and kindness from them. A considerable dissimilarity with the ones I had encountered in the first sphere. The bearded man nodded and acknowledged the fact that I had observed the potential between good and evil, and then he reminded me once more that The Great Spirit is willing to grant his divine love to any spirit or mortal who merely asks for it. He then urged me to pray each day and to earnestly continue to seek to desire the divine love from God, as only God can bestow the divine love to the human soul.

I sensed that he had concluded and that he wanted me to return to my earthly, material body. I was reluctant to do so at first, as I had enjoyed my new spiritual body immensely, and this beautiful, peaceful place in the third sphere. I told him that I could remain here forever. He paused, and then he said, 'you will when the time comes'. And later he stated that it will be much better than you perceive it to be now, because when you finally do cross over, the silver cord will be severed, and you will be entirely free of your garment of flesh, your earthly body, which weighs down your mortal sins and desires. He then said that I must return to the earth plane because all souls must answer for the sins done in the flesh, and it is not necessary that these penalties be paid in the spirit world. It would be better to pay the penalty while on earth to ensure that the progress of the spirit is enhanced once it has crossed over to the spirit world.

It was with great disinclination that I took heed to his advice and, immediately, found myself snapping, like that of a taut elastic band as if yanked rigorously, back into my material body on the granite ledge. As a result, I experienced an enormous burden of weight, which I believe to be the sudden presence of my physical body, which I had to endure once again having been quite contented as a weightless spirit.

Things got even worse once I had re-entered and passed through the Dissolvable Ghost Crystal, and had fallen to the floor on the other side in the theatre. I noticed that all the pupils had gone. I saw the two professors with two other tutors, I believe. I heard one announce that I was back, and another said 'over six hours, that was far too long'. Which alarmed me greatly, as I had only experienced a short length of time in the spiritual realms, but surely not as long as six hours? The last thing I heard was Professor Anne saying; 'we need to get him to the recovery room right now', and it was at that very moment that I passed out.

When I woke up, I was told later that I had recovered rather quickly, considering my recent plight with the Dissolvable Ghost Crystal. I was startled at the fact that I, once again, found myself lying on a golden throne, in a golden dome-shaped room, which brought back memories of the first time I had met Lord Bandersant, and his two Androgen, and of course, my beautiful Karla.

A joyful memory just crossed my mind, which made me look towards the door, I was able to clearly discern the outline of the golden door this time, unlike the first one, which I wasn't able to find at all; and I paused for a moment expecting it to open, and Karla would enter with Lord Bandersant. In all honesty, I would have suffered a cardiac seizure through pure fear, amongst other things, if this event had occurred precisely how I had imagined it, and there would have been an alternative explanation, which would, no doubt, clarify my existence in this paradise. In simple terms, I would have believed that I had indeed died, and all these events served only as a test and the prequel to my admittance and acceptance into the spirit world.

I suddenly heard a voice, or to be more precise; I perceived a voice, a distinctive voice. It was in my head, but not from my mind. I attempted to communicate with it, but not by sound. I felt the ability and the need to covey my thoughts on a higher level, so I greeted it and asked it to identify itself.

'Newton!' The voice said, rather surprised. 'You have survived the Second Revelation, and I see you have returned with much spiritual development and wisdom, and you assert your telepathic ability with great dexterity and pride.'

"Lord Bandersant, is that you?" I asked aloud, suddenly abandoning my telepathy. I stared at the closed door. The door suddenly opened quickly and quietly. Lord Bandersant bounded in wringing his hands and beaming. He approached me and shook my hand.

"I heard that you encountered some difficulty with Dissolvable Ghost Crystal? Perhaps it wasn't such a good idea to attempt to descend into the darker realms with this method, Newton." He said quietly, and sardonically, as he pressed a few buttons on the golden recovery throne.

"I guess I was overcome by the excitement of it all, and I became more inquisitive and self-confident," I replied, scratching my head like a naughty, nervous schoolboy, who had just been told off for disrupting the whole class.

"Yes," Lord Bandersant replied, "one cannot be over-confident and inquisitive both at the same time, especially in the lower worlds. You leave yourself vulnerable to corruption and spiritual mischief. You were lucky to have such a trusting guide to accompany you."

"Who exactly was the bearded man?" I asked.

"It is Cassiel, the wise spiritual guide who roams the spiritual realms in search of lost souls, and leads them to safety. Nobody knows much about him only that he passed over to the spiritual realms in AD 2520 around the time of the start of the spiritual movement. It is said that he accompanied the last ghost from the earth plane and brought her to the spiritual realms in AD 2599."

"The last ghost?" I asked, rather puzzled.

"Yes, Newton, the last ghost to occupy the earth."

"Are you saying that you have no ghosts on earth, Lord Bandersant? What about the new ones, surely people are dying every day, even in this wonderful and perfect world. I have met some of them?"

"Yes they are, Newton, you are correct in your assumption, but you are forgetting one little detail, the very instrument that makes this world what it is today.

"Ghost Crystal?"

"The very thing, Newton. In particular, the Revelation." He pressed some more buttons on the throne, and then he sat down on the edge of the seat. "Ghosts are simply disembodied spirits. They are lost souls that have left their bodies on earth and are too scared to cross over to the spiritual realms either because they do not believe that they are dead, or they are reluctant to cross over due to some violent or tragic event of the past such as murder, accidental death, and suicide. They can also be former people who died with unfulfilled wishes, so they continue to roam the earth plane for years on end. But since the advent of Ghost Crystal, it allowed our people to gain true knowledge of the afterlife before their passing, and this valuable information made them fully aware of the circumstances, which caused their death. Now, we understand death to such a degree that we welcome it without fear, and most of us in this world even look forward to it."

"I must admit," I began, as I made ready to stand up, "Since the second Revelation I feel different in a way that I cannot describe. I feel lighter and more energetic, and fearless too, Lord Bandersant – yes, fearless of death, I think because I understand it much more now that I have experienced it."

Lord Bandersant rose to his feet, looked me up and down, and said, "Well, Newton you have certainly recovered well from it. Your body functions seem normal and clear. Just take it easy for a few days, and in the meantime drink, and eat plenty of the good natural food that you adore so much, it will certainly help you to recover faster."

I thanked him and shook his hand, and then he left the room after he had said that he would see me later on but where I did not know. It was too late to ask him where I was, or where they had brought me. Although, I knew for sure that I was in a golden globe, or recovery room, what we would have referred to as a hospital back in my time, this one had but one bed, the golden throne, which contained the most bizarre and highly advanced technology. The whole contraption was capable of performing almost any physical healing or diagnostics. And I suspect it also could execute significant operations without having to make actual physical contact with the body of the patient.

I tried my new-found (ESP) Extra Sensory Perception to see if it would reveal my location but gave up halfway through. I blamed my failure on the fact that there was too much gold around for any mind signals to penetrate, which was a weak justification by any measure, as I had managed earlier to communicate successfully with Lord Bandersant while he was on the other side of the golden door.

I wondered what lies behind that door, as I approached it and touched the crystal button to command its opening. Was I still at the educational establishment, in their well-equipped recovery room? Or was I –

"Karla!"

She stood in the middle of the doorway wearing a huge smile, and a tight little pink mini dress. Her golden brown legs looked even more golden and much browner than usual, suggesting that she had taken even more sun than any young girl should in such a small space of time.

"I do suspect that you have been shopping, and sunbathing while I was suffering in Hades, Karla?"

Her big smile turned into a grin, and she leapt at me, as she always did when she hadn't seen me for a while. She must have been working out too; as I almost blacked out again as her smooth golden brown legs constricted my frail and tired torso.

I stumbled out into a hallway, which I did not recognise at all, trying desperately to maintain my balance with little Karla tightly clasping her petite self around me. With her warm lips pressed firmly against mine, in a kissing frenzy, which I was unable to break away from, I could not utter a word of protest. We struggled through another door to a further unknown room, but it was only when we were actually outside, staggering around on a well-kept lawn, that it came flooding back to me. I immediately recognised the very place I loved, as a veil of sheer happiness suddenly came over me. I found myself, once again, with great joy and delight, back on that vast floating vessel, 'The Island'.

CHAPTER 11

The Party

The one good thing about this place that they call Heaven on earth is the standard of living. I don't mean that regarding wealth from earnings gained by working your butt off all your life, as was common in my day on earth. After retiring later on in life and then perhaps you may be unfortunate enough to contract a debilitating condition, which could undermine your health or indeed end your days suddenly. Such an inevitable life-Patten has long gone and is no longer a requirement as endorsed and enforced by the establishment in my time. Living on earth now is better than any other time known to man throughout all history. We live here in such joy and happiness that it can only be comparable to that of a perpetual party.

If only our ignorant, belligerent forebears knew that the key to happiness was just to love one and other and to share everything equally, they could have saved themselves years of abject suffering, the stupid fools. I must add that since the second Revelation, I have become more susceptible to my own emotions as well as to those of others, which could be explained as one of the reasons for my recently discovered telepathic ability. I seem to have acquired a more profound affinity for the suffering, although no such unfortunate creature roams the earth today, I seem more concerned with those who have gone before me, and are now languishing in the lower realms. Dare I ask myself, should I feel a degree of guilt while I enjoy my life to the full while others languish in the lower Hells?

The point is there are no Hells as such, as I have learnt at my own cost that they don't exist because punishments are explicitly tailored to each of us individually. It would be impossible for me to bear the punishment for another person and vice versa. The spiritual law does not allow this, as there exists a law of compensation, which demands that a sinner must pay the penalty for his sins until there has been a full expiration, or until the requirement is satisfied. This law cannot be negotiated for a change in its operations, nor can any man avoid or escape its inevitable demands.

God is not the God of any race or nation, but of the individual. I am the oldest creature on this planet, and I know for sure that my people were wrong about almost everything they attempted to accomplish. According to them, life was all about conquering and victory over nations, but they overlooked the fact that God does not praise men or countries because of victory acquired through bloodshed, but only for those whose souls have been awakened to his love and victory over sin and evil.

I can safely say with confidence that I feel that I have acquired a great deal of the Divine Love from God since the first Revelation, more than I have ever received in my entire life on earth. I feel no guilt or shame due to the fortunate situation in which I find myself. I have learnt from the lower realms that all men have an equal chance to redeem their sins. The Great Spirit gives us all free will, and each of us is free to exercise this as we wish whether we are in the flesh, or in the spiritual realms. Because, regardless, we never die, and God is a God only of these things that never die, as he wishes us to conquer sin and appetites of the flesh.

"What are you thinking, Newton, appetites of the flesh?" Karla's voice rang out from the bedroom. I was sitting in the Jacuzzi at the side of our pool, just minding my own business, and thinking to myself, when she had picked up on my thoughts.

"Was I talking out loud, Karla?" I asked her.

"Of course not, Newton," she replied, "but your telepathic voice was shouting out loud!"

"Can you hear me now, Karla?" I said, in a jovial manner, "I want your gorgeous little torso in this Jacuzzi at once, or I am coming in to pick you up and throw you in fully clothed...or not"

"Oh, no, Newton, You can't do that, you'll ruin my new dress," she pleaded in a pseudo, superficial voice, "please don't… oh, my zip is stuck, I can't get the dress undone. Newton, wait, I need more time to undo this -." Her voice trailed off.

Immediately, I seised upon the opportunity in an attempt to play a trick on her, but it seems that her Celestial instinct and intelligence allowed her the upper hand, usually. I planned to let her sufficient time to resolve the problem with her dress and make her believe that I wasn't coming after her, and then suddenly sneak up on her, pick her up and throw her in the swimming pool. I stood at the door from the terrace, which led to the bedroom, looking in through the glass but I saw no sign of her anywhere. All of a sudden, I was completely drenched by a rapid gush of cold water from behind, or above, I could not tell exactly, only that it was freezing, even in the hot morning sunshine it had felt so cold. As I gasped for breath, my mind raced to find a solution or explanation as to what just occurred.

From the corner of my eye, which was blinking uncontrollably in a bid to clear the freezing water from it, I thought I saw Karla, bikini-clad, and laughing, as she ran towards the Jacuzzi and leapt in.

"How did you get there so quick?" I asked as I chased after her. "One minute you're in the bedroom - did you trick me with that story about the broken zip?"

I jumped into the Jacuzzi and grabbed her around the waist, and then I began to tickle her, profusely. She attempted a feeble protest, in between bouts of hysterics.

"Newton," she said, when we both had calmed down, "you left yourself open and vulnerable, I took advantage of that."

"Well, I guess I will have to work on my ESP then," I said. And it was at that precise moment that I was about to demonstrate this. We both paused for a moment as if we had heard something. Karla stared at me open-mouthed with a faint smile as if she knew something and was waiting for me to speak first. I did not physically hear anything, but I did sense a presence – at the front door.

"Darus!" I said, with a hint of too much excitement.

"Yes, that's good, Newton, your ESP has recovered. The cold shower did you well!"

"But I am unable to communicate with him, why?"

"No, you won't be able to, he's Androgen, and you will need a crystal translator.

She reached over to a small console, which had natural markings and some crystal buttons.

"Here, use this for now." She pressed one of the buttons that I had seen often and had been meaning to push to see what it did. I finally found out.

"Darus here," a voice said, "I have brought you some breakfast."

"OK, Darus, we will be there shortly," Karla replied, as she pressed the other crystal button.

"So, it's a door entry intercom? I exclaimed, rather relieved, "In a Jacuzzi?"

Karla smiled as she kissed my lips, and then she got out of the water to dry and change into a thick towel robe to meet Darus at the front door.

Darus congratulated me on the second Revelation, as we met him in the dining area. He brought us a fruit breakfast, which contained all the usual delights we were accustomed to on this giant luxury cruise vessel, plus some new varieties of exotic fruit picked this very morning. He set the large tray on the table. It looked so inviting, and I just couldn't wait to tuck in.

"There is a party later aboard Louden's balloon, and Muriel and Cassie would like you both to attend."

"Is it his birthday?" I asked, in an attempt to steer him away from Karla's scornful gaze.

"Oh, no," Darus replied in an innocent tone, "Louden won't be there himself, he had to go to the Antipodean Region for a few days, on a special expedition of some nature. He left the twins in charge of the balloon."

"Well – we will have to see because I -." I began, rather hesitantly to protect Karla, but suddenly, her countenance changed, surprisingly.

"Yes, we will be there." She interrupted, with a smile.

"Oh, there is one more thing," Darus continued, "The twins took the balloon down to the Southern Pacific and, by chance, they discovered the second anti-gravitational field, so they are planning to celebrate by hosting a game of Skyball to test it out."

"Yes, yes!" Karla yelled in jubilation, "Tell them that we will be most delighted to attend."

"I will tell them," Darus said, then he said that he had to go, and he would see us later on.

As soon as Darus was gone, I started on the breakfast platter. I kicked something over under the table while I was pulling a chair out to sit down. When I looked down, I saw that it was a bottle of golden Champagne.

"Darus is so kind, he must have left this for us, or perhaps it was meant as a gift for my Second Revelation, and he forgot to present it to me," I said to Karla, who was already seated at the table eating, struggling with a mouthful of juicy guava fruit. "Would you like some, dear Karla?"

"Yes please, Newton." She replied, eventually - after she had chewed and swallowed a large mouthful of the juicy tropical fruit.

The one thing about having fruit breakfast in the morning is that, no matter how much fruit you consume, you almost always feel a little hungry soon afterwards, especially when you foolishly wash it all down with too many glasses of the best golden Champagne.

I blame my sudden hearty appetite on the Revelation; the complexity of it must have drained my entire body of all its reserve energy, and now I find myself sitting in one of the best steak restaurants on the vessel in a bid to replenish myself of the loss.

Unlike the seafood restaurant that Darus had recommended to us, which was very exclusive indeed, this one was located on the opposite end of the Island, high up on the top level and with the same panoramic view. Here in this fabulous restaurant, they specialised in steak, cooked lovingly on a crystal grill no doubt, a somewhat futuristic looking contraption, which was capable of producing flames just like the gas or solid fuel barbeques back in my primitive era. In a brief conversation with one of the head chefs I asked, just out of interest, if he was familiar with gas or solid fuel, and did he ever use such methods, perhaps for sheer nostalgia rather than necessity. He laughed out loud, of course, and said that those things were ancient and only fit for cavemen and hermits and that they were confined to history books and museums. I had to agree with him modestly, and then I quickly changed the subject.

Karla enjoyed the ambience in this restaurant, not to mention the excellent wholesome food as well. Sometimes I struggled to cognise how a woman of such sylph-like physical proportions could consume food in the quantities as Karla did and yet remain so slim and graceful. She kept on telling me each time that it was a combination of her high metabolic rate and her solid-state crystal drive digestion system that was responsible for her adorable, physical attributes. I had always laughed at such statements that she made not knowing whether she was serious, or merely jesting with me. I usually responded by reminding her that she was Celestial with organic attributes and not Androgen.

As we sat at our table by the window, admiring the view and drinking red wine from my home country, the United Kingdom, not so united now, as the mainland, along with its isles, had drifted South and ended up next to Portugal.

I didn't notice her at first when she brought our menus over earlier, but it was when she had brought us the wine that I happened to recognise her.

"I suppose you identified her by her long slim legs, Newton?" Karla said to me as the waitress returned to our table.

"Do I sense a hint of jealousy in your voice, Karla? You cannot be Celestial. They are not supposed to feel jealousy."

She replied with a playful punch to my arm.

"So what are you two lovebirds doing tonight?" The waitress asked as she approached.

"Sorry we did not recognise you, Alana, we didn't expect you to be working here in the steak restaurant as well," I said, and then I received another playful punch from Karla.

"Stop that," she said, "we don't use that word anymore; it is not considered a good word."

"Have I said something unpleasant?" I asked, a little confused.

Karla leant towards me and mouthed something to me in a whisper, "That word 'work' we don't use it anymore to describe services that the Androgen provides in this world."

"Sorry," I said, but I was not so sure what I was sorry for.

Karla looked up at Alana, "He couldn't have been looking at your face, Alana, that's why he didn't recognise you."

"Come on, girls!" I said as I relaxed back in my chair thinking how fortunate I was for a moment, "Give me a break. I am new to this paradise; it is like Heaven, everything is made beautiful for the eye to see, and the heart to admire."

"You have to excuse him, Alana, he has just experienced the second Revelation."

"Oh, that's fantastic, Newton, and now you are both out celebrating?" Alana asked.

"Yes," I said, " then we are off to a party on Louden's balloon after this, Alana. Why don't you join us?"

Her eyes lit up with excitement, "I'm going to the party too!" She exclaimed, "I am in the Skyball team with the other girls. I think Darus is playing as well."

"This should be a fun night then," I said, as I wrung my hands. "Well, I never knew Darus was a Skyball fanatic. And you, Alana, flying around in the air in zero gravity, chasing the ball, I bet that's how you retain such an adorable figure."

"Take no notice of him, Alana, he knew nothing about Skyball before he saw it at the educational establishment," Karla said, as she delivered me a playful slap on my shoulder, "he only knows the ancient game they used to call, 'football.' They played it in fields, on the ground, hundreds of years ago. They ran around in a grass field kicking a ball with their feet, which they were not allowed to touch with their hands."

"Really?" Alana exclaimed, with her eyes opened wide with surprise.

"It wasn't that bad," I replied in my defence for what once considered was my national game. The beautiful game, no doubt. "Ours was a simple game, which could be played anywhere, by almost anybody, with just one ball, filled with air, the very thing we breathe. No complex zero gravity apparatus required."

After the girls had their laugh about my ancient national pastime, I jested to Alana about teaching her how to play one day. Karla thought it was a great idea, and she suggested that I could teach the pupils at the education establishment as well.

Lord Bandersant did mention about sharing my experiences with the younger people in this beautiful paradise. In particular, to assist in providing them with a basic understanding of how we came to destroy our world through selfishness, greed, corruption, and violence, and to ensure that it is not repeated in the future. Which I doubt very much would be possible, as the behaviour of mankind has changed considerably for the better since those dark days, and it continues to thrive with an abundance of love and happiness assured by the existence of Ghost Crystal which has, by far, proved to be so meritoriously faithful.

I put it to him the point and purpose of introducing such negative history to pupils whose lessons comprises nothing but peace, love, and kindness. He made a point about the meaning of the Revelation, stating that, although it served as a deterrent against evil by revealing the proper punishments available to each of us, it was also a handy tool to encourage morality, respect, virtuousness, and integrity. The distinction between good and evil can be balanced equally, and it is better understood by having full knowledge of history, in particular, the enmity and the disastrous mistakes of man.

I am not sure if the Revelation is supposed to affect my taste buds because the wine had such a distinctive and tangible flavour that I could almost visualise the region where it was grown. I dismissed it at first, but after my second glass, the visions seemed to become stronger. They were like quick flashes of a vivid dream. By the time I had started on my third glass, I had decided that I had to tell Karla.

"You have reached the second stage," she said, after freezing on the spot.

"Is it serious?" I asked, I think I froze too, with my fork in my hand, holding up a large piece of steak on the end of it, which I had just cut on my plate and was about to devour.

"Yes!" She cried, "Of course it's serious, Newton. It means that the Revelation has begun its full effect. It normally begins with the effect of food or drink. You experience what they call associative flashbacks, where you can perceive the energy from material things."

"Like a clairvoyant?" I asked.

"Yes, one who reads objects," Karla replied.

"Will it happen all the time, and just with food? And what about water?" I hesitated to put the steak in my mouth.

"Don't worry, Newton," she said softly, as she stroked my hand, "it is only happening like this initially, but later on you will learn how to control it. Now let's eat and drink and forget about the effects of the Revelation for now. We are supposed to be celebrating it."

I held my glass high, and we both toasted the effects of the Revelation. Then we continued eating and drinking until both plates were clean, and three empty wine bottles stood tall and proud in the middle of our table.

After a relaxing walk along the deck, which led from the steak restaurant, we made our way to my spacecraft, which I think should have been on the lawn on the lower deck, although, I cannot remember flying it back or even docking the vessel. Later on, as we were making our way to the lower deck to seek out my lost craft frantically, we met Darus. He informed me that Lord Bandersant had brought the craft back, with my unconscious body in it, and delivered me to the recovery room, so he must have docked it in its usual place. Well, that was the second time he had rescued me; first from my deep sleep, and now from this second sleep, a rest due mainly to the adverse effect of the second Revelation. We found the craft on the grass lawn next to the others. It was in the same position just as though it hadn't been moved.

After we boarded, I ascended high into the atmosphere to assure clear and safe airspace. I wondered how we were going to locate the balloon because it was supposed to be somewhere in the South Pacific, hovering over an anti-gravitational field, which was discovered by chance anyway, and to me, that would be the equivalent of searching for a needle in a haystack. Karla saved me, but not before she had her wicked way of a joke with me first. She put on her most serious expression and then informed me, without even the slightest giggle or chuckle, in her most serious voice, and said that to locate the balloon successfully, I would need to communicate with somebody on board using ESP. She almost duped me, due to my pure nature, and she would have succeeded as well if I hadn't stared intensely into her lying eyes with my serious expression, which, up until now, had never failed to break her. By the time I had finished reprimanding her with a severe and unrelenting tickling, she was exhausted and in fits of laughter. However, my lack of due care and attention to piloting caused us to alter course and end up somewhere over the North Antarctica coast.

Eventually, we managed to locate the balloon with a little assistance from the built-in auto craft finding system, a form of ultra-modern radar but with much more technical intelligence than the museum pieces that I used back in my days on earth. We spotted the balloon from high above, and descended towards it and floated about two hundred feet above it. The balloon looked formidable from this angle, as it hovered steadily above the ocean approximately one hundred feet from the surface of the water. Its huge gold, gas-filled envelope gleamed in the bright afternoon sun. We circled it twice to get a better view of this monstrous beast. I have seen air balloons, and I have piloted several back in my time, but I have never seen one as big as this one before in my whole life, not even in science fiction films. The gondola, or should I say, 'the large structure suspended beneath the balloon' resembled an old pirate ship from the late 16th Century, but with a more refined appearance and a somewhat futuristic distinctive form, to my ancient eyes, anyway.

The deck was huge, and it was made from a smooth, shiny, dark wood similar to English Oak, which I have never seen anywhere before. The grain was much more exciting than that of oak, as it displayed many vibrant shades of brown, interesting swirling patterns. We descended lower, where even more detail was evident. An outer perimeter deck surrounded the whole ship, which was sectioned off from the inner deck. It led to an extended area to the rear of the ship, where I could see some docked spacecraft.

"That's the docking area down there," I pointed out to Karla.

"Yes, I see it," she replied. She then paused, as if she had been listening to a voice, "Newton, land there next to the blue one," she ordered suddenly. She pointed to a small blue ship down on the deck, "and we will be required to tether, in auto-docking mode, when we land."

"Aye, aye captain," I said in jest. Which earned me nothing but a perplexed gaze, which lasted a few seconds.

I glided the ship down and made a perfect landing in the exact spot next to the blue ship. Karla explained to me the reason for auto docking mode. It was an advanced feature built into the craft, which enabled it to hover about one foot off the ground and remain there in case of any sudden turbulence, in particular aboard an ocean-going vessel in a storm or rough seas, so that it could compensate the movement and remain steady. She never elaborated on the technical aspects, but briefly informed me that it functioned by utilising a combination of anti-gravity, and a low idle of the ship's solid-state crystal drive system, which I understood to be an advanced form of mid-air suspension. My only concern was getting out of the door and having to jump down onto the deck. Of course, she thought that I was just flippant again and she paid me for my impertinence with a light punch to my arm.

As the door opened, I noticed we were not hovering at all, but firmly on the deck of the gondola. Karla pressed a few buttons and then she informed me that she was about to pre-select and engage the autodocking mode. We left the craft, allowing the door to close behind us. We passed through a gate on the deck of the gondola, which led us to the inner primary deck. As I looked back at my docked craft, I heard its engines murmur, and then I witnessed the craft as it lifted clear off the deck and suspended itself in mid-air about one foot above the wooden deck.

I was awestruck by the sheer size of the balloon high above us, right in the centre of the gondola. There was a structure underneath the balloon about fifteen feet above the deck; it was round, and it resembled a ships' crow's nest, but as we advanced, to obtain a clearer view, we could see that it was, in fact, a structure with windows all around its perimeter. There was a platform on the roof with wood railings all around the outside. This structure possibly served as some lookout platform, as the whole thing was supported by a tall, thick, robust looking, mast pole with an elegantly carved spiral staircase built expertly around it, which I believe to be a means of access to the crow's nest.

Many people were milling around in this area. Almost all of them were dressed in bright and colourful clothes of various styles, walking around holding glasses filled with colourful drinks, admiring the view and talking in small groups. It was apparently a party atmosphere. A live band played classical music from one of the balconies above the upper floor. We heard somebody shout from the crow's nest directly above us.

"Karla! Newton! Up here!"

We both looked up at the same time to see the twins, Muriel and Cassie, waving from the crow's nest observation platform. We waved back to them and watched as they both scrambled to the spiral staircase and rushed down to the deck to greet us.

"Be careful, you two," I said, as one of them launched herself at me and gave me a big hug, almost knocking me over in the process. "You'll hurt yourselves, rushing around like that… and you'll hurt me too with such a tight hug." The second twin, who hugged me even tighter, greeted me in the same manner.

"We missed you, Newton. How are you?" They both said, almost in unison.

"I'm fine, girls," I replied to them both, not knowing who was who. "Where's Louden? Is he here?" I asked, looking around at all the strange, smiling faces on the deck.

The twins looked at each other in silence for a moment, as if deciding on the most appropriate and favourable answer to provide me. They were both sincere, regardless of their hesitation, which was not intentional, as I was to find out later on.

After much hugging and kissing, we met up with Darus and my favourite little long legged waitress, Alana. Both of them were fired up and raring to go, ready for an energetic game of Skyball. I did some stroking too; it was immediately after a huge, ultra-soft, furry creature, none other than the pet tiger Alice, set upon me. She licked my face, relentlessly until I submitted, and offered her a warm cuddle followed by a severe stroking, which did much to subdue her over-excitement. I greeted little Sophista and asked her the whereabouts of her parents. She said that her mother was on the launch platform organising the Skyball game, and her father, Doctor Gabriel, was up on the upper viewing platform with the others, organising the conversation and drinking.

I left Kara with Sophista and the twins and made my way to the launch platform to see the phenomenon, the anti-gravitational field, in action, and also to speak to Prangalistra about some issues regarding the Luna Region (the moon).

When I got there, I could see people lined along the edge of the platform, leaning on the wood railings, looking over the side of the steep drop down into the deep blue Pacific Ocean below. But this was no ordinary ocean. I had to look twice to unravel this mystical phenomenon, which was plaguing my visual conception of normality. The crater must have been at least three hundred feet across, and fifty feet deep at its centre. It had a concave base, which was smooth as glass. It looked as if a giant had pressed a large glass bowl onto the surface of the sea and submerged it until the lip of the bowl was sea level, just enough to prevent water from flowing into the container. And then the bowl was removed leaving its exact, flawless imprint in the sea. But there was no glass involved here. This phenomenon was purely the work of natural gravity against the sea. Similar to the concave pitch that I visited at the education establishment, which was lined with a grass pitch on top of a solid base, from which one was able to push oneself off to propel themselves back up into the air. How they expected to achieve this in water and regulate a natural gravity field was far beyond my intellectual capacity.

I felt a sudden kiss on the side of my face. Thinking that Alice had followed me, it neither bothered nor startled me. I didn't inconvenience myself to look at her, I just said out loud, "Have you been following me again, you playful little tiger?"

A voice replied, which caused me such alarm that I almost jumped out of my skin with fright, "Would you be referring to that playful tiger over there, Newton?"

I looked behind, where Prangalistra was pointing and caught sight of Alice sitting on the deck, a few feet away from me, nonchalantly licking away at her paw. "Prangalistra, it's you. How are you?"

"I'm fine, Newton – Where is Sophista, has she left you to look after Alice?" She asked.

"No, I think the cat followed me. Sophista is with Karla and the twins on the main deck."

"I heard that your second revelation was a success," she said with a smile, "you are one of us now, Newton."

"Indeed I am," I replied. "A lot has changed since the first day I came to this place, but I still have much to take in." I moved towards the railings and pointed down towards the phenomenon in the sea, "Things such as this, Prangalistra, how does one regulate the gravitational field? And how will the players rebound off a wall of the sea and propel themselves back up to the balloon in mid-air?"

She looked at me wide-eyed and with a broad smile, "My dear Newton, were you not present when we both fled Fortinell's Androgen Processing Plant?"

"Gravity belts?" I asked, curiously.

"Well, we are hoping that, as the body reaches the area close to the surface of the anomaly, the force will reverse, and one will be able to return using this very force. It is a similar principle to the function of a gravity belt, but it occurs naturally, and will not require any artificial assistance under these circumstances."

I followed Prangalistra as we strolled, as I listened to her, not realising that we had ended up on the other side of the perimeter railings onto a large diving platform with no rails to the front, which offered a steep drop of almost one hundred feet down into the centre of the bowl.

"Who exactly is going to try it out?" I asked, and just as soon as I had finished the question, I saw Darus and Alana walking towards us. They were both wearing gravity belts.

"Don't worry, Newton; there is no danger here. The gravity belts are just a precaution and not a necessity. They have the option to switch them on if they need to, or we can do it from here, remotely if the need arises."

I saw a tall Androgen man standing by the railings holding a small square crystal device in his hand. I tried to speak to Alana, but before I could get her attention, she had already disappeared off the edge of the platform. Darus immediately followed her. I quickly made my way to the side of the railings to try to get a better view of their impending fate. I caught a glimpse of the two Androgens free falling in mid-air. They suddenly adopted an incredible acrobatic swan dive position, much to the amusement of the crowd. It was evident that they were enjoying their free-fall and rapid descent into the unknown. The crowd gasped as they both neared the surface of the ocean. Their gasps turned to cheers as soon as they had witnessed the two divers decelerating rapidly, and then they slowed right down and almost came to a sudden stop just feet from the wall of water at the bottom of the bowl. I saw Darus reach out and stroke the surface of the water just before they began their ascent to the top of the bowl. But they were reluctant to return to the platform. Their mission was a success, and the crowd enjoyed their performance. Darus and Alana were both determined to make the most of their success by performing as much acrobatics as their talents would allow, flying up and down, and across and over each other without once touching the water.

The rest of the team were already on the platform, all fired up with vitality and enthusiasm, ready to descend into the arena. One had a giant orange ball in her hand.

"Fantastic!" Prangalistra shouted, "It's a perfect, naturally-occurring, anti-gravitational field, ideal conditions for Skyball."

"You can't control the strength of the field. Will that present any problems?" I asked.

"It doesn't matter, Newton... you saw them. Look at their acrobatics...they are both dry, and in full control, and the gravity belts have not even been switched on yet. There is no need to control the field."

"Where's Louden, Prangalistra?" I asked, taking full advantage of the uproarious crowd, clapping and cheering. Soon, music began to play from the crow's nest. The whole vessel was alive with unrestrained festivity.

"He was taken, – " Is all she said when her voice was drowned out by the noise.

When I looked back over the railings, I saw bodies swooping down into the ocean. The whole team had plunged over the side. First the girl with the ball, and then the others followed one by one in rapid succession. Each one was swooping down in perfect formation, like swifts, towards the pit, and then each one diverged and went their separate way. Remarkably, I saw no collisions or near misses. I tried to reach Prangalistra once again, but there were too many people around her. The situation was made worse by the sudden appearance of a group of scantily clad female dancers. I couldn't tell whether they were Androgen or human. Celestial didn't even cross my mind until I heard somebody behind me explicitly say that they were indeed Celestial. I turned around to find Doctor Gabriel standing there with a drink in his hand. Some of the dancing girls brushed past me, deliberately gyrating up against my body, one girl, in particular, seemed to delay the whole flow of the performance by purposely prolonging her dance routine with me, while the others took their turn and moved along quickly towards the landing deck.

"I think she likes you." Doctor Gabriel said, with a broad smile.

I stepped back, as Doctor Gabriel retreated to the other side of the railings, where there were more room and fewer people. I followed him, and we ended up standing not too far from the mast.

"Do you where Louden is?" I asked him.

Doctor Gabriel took a mouthful of drink from his glass and savoured the flavour of the liquid for a moment before he answered my question. "Louden is on the mainland of the Antipodean region; he is partaking in an experiment with a newly developed Ghost Crystal which is more powerful than any others in existence in the world today."

"That stands to reason," I said, "is it necessary for him to receive a third dose of the Revelation?" I asked, somewhat nonchalantly.

"This will be his second," Doctor Gabriel replied, which surprised me. And he noticed it in my reaction, which I should have controlled better. He probably knew from ESP anyway. "Louden had somehow evaded the second Revelation. He went off exploring in this contraption. He built it himself, you know, a remarkable feat for one man. You see, Newton, how unique life is in this place? With the power of the Great Spirit, and through Divine Love, knowledge, and wisdom, one can achieve many great feats in this beautiful world with a little effort and a little faith. Even more so with the aid of the second Revelation. By the way, how are you feeling after yours? I heard that you performed it in the educational establishment with the students? What a great example to them, something that they shall cherish and talk highly of for years to come.

"It was quite demanding," I replied, "but enormously beneficial to me, as my mind is much clearer now, and my ESP has improved greatly. The Monkey Mind has vanished completely, and I don't think it will ever return because I strongly feel that all those earthly desires of the past are now extinct."

"Good, Newton," he replied, "Very good. Once you have acquired a degree of the Divine Love through the Revelation, there is no going back, unless you desire to seek earnestly to delve down into the depths of the lower worlds, which would require much effort and desire in the physical and mental recital of evil and malicious behaviour. Newton, we have prepared a dwelling for you and Karla. It is located just on the outskirts of the city, in the countryside region, where silence prevails, and nature is rife. I'm sure it will satisfy your soul. It is perfect for you both."

"I do suspect that you have been talking to Karla?" I asked as I chuckled.

"Well -," he said, shaking his empty glass, "she was kind enough to provide some input on the design aspect – on your behalf, I must add. She certainly knows what you like, Newton...is that Alice over there? "Doctor Gabriel suddenly asked after a short pause.

"Yes, it is," I replied, pretending not to have seen her, "she's been following me around but has kept her distance, until now. Sophista is with Karla and the twins, somewhere on the contraption. They could be watching Skyball."

"I'd better go and find them. Newton, you must try the Black Champagne. It is new from the Zealand Islands." Doctor Gabriel said, as he reached out and grabbed Alice by her collar. She growled, and she kept on turning her head, to look back at me as she was being almost dragged away by Doctor Gabriel. I looked back at her, and I shook my head and mouthed, 'no, I 'm not coming with you'. I think she understood me.

I couldn't see how the game was progressing if there was one going on because the festivity had eased a little. There was still the odd cheer or holler to be heard now and then, over a steady beat of the music, which came from the bar area on the upper deck, where I soon found myself heading.

This contraption, as Doctor Gabriel called it, was no Island. It was huge, as far as balloon boats are concerned, whatever they were, as I have never seen one on earth back in my time. You either had a balloon, or you had a boat, or both if you were lucky, or wealthy enough, and neither if you were poor. Here in this perfect world, there is no requirement to desire any riches, because riches come straight from the heart. One is only as rich as the condition of their soul, as there are no banks or bank balances to support this. The goodness of the individual's soul will determine the extent of his wealth, just as the amount of punishment that a man receives is determined by the condition of his soul.

I was so engrossed in my thinking, something I hadn't felt or experienced before the Revelation, that I could not remember how I had managed to find myself suddenly standing on the upper deck, as I could not remember going there. There I stood, at the bar, surrounded by some happy carousers, and with a thought in my head that I was just about to ask the bartender for black champagne. The tall Androgen had only served my drink, and I finished thanking him when I heard a voice to the left of me. Thinking that it was just my ESP again, or perhaps somebody talking with slightly more enthusiasm than usual, I chose to ignore it initially.

"Bumptious man thinks that death and punishment are the same for everyone, but it is not." The voice said, quite clearly.

I turned to see a man standing beside me holding a bottle of black champagne in one hand, as he thrust his other hand towards me. He was sporting a colourful robe.

"Hi, Newton, my name is Nesasigamany, I am the ruler of the Luna Region, the sole sovereign and domain of King Fulk and Queen Fulk."

"I am pleased to meet you, Nesasigamany. How do you know of me, and what are you doing on the moon when we have a lovely planet down here to live on?"

"Newton, who has not heard of the man who slept a thousand sleeps, and awakens to walk the earth once more?"

"They'll be writing songs next," I said, under my breath.

"We mine crystals on the moon." He said, proudly, "Under the auspices of King and Queen."

"I didn't know there were any crystals on the moon, not enough for a mining operation, anyway, let alone a Monarchy as well?"

"Probably not in your time, Newton, but until about four hundred and fifty years ago. They found water deep below the surface during a routine survey operation. That is when they discovered the crystal, Moldavite, a tektite (small dark glassy rock), a stone of intense frequency and high vibration, used mainly during the process of Ghost crystal, and also for healing in medical science."

"Do you process it on the moon?" I asked, with great interest.

"Indeed, we do process the crystal, but the making of Ghost Crystal itself is a different matter entirely. This surreptitious task is performed in the sealed chambers, by the Strict Androgen."

"I'm sorry, Nesasigamany, you will have to elaborate, I have never heard of Strict Androgen. In any case, I was informed that the moon was dead and unoccupied."

Just one glass of the Zealand Black Champagne was causing my head to spin. Doctor Gabriel should have warned me about its potency. I suppose he thought I was capable enough to read his thoughts, so I should have known anyway.

"They have never informed you about the making of Ghost Crystal, Newton?" He said, in a derisive tone of voice. "Newton, they don't even know about the making of Ghost Crystal themselves. It is not for the eyes of man to see such things, lest he interfere and meddle, and cause havoc like he always did so in the past, with great success. Only you could understand such things, Newton. That is the prime reason why humans no longer involve themselves with manufacturing; they leave it to us Androgen. We have a selection and type which we refer to as Strict Androgen; they perform their duties in sealed chambers making themselves inaccessible to humans so that nobody can interfere with the process."

"Do I suspect some top secret operation?" I asked.

"Newton, this is the thirtieth Century, not the twenty-first. Man abolished manual labour over one hundred years ago when he developed Androgen to perform most of the manual tasks, which he did not desire to do himself, including manufacturing."

"So I've been told. What about the processing plant in the Antipodean Region?" I asked him.

"What about it, Newton? Because you must understand that I don't have any association with that place, despite being Androgen; Cyberscience is not my field in any case."

"Were you created there?"

"Indeed not, Newton, however, we Androgen are all assembled there, but previous to that we are created in the Luna Region like most other things, which are utilised by man. There are no industries left on earth, Samuel Page saw to that saw to that back in AD 2520 when he transferred all heavy industry to the Luna Region. He wasn't thrilled with your brothers from the past, Newton. Page was given the arduous task to clean up their rotten pollution from the last war before he was able to begin any construction work."

I almost dropped my full bottle of Black Champagne, which was handed to me earlier by one of the waiters, that was when he had said to me that I couldn't enjoy watching a game of Skyball while holding an empty glass, or stomach, for that matter. I poured the potent black nectar into the glass and had held it in my hand all this time just to appease him. "I thought you had no more war on earth after the holocaust in AD 2020?"

"That's the very war I was referring to, Newton. No other war but the one instigated by your brothers in your reign, in the very year of AD 2020."

"I understand that this so-called construction took place on the dark side for reasons of confidentiality? Why didn't Samuel Page construct his facility somewhere else, away from the polluted area?" I asked, slightly perplexed.

Nesasigamany took a deep sigh, "Newton, the legacy left by your war mongers is a rather complex one. There are some technical reasons to do with existing airshafts and deep foundations, which were excavated by your people, Newton. Samuel Page needed to utilise and adapt these to serve as foundations for his new facility, so he had no choice but to relocate all the top-secret material first."

"Top secret?" I asked, curiously.

Nesasigamany waved his hand in a dismissive gesture. "Oh, those are things of the past, Newton. They have no consequence in new matters of today."

"Have you seen any of this top secret material?" I asked, eager for an answer.

He sighed again, this time it was deeper than before, "Newton, why would I waste time on futile matters of the past? Your ancestor's deadly contraptions of conspiracy and war? And their ineffective experimental devices, which serve no purpose in this world but to pollute and destroy? They are all long gone; sealed in the tomb of dread and destruction, never to see the light of heaven again."

He took a long swig from his black bottle. As he did so, a loud cheer erupted from the platform. I noticed that a few people from the bar had walked along the upper platform and out onto a deck, perhaps to attain a better view of the action in the arena. I told Nesasigamany that I must go and watch my two Androgen friends perform in the Skyball game and that he should come with me if he so wished. He said that he had to get back to the Island, where he was staying for a couple of days until he returned to the Luna Region. I told him that we might meet again somewhere on the Island, as we too are staying on the cruiser for a while, perhaps until it has completed its circumnavigation of the Antipodean Region.

I had a beautiful uninterrupted view of the ocean arena from the upper platform. It looked as if the Skyball game was in full swing. I could see bodies flying up into the air, some hitting the ball with their arms, legs, and head, and others zooming around and across the arena in a desperate bid to thwart their opponents. Some of the players were successful, while others were not so successful. The unlucky ones ended up heading towards the formidable looking watery wall of the sizeable bowl-shaped anomaly, almost crashing into its still, glass-like surface. Only to be saved at the last minute by some deft, self-induced manoeuvre such as a somersault or a backflip.

The whole scene was fast and furious, entertaining, and funny. I spotted Darus; he was the star of the crowd. Each time he hit the ball they would erupt in a tumult. Luckily, he had Alana on his side; she demonstrated such deft acrobatic skills, which I have never seen before. I didn't realise that she was so supple, and I began to wonder if all Androgen possessed this ability, to flex with such legerdemain. I know that Karla was extremely flexible, as she had demonstrated this quite regularly much to my delight. But she was Celestial, which is organic based. Celestials were encouraged to practise regular training and exercise from an early age, so Karla had told me, no doubt.

My inebriety from the effects of the Black Champagne had worn off very quickly which made me wonder if it was because of its weak potency, or could it be my induced power caused by the Revelation. I was speaking casually to the barman when I decided to order another bottle. During our conversation he disappointed me by revealing that the kids drink it to experience inebriation, and when he saw my jaw drop he quickly reassured me not to worry, as this stuff is completely harmless as it is composed only of pure organic grape juice from the giant black grapevine.He said that there is no toxic alcohol present, not like the quantities and chemical content that I had to endure in my days. The ingredients provide the drinker with a simple, artificial intoxication effect that wears off quickly. Most of the fruit grown today is derived from a new form of pomology combined with crystallography, the likes of which were not available in my days. He said that the education establishments use the Black Champagne to demonstrate the effects of intoxication and to attempt to explain to the pupils the reasons why futile men of my era drank themselves to a stupor and intoxicated themselves with alcohol to such a state of illness and depression that they could no longer stand up straight. But the pupils could never understand how drinkers became addicted to the stuff, as addiction does not exist in the world today.

I must have gulped that last bottle down after he had fed me such disturbing information, and I was somewhat discouraged from sampling any more. Instead, I decided to quench my taste buds with the plethora of colourful fruit juices on offer. One after the other, one colour at a time, and each one tasted much sweeter than the Black Champagne.

"So, I see you have started the party without me?" Karla said when she had sneaked up behind me and whispered in my ear. Perhaps I should not have ordered five drinks all in one go.

I recognised her voice immediately, despite the effects of my pseudo intoxication, which was almost about to wear off. It was, somehow, a mitigating effect to that of real alcohol in my time. I turned around and smiled at her as I flung my arms around her and gave her a long kiss on her soft, warm lips as I squeezed her tightly, almost lifting her slender body off the floor.

"You two will swallow each other one day," Sophista said as she squatted down behind us to hug Alice. We ignored them until we had satisfied ourselves with our extended caress.

"What's the matter with you, Alice?" I said to the fluffy man-eater, "Why aren't you jumping up to greet me like you usually do?" I noticed that her eyes looked drowsy and watery. I pointed this out to little Sophista, who was busy greeting me with a hug.

"She had some Black Champagne," Karla said, "It is quite safe for animals, and it should wear off soon."

I knelt down to stroke her soft fur. It was satisfying and peaceful making such a connection with a beautiful, intelligent animal such as this, without the fear of being mauled, and pawed, or licked to death, in Alice's' case.

Louden did explain to me how a large proportion of the animals on earth today had effected a change in perception and behaviour. In particular, the more intelligent ones did to such a degree that they no longer feared man. However, had this phenomenon occurred in my time man would have surely taken full advantage of the situation to satiate his egocentric nature, and the only achievement gained would be the total annihilation and extinction of these innocent animals along with a variety of other species for good measure. I learnt that nearly all the animals that we had once considered wild and dangerous in my time were now tame and innocent. Some say it was the result of the effects of Ghost Crystal, initiated by intelligent Chimpanzees. Supposedly, they had somehow managed to experience the Revelation and then by miracle or nature, used their animal communication to relay this experience throughout the animal kingdom. The result caused a revolution of awareness and perception in the animal kingdom.

There must be some credibility in this theory because shortly after there were many reports of strange behaviour in individual animals, which increased rapidly throughout the world in a short space of time. These included dangerous animals, such as tigers and bears, suddenly losing their fear of man, and then gradually attempting to integrate socially with him. One incident I can recall around AD 2521, taken from the archives, involves a family who woke up one morning to find a giant grizzly bear sitting on the floor in their kitchen. The animal was seen holding a cup in its paw, just like a human, and drinking water from it, which he must have taken by himself from the kitchen sink behind him. There were no running or dripping taps to be found anywhere in the house, so it was assumed at the time that the bear, no doubt a well-mannered one, must have turned the water off after he had filled his cup.

Incidences such as these increased rapidly throughout the world, and in a few years or so, wild animals became scarce, and instead, they lived either in the wild as tame, or with humans, as pets, just like Alice.

The Black Champagne had subdued her momentarily, while I took full advantage of the caressing her massive head and neck. Her soporific state afforded me the opportunity to scrutinise her facial features in great detail without the fear of her lashing wet tongue.

"Karla, have you been out house hunting lately?" I said, suddenly, while I continued caressing Alice's soft fur.

"Newton!" She exclaimed, rather surprised, "Have you been conversing with Lord Bandersant?"

"No, Karla, but I did speak to Doctor Gabriel, just a while ago. Was it Lord Bandersant's' idea?"

"Both of them were responsible. It was meant as a surprise, Newton, but I expect Doctor Gabriel thought that you already knew of the details. It's difficult to keep any secrets here."

"I should think so too, Karla, with the amount of ESP floating around in the ether, and the Ghost Crystal," I added, but was quickly interjected by little Sophista.

"We never use Ghost Crystal for clairvoyance." She said, as she knelt beside me and began stroking Alice too in, what appeared to be, a stroking competition. I conceded, and let her win, as she seemed far more experienced in big cat stroking than I. She began her apprenticeship way back when Alice was a cub. I ruffled Sophista's hair as a gesture of my submission before I stood up.

"Life would be quite dull and unpredictable if we were to rely on discarnate entities to make decisions for us," Karla said.

"I suppose it could present problems such as evil spirits, who had a grudge, or two." I added, "The temptation for evil spirits to recreate a society like the one I used to live in would be enormous. I don't think that Ghost Crystal Clairvoyance would benefit this wonderful place in any case."

"That is why we avoid such practice here, Newton." A deep, familiar, female voice came from behind me.

"Hello again, Prangalistra," I said, as I turned to greet her. She gave me a lingering kiss on the side of the cheek, followed by a tight hug, and then she turned to Sophista to greet her with a little hug and kiss before she began a cheerful conversation with her about Alice.

"What's the matter?" I enquired when I saw Karla's covetous expression.

"She likes you, Newton." She said as she gestured to Prangalistra with folded arms.

"Karla, I am surprised at you!" I replied in a loud whisper, "Do I detect a hint of jealousy, Karla?" I took her in my arms and hugged her tightly, but only immediately after she had already delivered a playful punch to my arm.

Later on, when the Skyball game had finished, and the players were exhausted, the whole airship seemed to come to life with colourful lights, and beautiful melodious music. People in the most vivid costumes danced and drank fine wines and ate fabulous tasting food. I could imagine the view from above, with the whole airship gleaming in the twilight and looking much like a colourful, precious jewel set in a luminous sapphire sea. I was tempted to take off in my craft and fly high just to prove my presumption. However, I wasn't about to miss the grand feast, which was only that. A line of tables stretched across the centre of the main deck, from bow to stern, and draped with beautiful silk covering, on which I had witnessed the grandest banquet I had ever seen. So copious was the meat that, at first thought, I genuinely believed that those wonderful Androgen chefs had made an allowance of one whole full-sized bird for each person on board. Not to mention the fish, the Seafood, the pies, the vegetables, and a whole medley of other appetising foodstuffs that this beautiful world had to offer.

I saw no fruit or sweet cakes; there was no room on the table for desserts yet, or drinks, except for a single golden goblet at each place, for the Black Champagne, I stress. The sweet would have to wait its turn for the second sitting after the main course was voraciously devoured, and the tables cleared by the busy, industrious, Androgen waiters.

"Are you not joining them?" I asked Darus, light-heartedly, as we took our places at the long table. We chose the middle near to the balloon, below the crow's nest.

"Today, I'm a gamer, a Skyball champion," Darus announced proudly. "Not a waiter. Only on the Island, I wait. There are enough waiters here anyway, Newton."

"You don't know the results yet, Darus, so don't presume yet," Muriel replied, as she walked past him and gave him a little playful shove. She sat opposite Alana because they wished to continue their conversation about the Skyball game. They were both reasonably good players.

"What do you think of the newly discovered anti-gravitational field, Alana?" I asked her. I leant to my left, past little Sophista to get her attention.

"Did it reach your expectations, Alana?" Doctor Gabriel asked, seated opposite me to my right.

"It was deep!" Alana replied, "And so powerful."

"That is because it is natural," Doctor Gabriel said, "unlike our artificial version in the educational establishments."

"Powerful, all the same," I said, "As I witnessed recently."

"Did you play, Newton?" Cassie asked, rather excited.

"No, Cassie. I watched from the safety of the glass tunnel. It wasn't as formidable as this natural one, but they could vary the speed and velocity."

"Even the maximum setting would not equal the power of this natural field," Prangalistra added, as she gave me a broad smile from where she was sitting, directly opposite me. I caught a nudge from Karla to my right. She whispered in my ear.

"Why is she sitting directly opposite you?" She asked. But I sensed a playful tone in her voice.

"You are sitting opposite Doctor Gabriel," I whispered back to her, "should I have any cause for concern there, Karla?"

A sudden, distant cheer emanated from the stern, on my right, and it increased as it travelled towards us, and then it faded.

"They must be serving up the Champagne," Doctor Gabriel said, rubbing his hands together.

"Is it the black?" I asked.

"Oh no, Newton, this is the best one," he replied. "It is made on Louden's ranch. Trust me, Newton you will like it."

Two waiters descended upon us from nowhere, both carrying a silver tray with several black bottles, which I presumed to be the Black Champagne. Sure enough, they began filling each golden goblet in turn. Later on, we proposed a toast for something important like a hearty and sumptuous meal before tucking into the delightful spread. About halfway through, when our mouths were far too full to speak or make conversation of any kind, Sophista stood up and proposed a toast to her pet tiger, Alice. After much laughter from our full mouths, little Pranga decided to propose one for me. She said, 'may the traveller have a safe journey back to his world', or something of that ilk, which I could not recall exactly, because of the mayhem and the laughter that followed. I had lost count of the number of golden goblets I had poured down my throat that night. This stuff was good. It wasn't so potent like the Black Champagne, and it didn't cause any temporary inebriation either. Its natural chemical combination succeeded in delivering an overall feeling of euphoria without any detrimental effects on the body. The result enhanced one's awareness, perception, and assertiveness to such a level as to transform an introvert into a gregarious extrovert.

If I had Louden's recipe, and I was scheduled to return to my world, that would be the one thing that I would take back with me, along with a few crates of the champagne too, of course. Darus laughed when I told him my supposed plan of becoming a Champagne mogul.

"First of all, you would need to become a time traveller, and secondly, you could not make our white Champagne in your polluted world." He said, somewhat seriously.

Doctor Gabriel agreed with him, and then he demystified my idea even further with geological facts, which he said pertained to specific climate and soil conditions peculiar to that region alone, and not found anywhere else on earth. And he also added, for good measure, that it would take a holocaust, followed by a geological reformation, to occur and continue transforming the surface for over a period of half a millennium to replicate such conditions to successfully grow this type of grape to produce this particular Champagne.

I was in a Psychological state never experienced before, due to the natural substances contained in the fruit, and the process, which affected the result. Prangalistra assured me that this was harmless as long as you kept away from the edge of the ship. I learned later that one of the side effects of this natural elixir was the sudden urge to jump into deep water. I have seen the formidable vortex they called the Skyball arena, and I didn't fancy my chances in there, not after I was informed that the ocean floor was at least fifty thousand feet beneath our feet. A surprising increase in depth, I later learnt, caused by the terrain reformation, which ended in AD 2414. I finished the last mouthful of champagne and refilled the goblet with a pleasant, passive fruit juice.

When we were done eating and drinking, the tables were cleared of main course leftovers, which were very few, and then replaced with cakes and sweets, and tropical fruit of various delicious and appetising varieties. I knew that these were natural, and more nutritious than any of the fruit from my time on earth because Karla had told me, in detail. She was an expert on food. She consumed copious amounts, in particular, the sweet variety, without even gaining a grain of extra weight. Unlike most of the population in my time who ate such food on a regular basis, and unfortunately had suffered the consequences in the form of diabetes, obesity, tooth decay, and all other detrimental diet-related ailments associated with sweet, desirable, and irresistible foods.

Karla would tell me that there was nothing unfortunate about it, as these were natural, organic foods, so long as you kept them so. It was man's greed for profit that motivated him to make dangerous additions and subtractions to its nutrient content rendering it inedible and, at the same time, making it commercially marketable. She always said to me that, his most significant mistake was his desire for greed and profit, instead of health and well-being.

Right at this moment, I was holding her in my arms, close to me, dancing on the shiny deck to sweet, slow, romantic music. All the food had been consumed by now, and the tables and chairs had been cleared away rather quickly by an army of Androgen waiters, leaving the deck free for dancers. Prangalistra and Doctor Gabriel were intertwined and moved rhythmically to the beat of the music. Darus and Alana were dancing to a rhythm that was slightly ahead of the beat. I also caught a glimpse of bright orange and black stripes lying on the deck under the gondola, next to the mast, and somebody's hand, I presume to be that of little Sophista, stroking the subdued cat. I just hope she hadn't consumed any of the champagne!

I was looking up at the huge balloon, which kept the vessel hovering in the air just above sea level, and I wondered how high and fast this beast was capable of reaching if it were to be let loose at maximum thrust.

"Nowhere near the speed of your spacecraft, Newton." A voice said to me, which I thought was somebody playing an ESP trick on me until I discovered that it was Doctor Gabriel, he and Prangalistra still entwined but now moving much slower on the dance floor, had sneaked into my field of view from my blind side. Karla had her head against mine, which obscured my left eye completely.

"Are you going back to the Island, Newton?" He asked.

"Not until I've seen that beautiful house that Karla's been telling me about," I replied.

"And then what?"

246

"More exploration, I guess. I will do some lecturing in the educational establishment with Professor Anne and Professor Stagston, in between, but there is a lot more I need to know about this world first."

"Yes, Newton, there is always a lot to learn, I understand, but who in this world today has more experience about life than yourself? Almost a thousand years?"

"During most of that time, I was asleep in suspension. I can hardly attribute those lost years to experience unless I have total recall. Who knows where my spirit had travelled during that period?"

"Newton, time moves much slower in the spiritual realms due to the higher vibration of matter. Every hour you spend in Heaven is equal to forty-one years in the material world, on earth. Although you have been asleep on earth for almost a millennia, your time in the spiritual realms merely equates to about twenty-two hours."

"I understand that, Doctor Gabriel that is why I wish to learn more."

"Where will you go to learn more except to consult the Ghost Crystal?"

"I spoke to Nesasigamany earlier on today about the Luna Region."

"You won't find any answers there, Newton, only antiques from the past, and other dusty vestiges, perhaps."

"What about the creation process of the Celestials, and the manufacturing of Ghost Crystal?"

"Most of our manufacturing is carried out in the Luna Region, Newton, that much is true. And, yes, there is an Androgen facility there too, and indeed, a Celestial one but they are sealed and secure. We have no idea of the details or methods that they use to process things up there; we leave that in the capable hands of the Androgen. They continue to demonstrate, quite flawlessly, their true capability and complete trustworthiness of the handling of all of the earth's manufacturing process, as they have done so for years. It is not in our interest to interfere with anything they do up there in that region. No Androgen can permit you entry to any of the manufacturing facilities, and in any case, Newton you would not survive in the chambers as they are considered hostile environments."

"Hostile?" I exclaimed, rather surprised. "They have weapons?"

He laughed. "No, Newton, the dangers you face are not from weapons, or hostile Androgen, as no such thing exists in this solar system. Your only concern would be the dangers within the manufacturing chambers if you were to attempt to enter any of them to observe the process. The chambers are pressurised vacuums, and some contain ionised gases similar to the basic plasma, which your ancestors used in early experiments but a more highly developed form, which is so precarious that any bodily contact would cause the entire human body to vaporise instantaneously."

"I have no intention of entering any of the manufacturing chambers, doctor Gabriel. It would be of no benefit to me to know or study the process of Ghost Crystal production. My only concern is with my ancestors, and the hope of finding any evidence they may have left in connection with scientific research or experiments which relate to life support systems."

"You won't find much up there, Newton. We don't even have any details in our archives concerning activity on the Luna Region in the past, especially in your time. Your basic, primitive craft was rather cumbersome and highly inefficient with fuel consumption, dangerous too! And so slow, it took days just to travel there from earth. All you will find there are ruins of a crude space station, which we filled in and used as a secure foundation for our manufacturing chambers when they were constructed about one hundred years ago."

"Well my trip shall be a short fly by then, Doctor Gabriel," I said, as I swung Karla around twice, and then pulled her towards me in time with the end of the music.

"Take me home, Newton," a very sleepy voice whispered in my ear.

"I thought you Celestials were immune to tiredness." I quipped.

"Newton, Celestials are not immune to the effects of Black Champagne," she whispered.

"They would be if they didn't drink so much of it," I replied, and I almost let go of her in my feeble attempt to fend off one of her playful punches. She paid me with one more, on the other arm, for being so careless.

Karla was so tired from the combined effects of excessive champagne and dancing that she was unable to make it to the craft without a little assistance from my good self. I received another playful punch on the arm from her when I jested and said, 'it was a good thing one of us had adopted some self-control tonight'. Her condition was not likely to persist, as the effects usually wear off in a few hours, even less for a tough little Celestial like her. Although I must admit, I have never seen her yet in such condition, since the day we had met, after drinking champagne. However, this was no ordinary champagne. It was Louden's champagne.

I had to carry her into the spacecraft and then strap her into her seat before taking off from the balloon. I was right; the balloon did look magnificent from the air with all its colourful lights glowing. Even the fabric of the balloon was illuminated by a multitude of soft rays, which emanated from various angles around the deck, and I presume the upper decks. It was somewhat difficult to spot exactly where the source of light had come from because there were no straight beams to follow. The light did not behave obediently like it did in my time, not in this advanced century. They had defeated such laws of science, which we had worshipped slavishly for years without even thinking of other possibilities. They could make the light bend, twist, and turn in all directions before it found its target, which resulted in a more pleasing and exciting display.

Karla wanted a comfortable bed and a large glass of guava juice, she said it would help her condition and revive her. She also expressed her reluctance to travel the long distance back to the City anyway. Even the temptation of spending our first night in our new home was not enough to persuade her to consider suffering the arduous journey, as one could only cruise at a steady speed at night. In the end, we decided to return to our floating piece of luxury that we had recently become accustomed to, for now.

I climbed high into the night sky in the hope that I would spot the lights of the Island. A little, tired voice gave me specific instructions to head south and look for the laser hologram in the sky. She baffled me greatly with her power of perception. How Karla managed to know such detailed information concerning our exact position, speed, and trajectory, while she had her head tilted back, and her eyes tightly closed, I know for sure that she didn't open them once, while under the influence of potent champagne, I shall never know. I decided not to challenge her while she was half asleep; instead I headed south, and after a few minutes sure enough, I caught sight of the giant hologram in the sky below us, which clearly marked the exact position of that most welcoming floating paradise, the Island.

CHAPTER 12

The Luna Region

There was definitely something very different about this morning. I tried hard to think what, exactly, but to no avail. Admittedly, not the effects of last night's Black Champagne, I hope. I had stopped drinking long before Karla and had cautiously, and cravenly, reverted to the fresh fruit juice instead. I was well enough this morning to physically carry her all the way from the park, where I had docked the spacecraft, and to our cabin, the honeymoon suite. I can't remember ever stopping on the way, or putting her down anywhere and leaving her unattended for any length of time. With that thought in my mind, I reached over to her side of the bed and pulled the silk sheet gently away from her head, only to reveal her appealing light, golden blonde hair. I needed no further confirmation that she was indeed my little Karla. There was no requirement to deliberately prod or poke her to cause her to stir in her restful sleep, just to catch a glimpse of her flawless face, her beautiful slender lips, or her gorgeous emerald green eyes, only to satisfy my curiosity.

I got out of bed slowly and quietly trying my best not to alert Karla. I noticed two large crystal jugs on her bedside table. One of them was empty, and the other contained a drop of colourful liquid, which I recognised immediately as Guava juice. Did she consume two jugs? I asked myself in a silent whisper. Then I spotted an empty glass on my table with a trace of the same liquid. I swallowed it and confirmed that it too contained the sweet Guava juice. We must have had a jug each this morning. Outside looked much brighter than usual, and much more colourful also, as I walked out through the open glass door, into the patio area. The water in the pool looked still and bright, and deep blue, just like the vivid colours in a dream. I remember that I had experienced a similar feeling in this very place, in this room, the Honeymoon Suite, when Darus first showed me around. Could it be spiritual? I thought to myself, but there are no hauntings on earth. All ghosts had left the earth plane in AD 2599. Could it be due to my recently developed, enhanced awareness of the second Revelation, or perhaps a spirit communication? They don't necessarily need to be on earth to contact us. Maybe I need to consult the Ghost Crystal to find out, as my Extra Sensual Perception may be too weak to effect a successful communication?

I walked to the end of the patio and looked out at the ocean. The water appeared strange too, as it seemed much calmer than usual as if the waves had subdued temporarily for a particular reason. Its colour was of a more profound blue than that of the pool; it was as if I was looking at it through an optical colour filter. I decided that this unique strangeness was indeed a subtle sign, and I needed to communicate to find out more, but was in two minds whether to wake Karla and take her with me or just leave her here to sleep. She looked so peaceful, in her little world; I decided that it would be better to leave her where she was for now, as I wasn't planning on being out too long, and she needed the rest after all that Champagne last night.

I made my way down to the lower levels of the vessel to one of the more lively areas, which reminded me of a particular street back in the city, where I had strolled along with Karla on the night before the first Revelation. It was alive with friendly, happy faces; each had their good reasons to be cheerful. But none were sad at all, not here in this beautiful place.

The restaurants and bars were full of spiritually affluent beings, all in merry conversation about important matters. Nothing was heard or mentioned about money, greed, power, or other earthly issues of the past, only issues about the well being of the body, spiritual development and awareness, and growth to develop a higher consciousness, were discussed here. I wasn't so eager, previous to the Revelation, as I am now to involve myself in such matters, which I had limited knowledge of at that time. Now, after the second Revelation, I can proudly admit that I had managed to liberate myself entirely from the, aptly named, 'Monkey Mind' which now left me free to concentrate on developing qualities such as unconditional love, joy, self-honesty, modesty, and humility.

I tried my best to explain this to Nesasigamany when I caught up with him in one of the breakfast restaurants. I walked past rather slowly, as I had found myself deliberately procrastinating yet again so that I could admire the magnificent architecture. I heard somebody call my name, as I was looking up at the façade. I spotted a hooded man sitting at one of the tables on the terrace. I guessed he had just finished a hearty breakfast because he had a large, empty plate in front of him.

"Isn't it a bit warm to be wearing a hoodie, isn't it?" I asked, and then I realised that he might not be familiar with the twenty-first-century term. I was correct in my assumption.

"Wearing a what, Newton?" He replied, looking somewhat perplexed.

"Why do you cover your head in this heat?" I asked.

"I dwell on the Luna Region, Newton, the dark side. We have no sun there, only artificial crystal light. I am not accustomed to all this bright sun."

I sat down at his table to join him for a coffee and a chat. Before I could land in the comfortable soft chair, a waiter approached carrying a tray with coffee and two cups, which he set down on the table, and he promptly took away the empty breakfast plate.

"Well, one of you must have read my mind," I said, as I made myself comfortable. I reached for the coffee. "Are you leaving for the Luna Region today?" I asked him because he appeared to be dressed and ready for a voyage.

"I changed my plans and decided to leave early this morning." He replied.

"So what happened, Nesasigamany?"

"There's a problem with the craft."

I was astounded to hear him deliver such a negative remark in such a near perfect world as this. All my hopes and dreams of a trouble-free world where nothing ever goes wrong, because of the high level of technologically advanced perfection, which they developed and had mastered some time ago. "Nesasigamany, how could you have a problem with the craft? They are almost infallible."

"It's not so much the craft that has the problem, but it is what's inside it, Newton." He took a long mouthful of coffee, while I waited patiently in anticipation for the rest of his explanation, which I half expected to be a portentous one.

"What exactly did you find inside the craft, Nesasigamany?" I asked, impatiently.

"Nothing, inside the craft, Newton, but inside the photon jets, there was an obstruction. The drive system was choked with silicon dioxide fine glass dust from the Luna surface, and some small rocks as well, which had larger glass crystals embedded in them. I have two Strict-Androgen working on it now. They said that when they started the engines this morning, the photon jets fired into the crystal in the rock debris and caused the photon beam to refract, which resulted in internal fission in the engine. I don't think that we will be going anywhere today."

"Where is the craft now?"

"On Louden's balloon, out in the Pacific Ocean."

"Those Androgen you spoke of, the strict type, are they allowed to leave the Luna Region?"

"No, Newton," he replied in a whisper, "they only work under strict conditions, in vacuums, under water, and in other dangerous environments where the risk of contamination is high. They are not even allowed to leave the Luna Region."

"I did wonder how you managed to complete all the dirty work here in this wonderful clean place. I presume that these Androgen are responsible for the tunnelling work for the subterranean transport system?"

"I believe so, Newton, about one hundred years ago, work began and is still going on today. Your primitive folk had excavated some too, back in the twenty-first century, inside the disruptive zone, but your kin used old machinery and methods to disturb the terrain. Your bombs did not do much to help either."

"I'm sorry, Nesasigamany, on behalf of my primitive kinfolk, for messing up your terrain with our antediluvian machines," I said with a slight hint of light-heartedness and jest, "but it wasn't us who honeycombed the world with tunnels to build an underground railway system. What happened to all the roads that we constructed anyway?"

He waved his hand in a dismissive gesture, "You polluted the air with your land vehicles, and we weren't going to follow you down that same route and slavishly repeat history, not in Heaven. We abandoned the roads long ago and gave the land back to nature. Taking to the skies as a natural means of transportation for all would have been chaotic. We achieved more efficiency with electromagnetic technology, and we had much-improved tunnelling machines with crystal laser cutters that could cut through rock with great ease, and with no waste, as everything is compressed back into the walls, so there is no extracting, or additional tunnel lining required."

"That is highly ingenious," I said, with excitement, "I would like to see one of the tunnels, to feel its walls. They must be as smooth as glass."

"Even smoother, Newton, and super water-tight too, but you can't see one, not here on earth. You cannot gain access to the tunnels; it is far too dangerous to go down there. Those golden pods can cover a distance of one thousand miles or so in a matter of minutes. You wouldn't want to be hit by one of those, Newton! Unless you desire to become a portrait on the smooth, shiny tunnel wall."

I was curious to know more. I poured us more coffee; its fresh, natural taste aroused my power of perception. The waiter brought us a variety of fresh cream cakes on a tray and set them down on our table.

"Can you show me the disruptive zone, Nesasigamany?"

He laughed, with a face full of fresh cream. "You have already seen it, Newton."

I thought for a moment that he was joking yet again. I stared at him for a brief second in the hope that he would give up and admit his fooling around, and break out in a smile. I could have waited forever. Only his most serious visage graced his face. He was truly serious.

"During the Revelation?" I asked, curiously.

"No, way before that — You were found in a place deep in the sub-terrain, as I have been told by others, in a land, which was once given the name, The United Kingdom."

It was his turn now to stare at my dumbfounded expression, as he awaited my reaction to the confusing information that he had just given me.

"You found me in the United Kingdom? I cannot recall any memory of my country of origin, although I had been under the assumption that I was from the United Kingdom, nor can anyone here recognise my origin from my accent, because you don't have indigenous accents or dialect like we had all those years ago. So I have been told by Doctor Gabriel. Nesasigamany, do you have any other information in the archives which relate to where you found me?"

He thought deeply for a time, and then just as I was about to engross myself with optimism, he grabbed another cream cake and took a large bite of it and began chewing it devotedly. I just resigned myself to patiently wait as he devoured the whole cake piecemeal, at the rate of one pleasurable mouthful at a time. In the meantime, I would just sit there and admire the tranquil scene, and watch the happy people going past the restaurant.

"Newton," he said, eventually, just as he was about to swallow the last piece of cake, "I was in the area where we found you just after Lord Bandersant removed your body from the life support pod, or whatever the contraption was that he found you in. I can distinctly recall that there was a high reading of seismic activity in that area. A sinkhole, or something similar, caused the terrain to collapse, so we were unable to retrieve anything else."

"Nesasigamany," I pleaded, "was there anything else that you can remember – like markings, words or symbols on the pod?"

"Newton, we had to get out of there quickly, we had no time to read signs."

"So there were signs?"

"Newton, I can't remember any details….

"You must try to remember, Nesasigamany, it is important that I know about my past. I have tried consulting the spirits through Ghost Crystal, but all I get from them is cryptic clues, and they don't seem to know much about me or my past, to tell me anything of importance."

"Newton, you waste your time with the spirits. An ignorant man, who walks the earth, when he dies and crosses over to the other side, is still an ignorant man, until he learns differently through higher spiritual development. The mere act of crossing over to the spiritual realms does not guarantee enlightenment. Even those unenlightened men in your time, Newton, they have all died, but even now they may still be, to this very day, without spiritual advancement. How do you think they are going to be able to help you here on earth, when they cannot even help themselves in the afterlife?"

"I will find a spirit with the answers, Nesasigamany, I must find one. I am on my way to the theatre to consult the Ghost Crystal right now."

He waved his hand, dismissively once again. "Newton, you want answers about your past, then look at material things of the past. Your ancestors used the Luna Region as a base, and perhaps you should look there for your answers."

"I was informed that nothing exists on the moon from our past anymore, except your manufacturing, and the mining."

"Yes, Newton, you are correct, but your corrupt thugs from the past used the old base as a storage facility for their disgusting, murderous weapons, as well as a crude facility for their futile experiments."

"Experiments?" I exclaimed, in surprise.

He waved his hands again, this time both arms flayed the air, with dismissive vigour, "No, Newton, don't go asking me any questions about the activities of your corrupt ancestors. I know nothing about their insane practices in the Luna Region."

"Take me there, Nesasigamany!" I insisted, vehemently.

"I'm not going anywhere today, Newton, my spacecraft is out of action, remember? I have Strict Androgen working on it right now."

I stood up immediately, "OK, I will take you there in my craft, Nesasigamany. You can show me the way."

All the way to my ship, and halfway through our journey to the Luna Region, while we were travelling through space at around two hundred thousand miles per hour, Nesasigamany had repeated himself several times about his reluctance to divulge any information to me about the Luna Region. He also added that both King and Queen Fulk would share their passionate disapproval of an earth human visiting their domain.

"Are they Androgen, or Celestials?" I asked him.

"Oh, neither," he replied, succinctly.

"So they must be humans?" I said, tentatively, slightly concerned with his sanity at this stage.

"Not really," Nesasigamany replied.

It was at this stage that I almost lost my own. I was in two minds whether to go to light speed to get there faster before he lost his mind completely, then he would be no use to me at all. In the end, I decided against it, as it would not be safe to do so on such a short distance, as the possibilities and danger of a collision with satellites and other obstructions would be significantly increased, especially in unknown areas such as the less attractive dark side of the Luna Region. I am genuinely the proud pilot of an un-crashable spacecraft, a degree of caution will still need to be upheld, respected, and regarded.

"All right, Nesasigamany, no procrastinating now, I want you to show me exactly where our location is so that I can land this craft." I insisted, as soon as we neared what I believed to be our destination after much aimless orbiting around the dark side of the Luna Region.

The instruments were not functioning correctly at all, which was slightly frustrating. They all seemed to be going crazy. None of them was responding to the terrain. It was as if someone, or something, had been deliberately scrambling all the sensors, in a sinister bid to prevent any craft from landing.

"How do you manage your craft, Nesasigamany, do you have this much trouble coming home each time?" I asked him.

"Newton, it is not for the eyes of man to see such things as our delicate manufacturing operation here in the Luna Region. Do you think that they are just going to invite you here with open arms? Besides, I don't get out much, and my craft is certainly much smoother than this one."

"Hang on tight!" I shouted, and just then I suddenly decided that it was time to stop this perpetual orbiting, and buffeting around, above this barren ball of rock and quickly find somewhere to land. I descended rapidly, in the hope that he would recognise something, which would jog his memory. I could see the concern in his eyes, as he gripped his seat tightly.

"Take it easy, Newton, they will see us. You're flying too low."

"And what do you suppose they will do, Nesasigamany, fire lasers at us? This earth is Heaven now, and there is no aggression here."

"This is the Luna Region, Newton. It is not the region of or for humans to rule over like on earth. Your rules apply on your planet, not here in the Luna Region."

"Oh come now, Nesasigamany, you talk as if you were born on this barren rock. It is not a habitable planet. It is just a satellite of silicon and iron."

"It controls your tides, on your earth." He quipped.

"Our earth, Nesasigamany. The one thing you don't have is air. How are we going to get into these buildings, we can't just get out and go and knock on the door?"

"Don't despair, Newton, we may not have an atmosphere like you, but we have plenty of air. We need to find an airlock to fly into and dock the spacecraft, that is why we have the Strict Androgen."

"How are they doing? Are they still with us?" I asked, as I looked out of the clear front and roof canopy for signs of life, but could see none.

We had flown by and collected the two Strict Androgen from Nesasigamany's damaged craft, on Louden's balloon, just before we began our journey to the Luna Region. In spite of having the exact physical appearance of Androgen, the Strict type were more robust, designed specifically for industrial use only, to work in dangerous and hazardous conditions where humans would not be able to survive for more than two seconds. These resistant humanoids were accustomed to such conditions, so were not permitted to hop into, or onto, any spacecraft and travel anywhere with humans or Celestials, and indeed ordinary Androgen. They were not even allowed to visit the earth for any reason for fear of contamination. Nesasigamany's spaceship was explicitly designed for the transportation of Strict Androgen, but they were required only to travel on the outside of the craft on a specially constructed pod.

My little spacecraft was not designed to carry stowaways on the inside, let alone on the outside. I was particularly worried about the fact that the Strict Androgen would not be able to hold on to anything out there. There was no provision for external travelling passengers, or even worse, they might damage a vital part of the craft with excessive force, which they had in abundance, being of the industrial grade. They only had to squeeze something a little too tight to cause extensive damage to the delicate apparatus, such as the cooling tubes, and as a result, we would witness Androgen and ship debris floating away into space.

Luckily this was not the case. It was confirmed when I found the button for the external cameras, a button which I could have made good use of if only I had discovered it when I took the craft out on its first voyage. Lord Bandersant couldn't show me all the controls, as they were far too complicated and too numerous to explain in every detail. I had to discover and master them in my own time, which I have accomplished quite successfully up to now.

We spotted the two figures, in dark suits, both Strict Androgen outside of the spacecraft, each with their hands flat against the fuselage. I learnt later that they had used some form of powerful magnetic induction from the crafts' engines to secure themselves safely onto the smooth surface of the fuselage.

"Look! Down there!" Nesasigamany shouted suddenly, as he pointed to a cluster of buildings, and a large rusty looking door with some faded markings on the front of it. I could see the door, but the markings were too far for me to make them out. I informed Nesasigamany that I was about to go in closer to get a better view. I made my descent to about three hundred feet above the surface, and then circled slowly around that area.

"Nesasigamany, what can you see?"

"Down there! On that cargo bay door; I have seen those markings before."

"What is this place?" I asked.

"It's the old test facility. I have never been in there, Newton. It is probably not guarded; we have no use for such a place anymore. I believe that your people used it for storage."

"Can we open it?"

"I will send the Strict Androgen down on a preliminary investigation, and to see if they can open it."

The two Androgen, as soon as he gave them the order via a small illuminated crystal tablet, which he withdrew from his pocket. They immediately released themselves from the craft and, like a pair of eagles swooping down on their prey, they descended to the surface and landed gracefully on their feet close to the vast cargo bay door. They proceeded, without hesitation towards the control panel on the side of the frame.

After much button pressing, we heard a loud clunk, and then a creak, and to our surprise, the vast cargo door began to open. Like an over-sized garage door, it opened upwards groaning and creaking all the way until it was at its maximum, agape so full as that of some giant moon serpent that had just emerged from deep within the Luna crust in search of food. My spacecraft.

The cessation of the flashing beacon was promptly followed by a steady green light, which was my cue to begin my entry into the mouth of this vast unknown. I didn't wait for Nesasigamany to invite me to enter; I just steered the ship in through the huge opening at a very slow speed, taking care not to cause any unforeseen collision, which could cause damage to the craft. That was until Nesasigamany, using his best tone of sarcasm, informed me that I have more than enough clearance on all sides to accommodate a whole fleet of medium-sized spacecraft.

"Just land on there, Newton." He said pointing to a large raised platform in the middle of the huge space inside. When I had turned the craft about to face the bay doors, I brought it down gently onto the platform, and then I shut off the engines.

"It is advisable to wait a while until the atmosphere equalises before we can leave the ship," Nesasigamany said, as he caressed with his light tablet. "The Strict Androgen will wait here with the craft while we go and take a look around. I shall call them if we need them."

"Shouldn't we take them with us for protection?" I asked, with a hint of urgency.

"Protection from what, Newton?" There is no life in this sector, only relics from the people from your era, and their primitive machines. Besides, the air was regenerated and pumped through just a while ago, when the Strict Androgen initialised the cargo doors. No organic life forms can survive down here without oxygen."

"It's not the organic ones that I am concerned about," I told him, but he did not answer.

Nesasigamany informs me that there exists a crystal generator on the sunny side of the Luna Region, which provides enough energy to supply and run the entire base, including the manufacturing sector, which was about one mile from where we had landed. This area, although it could be reached via the vast network of underground tunnels beneath us, it was most definitely out of bounds to humans. I wasn't too concerned about that; I just wanted to find and explore the test facility.

When it was safe to leave the craft, I held my breath through fear of suddenly being sucked out just as soon as I opened the door of the craft.

"That is impossible, Newton," Nesasigamany retorted, when I told him, "Your spacecraft would never allow you to open the doors under such perilous conditions outside of it. There is a great deal of advanced technology built into this little craft, Newton, far more than you can even begin to comprehend."

"Well, thanks for putting my mind at rest, Nesasigamany," I quipped, as I followed him through the door and onto the landing gantry. The area was vast; it had apparently been used as a cargo depot for ships travelling to and from earth at one time. These ships must have been truly enormous, as everything we see before us must have come from earth at one stage. Nesasigamany laughed, of course, I did expect him to.

"The ships of the past were large, true, Newton, but they were also cumbersome and slow, and they consumed a lot of dangerous, highly combustible fuel. Perhaps you haven't seen a large cargo ship of today? I don't doubt it because they are rather scarce and only required when a vast amount of material needs to be transported to and from the Luna Region for example. Newton, these modern cargo ships are one-quarter of a mile in length."

He made me laugh now. The sound of it reverberated down the narrow corridor, which led to a large elevator at the end of it. I suggested that we used the stairs, but Nesasigamany doubted my choice of transport. I was soon in full agreement with his decision once he had informed me that there was the slight possibility that we might have to descend to a depth of one hundred feet or more. My only concern was with the safety and reliability of this ancient contraption. He reassured me that the elevator was powered and controlled by modern, up-to-date technology and that it was genuinely reliable and safe. He waited until we were inside and descending at high speed before he mentioned that he could not guarantee its structural condition, as it was so old, and hardly ever maintained.

We dropped down to one hundred feet, or more within a space of a few seconds, and found ourselves in another chamber leading into a long corridor, which was reminiscent of a scene from one of those scary science fiction films that I used to watch back in my days. Any minute now, I expected to see a large, hideous creature emerge from the crystal lit, shadowy coves. But I saw nothing but shadows and encountered nothing along the way but airlock doors, which Nesasigamany, with his magic light tablet and dextrous Androgen fingers, managed to defeat every time. I sighed with relief at the hissing-clunk sound of each two-tonne door he vanquished. I was thinking of Karla, and my idyllic lifestyle back on earth, in the Heaven, which man had finally managed to create. I was in a semi tranquil state, thinking of all the good memories, while my sub-conscious was busy controlling my body, just walking along the never-ending corridor when I was awakened and startled by a voice.

"Shhhh!" Nesasigamany suddenly interjected as he stopped abruptly without any warning.

My heart leapt. I could feel it beating hard against my shirt. "What is it?" I whispered loudly.

He retrieved his light tablet from his pocket. "I can hear something, like a humming sound."

"Is it a Strict Androgen?" I asked in a whisper, which was hardly audible.

"There are no Androgen down here, Newton – Wait! It is coming from in here! This way!" He moved slowly towards a door, which was hidden in one of the coves on the right side of the corridor. He looked through the round glass porthole at the top of the door, but he didn't reveal to me what he saw. I could only read the fear on his face.

I held my breath and decided to take a look for myself. I slowly approached the glass porthole with great caution, in fear of what I was about to witness through the soiled, obscured glass. This glass was no thirtieth-century clear crystal; it was tainted, scratched, and worn like the glass of the twenty-first century. This part of the facility was ancient to those earth dwellers of this century. To me, the scratches and the dirty glass were indicative of my past, the one that I had a limited memory of.

What I witnessed through the porthole was a terrifying testament to my past, but I had positive memories of such things. I could recall them as well as create them vaguely in my mind. I wanted to get inside to see more, but I needed first to eliminate stiff opposition from the gatekeeper.

"It's an abomination in the eyes of the Lord," Nesasigamany preached to me, "You should be aware of that, Newton. You have seen the Revelation."

"Yes, Nesasigamany, I understand fully, but I need answers, or all this will have been in vain."

"Why, Newton? You cannot take them back to earth with you, they brought shame on mankind and caused death and destruction, that is why they were brought here and locked away for all eternity."

"And here they will stay, Nesasigamany. Do you think for a moment that I would risk everything I have on earth now? And for what? Money? It no longer exists. Power? It is no longer required. Wealth? I already have it, in abundance. How about greed? Am I about to risk everything for the sake of greed? No, Nesasigamany, I already have everything that I need on earth to make my life as comfortable as it can ever be, and I am truly happy. I am living in a world that is so perfect, a world that men in my time could only dream about; some even doubted, with passion, that a perfect way of life on earth was impossible, just as they doubted the abolition of currency, which they argued could never be achievable. I am truly fortunate to be in a position where I can look back and observe, and learn from these wonderful achievements, and hopefully pass on the important lessons of ignorance, scepticism, and greed, and persuade your good people not to make the same mistakes as we did in the past. Nesasigamany, do you know what the most important thing of all that I desire to preserve more than anything else in this Heavenly world is?" I paused for a moment, while he was in deep thought, deciding whether to grant me access to death and then I continued, "It is Peace, Nesasigamany, precious peace!"

He nodded in agreement with a smile, and then, without further hesitation, he approached the door and, without uttering another word, produced his light tablet, and offered it up to the door controller panel. The sound of the bolts in the stable steel door could be heard reverberating off the walls and down through the long, empty corridor, only to be dissipated throughout the vast labyrinth beyond.

My heart was racing fast, why, I do not know, or I wasn't entirely sure. Whether it was through fear, expectation, or excitement, I could not discern. Nesasigamany chose not to enter the room with me. He sat on the floor outside in the corridor with his head in his hands lamenting over the wretchedness of mankind. He left me, by my volition, to enter the den of evil, but not before I had pledged mankind not to touch anything, or take anything from this room. He insisted that nothing shall pass over the threshold of the opening where the two feet thick, solid metal door hung, ajar, awaiting my return, and speedy exit, in case of some accidental or unforeseen incident. I agreed readily, because of some of these monsters, apart from looking quite menacing, appeared frighteningly heavy too. I was in no mood to attempt to disturb any of them for fear of awakening them.

There was a sudden flash of light, which startled me at first until I realised that it was just the automatic lighting kicking in. It was at that moment that the sinister secret of this vast storage facility had suddenly revealed itself fully. The light revealed row upon row of cages, each of them stacked with warheads, the very weapons of mass destruction. I kept on reminding myself that I was living on earth, in an idyllic world, analogous to Heaven. Heaven on earth, to be more precise, in a world populated with angelic beings, who had managed, over some years, to eradicate war, along with the seven deadly sins, Lust, Gluttony, Greed, Sloth, Wrath, Envy, and Pride. Those virtuous inhabitants, fed up with war, must have gathered the entire world stock of deadly weapons and brought them all here to this dark, desolate place, where they could be safely locked away from the wicked, devilish hands of the malevolent warmongers, forever.

So abundant in number were the large steel cages, each one taller than a man and stacked ten or twenty high. My eyes tried to focus, and they ached and strained as I challenged myself to read as many labels as I could in the limited time I had. I scanned each tag while walking briskly from cage to cage. Each warhead displayed the familiar nuclear symbol. I reached in to touch one; its cold metallic surface sent an icy shiver down my spine. These metallic monoliths were responsible for the demise of my old world; my family, my friends, my wife and children, if ever I had them, or better still, if I was able to remember the love and the happiness we had once shared in my long forgotten fragile world.

I soon gave up trying to read every single label when I discovered something on the side of each cage, and instead, I began to rush from cage to cage to save more time. All my fears were confirmed. I noticed that this marking was a small sticker label on the side of each cage printed with a flag for each country of origin. I saw Russia, on the first one, the United States, on the next one, and then subsequently, France, China, the United Kingdom, Pakistan, India, Israel, and North Korea, by the time I had gone much further into the room. There was another section in the place, on the opposite wall to the cages, which contained shelves; a complete wall of deep steel shelving, stacked with long, steel containers arranged neatly in rows. Each container had a label on the end with a printed schematic photo of a particular firearm. There were hundreds of boxes stored higher than the light could reach, giving the illusion that the stack continued into infinity and beyond. I didn't even begin to count the variety of weapons depicted on each label, and there was no indication of the quantity that each container held. There were handguns, rifles, bazookas, and others, which I did not recognise, probably because they were invented some years after the nuclear holocaust, presumably while I was still in a deep sleep.

I had seen enough of this devil's den of death and destruction. I cherished my blessings and good fortune that I was not present to witness the final nuclear holocaust, the war that ended all wars, and with that thought, my desire to return to my Heavenly paradise of peace and tranquillity grew even stronger.

I can fully understand now why Nesasigamany was so reluctant to open the door to this Godforsaken temple of doom and destruction, and of his refusal to even cross its threshold. With that thought in my mind, I made a futile apology for man's iniquity to man, and then I prayed and asked earnestly for Divine love, direct from the Great Spirit. I hastily made my way back to Nesasigamany, whom I found still seated in the same position, on the floor in the corridor, where I had left him.

"Seal this up, Nesasigamany!" I shouted to him, as I bolted out into the corridor, "I never want to see this den of destruction, ever again. No human shall ever cross this threshold or look upon this deadly cargo!"

He quickly rose to his feet, "Newton, I told you that in the beginning, that is why this treacherous cargo remains here, locked away safely out of the reach of mankind." He said. But he had a worried look on his face, and he kept looking at his light tablet, and each time he did so his worried face turned into a troubled one.

We moved further down the corridor and eventually came to another door, which was similar in design to the one for the weapons store, but this one was smaller.

"Oh no," I said with a deep sigh, "not more weapons, please."

But Nesasigamany did not reply. Instead, he was staring inquisitively at the door. But I saw nothing on the door to warrant his keen interest, not even a porthole to look through. Until he reached closer to it and he brushed away some dust only to reveal a small square metallic label, which had a symbol on it. He stared pryingly at the label, and then he looked me in the eye.

"What is it, Nesasigamany?" I asked, relatively worried now because the look on his face indicated to me that he had discovered something much more worrying than nuclear weapons and guns.

"I have seen this symbol before," he said, with a nervous tone.

"I haven't." I replied, "Is it bad, Nesasigamany?"

"Yes, it is bad." He replied as he pressed some buttons on his light tablet.

"Why are you opening the door if it is bad?" I asked, curiously.

"There is no bad danger in here, Newton, only corruption and deceit."

Suddenly a clunking sound came from inside the door, followed by a succession of locks disengaging one after the other. The small, thick solid steel door swung open slowly. As it did so, the whole room inside illuminated with clean white light, which was helped much by the whiteness of the room itself.

We entered what looked much like a clean laboratory. Almost everything was white and hygienic. The benches, the chairs, the wall cabinets, even the floor, ceiling, and walls. There was a large glass partition wall at the rear of the room, which stretched from floor to ceiling.

"I take it that you are unaware of the existence of this facility, Nesasigamany?"

"I have heard vague rumours, but never anything definite about its existence." He replied.

"What was it used for?" I asked. His questionable stare was all I needed to confirm that something somewhat sinister took place here. I had to look for myself while Nesasigamany messed around with a computer console. After all, there was no danger in here; it was an innocent laboratory facility.

I left Nesasigamany to press buttons and scrutinise the computer screen while I went off to investigate behind the glass partition wall at the end of the room. I found a door with a code lock, which had no illuminated lights on its small screen. I pressed some of the buttons at random, but nothing happened. I pushed harder in frustration, and to my surprise, the door clicked open, as if somebody had been watching me on a monitor, or by other means, and had felt my frustration too, and at that precise moment had somehow remotely released the door for me.

I entered the room with caution. There were no lights on, nor did any illuminate automatically. I went back to the door and, after some fumbling around, I found a button. Immediately as I had pressed it, the whole lab lit up, revealing its dangerous and worrying contents. My heart raced as I approached the large vertical, cylindrical tanks. Each one was filled almost to the top with a clear liquid, which I assumed to be water, or saline, perhaps. All four tanks had tubes of various colours and sizes leading from the top, and the base of each container, which led to, and terminated, in the back of a large portable console on wheels. This console had large, flexible cable and various tubes trailing from it, and they disappeared into a panel in a control room on a mezzanine floor above.

I stood gaping at the tanks for a moment, thinking who, or what manner of strange and wretched creature did these people keep in such hideous vessels, and indeed for what purpose or intention.

"Celestials, Newton!" A voice called out directly behind me, causing me to almost jump out of my skin.

"Nesasigamany, I didn't hear you knock first. You startled me. How is it that my perception is so bad here? Am I losing it?"

"No, Newton you have not lost anything," he said, as he battled with his light tablet. "It is not only your perception; everything is bad here. There is an ESP block in force on the entire Luna Region. Even the discarnate spirits are prohibited from this place, for security reasons."

"What on earth went on in here?" I enquired earnestly.

"This is an experimental laboratory, Newton, for the first Celestials. They created the prototypes here in the twenty-ninth century." He continued to press buttons frantically. He displayed a frightful expression, which caused me great concern. I asked him a question about a door in the corner of the lab marked with a large red 'X', but he did not answer me; his mind was occupied elsewhere, worried about something else more urgent. I had never seen him in this state before. I decided not to disturb him with further questioning, but to continue to investigate the door on my own.

I was met with yet another code lock. I pushed the door, and again, to my utter surprise, it opened without any resistance. I thought I heard Nesasigamany shout out something; his voice was faint but firm.

"Don't go in there, Newton, we haven't got much time. We must get back to the spacecraft!"

I didn't turn back, and I did not look back either, because my mind was concerned now, at what stood in the room before me. I approached these familiar-looking objects, which had somehow, suddenly caused my memory to recall, and for the first time since I had been revived, I was able to remember flashbacks from the past which were somehow suddenly imparted into my memory as a juxtaposition of sporadic events.

Nesasigamany burst in shouting, "Don't look in here, Newton! We have to get back to the spacecraft, now!"

But it was too late. Nesasigamany found me slumped on the floor, on my knees, with my head buried in my hands, in a state of deep lament and sorrow. He didn't console me; instead, he brushed past me and headed for the two familiar objects, which he thought more important than my sorry, emotional state.

"Newton, did you press the 'Revive' button?" He kept on asking me, and I kept on replying the same word, over and over again.

"Karla! Karla!"

"Newton," he pleaded with me, as he held his light tablet, glancing at it anxiously, "listen to me, we have to get back to the craft now. We are in great danger."

I looked up at him through the tears in my eyes, unable to focus on his real expression of concern, which was just as well. "There is no danger here; This is Heaven," I said.

"No, Newton," he pleaded, "This is the Luna Region. I think we are being pursued; we must leave now."

"Strict Androgen?" I asked.

"No," he replied, "not Strict Androgen, or Celestial, or Human. Not even Animal!"

"Then what?" I asked, somewhat puzzled, and for the first time since I have been here, terrified. I was forced to abandon my emotions as my survival instinct kicked in, as I quickly rose to my feet.

"That is the problem," he said, "I am picking up an entity in pursuit, which is registering on my light tablet as a form of life, yet the memory banks indicate that the form is unknown."

"Perhaps your tablet is faulty, Nesasigamany?"

He laughed, and then he said something about the efficiency of crystal technology, that it was incomparable to my ancient, caveman, technology. I wasn't taking any of it in, despite the impending danger. I guess I didn't care at this stage. My mind was focussed elsewhere. I just had to have one more look before we left this Godforsaken place. I approached the two life support pods, which were both lying side by side. I ran my fingers over the metal plate on the base of the pod, which bared the name of its occupant. This time I prayed that I am released from this nightmare. I closed my eyes, and hoped harder than I have ever done in my entire life, that when I open them again, I will be at home in the City, or back on the cosy Cruiser, The Island, together with my loved one.

I must have cried out loud in a moment of lost consciousness, because the next thing I knew, Nesasigamany was right beside me urging me to keep quiet, and reiterating yet again that it was crucial that we vacate this place immediately. But my only concern was of the names etched onto those metallic plates attached to each of the pods, in bold text, which I thoroughly understood read, 'KARLA FLOTMAN' and on the other pod it read, 'NEWTON FLOTMAN'

"How could this be, Nesasigamany?" I pleaded with him, "Can you explain this to me?"

I moved aside while he examined the pods in turn. He scrutinised each nameplate in turn. I studied his face for clues. I could find none because he revealed nothing. He too was genuinely affected by this bizarre discovery, I could discern from the mystified look on his face, that he found this situation strange and inexplicable. He shook his head, and then suddenly realised something, which prompted him to look below the nameplate, where he discovered a hidden console. He had to bend down to access it.

"These are old machines," he said as he fondled the buttons, "but you have to be very careful, as Celebrias was notorious for his hidden surprises. He'd often design them into his inventions as a preventative measure just in case they got into the wrong hands."

"Are you saying that he put a booby trap in there as well?" I shouted in utter surprise and objection, as I stood up and began to pace the room like a lost dog.

"That's an ancient word, Newton. Not to worry though, these things were only dangerous when in the wrong hands."

Suddenly there was a loud clicking sound, and several coloured lights illuminated and began to flash at random on the console of both pods, which was shortly followed by an alarm sound, which came from my pod. I was startled, so much so that I stopped pacing and approached Nesasigamany. He was busy fiddling with his light tablet.

"Have you triggered it, Nesasigamany? Is it going to blow?" I asked him, as I wiped the sweat from my brows.

"Relax, Newton," he replied calmly, and then he looked at me with a half smile on his face, "it is going to open." He said, with a broad smile.

Before I could express my surprise or anything else for that matter, my ears endured a harsh and sudden pain. The loud hissing sound, which followed, induced a sudden burst of tinnitus. In a single moment, before I had time to cover my ears in defence, the lid of the pod flew wide open. Nesasigamany stood up and pointed his light tablet towards the pods, while pressing buttons. My heart pounded as I craned my neck to look into the pod at the one that bared my name.

I felt the blood drain from my head when I looked at it. Nesasigamany was staring at me, wide-eyed and open-mouthed. "It's empty!" I shouted to him half surprised, and half doubtful.

He approached, looked into the empty pod, and then scratched his head. He reverted to his light tablet.

"Open this one!" I shouted to him, as I cradled Karla's pod, frantically looking about it in vain for a button, any button, perhaps one with the words marked 'open'.

"No, Newton!" Nesasigamany shouted. I noticed an intimation of urgency in his voice. His eyes stared differently at the light tablet, as he held it close to his face. The reflection of its light made his eyes pleasing and contented. "No, Newton, you must trust my judgment now," he said, with a sense of calmness, as he smiled into the tablet. "We cannot open this pod, Newton! We must get back to the spacecraft and leave this place right now!"

A thousand mixed up thoughts passed through my head in a split second. I wanted to open the pod, but I knew that it would be dangerous. Nesasigamany admitted later on that he was unable to open it anyway, for some unknown reason. I followed him out of the room and along the empty corridors. My next concern was the entity in pursuit, and I wondered how close it was to us at this stage. He said that it was gaining on us fast, as we had lost some time messing around with the pods, which made me feel a slight sense of guilt, as I should not have entered the room in the first instance. I have no regrets, however, as I know more now than I ever did before. In any case, I was quite confident that I had been persuaded into action by some unknown force or entity.

We had to take a different route back to the spacecraft. We ran as fast as we could, without stopping for anything. We didn't even slow down to investigate the strange noises that we heard coming from the Incarceration Sector. Our only concern at this moment was to get back to the docking bay quickly, and then fly straight back to earth, where we would be safe from whatever it was that was that was pursuing us.

When we reached the craft, we wasted no time boarding, although we had to delay a while for the main cargo doors to open so that we were able to fly into the pressurisation airlock, and then out through the doors at the other end, into space. Nesasigamany had his eyes fixed on his light tablet while I struggled with the steering.

"It looks like we've lost it, whatever it was, Newton," he said, as his eyes roamed frantically up and down the screen, " It must have realised that we were heading to earth, and decided to turn back." He concluded with a smile, and then he put the light tablet away in his pocket.

But he was mistaken, as we would learn later on. The entity had not gone back at all. It had already entered the ship while we were still on the platform, awaiting take off. Something stirred, and then settled in the small cargo hold beneath us in the belly of the spacecraft, out of sight, waiting patiently, silently, unnoticed, until it reached its final destination, planet earth, where it would eventually manifest itself.

I entered the earth's atmosphere at high speed, first with a troubled mind, and then the moment we had breached the stratosphere, I experienced a sudden catharsis similar to a fragment of enlightenment felt during the second Revelation. Nesasigamany commented on my speed on approach and said that it wasn't necessary, as the unknown entity was no longer pursuing us and, in any case, we were safe here under the protection of the Great Spirit. He explained that the feeling that I had experienced was probably due to spiritual security within the confines of the earth plane. I wanted him to explain it in more detail about what we had found in the laboratory. He appeared reluctant at first because he believed that his theory was only a rough intuition without plausible facts. I would need to consult somebody in higher authority such as Lord Bandersant, or Doctor Gabriel, for a more detailed and specified explanation.

I landed on Louden's balloon close to where Nesasigamany had left his craft, along with the two prohibited Strict Androgen, who had to remain concealed for obvious reasons. He informed me that it was imperative that he returned to the Luna Region immediately, taking his industrial Androgen with him, before somebody discovers them, which could invite even more misfortune.

"I am probably in trouble with the King and Queen, in any case. Somebody must have seen us on the monitors up there," he explained, as he stood up and began to fumble around in his pockets, "they will summon me to appear before them to explain why I had brought an unauthorised human to the Luna Region."

"Can't you just tell them the truth, Nesasigamany?" I suggested.

"Sure, Newton, I'll just tell King and Queen Fulk that we broke into their old storage facility to examine the weapon stockpile, and while we were there we happen to discover a laboratory where Celebrias and his kin performed experiments on humans, and cloned Celestials using human DNA!" Realizing that he had been rather overzealous with supposition, he suddenly changed his tone from a facetious one to a more serious and subdued one, "What is it your ancient folk used to say, Newton? 'Such a story would go down like a lead balloon?'"

"OK, Nesasigamany, yes it was something along those lines. I will leave it up to you to explain to your King and Queen of the Luna Region if ever they exist. Now perhaps you would be kind enough to explain to me what happened to Karla up there, are you saying that they cloned her?"

He suddenly found what he was looking for in one of his many pockets. He ignored my question, or avoided it, and instead he handed me two small oblong crystal tablets. "Here, Newton, this is all I have; I managed to retrieve these records from the database in the laboratory. I don't know what happened up there; I can only provide my theory, which may be inaccurate. The database may contain vital and helpful information, which could be more helpful to you. Gabriel or Bandersant will know how to extract data from them. Good luck Newton, I must take myself and the two strict ones back to where we belong, lest the Monarchy send a search party out to hunt me down like a lame quadruped... Oh, don't worry, Newton you are quite safe here on earth, they won't trouble you, provided you don't plan any more visits to the Luna Region."

Nesasigamany shook my hand and then he advised me to remain inside the ship until he had taken off, for my safety because he would be blasting off at high velocity to escape the earth's atmosphere as quickly as possible, to limit the chances of detection. I thanked him, and then I opened the hatch to let him out. I watched him, through the front screen, as he walked to his ship. The hatch opened, and I caught a glimpse of two figures standing in an area of darkness by the spacecraft, but I couldn't see the upper half of their bodies, only legs clothed in black trousers. Nesasigamany said something to them. I guessed that he had asked them if the repairs were successful, because immediately afterwards he gave me the thumbs up and then he disappeared up the ramp into the belly of his large spacecraft. I watched the hatch as it slowly closed. There was a bright flash of pure white light, which engulfed the entire screen of my craft, and then it diminished. In a split second, and his whole ship had gone. It had taken off with such high velocity that it appeared to have entirely vanished from the deck, immediately, during the bright flash of light.

I opened my hatch and went outside to witness the near light speed departure. High up in the deep blue sky I could see tiny white object trailing a bright glowing tail, like that of a comet, as it headed towards the Luna Region. It burned for a while, reducing in size until it eventually faded away and blended into the blue sky.

Something extraordinary happened to me when I returned to the Island. I flew down and landed on the green lawn, where I had usually docked my craft, next to the other spacecraft. The inexplicable phenomenon occurred after I had opened the hatch and stepped outside of the craft. I stood there for a moment gazing at all the happy people, wearing their usual happy, smiling faces, and walking around enjoying the warm sunshine. I had just turned around to look back into the open hatch of my ship reminiscing about the perilous adventure back on the Luna Region when I suddenly felt a fresh breeze blow towards me. The pressure was not from the sea, as one would expect, but it seemed to have come directly from the inside of the craft. It felt cool, as it struck my face, but it didn't just dissipate, once it had kissed my face, it felt as if it had penetrated my entire body and departed through the other side of it. Bizarrely though, at that very moment that it left me. I had a clear and most potent thought of Karla, which caused me to experience a sudden feeling of apprehension, about what, precisely, I could not discern, but it prompted me to action.

I was running fast, heading straight for the Honeymoon Suite, where I had left my Karla in bed Sleeping off a lousy dose of Louden's debauched, Green Rum when I had left her unexpectedly and had gone to the Luna Region with Nesasigamany. I felt a degree of guilt because I had not told her where I was going at the time; however, my trip to the Luna Region wasn't planned, as my prime intention was to visit the Auditorium on the Island to consult the spirits for some advice. I guess that she will be quite upset with me. I should not be so presumptuous as to expect the same unbridled welcome that I had been accustomed to. And indeed I should not assume or expect the same level of affection and hope that she would constrict me with her slender bronzed legs, and greet me with kisses and contentment. Instead, I should prepare myself for something much more unreceptive, maybe one of her playful slaps around the head, but not particularly as playful as I would anticipate, and perhaps if I apologise obsequiously enough, she might just spare me a clenched fist and substitute it for a soft, open hand.

As I reached the plush entrance to our suite, I worried greatly about how I was going to break the news to Karla about the sinister discovery in the laboratory on the Luna Region. I needed to get her undivided attention first, and then break it to her gently before she had time to express her disappointment about my sudden absence. I sat on the well-upholstered seat in the corner of the entrance area, and pondered, for a while, thinking carefully about the exact choice of suitable words to use to mitigate my predicament.

"There you are, Newton!" A voice startled me, as it echoed across the reception area, "We've been looking everywhere for you."

I looked up to see Darus, the skating waiter, standing before me with a tray in his hand, which had a large clear bottle of an orangey red juice that looked truly refreshing.

"Here," he said, as he set the tray down in front of me on a small, round wooden table, "you will need this. It is a new recipe called 'Island Sunrise' I created it myself. Go on, try it."

I picked up the bottle, and I immediately noticed that, contrary to its icy appearance, the bottle felt quite warm in my hand. "Do I drink it out of the bottle, Darus?"

"Yes, Newton. It is best drunk that way, and don't worry if it is warm to the touch, the real surprise comes when the liquid is taken in the mouth."

I took a large mouthful from the bottle, and in an instant, I could feel the cooling, fresh sensation on my taste buds. And then I gulped it down, and almost immediately, I experienced the most desirable, indescribable quenching sensation in my throat, which I enjoyed so much that I had to take a second mouthful. I completely emptied the whole bottle without even realising it.

"Darus, that is a good recipe. I must make this my regular drink." I said as I savoured the last drop. I then adopted a more serious tone. "Why have you been looking for me, Darus?"

"Have you been in to see Karla yet?" He asked, in a manner that did not alert my suspicion in any way.

I stood up, "I was just on my way now. I only got back moments ago." I replied, and then I began to make my way to the Honeymoon Suite, rather confused and apprehensive.

I was further astounded when I was startled by the sudden presence of Lord Bandersant and Doctor Gabriel outside the door to the suite, who both greeted me vehemently. Lord Bandersant looked straight towards me and said, "Are you sure that you saw it come this way?"

I was bewildered now, and I was just about to reply to him when I heard a voice directly behind me. It was Darus, who he had been addressing, behind me, while his sorrowful eyes were looking at me.

"Yes Lord Bandersant. I was skating along the main walkway, and I noticed it in the corner of my eye. I didn't see it again until I entered the main reception, and I decided to follow it." Darus replied, somewhat nervously.

"And it led you here, Darus, outside Newton's door?" Doctor Gabriel enquired.

"Yes, it stopped right here, in the hallway, and then it glowed brightly."

Immediately I feared the worst. All the horror and disgust of the dark Luna Region came flooding back in an instant. My mind raced as it frantically searched for an intimation of what Darus was describing that he had seen here outside my room; Karla's room; our cosy little place on this paradise. My whole body turned cold, as I suddenly had a disturbing thought about the mysterious entity that Nesasigamany had located on his light tablet. Had I defied the code of peace and invited danger to this peaceful world by allowing, and causing, a disembodied entity to follow us back to earth? Perhaps I should own up to my deceitfulness? I hope Karla is safe. I had to find out. I had to see if she was safe.

"What is happening here?" I asked Lord Bandersant, "Is Karla OK?"

"What happened after it glowed brightly?" Lord Bandersant asked Darus, while he avoided my question and looked beyond my gaze, towards Darus.

"It went – " Darus hesitated, and then he glanced at me for a split second and then he turned back to Lord Bandersant. " - It went straight through Newton's door." He said, as his eyes filled with sorrow and then with fear.

"I must see Karla!" I demanded. "It was my fault, the entity followed us back from the Luna Region. I was there with Nesasigamany, he tracked it on his light tablet, and then we lost contact with it when we left the Luna Region. It must have followed us back to earth."

"Relax, Newton," Lord Bandersant said, "we are not sure what we are dealing with here, as yet."

"I must see her," I demanded, as I moved towards the door.

Lord Bandersant raised his hand, "OK, Newton, but you must open the door slowly and tread carefully, we don't want to scare it away. I am sure if it were harmful it would have harmed you by now, especially if you brought it back here from the Luna Region, as you claim."

"We will be right behind you, Newton," Doctor Gabriel said, as he reached into his pocket for his Crystal Light Tablet.

"You have weapons?" I asked before I had caught sight of the simple device, which he had retrieved from deep in his pocket.

"Newton, you know the rules. Even if we did have weapons, they would be of no use in any case. You cannot fight the non-physical with physical," Doctor Gabriel said. "This thing can penetrate solid objects."

"Lasers would suffice, would they not?" I asked in desperation, as I grabbed the door handle nervously, and prepared myself to enter the room.

"In the last century perhaps, Newton. But today, if we had any cause to develop weapons, they would consist of the Solid State Crystal Laser Device, and even an extremely low powered weapon would be too excessive for this task. Its capability would allow it generate enough energy to obliterate this entire suite, and us with it." Doctor Gabriel replied.

"And, such an entity, which is capable of passing through solid walls, would indeed have the advantage, and could escape at will, before we could get a clear shot at it with our murderous weapons." Lord Bandersant added, in support. He then turned to Darus and instructed him to stay out in the hallway and wait for his men, and not to enter the room under any circumstances.

I guessed that he meant his two men in black, which I have not seen for some time. I was worried that I was about to enter a room to confront an unknown force, which, I believe, had followed us to earth from the Luna Region, and none of us knew anything about its capabilities or its intentions. If it wanted to do us harm, I suppose it would have done so already. Perhaps it was playing around with us? It seems to have a keen interest in Karla. I will not let it harm her. I just cannot allow such an act to be committed here in my happy world, in our Honeymoon Suite.

The combination of my high emotions bolstered by the effects of Darus' new Island Sunrise drink concoction, served to suppress my fears. I was worried about my Karla too, apparently, but somehow within my inner spirit body, I could sense a degree of calmness, which I am not able to explain. Perhaps Lord Bandersant and Doctor Gabriel are experiencing similar emotions, because they both seem calm considering the impending chaos which we believe could potentially unfold right here before our eyes, in my Suite.

I opened the door, slowly to begin with, and then with boosted confidence, I swung it much faster because I couldn't see anything in the room. I guess I swung it too much, as it almost collided with the wall behind it. I turned in time to see Lord Bandersant, who was right behind me. He gave me a look of disdain. Doctor Gabriel entered the room behind us, holding his tablet.

"It is in here somewhere." He said with confidence.

"What about Karla?" I asked, slightly worried and nervous at the same time.

"She's in the bedroom," Doctor Gabriel replied, "Wait!" He shouted suddenly. I felt the hairs on the back of my neck tingle, as we all stood still. At that moment, I thought of picking up something to hit it with, or at least to defend myself in the event of an attack. I immediately changed my mind, and then I began to think how pitifully absurd and banal was such a thought because I was fully aware that it would be a futile action to challenge an entity with, a real weapon, that possessed such capabilities as to pass right through solid objects. I was unable to find anything in our pristinely kept suite in any case, except one of Karla's little Bolero cardigans, which was hanging over the back of a chair. And it was too late to go into the kitchen to find a laser knife, or something similar to try out on the creature.

Doctor Gabriel's warning was loud enough to cause my heart to jump. He announced that the thing was by the Jacuzzi, out on the patio, and it was slowly heading our way. We waited in anticipation, the three of us, poised in front of the wide-open glass patio doors; all of us under the assumption that the entity would choose to enter again the same way which it had gone out because it wouldn't be bothered to go through the solid glass further along. Perhaps it required more energy to permeate solid matter, and it wished to conserve it?

I held my breath as Doctor Gabriel announced once again that it was heading straight for us. I had my eyes completely fixed on the opening. I had no idea of the exact position in the room of Lord Bandersant or Doctor Gabriel. I could only hear their voices. Suddenly time seemed to slow down, just like one would experience during an unfavourable event like an accident, or a near death experience (an NDE).

I heard a voice, but I was unable to discern from whom or whence it came. The voice mentioned the term, 'higher vibration'. Were we about to experience a chronological shift? My eyes suddenly received a slow burst of brilliant white light. Its radiance was like no other light seen even here on earth since my awakening. Not even from the blast of a solid-state crystal drive photon jet, which, I dare say, can engender more power than any nuclear fusion system from the twenty-first century. The thing that was most frightening and bizarre was the fact that I was able to withstand the intensity of the light, despite my squinting, which I thoroughly accepted as a natural, instinctive human reaction, which wasn't necessary anyway. My fear and concern increased when I began to equate this experience with that of a similar one I had during the second Revelation. Was my time here in this paradise indeed over? Did the divine Spirit send an archangel down to fetch my soul and cast my spirit into the heavenly realms?

I watched as the light grew intense, and then it diminished and glowed with a golden hue. Time reverted to normality, except for the golden glow, which hovered at the entrance of the opened patio door.

"What is it, an angel?" I asked, although not hoping much for an answer because I wasn't sure if they could hear me.

"Perhaps a spirit of some sort." Lord Bandersant replied.

"It must be an important one," I said, as I moved closer to examine it in more detail.

"It is a spirit indeed," Doctor Gabriel confirmed with confidence, "and it has returned from somewhere; captivity perhaps."

"I thought you said all ghosts left the earth in the year AD 2599, how did this one become trapped on earth? Could they have missed it?" I enquired.

"Who said it was trapped on earth, Newton?" Lord Bandersant said, which sent a shiver down my spine, once again.

Doctor Gabriel stared intensely at his tablet and then he looked up at the glowing spirit a few times. His actions indicated that he had stumbled upon something.

"It looks like we are about to find out," He said with a grin, and just as he did so, the spirit moved slowly towards the bedroom.

I was concerned about Karla, as she had continuously slept since I had left for the Luna Region, and nobody knew precisely if she ever woke up after I had left with Nesasigamany. There was no sightings of her anywhere on the Island, and as we were inseparable, most people assumed that she had gone somewhere with me.

I made sure that I was the first one to enter the bedroom. Both men gave way to me out of the kindness of their hearts in any case, and I strolled in expecting to see Karla lying in bed. The spirit was hovering above the bed close to the ceiling. The initial sight of seeing Karla caused me sudden fear, albeit for a split second, until my mind had adjusted to my dismay.

Karla wasn't in bed asleep as we all expected her to be, she wasn't wide-awake either. She was sitting upright, and entirely still, but on top of a perfectly made bed, with her legs crossed, and her eyes closed. Both of her hands were resting upon her knees, with her palms facing the ceiling as if she had been praying. She did not open her eyes or acknowledge our presence in any way whatsoever.

"Doctor Gabriel, what does this mean?" I asked, my voice shaking with fear.

"My God!" Lord Bandersant exclaimed, which only served to compound my fear.

"Relax, Newton," Doctor Gabriel said, as he smiled reassuringly, and he looked up to the ceiling at the hovering spirit.

Lord Bandersant glanced at Doctor Gabriel, and then he addressed me, "Whatever happens, Newton, do not touch her; do not talk to her or ask her any questions. Do not attempt any communication with her, which could alert her in any way whatsoever."

"It led us here." Doctor Gabriel said with glee, "It wanted us to know."

We watched as the spirit bounced up and down twice as if to acknowledge something, and then it did something so remarkable, which no man on earth has, undoubtedly, ever witnessed throughout all of history.

The bright spirit descended slowly towards the top of Karla's head, and then entered through the crown and down into her body, where it eventually dissolved into it, and then it was gone. From what we had just witnessed, I still pondered over the possibility and the reason why a spirit had entered into Karla's body through the top of her head.

Before I could begin to express my concern about her present condition, Karla flinched, and then she took a deep breath and sighed. I took this to be an acknowledgement that she was okay, and this foe was friendly, and it did not harm her. Lord Bandersant was ecstatic.

"Harm, Newton?" He exclaimed when I had asked him the question, "Of course not. I must admit we were somewhat confused at first, particularly when we had assumed that it was hostile, but this action is proof in itself. She will be fine now, Newton. Don't you worry."

Doctor Gabriel was walking around the room holding his light tablet, taking readings, or looking for something else; perhaps another spirit? I was busy tending to Karla. She was awake but dazed. I kissed her on the forehead and caressed her hands. She looked straight out of the bedroom patio door and then she began to whisper something, which sounded much like a chant at first, but then I realised it was a prayer.

"What is she doing now, Newton?" Doctor Gabriel asked as he paced by the patio doors.

"She's – She is praying!" I replied, in a somewhat uncertain tone.

"That is good," Doctor Gabriel said, with much zeal, "that is perfect."

"Yes, Newton, do not appease he too much, just stroke her hair to reassure her." Lord Bandersant said, as he stood outside on the patio, where Doctor Gabriel joined him.

I made my assumption of what happened to Karla, but I was eager to hear both Gabriel and Bandersant's theory first since they appeared to have understood the reason for this phenomenal episode which had just taken place right here in our Honeymoon Suite. I wondered if they knew anything about the details of our escapade in the Luna Region? I only told them that the spirit followed us back to earth, and that was just a presumption. It could have made its way here, or perhaps it hitched a ride in my spacecraft. Who knows for sure? I needed to know for sure.

I stopped stroking Karla's hair and made my way out onto the patio, where the two men were standing, and in conversation.

"I thought only humans had spirits?" I addressed both men.

"We are just as confused as you are, Newton," Lord Bandersant replied, "Newton, you've had a long day, and poor Karla needs some rest now, after her ordeal. Why don't we leave you both in peace for now, and tomorrow you can take Karla home to your new house, and perhaps we can all meet there later on?"

"We shall do some research into this matter, and by tomorrow we will have more information to share with you both." Doctor Gabriel added, with a smile.

Both men looked as if they could do with some sleep as well, as the look in their eyes conveyed an expression of tiredness and fatigue. I too was tired out, and impatient to learn what exactly had happened to my little Karla, but I knew that I stood a better chance of a more detailed report after both men had conducted further investigations in the morning.

I looked back at Karla asleep on the bed. She was lying down now, looking cosy under the sheets. She seemed somewhat secure and snug. I didn't want to disturb her further. Besides, I was tired as well after that episode in the Luna Region, so I decided to close this case for today and rest until tomorrow. Perhaps after a good, long sleep, my mind will work better, and I may acquire an improved understanding of this puzzle. First of all, I had to quench my thirst with a large jug of Darus' Island Sunrise. As soon as the others had left, I instructed Darus to find the largest bottle and fill it with his new creation. He informed me that they only come in the regular size special bottles, and it would spoil the flavour if it were decanted.

"Anyway, you would struggle to drink more than three of those, Newton!" He teased.

"OK, Darus bring me all you can carry, and I'll show you the empty bottles in the morning!"

I wish I hadn't suggested such a crazy challenge. I had forgotten how intense the Androgen were, regardless of their size and gender; they all possessed hidden strength, which was a primary requirement included in their creation, to assist and serve mankind for manual labour. Darus wasn't disposed to showing off his hidden strengths. These complex humanoids were void of ego, in fact, self-esteem and inflated opinion were extinct in this new world in the year of our Lord AD 2914, it was defunct as money and as scarce as the banks that contained it. In fact, not even the animals had a hint of it left in their bones, not that they ever did so in my time on earth, save for the domesticated ones, who may have inherited it from their owners in any case.

Darus brought me two! – Two crates! And each crate contained twelve bottles! He strolled into the room, calm and collective, carrying a container in each hand. I joked with him about using a hoverboard. His unique sense of humour kicked in, and he smirked and told me that 'in that case, I have already been defeated' because he could load at least eight crates on an averagely sized hoverboard. I guess I will have to take a crate back to our new home for later.

I sat up until almost midnight staring at the crystal tablets, which contained all the information from the Luna region, wondering what dark and surreptitious secrets they would reveal. Was there some clandestine research and experiments going on up there, and did Nesasigamany know more about it than he was prepared to explain? And who exactly were King and queen Faulk? If they ever existed. I almost lost a bottle of Darus' nectar through my limp and tired fingers, in a moment of total relaxation and loss of concentration, which I acknowledged as a warning that my body required sleep, right now. I looked at Karla in the bed; she was fast asleep under the cosy silk sheets. I promptly downed the last drop of Island Sunrise before retiring in Karla's cosy nest, which her slender body had kept warm for me.

I have seen my fair share of luxury houses in my time on earth, mostly in publications, which related to property for sale to the elite or the fortunate members of society, and indeed, I might have also visited a few, if only I could remember. I had to ensure that Karla had led me to the right place because my humble self had expected something less opulent. I could see from above, as we made our descent that the neighbouring properties were similar in size, so ours had to be one of these enormous structures.

Karla, in her most bossy manner, instructed me to land on the landing surface in front of the house, as she had recognised a particular landmark and insisted that this was the correct abode. She confirmed this with a punch to my right arm, a playful one, I must add, which elated me greatly as this also corroborated the fact that my Karla had not lost any of her unique and distinctive personality, in spite of her recent trauma.

I decided not to reveal anything about what happened to her yesterday, nor did I push her with any awkward questions. Although I was extremely eager to find out, I fought myself to hold back until Lord Bandersant, and Doctor Gabriel arrived later on armed with all the facts.

The architect and designers of this fantastic abode must have somehow used ESP or Ghost Crystal to tap directly into my spiritual energy field to learn of my exact preferences to complete the design of the external areas of this property. They were correct in every detail of choice, right down to the type, colour, and pattern of the natural wood floors throughout. Karla said that she had supplied them with all the information that they needed for that purpose, and she went on to boast that she knew all about my preferences in detail. I did not argue with her. I was slightly concerned about one little change in her personality. It seemed evident to me that she showed an increased interest in heavenly matters, and was equally less worried about earthly things, which led me to believe that one of my assumed explanations could well be right.

"I always thought that Celestials were less concerned with the spiritual side, as they were not human, and they were void of a soul," I said to Lord Bandersant, later that day when I greeted him and Doctor Gabriel at the front door. I led them through the spacious hallway, and into the vast lounge, where they both sat down on the settee. Karla was in the kitchen preparing some refreshments.

"I see you have settled in nicely. Is everything to your liking, Newton?" Doctor Gabriel asked.

"Yes thank you, Doctor Gabriel. This place is fantastic. It has everything I ever wanted, and it is enormous. I haven't even explored the grounds yet." I replied, somewhat excited like a child with a new toy.

Karla entered the room with a tray of refreshments, a variety of fresh exotic fruit and some seafood, which she set down onto the low table in the centre of the settees, which were arranged in a 'U' shape formation around the table.

"I have something you must try," I announced, as I pulled out two bottles from a crate on the floor by the side of my seat. I handed Lord Bandersant and Doctor Gabriel each a bottle of Darus' Island Sunrise drink. "Drink it slowly, and you will enjoy it thoroughly. It is one of Darus' latest creations. He has called it, Island Sunrise."

"Is this what you have been drinking all last night, Newton?" Karla asked as she sat down next to me on the settee. "Here, let me try one," she said, and she held her hand out for a bottle, which I handed to her.

"In answer to your enquiry, Newton," Lord Bandersant began, as he sat back on the settee to make himself more comfortable, "Concerning Celestials devoid of a soul, I am afraid we have some news which conflicts with earlier research. Also some facts and findings of our history."

"You mean, you were wrong?" I asked.

"Not necessarily," Lord Bandersant replied, "We were certain that it was not possible for a spirit to incarnate into a celestial body, but no investigations or experiments were carried out to prove this theory. There was simply no need. It wasn't in our interest to conduct such science or to seek and discover such evidence, as the Celestials were considered highly complex organic humanoids, and not human."

I caught Carla's gaze just as I turned towards her next to me on the settee. She smirked and clenched her fist. I smiled back, and then I turned to Lord Bandersant.

"So what happened in Karla's case? Am I to believe that the entity we witnessed yesterday was a spirit, if so, whose spirit?"

Lord Bandersant turned to Doctor Gabriel, who had his light tablet in his hand. He glanced at it as he spoke.

"It was a spirit indeed, Newton," Doctor Gabriel said, "and we think it was the spirit of Karla."

"Are you saying that Karla is not Celestial?" I asked.

"I shall tell you all the information that we have found, Newton," Doctor Gabriel replied, "as it is quite difficult to find exact history, even with these memory crystals." He threw the small crystals down onto the table in the middle of the seating arrangement. "This history began in your time, Newton, and some of it was undoubtedly misplaced or lost after the holocaust."

"Karla was around at that time?" I asked, somewhat surprised.

"Yes, Newton," Doctor Gabriel replied, and he pointed to Karla, "However, not this Karla. Celestials were not created until AD 2814, almost eight hundred years later." He inhaled, and then he sighed, "I am afraid to tell you, Newton, that the Karla in the life support pod, on the Luna Region is the human Karla..."

I was speechless, and a little shaken too. However, I was expecting news of a similar nature, but nothing could have been worse than the moment we had discovered the life support pods. I braced myself for more news.

"...She was, we assume, your wife, Newton..." There was more silence. This time I grabbed Karla's hand and began to rub it gently. I could see tears welling up in her eyes.

Doctor Gabriel continued, "The other pod was for you, Newton."
Lord Bandersant began to speak, "Newton, we knew nothing of
these experiments, as they were highly secret and the fact that they
took place before the holocaust made it virtually impossible to trace
their history."

"That's right," Doctor Gabriel confirmed. "When we found your
life support pod on earth, we never suspected that there were two.
We now realise that Karla had been taken to the Luna Region in a
pod similar to the one we found you in on earth. Just before nuclear
war broke out, perhaps for safety reasons, or for the scientists at
that time to continue with their experiments in zero gravity, or
perhaps in a safe environment away from the war. Your scientists
transferred her to the pod that you found on the Luna Region. The
other one was obviously ready for you, but unfortunately, they
were unable to complete the transfer for some unknown reason,
perhaps because of certain developments of the nuclear holocaust.
They had no means of getting to the Luna Region, which I believe
you referred to as the Moon in your time, Newton because the base
had been totally destroyed along with most or all of its spacecraft.
In effect you were stranded here, Newton, deep underground, in a
primitive life-support pod, in a deep sleep, accompanied by a
handful of scientists to tend to all your needs. They remained there
until they were overcome by something hazardous or perilous that
had ultimately caused their demise; starvation, suffocation,
radiation poisoning. We shall never know for sure exactly because
the terrain had suffered such an excessive amount of seismic
activity over the years, that it became unsafe to attempt any
exploration there. It was all forgotten about right up until recently
when Lord Bandersant and his men discovered you, they were
fortunate to get you out of there in time before the whole area
became completely unstable as a result of the geological
disruption."

"What about Karla? How did she survive on the moon, the Luna
Region?" I asked.

"Karla, your wife, having being transferred to another pod on the Luna Region, was kept there at the base for how long, we shall never know." Doctor Gabriel went on, "We do know that she was kept there at the Luna base station which your people built just before the war. They discovered a crystal, which they mined and used on earth for their communications technology and advanced laser weapons. How surprising! Little did they know that this type of crystal was to become extremely valuable to us and it would serve as a prime ingredient in the manufacture of Ghost Crystal. Its properties included the ability to harness energy from light and to repel spirits.

"Even your miserable scientists failed to discover these important uses. They were so engrossed in war and destruction that they failed to recognise something so valuable, which had the potential to propel them out of the Stone Age."

"So how did they apply it to war?" I asked.

"They crushed it and used it as a propellant for their missiles... Cavemen! They even tried it in their nuclear missiles."

"And what happened?" I asked, expecting him to say that it improved the range.

"Armageddon, Newton! Armageddon!"

"What happened to the Luna Region after the war?" I enquired to Doctor Gabriel.

"It remained a base until AD 2520 when all manufacturing ceased on earth and was transferred and carried out on the Luna Region. Nobody knows for sure what happened to Karla, your wife. We think that with the invention of Ghost Crystal, Samuel Page began constructing manufacturing plants, a new laboratory, and even a prison for disgruntled criminals from earth, and her pod was kept deep underground in the old laboratory, which they originally excavated from pure crystal."

"The Spirit repelling one?" I asked.

"Yes, Newton, and I think you know what I am going to tell you next? This crystal, in its abundance, prevented her spirit from leaving her body, although she was alive but in a deep sleep, the body could not yield and give up its soul, but only allow the spirit to travel as far as the silver cord would permit."

"Are you saying that this went on for years, Doctor Gabriel?"

"I'm afraid so, Newton."

"They couldn't open the pod or wake her?" I asked as I felt the tears welling up in my eyes. Karla could sense my emotions too. She squeezed my hand in an attempt to comfort me.

"No," Doctor Gabriel replied, "It would have been of no use, as she could not have been woken without the specific equipment from earth, which I believe was with you, Newton, in your laboratory here on earth. Deep below the terrain, hidden away until the day we discovered you. And all the scientists with the required knowledge to operate such paraphernalia had either died in the holocaust or had gone off to other parts of the world after the war had ended.

"It was only after the inception of Androgen Cyberscience In AD 2814 that Celebrias and his team began to progress greatly in the development of Androgen and Celestials. We are not sure of the exact date, but he created his first prototype, a character by the name of, Fortinell, who is still around today."

"Yes, Doctor Gabriel, I am aware of him," I interjected, "He currently runs the Androgen facility in the Antipodean Region, and is partial to a drop or two of the Green Rum."

"Inherited traits from his creator, we believe," Doctor Gabriel said. "Despite his bouts of inebriation from time to time, his work was outstanding. We left his team to control and run the entire Luna Region. They were responsible for the creation of all organic and non-organic humanoids that helped to create this wonderful world which we live in today; Heaven on Earth, Newton." He took a long mouthful of Island Sunrise.

Lord Bandersant stood up. He looked as if he desired to stretch his legs. "As Doctor Gabriel was saying, Newton, we do know that Celebrias and his team of research scientists conducted experiments with human DNA at some stage."

"Is that how they created Celestials?" I asked Lord Bandersant, as my eyes attempted to follow him up and down the room.

"No," he replied. "Celestials are created by the utilisation and the fusing of the male and female Gametes in a complicated process which involves the use of high vibration crystal energy from a combination of stones such as Herkimer, Moldavite, Datolite, and Elestial Quartz. I do trust that this is a totally new concept of technology to you, Newton."

I gave up turning in my seat to keep up with his pacing. I sat back and relaxed, and naturally raised the volume of my voice to drown out the sound of his leather soles against the rich oak panelled floor. "And they used DNA instead?" I asked, hoping that he would disagree.

"They took DNA..." He stopped pacing and stood still by the table directly in front of Karla and me. "I'm afraid that they took DNA from Karla. From the body of your wife, Newton..." He then approached me, and then he stood directly in front of Karla, "They then used it to create...Karla."

I pulled Karla towards me and cuddled her in my arms. I could feel her warm tears on my arm, "This Karla? My Karla? The Celestial Karla, Lord Bandersant?"

Lord Bandersant nodded his head and walked back to his seat and sat down without uttering another word. My eyes followed him, and I watched as he sat himself down awkwardly onto the sofa next to Doctor Gabriel, I continued to stare at each of them in turn, half expecting a little more information. I searched, and I sought to ask more questions, but which I could not deliver because I had suffered a momentary loss of perceptiveness. Karla had her head leant back and resting against the headrest, with her eyes tightly closed.

Doctor Gabriel pulled himself forward almost to the edge of his seat. "She was in a state of sleep, much deeper than yours, Newton," he began, "due to the difference in atmospheric properties between the earth and the Luna Region. However, her spirit, just like yours, still attached, but was only able to roam restrictively due to the prohibitive properties of the crystal formation on the Luna Region."

"For such a long period of time?" I said, almost repulsed at the thought of her supposed suffering. Such suffering of a spirit must have been equal to the grief felt by those discarnate souls that dwell in the lower worlds; to be trapped, in abeyance, waiting almost forever, to be released.

"Newton, I am positive that your awareness and understanding of the concept of differences in time between the material and spiritual worlds is quite clear," he replied. "Her suffering was no greater than yours, during your time in deep sleep, as any degree of punishment depends largely upon the condition of the soul. Your wife must have had a great deal of purity in her heart for spiritual law to permit her soul to travel to earth regularly for a transitory possession of her Celestial body."

"With the silver cord still attached?" I asked.

"Yes, Newton. The silver cord, which connects the soul to the central nervous system of the physical body."

"She knew all along where I was, and she used Karla's Celestial body to be with me?"

"I doubt that it was as straightforward as that, Newton, but, yes, that's the most truthful and feasible explanation we can find."

"None of the spirits in the afterlife told me about this during my consultations with the Ghost Crystal, why is that?"

"Even the spiritual realm has its laws, Newton. That is the Spiritual Law, and it must be obeyed. We are still unsure why your wife's soul was able to divide itself between her body and Karla's clone. Perhaps a sense of remorse was to blame? The fact that that the soul had been trapped on the Luna Region in a half-dead body, inside a life support capsule unable to release itself, was sufficient suffering for the higher spirits in the kingdom to grant philosophic acquiescence and allow it to transfer into the clone body."

Something immediately switched on in my head. I know that Karla had felt it too because she reacted in the same way. She lifted her head and sat up, with eyes wide open. I looked straight into her eyes and saw a revived Karla, regenerated with faith, love and hope.

"I cannot recall any physical features of my wife, Doctor Gabriel, neither am I to believe that Karla here is an exact clone of my wife? Physically, that is, in every exact detail?" I asked, with my eyes filled with hope, staring deep into Karla's.

"I do believe that to be correct, Newton. I cannot see any reason for any doubt with this advanced method of cloning, as its accuracy is supreme, one of the reasons why it is considered an outlawed, and out-dated procedure today. Historically, it has been known to have caused great confusion because of its accuracy to replicate."

I held Karla tightly in my arms, as we embraced tightly. I stroked her hair, and I fondled it for a while. My hand moved down to the back of her neck, where I continued to stroke her gently but tentatively. I caressed her nape, pausing along the spinal cord. I stopped and turned to look at Doctor Gabriel.

"Newton, you must be aware by now that the vertebrae of all Celestials are made entirely of organic crystal," he said, and then he took a mouthful of Island Sunrise. "That is a fact, and it does not have any bearing on spiritual development, as it is merely physical. The soul of your departed wife was somehow permitted to follow you from the Luna Region to earth and is now with Karla. This can only mean one thing, Newton. That Karla must be your true soulmate."

I hugged her tightly, "Did you know all this, Karla?" I whispered in her ear. I felt her as she shook her head, and then she whispered into my ear.

"Newton, my darling, I'm as confused as you are. All I ever felt for you was love, which has been growing each and every day. I have had many dreams of us flying together. Up until now, I struggled to understand the meaning of such dreams. But recently I have felt very different; my feelings are more intense; my love for you is deeper than ever. I feel a comfortable sense of familiarity when I am with you, Newton. I feel that we belong together and that we are one, and nothing can ever separate us."

"Then we are truly soulmates, my darling, Karla," I whispered back to her, as we embraced lovingly.

I never did regain my memory entirely or indeed partially, despite realising further truths about my past. I discovered later, with the help of the crystal database, which Nesasigamany had found on the Luna Region, that I was indeed born in the United Kingdom as I had assumed all along. In the county of Norfolk on a secret military base where my mother resided and worked as a scientist on highly specific, top secret projects related to astrophysics.

Although I knew nothing more of the actual nature of her work, or who my father was and whether he worked on the base as well. I found out that she had named me after the place where I was born, but discovered nothing more after that, as I was unable to check the history because there were no longer any maps available in existence dated around this time, AD 1985.

I firmly believe in fate, and the fact that there is a reason for all our actions, almost everything we do and say in the flesh, in this material world. My newfound spiritual enlightenment had convinced me that all events in my past, which relates to physical matters, were indeed futile and insignificant and had no place in the spiritual development and advancement of my soul. However, there is still a reason for those crucial actions that we perform or say to others in the physical world. Each one has some significance and life-altering effect upon us all, and it is up to us to identify and understand the reason, and the cause and effect of such actions so that we can admit to them and adapt our lives accordingly.

No man is more important than another, as we are all given the same free will by the Great Spirit, which he already permitted us to implement as we please, but not without the consequences for which the law has already been put into place, and this cannot be altered by man. So I say to you all, with all my heart, I know for certain, having suffered two Revelations, that mankind is indeed equal, and none can claim to be greater than others contrary to what you are told by man.

When I last walked the earth in the twenty-first century, some men firmly believed that they were higher than others for simple reasons. They created a regime where all men engaged in trade and became collectors. Each of them was judged by his ability and success as a collector, which they performed with great zeal. It soon became a competition, which gave them even greater incentive to lie and cheat in a way that it increased their wealth, and as they grew, they became adept collectors just from the results of their moral and immoral occupations.

They called this unmerited practice 'business', and then they created their own laws to indemnify themselves against unforeseen events and other measures in their own favour. Their goal was constantly based on their success as collectors, which they deemed as 'profit', but this was, unfortunately, the wrong 'profit'. Instead, they should have listened to the true words of the 'Prophet' and followed his ways towards true success and spiritual enlightenment.

The real problem with those fools of the twenty-first century was their stubborn inability to accept the truth about the existence of the afterlife, even though in many instances adequate proof was provided. Their own scientists had provided concrete evidence of the existence of such phenomena, but still, their inept minds retained its stubbornness and incredulity, and so they chose to ignore this truth for fear of revealing something greater and more powerful than themselves.

Two thousand years before, when the Great Prophet came to earth to show us the way back to spiritual perfection, which we had previously lost, there were doubters and disbelievers then who expressed their scepticism and doubt despite being given adequate and feasible proof. Not much had changed over the next two thousand years, until now.

Shortly after our meeting, with Lord Bandersant and Doctor Gabriel, the two men said their goodbyes and left the house. As they were departing, they noted that Karla and I needed some time alone together after such an inspiring episode. We did indeed spend time together, lots of time, but not before we had adequately explored our new house.

Although she had a great deal of input in the designing of the new abode, Karla had not actually reconnoitred the finished project, so she was equally surprised with the results, just as I was when we had conducted a detailed exploration room by room.

The best thing about this beautiful world, or the way this fascinating world is currently managed, there are no adverse issues, ideas, or requirements such as slaving for somebody else. For the evil tender, the prime cause of all evil, which had been abolished a long time ago and is now confined to history. Virtually all manual labour is controlled and undertaken by Androgen Humanoids that are so highly advanced and efficient that one would struggle to distinguish them from us humans. I naively thought that these beings were just hard working humans when I first encountered them.

I fully realise now where we had gone wrong as a nation, and indeed a planet, with what we had once considered as the first world, in comparison, was indeed, in reality, worse than the third world. We conducted ourselves as selfish and uncaring creatures, and we abandoned our religion and our real purpose in life, which was to follow the teachings of the Great Prophet, and to seek the Divine Love from the Great Spirit, God.

The teachings administered to us by the Great Prophet were long forgotten by the so-called modern man in my time. And our obsession for wealth and power, and our lack of love for our fellow man created nothing but poverty and sickness throughout the entire world, and in the process, we created a mere handful of wealthy and super-rich men to run the world. Into the ground, I should say, as these selfish, overfed, and over-rewarded, greedy cretins would say, as they choked on mouthfuls of caviar and foie gras, 'there will always be poor people in the world'. Yes, there will undoubtedly be poor people in the world so long as the greedy few continue with their senseless greed and insist on taking more than their fair share.

I live now in the same world that you greedy and selfish men once occupied, the same world that you claimed was running low on water, on food, and natural resources; a world which is now free from conflict, greed, and poverty, yet all humans here are wealthy and in good health. They all enjoy nourishment through human and divine love and have an abundance of material possessions. There is no starvation here now. And money, which was once considered the bane of life, has become extinct. If I am thirsty, I drink; when I feel hungry, I eat, and I have a choice from any one of the high-class restaurants located in and around the city that are all well run by the Androgen, who continue with their avid eagerness to please and to serve.

Work and employment, as it was in my time on earth, has melded into recreation. All the manufacturing, which was once carried out by humans on earth, has now been transferred to the Luna region and is now controlled by Strict Androgen. Which leaves us, humans, free to choose from the more excellent and exciting subjects, from the most important group, which include caring, teaching, and scientific research and design, all of which contributed much towards the creation of this blissful kingdom here on earth.

Nothing is mandatory here, and they do not synchronise their activities with time, as time is not recognised in Heaven, Lord Bandersant would say. This is the reason why they called it Heaven. In fact, it was, Heaven on Earth, because it was planned, created and developed over the last five hundred years or so, from around AD 2414, with Heaven in mind. They had attempted to replicate every detail of Heaven on earth, and they were hugely successful, to say the least, primarily after Ghost Crystal was invented and developed by the late Samuel Page during the Spiritualist Movement around AD 2520.

I do not know the reason why I have found myself here on earth in the year AD 2914, although I am now aware of how I came to be in this situation. Now that my Karla, and the spirit of my wife Karla, is much involved in this saga, it seems to make more sense now. I am thinking, perhaps, that her soul, which had been inadvertently denied life through incarceration on the Luna Region, was now free and, in this extremely rare circumstance according to spiritual law, has found itself incarnated into my Celestial Karla (an exact clone of my wife, Karla). I am here too, currently living in the flesh, awoken almost nine hundred years later, in the same body I had from birth, reunited with the spirit of my wife, Karla.

I will undoubtedly continue to enjoy my life in this beautiful, happy world, surrounded by my newly found loved ones. While I divide my time between lecturing to the young at the Educational Establishment, on subjects such as how not to run a world, and scientific research and development at the Scientific Research Centre, where I am attempting to understand their highly complex crystal technology.

The rest of the time is spent with Karla, my true soul mate, travelling and socializing, sometimes on my favourite vessel, The Island, as often as possible, I must add. I consult the Ghost Crystal on a regular basis, as I can only endeavour to develop my spiritual well being much further. And I shall continue to earnestly seek the divine love from the Great Spirit until such time when I shall cross the threshold of life without fear and enter into the spiritual realms, and perhaps then all this will be made clear to me as 'to live you have to die'.

Professor Newton Flotman, June 10th AD 2917.

38317200R00167

Made in the USA
Columbia, SC
10 December 2018